About the author

Now happily retired, I often wonder why I devoted so much energy to a transient career, now that I have discovered something I truly enjoy. This is my first published novel and, I hope, not the last.

I had a passion to write this story because of its connection to my father and the uncanny echoes with my own life. Through writing it, I have learned a lot about both of us.

To find out more about me and the background to this novel, please visit my website www.chrismapp.com.

Songs of Expectation

Chris Mapp

Copyright © 2026 Chris Mapp

The moral right of the author has been asserted.

Apart from any fair dealing for the purposes of research or private study, or criticism or review, as permitted under the Copyright, Designs and Patents Act 1988, this publication may only be reproduced, stored or transmitted, in any form or by any means, with the prior permission in writing of the publishers, or in the case of reprographic reproduction in accordance with the terms of licences issued by the Copyright Licensing Agency. Enquiries concerning reproduction outside those terms should be sent to the publishers.

The manufacturer's authorised representative in the EU for product safety is Authorised Rep Compliance Ltd,
71 Lower Baggot Street, Dublin D02 P593 Ireland (www.arccompliance.com)

This is a work of fiction. Names, characters, businesses, places, events and incidents are either the products of the author's imagination or used in a fictitious manner.

Troubador Publishing Ltd
Unit E2 Airfield Business Park,
Harrison Road, Market Harborough,
Leicestershire. LE16 7UL
Tel: 0116 2792299
Email: books@troubador.co.uk
Web: www.troubador.co.uk

ISBN 9781806342051

British Library Cataloguing in Publication Data.
A catalogue record for this book is available from the British Library.

Printed and bound by CPI Group (UK) Ltd, Croydon, CR0 4YY
Typeset in 10.5pt Adobe Garamond Pro by Troubador Publishing Ltd, Leicester, UK

For my father and the other 100,000 children

Foreword

Songs of Expectation is a work of fiction but is based on actual events that played out over a period of seventy years. From the late 1860s until 1939, around 100,000 British children from pauper backgrounds were sent to Canada, and most of them never returned: more than 10% of Canada's current population is said to be descended from these children. Orphaned, abandoned, or otherwise 'rescued' from the workhouses and slums of Britain, they were shipped across the Atlantic by a plethora of individuals and organisations, with many leaving behind parents and siblings that they would never see again. They are known as the 'British Home Children'.

When these children arrived in Canada, they were placed with individual families, but apart from the very youngest, they were not to be fostered or adopted as we would know it. Instead they were set to work: their relationship with their new families was governed by a contract of employment rather than an emotional connection.

Songs of Expectation is inspired by these children, and particularly by my father, who was a Home Child himself. In this novel, I have included some real events, including a couple from my father's life. Otherwise, as you will often see quoted at the start of a TV drama, 'characters and scenes have been created for dramatic purposes.' Rather a lot of them, in fact. And some liberties have been taken with dates. It is not my intention to add to the excellent library of academic and factual books on this subject. But while the characters in *Songs of Expectation* are fictional, I believe the book provides a true insight into the lives of those involved in the child emigration movement in the 1880s, the period largely covered by the novel. It is meant to be intrinsically and emotionally accurate, and I think it is. The individual stories are typical of those experienced by the Home Children: the challenges and prejudice they faced; the triumph against the odds that some enjoyed; the hardship and abuse suffered by others. Some adult characters are loosely based on actual participants, with fictional elements added that are in keeping with their modus operandi; others are pure inventions but grounded in real life. The political backdrop is consistent with reality. And while this is a story from the past, much of it still resonates with what we see in the world today. I will leave it to the reader to draw their own conclusions about this.

To find out more about the British Home Children, please visit my website www.chrismapp.com.

One

'Stand still, you little demons! How can I count you if you're scuttling about like mice in a pantry?'

On a July morning, in the year of our Lord 1881, one hundred orphans and foundlings had been mustered in a London street, and they were revelling in their temporary freedom.

'I can't hear myself think with all your shouting!'

It was a gathering of innocents and not-so-innocents of all ages, from runts who could barely buckle their shoe to bruisers whose judgement had not always kept pace with their physique. Their stories were many and various but joined by a common thread. Some had been thrown away as unloved and inconvenient; left to fend for themselves, or not, as the case may be – it could go one of two ways. For others, the abandonment was an act of desperation by those who could see no alternative, whilst plenty had run away of their own volition; there was only so much one could take. A cluster had been harvested from the nation's workhouses, repositories of privation and want, where altruism met harsh reality and came off a poor second. Others found themselves alone through the intervention of the Grim Reaper or Her Majesty's constabulary and were forced to seek sanctuary wherever they could find it.

And there were those whose parents, with all hope lost, had pleaded that their child be taken, their absence being the one gift they could bestow, the ultimate act of love.

Over the previous months and years all had found their way, by one means or another, to the Alice Hamilton Home for the Salvation and Advancement of Destitute Children; 'the SAD children', as people called them, much to the founder's disgust.

The harassed matron of the home was taking a register. She might as well have tried to catch the breeze that gently ruffled her papers. 'William Stretton, I have ticked you three times now. I will have to tie you to those railings if you won't stand still… I can't recognise you by the back of your head, boy. Turn around… You, with your hand raised. If you stopped singing, you might hear your name… Are you Esther or Emily? I've never known which twin is which… No, Bob Cooper, you do not have a twin. There is no one else remotely like you.'

It was the height of the emigration season. Throughout the summer British ships had been sailing for Canada, laden with children, dispatched to provide labour for a country whose appetite matched its boundless acreage. Now it was time to fill another.

Older than their years, but yet to enjoy a childhood that might be recognised as such, the latest shipment had been scrubbed up, kitted out and furnished with the promise of a new beginning and a better life. And on their last day in England they were skittish and contrary, having been whipped into a frenzy of expectation.

'Which child are you?'

'That's mad Maisie,' someone shouted. 'She's here, but she's not all there.'

Cue laughter and a slap from the girl.

'Stinky Joe is here, Matron. I can smell him.'

More hilarity and a boot delivered to a backside.

'Jack Somers?'

Three voices said 'yes' and shrieked in pleasure at their mischief.

A very small voice cut though a sudden quiet. 'I've changed my mind, ma'am. I don't want to go.'

Big steps for little feet.

A carriage pulled up at the front of the melee and a woman alighted awkwardly; the step had clearly been designed for a taller person. Her dress – businesslike and avoiding any sense of frippery – gave no clue as to what the season might be, and in a gloved hand she clutched an umbrella, despite there being no obvious need for it. Her hair might once have been an attractive chestnut but now tended to grey, with just a hint of its former glory, peeping out from beneath a hat that was more functional than decorative.

Alice Hamilton surveyed her charges with a piercing eye, instinctively disapproving of their irreverent spontaneity. There was a time and place for everything, and this was not it. Her gaze speared one child, transfixing him into silence and rooting him to the spot, then she skewered another, and soon a third was spiked. Having dealt with those within range, she smacked her umbrella fiercely on the frame of the carriage until even the most distracted child could not help but notice. The hubbub gradually subsided into a burble of impish whispers and giggles. She knew it was as good as it would get.

A servant produced a box and Alice stood on it.

'O happy travellers!' she boomed at the children. In her rapture, she stretched her arms out as far as they would go. 'O happiest of days!' She paused for dramatic effect, although the impact was largely negated by the sudden blowing of a raspberry and the nervous laughter that followed it. Alice glared thunderously in the direction of the offence until a semblance of dignity was restored.

'My brave souls!' she continued, satisfied there would be no repeat. 'On this bright morning you will write your names in my roll of honour as you march through our great city, bidding farewell to your humble past and striding fearlessly towards the brightest of futures. And folk of all persuasions shall witness your passing and will marvel at the transformation in your destiny. You are surely the fortunate ones, upon whom God has smiled.'

The more compliant children attempted to portray what 'fortunate' might look like.

'For some, this has been your home for many years, while for others it is merely a staging post along that glorious road to salvation. But each one of you will have been touched by our mission and all will remain in our prayers.' Alice smiled benevolently. 'The Good Lord has graced you with this opportunity, which I know you will grasp with willing hands and joyful hearts. And just as you are reborn as colonists of great resolve, the life of our glorious Empire is also renewed and enhanced.'

She paused and surveyed her flock, arms still outstretched, but now wavering, as the expected 'hurrah' did not materialise. Instead, the children were starting to fidget, and a fight had broken out at the rear of the gathering. With a growl of displeasure, Alice let her arms fall and swiftly moved to a conclusion. 'So now let us proudly march to the railway terminus at Euston, from whence you will be conveyed to the Port of Liverpool. There, your passage awaits you.' Now there was gravity in her voice, and just a hint of resignation. 'And may I remind you that throughout the parade you will be on public display, and among the crowds will be those with deep pockets and charitable intent, who will need some persuasion to part with their guineas. We rely upon their generosity, so I trust you will not let me down. Otherwise I might just as well pile you onto the back of a cart.'

Her eyes scorched through the morning sunshine, demanding discipline and order. It was time to put away childish things, as the Good Book said.

A sizeable audience had assembled to see the marchers on their way. There were onlookers at windows, and passers-by stood for a moment in curiosity. The staff of the home formed a semi-circle with the 'perhaps next time' children, ensuring that they remained separate from the travellers; there had been an unfortunate incident two years previously. Alice had insisted that certain representatives of the press should be present to record the occasion, and they stood in a huddle, passing around a bottle of something stronger than the hour demanded. A line of carriages waited for the road to clear, their occupants peering out and scowling, harumphing with impatience. But no mother or father or sister or brother were in attendance, even if any survived and lived close at hand.

'A clean break is essential,' Alice claimed in justifying their absence. 'Such a presence would put doubt into the mind of the child, even if that were not their purpose. We must make it as easy as possible for the poor mites, they have enough to think on.'

And in case any parent should get wind of proceedings, several large gentlemen were employed to minimise their involvement.

The children bade farewell to those who had cared for them. For many, it was the only family they had known or could remember. Some staff had a keepsake for those they favoured, perhaps a trinket or a handkerchief, and these would be cherished. All had a kind word. There was bravado from the older boys, who exuded confidence and belief, whether they felt it or not. The senior girls were outwardly calm but wiped their eyes when they thought no one was looking. There was a fretful grizzle among the most junior. Not all seemed to fully understand what was being asked of them.

'I will see you when I get back from my trip,' one eight-year-old said to the matron, who could not find the words to contradict her.

And then it was time to go. Banners were raised, fell and were raised again. Caps were thrown and retrieved. Children jostled and fought to walk beside their most trusted friends. Siblings clasped hands. The youngest were reluctant to move, and a girl called for her mother. Staff shouted and clouted. The scrimmage gradually dissolved into a semblance of straightness and shuffled off, with Alice's carriage in the vanguard, Boudicca leading her tribe into battle. The home's very own marching band struck up a spirited, if largely dissonant, accompaniment. Gaps soon appeared in the crocodile as those with the shortest legs fell behind their longer-legged peers, and from the front there was a constant refrain of 'keep up'. Coats were removed as the temperature rose, and shoes that once were clean fell prey to the filth of the street. There was excitement and hope, chatter and silence, sadness and fear. And as they straggled down Bethnal Green Road for the last time, more than one child looked back at the home and shed a tear.

Two

'Hey, mister, pick a card and I'll bet you a ha'penny I can name it.'

Arthur Dilkes, twelve years going on twenty, was up to his usual tricks. The parade of the SAD children had reached the City of London, and suddenly the streets were busy with carriages and omnibuses and people who had business to go about. As was customary, Arthur had dragooned Sam Barney into his service.

'Look, Sam, targets by the score. Let's see if we can make us some pocket money. Might come in handy later.'

'I don't know about that. Miss Alice won't like it.'

Most days Sam found himself trying to rein in his friend, usually in vain, and he often complained that his life was more taxing than it needed to be, although undoubtedly more interesting. The boys were inseparable; they had lost count of how long they had been in each other's pockets, but it was a sizeable chunk of their short lives. Together they haunted the city and the stations that served it, begging for a crust, never short of a story to tug at the heartstrings, with Arthur the raconteur and Sam arranged pathetically at his feet. They were an effective team in relieving street sellers of produce, Arthur a distraction with his silver tongue, and Sam taking the risk and claiming the spoils. They mudlarked their way along the Thames in search of valuables, and if they found a ring or bracelet, they could eat well that day. They scrounged paid work where they could find it, and if it was within the law, so much the better. Then one day they tried to take Alice Hamilton for a dupe and, as an alternative to the constabulary getting involved, they allowed themselves to be saved.

'Come on, Sam. Just like old times. We can't turn this down.'

And, as always, Sam allowed himself to be persuaded. The boys detached themselves from the ranks of the SAD children and headed for the hustle and bustle, scanning the scene in search of prey. But with fortunes to protect or acquire, most passers-by would not be stopped or even slowed, and Arthur's patter fell on stony ground. Then out of the corner of his eye, he spied an opportunity. 'There's one, Sam. Waiting for a hansom. He ain't going to move. He's trapped.'

A man stood at the side of the thoroughfare, his gaze impatiently travelling up and down the road, his arm poised for the moment when a cab might come within hailing distance. The boys moved in for the kill. Sam stood in front of the man, waving brightly coloured cards in his face and obscuring his view of the street, while Arthur spun a yarn about his magical powers. Eventually they wore him down.

'Go on, mister, just one card. It'll help you pass the time.'

'Very well. If it will get rid of you.' The man chose a card and held it as instructed.

'It's a queen … the queen of diamonds!' Arthur announced triumphantly, having read the markings on its back.

'And you are a pair of knaves.'

The boys spun round at the sound of a familiar voice. Alice Hamilton was not amused, and she dealt out a smack to each. The man took the opportunity to escape, vigorously gesturing at a hansom that was coming his way.

'You owe me a ha'penny, mister,' Arthur called over his shoulder as he was escorted back to the parade, and another smack landed before he had finished the sentence.

Alice placed the boys at the front of the crocodile, so they could be monitored more easily, and gave them flags to carry which might provide work for their idle hands.

'I'm telling you, that woman has eyes in the back of her head,' Sam muttered.

'More likely someone told on us.'

The procession meandered up Leadenhall Street and Cornhill, past the mighty Bank of England, weaving in and out of traffic that asserted its authority and made sure the marchers knew their place. Urchins, who might one day be SAD boys themselves, scampered in and out of the crowd, clearing a corridor through mud and filth for an important man or visiting lady, hoping to earn a penny for their trouble. There might have been a forlorn parent or two following at a distance, hoping to catch a final glimpse of a child they had surrendered or lost or had taken from them but, if so, they knew better than to make themselves known. The band played after a fashion and the children sang as they walked, some more enthusiastically and tunefully than others:

> 'Singing Songs of Expectation,
> Onward goes the pilgrim band.
> Through the night of doubt and sorrow,
> Marching to the Promised Land.'

Alice Hamilton clattered uncomfortably along, her carriage dwarfed by the big beasts that also drove along the road, an irritant to their progress and vulnerable to their bullying, a David in the land of Goliaths. She relished the challenge. Always on the lookout for new patrons, she waved imperiously at anyone whose gaze strayed in her direction; some showed signs of recognition, but most quickly looked away with a scowl. No matter, it was a numbers game, she reasoned; just one enquiry could be counted a success.

Eventually, the miles took their toll on the children, and the parade ambled to a temporary halt around midday. They took over a grassed area in a central square and spread themselves out. Alice read a sign suggesting that the area might be private and made a point of ignoring it.

'She's as bad as us for taking liberties,' Arthur noted approvingly, while Sam nervously looked around for any sign of a constable. There were none to be seen.

A cart had been following the procession, carrying supplies of bread and water for the marchers, and something more appetising for Alice Hamilton. Whatever the fare, it was eagerly consumed. The children sprawled amid the novelty of grass and trees, rejuvenating tired limbs by wiggling fingers and toes in the greenery. The youngest closed their eyes and the birds sang them to sleep. For a few moments there was tranquillity.

'I shall want more of this bread,' Arthur whispered to Sam as they sat in the shade of a London plane.

'We've had our share, and they know us too well to give us more by accident.'

'Watch this and do as I do.' Arthur cajoled a boy with a particularly large head to lend him his cap. Pulling it over his eyes, he rejoined the queue and, with head bowed and hands upraised, he smugly received another helping, chuckling as he made his escape.

'Now it's your turn.'

Sam took the cap, but it seemed to afford him less coverage. Either that, or it was itself memorable enough to be recognised so soon after its last appearance. Or maybe he just hadn't the confidence to carry off the deceit. But when he raised his hands for bread, his only reward was a clip round the ear by the server. 'You've had yours, greedy child. Be off with you.'

All Sam could hear was Arthur's cackle as he made his way back to the tree.

'Not speaking to you,' he mumbled, and he sulked for the rest of the afternoon, much to Arthur's annoyance and ridicule.

Soon the calm was ended by Alice Hamilton in full flow. 'We are a charitable organisation and cannot afford the hire of premises. Would you have the children walk until they fell down with exhaustion?'

A constable had appeared and instantly regretted that he had not taken longer in his approach or found a more pressing engagement altogether. As he was being appraised of his personal shortcomings and those of his employer, the children quietly organised themselves. For many, the excitement of the day was spent, yet they had miles still to go. Each step was more hesitant than the last, as doubt began to cast its insidious spell. The band had long since exhausted its repertoire and turned back to Bethnal Green, the last squawk of a trumpet fading into the distance. As the parade moved off again, the rain began to fall: London shedding tears for its lost children.

Towards the rear, Mary Oliver, a senior citizen at thirteen years old, took protective charge over brother Percy. He was four years her junior, but she treated him as if the gap was much wider. As they passed through the less salubrious districts, Mary clasped his hand tightly, forever on guard and deflecting his attention from sights that young eyes should not see.

Percy entertained himself by teasing her. 'Hey, sis, what's that lady doing?' he asked innocently, having a good idea of the answer. 'And why is that man leaning up against a wall?'

'You know full well, Percy Oliver. Now keep your eyes to the ground so you don't step in anything nasty. I can hardly move for it.'

And much to Percy's delight, as the day got longer and his steps ever shorter, Mary enquired whether he might like to be carried. He could not resist overstating his tiredness.

The party stumbled along Holborn, wheeling to the right up Southampton Row, and skirting the remains of the St Giles rookery, with its gin palaces and brothels that some of the children would have recognised, perhaps even from the inside. Alice had exhausted her waving arm and sat motionless with her thoughts: vindicated in her belief that even the most lowly might be saved and given hope through emigration, pride that she was the first to see it, and contempt for those that claimed at least an equal share of the idea (of whom there were several).

Finally, after a turn onto Euston Road, their destination stood before them, its entrance a fluster of scurrying feet as travellers did battle with clock and timetable.

The children gathered around Alice and her helpers. The station was thick with smoke from the trains – great metal beasts pawing the ground as they awaited their release. There were final instructions, barely audible above the shouting of the railwaymen and the answering roar of the engines, then, travel bags in hand, the children climbed on board, bound for the emigration docks at Liverpool and thence to Canada. Their trunks were already stacked in the luggage van, each containing everything a prospective pioneer might need: clothing suitable for Canadian extremes of weather, or the closest that Alice could find in more temperate London; a Bible, inscribed with the date of emigration; a Sankey hymn book; a copy of *The Pilgrim's Progress*. Suddenly, all was excitement again and there were screams of wonder as unfamiliar worlds flashed by at unimaginable speed. Alice settled into her private compartment and, satisfied that she could not be seen, took a surreptitious swig from a hip flask. And then she took another and yet another until finally her eyes closed and she could get some peace.

Three

As the SAD children rattled at speed towards their destiny, Mary Oliver was deep in thought, staring absently at the passing landscape, reliving the chain of events that had led to this moment. Brother Percy's head nestled on her shoulder as he drifted in and out of sleep, a trail of dribble darkening the fabric of her dress.

Trains were in their blood. Their father had been a stoker on the mighty London and North Western Railway, riding the cab up to Liverpool and Manchester, shovelling coal into the bowels of the engine, taking pride in its progress. He may have worked the very train on which they sat.

Mary could barely remember her mother, whose luck ran out most brutally at the birth of her third child. After twelve desperate hours of unstoppable flow and unspeakable pain, both were gone, the baby first, then the mother. Mary and Percy had been spared the worst of it, having been packed off to an aunt for Ma's confinement, and they did not return until after the burials. And when her father opened the door to them, Mary saw a different man to the one she had left: shrunken of face and drained of spirit, a man hollowed out by grief and loss.

They said very little that first day. Mary was impatient for him to talk; for it not to be acknowledged and spoken about, it was as if Ma had just disappeared into thin air without anyone noticing, and she deserved more than that. And without saying what each of them felt, it would imply that she might not be missed. Then there was the future: how would they live now that she was gone?

It was the next evening before her father was able to speak. Percy was safely asleep, and Pa sat in their one comfortable chair, Mary at his feet. She could see him struggling to find the right words and encouraged him by intermittently squeezing his hand. Otherwise she let him pick his moment. Even her six-year-old self had some sense of how hard it must be for him, as it was for her.

'It was a girl. We'd wanted a girl.'

Out of nowhere, the ice was broken. Mary stared sadly into the blankness of his eyes. 'I'd have liked a sister.'

Her father did not hear, or if he did, he made no acknowledgement, being back in that room with his wife once more.

'So cruel for her to die, seeing that the child was lost and knowing that her own passing was in vain.'

'And cruel for us. With 'em both gone and us still here.'

'You're right.' Now he was back with her. 'I'll say as much, but no more than you need to know, about what happened. There are things a child shouldn't hear.' He poured himself a pot of beer and offered Mary a sip, but she recoiled from the bitterness of the taste.

'How can you drink that evil brew?'

'Very easily, I think you'll find.' And he was true to his word.

They talked all evening, long past the hour when they would usually have been abed. Sometimes her father spoke openly, and Mary almost felt that she was there beside him in that terrible room, but at times he was distant and could barely bring himself to reply. And she herself was distracted by the ghosts that danced around her head. Her loss was as intense as her father's but, in some ways, different, more sculpted by a fear of the unknown than the absence of an emotional support. That would come later. First, there were more immediate concerns. What should I say? How can I help? Then, layered on top, sat a deep disquiet about the future: for her father, a man she had only ever known as solid and untroubled, and, by implication, for herself and Percy. How would they recover from this?

'Were you alone?' she suddenly asked. 'I'd hate to think that.'

'Two women from the block helped out. But there could have been a hundred or more, and it would still have felt a lonely place.'

Mary did not know what to say to that. She gave a big squeeze of her father's hand, and it was several minutes before the silence was broken.

As the conversation meandered around, there was one point that Mary was not shy of making. 'I've not said goodbye to her. Not had the chance.' she accused, steel in her voice. 'Surely, I could have seen her buried and said my farewells then.' She saw her father flinch and immediately regretted her tone. And when he spoke it was with regret.

'I thought you both too young, but perhaps I was wrong in that. Anyhow, I'll show you where she is, and then you can say whatever needs to be said.'

'I just want her to know that I shall miss her greatly. In case she's looking down and listening.' Mary dabbed her eyes with her only handkerchief. 'I loved her very much,' she whispered.

"She was a woman where that came easy.'

It was not all sadness and despair. There was also time for joyful memories, and it felt right that there should be laughter.

'Remember the time that woman emptied a latrine bucket out of her window without looking, and Ma got a drenching? I never heard such language from a lady.'

'And she was always shouting at someone or other, and most times I never knew why. Didn't take much to get her mad.'

'Aye, she'd a temper, your ma, and she didn't mind who felt it. Luckily, you seem to have been blessed with my sweet nature.'

And at other times they cried together.

'I can still see you in her arms, all freshly born. That was a good day.'

Finally, it could not be put off any longer. It was time for Mary to ask the question that most concerned her. 'What is to become of us?'

Her father shifted uncomfortably in his chair. 'I'll need you to grow up fast, my lovely,' he murmured, clearly hating himself for having to say it. 'I must go back to work; they won't pay me for sitting here. You must take her place as best you can, for all our sakes.'

Mary's heart sank. Even though she had half expected it, it was still a shock to hear it confirmed.

'It's awful unfair on you, but if I can't work then we'll be paupers, and you've seen what happens to them.'

'But Pa, how can I—'

'You've seen her wash and scrub. It just takes a bit of elbow grease.'

'But that's heavy work. I ain't got the strength—'

Pa ignored the increasing panic on Mary's face. 'It don't matter if it's not perfect. A bit cleaner than before will do. And the same with the floor and the rest of this place.'

'I can do that, maybe…'

'And she taught you to mend?'

'Not much, Pa, just a little.'

'A little is all we need. And you helped her cook?'

'I can make a pot of something if I know what to put in it, and I can rest it on the fire if someone shows me how to make one.'

'I'll teach you that, and there's women here you can ask about the rest.'

Mary shuddered. She could imagine how some of the fearsome women of the block might react to being troubled with her questioning.

'And most important of all, there's the boy to look after. I sees you doing it already, so I have no fear of that.'

And even in her state of fluster, Mary felt very proud that her father should place such trust in her, and she was determined to prove him right to do so. 'I'll try my best, Pa, but I'm scared. What if I get it all wrong?' She hugged her father with all her might, as if in doing so she might absorb some of his strength and knowledge.

He gently stroked her hair. 'I know you, Mary Oliver. Your best will be more than good enough.'

And so a routine was established. While her father worked, Mary slowly became the mother she had lost, learning through trial and frequent error, and hiding her grief beneath a mountain of chores. Slowly her confidence grew, and Pa would never complain, no matter what shortcomings were exposed.

'That's very tasty, my lovely,' he would always say, even if served up something unrecognisable, or 'Don't worry, I can do without that shirt another day.'

Mary often visited Ma's grave and asked for her advice. Finding some comfort in it, she would generally muddle through. Almost by accident, she discovered that she had a singing voice and found that if she used it, time passed more agreeably. And sometimes other women would join in, and the tenement would be regaled with the latest ditty from the music halls, the words and notes being less important than the act of singing them; briefly they could escape the world as they knew it; it reminded them that they were not alone.

Most importantly, Mary attended to Percy's needs and kept him safe and entertained, watching him grow from infant to boy, observing his health and contentment with satisfaction and much relief. All in all, she did not think very much about whether she was happy, and consequently she was.

While she had not been a witness to her mother's fate, Mary could see, and almost hear, her father slowly fading away. It was an illness that crept up on its victim, with today being little different from yesterday, which was not unrecognisable from the day before. The damage was only obvious in hindsight. Unknown to Pa, each shovel of coal that he hurled into the furnace took its revenge on him: its offspring particles, now independent and homeless, sought sanctuary and found it each time he breathed in. At first it was a mild cough, nothing out of the ordinary; all city dwellers inhaled their share of soot just by walking about or opening a window. But soon you could hear him approaching from a distance, retching with the effort of clearing his chest, and in time he barely had the puff to walk even the shortest distance or perform the simplest task. Still, he greeted each day, shovel at the ready, dragging himself to the station for the early train, stoking the fire from reserves of willpower and stubbornness.

'You must find other work, Pa,' Mary begged him, time and time again.

'I don't know nothing else, my lovely, and we must eat.'

'But what if it kills you, Pa? What will happen to us?'

'I can rely on you, my child. You have so much of your mother in you. But promise me you'll care for the boy. Until he's old enough to care for you.'

And of course she promised, but she fretted that it might

come to this. 'Your pig-headedness will break my heart,' she once told him. 'I can see it coming.'

Then one day, just short of Mary's tenth birthday, her father did not return from work at his usual time, and it was after midnight before a railwayman called to break the news. His body was returned to London on the mail train, and he was given something better than a pauper's funeral, courtesy of the burial club to which he had subscribed. And so Ma and Pa lay together once more.

'Stupid man, look what you done now,' was all Mary could think as the coffin was lowered. But she remembered her promise. And she tried not to let Percy see how scared she was: after all, she was Big Sister and must act the part. As they stood together at their parents' graveside, she was already thinking ahead. 'We can't stay where we are, Percy.'

'Why not, sis?'

'We've no money for the rent, and I can't leave you while I earn some.'

'What will we do, sis?'

'I have a plan.'

The children went home to pack up their belongings, such as they were, and two days later they found themselves outside their aunt's lodgings, seeking entry. It took three attempts for the sound of their knocking to exceed the noise within, but eventually the door was opened by a woman who was clearly having a difficult day.

'You can hear them inside, shouting and screaming and wanting things. And you think I've room for two more?'

'You promised Ma you'd care for us if we needed it. Pa said you did, and he weren't no liar.'

The aunt could recall the pledge, made while her mind was mellowed by something strong, and in the expectation that she would never have to honour it.

'I weren't in my right mind when I said it. People say all sorts they don't mean.'

'So, you'd see your sister's children starve, would you?'

'My own aren't much better off. And neither am I.'

'Still better than our situation.' Mary folded her arms and stood her ground.

The aunt continued with her excuses. 'Look, I know I said I would, but a lot's happened since then. My previous man might have been all right with it, like when you stayed before, but the new one's a very different kettle of fish. Not the charitable sort. And I've more of my own now to think on. They just keep coming. Can't seem to stop 'em.'

'Tell him I'll do all the looking after for Percy. I wouldn't trust no one else anyway. And I'll help with yours. We just need a bed and a few pence a week to live on.'

'You'll help with mine?' The aunt's eyes lit up and suddenly she was all smiles. 'Very well, I'll hold you to that. I'll ask his lordship, and while I can't vouch for what he'll say, I'll do my best.'

She closed the door, although almost every word was still audible through its splintered skin. It transpired that her man had a great deal to say, and none of it was sympathetic to the idea.

'We ain't got the money for two extra mouths.'

'We would have if you didn't drink it.'

'I work hard. I deserve my drink.'

'Work hard! It's me that fetches the most in.'

'I bring you gin and ale. What more do you want?'

'All you bring me is trouble and yet more children.'

The back and forth continued for some time, its volume rising in line with its malice. Ear to the door, Mary was increasingly unsure whether she wanted her aunt to prevail, with visions of their likely experience flickering before her eyes. The sound of objects being thrown was the final straw.

'We can't stay here,' she said, grabbing Percy's hand. 'I've got an idea where we can go.'

'Where's that, sis?'

'You'll see.'

Meanwhile, inside the lodgings the debate was reaching a conclusion. 'All right, you can have 'em, but don't expect me to lift a finger to help.'

'No change there, then.'

And there was a final crash – perhaps a plate meeting a sorry end – and the cry of a man who might have been the target. But when their aunt finally appeared at her door, Mary and Percy were gone. Her face darkened and her body slumped as if all hope had suddenly been drained away. 'She promised to help with mine,' she repeated pathetically over and over again. And then she identified the real culprit. 'It's all your fault,' she screamed at the man inside, and re-entered the fray with renewed purpose.

Mary led Percy through the streets towards Bethnal Green. An hour later they stood shivering outside Alice Hamilton's Home for the Salvation and Advancement of Destitute Children, nervously clutching each other's hand.

'They'll take us in and treat us right. Or so people say.'

'You sure, sis?'

'I've heard of others that stood here and not regretted it.' Mary's confident voice was for her own benefit as much as Percy's. They looked anxiously up at the blackened windows and weathered brickwork, and the sculpted figurines that might be gargoyles.

'They're a likeness of the children inside,' Mary teased, trying to raise a smile.

They approached the entrance, a forbidding wooden door with a metal grille through which a wary eye could be cast over any newcomers.

'See the mouth of the great beast, waiting to feast on little boys that pass its way.' Mary pinched Percy's arm so that he cried out and then laughed. But while she wore the bravest of faces, Mary's stomach turned somersaults that an acrobat would have admired.

'You sure this is the right place, sis?'

'This is the place. And remember that, whatever awaits us, we still have each other.' She clasped Percy's hand a little tighter, and with the other she knocked timidly upon the door.

Four

The 'Orphan Express', as some termed it, swept into Liverpool docks and decanted its passengers onto the quayside, celebrating their release through whistle and steam. Gaggles of children milled about awaiting instruction, while helpers tried to agree on what that instruction should be. Already sporting battle scars, the children's trunks were swung brusquely onto handcarts by impatient men and wheeled up the quayside, where they would suffer further indignities in being loaded for Canada. Several mites had misplaced items from their travel bags, overcome by the temptation to take out and touch some basic accessories, with ownership still a novelty for many; there was a delay and some muttering as these were found and restored to their grateful owners.

Alice Hamilton emerged from her compartment, somewhat bleary-eyed, and was soon barking orders at flustered helpers. 'You! Yes, you! Take this first group up to where we are berthed. What do you mean, "where is it"? Find something that looks like a ship and stay there. And you! Round up the stragglers and follow suit. And keep them well away from the edge of the quay. I am not dressed for fishing them out.'

And after tears and tantrums from children and staff alike, eventually all were manoeuvred to more or less the right place.

The children gaped at the SS *Parisian*, silhouetted against the setting sun, that was to be their carriage across the perilous Atlantic. Most had seen great vessels steaming up the Thames to shed their cargo in the Port of London but had never thought they might have the adventure of boarding such a beast. There were open mouths, wide eyes and nervous smiles aplenty.

'It's a sea monster!' squealed one.

'The size of a town!' added another.

'It won't seem so big once we're out there,' cautioned a third. 'I've heard stories.'

And those helpers who had sailed before exchanged knowing glances.

Arthur Dilkes was unimpressed. 'Course, I went to sea once,' he boasted.

'And how did that come about?'

Alice Hamilton happened to be passing and gave Arthur her most withering stare. She had heard her share of tall stories and outright lies, and not just those told by children, and she always found some sport in deflating an ego or cutting an exaggeration down to size. Arthur had expected to deliver his tale to an admiring audience and was temporarily flummoxed. 'Well, it was more of a barge, actually,' he spluttered. 'I jumped on at Maidstone, then up the Medway, round the corner to the Thames, and on to London…'

'It is hardly going to sea, is it?'

There were giggles from listening children, unused to Arthur being ridiculed.

'Nearer than most have been, miss. Same water, just placed different.'

'So, can you swim?' Sam butted in. 'I'll wager you can.'

'I expect so.'

'If the ship goes down, being able to swim won't help you much.' And with that happy thought, Alice stomped off.

Further down the quay a shambles of men and women stood or sprawled, according to taste, clutching one-way tickets and on much the same mission as the children. Shabby and sullen, many swigged from bottles or flasks as they waited their turn to board, becoming more dishevelled by the mouthful. They would be the children's roommates in steerage and would have Alice Hamilton to deal with if there was any trouble. Meanwhile, those destined to enjoy a more comfortable passage arrived in a clutter of transports: broughams and landaus for the gentlemen, Victorias for the ladies. They were followed at a respectful distance by wagonettes, groaning under the weight of their masters' luggage, elbowing past each other in a delicate waltz of hoof and wheel. Some had friends or family to wave them farewell, and tears were shed at their departure.

There was no one to say goodbye to the children. The order to embark broke the silence. Looking nervously about, they walked hand in hand up the gangway into their ark.

'Are you sure about this?' whispered Sam, looking hesitantly down at the quayside from the deck of the *Parisian*. Night had fallen and the ship was about to sail. Soon they would be out of sight of the mother country and all they had known.

'Too late now even if I weren't.'

'We will be together, won't we? When we get placed, I mean.'

'Don't see why not.'

Sam stared at his friend. 'Sure you want that?' he asked timidly.

'Course I do. Said so before, didn't I?'

But Sam wouldn't let it go. 'I told Miss Alice to arrange it, but I'm not sure she heard.'

'She hears what she wants to hear.' Arthur's voice betrayed some impatience. 'Look, I'll speak to her as well. If she'll listen.'

'I know it's more important to me than to you,' Sam said quietly.

The boys were silent in a way that they had rarely been before.

'Suppose we'll be sent to a farm, then'. Sam ventured to fill the gap.

'It's that or parade about as a maidservant, and I doubt I'll look good in a pinny.' Arthur laughed perhaps a little too heartily.

'But we never done farm work before.'

'Can't be that difficult. Farmers seem all right with it.'

Another awkward silence.

'Course, what I'd really like is a family to call my own.' Sam gazed wistfully out into the darkness. 'Not one that just sees you as a worker, but as something more.'

Arthur winced. 'You might have mentioned it. About a thousand times,' he exaggerated. It was probably only in the hundreds.

'Don't you want that?'

For a moment Arthur looked uncomfortable. 'If it comes along, fine, but I'll not lose sleep over it.'

Too proud to admit it, Sam thought. 'Miss Alice said we might get one of those,' he continued.

'See, you don't need me after all.'

Sam wiped his eyes. 'Won't happen, though, will it?'

Arthur sighed and set off to explore the ship. 'I've got a good feeling about Canada,' he shouted over his shoulder.

Sam's gut was telling him a different story.

Below decks, Mary Oliver was inspecting the sleeping arrangements and laying claim to what appeared to be the safest and most private space for Percy, making sure she could also squeeze in beside him. Others had the same idea, and Mary had to fight off some competition for a prime slot, but she was older than most and tall for her age and was not above some push and shove in the line of duty. The beds were nothing more than straw mattresses, and doubtless had stories of their own to tell, while the children's travel bags would have to serve as pillows; there would be little comfort here. The first night, Mary was awake until all was quiet, in case the drinking and the singing of the men in steerage evolved into something more threatening.

The *Parisian* cast off and edged down the estuary, still protected by the proximity of the land, and with the sea yet to show its true colours. But even that was more than some constitutions could bear, and the children took comfort in dreaming of the reception they had been promised at the end of their voyage.

'They'll be getting out the flags for us,' Arthur confidently predicted. And soon he was dead to the world. Sam was awake for rather longer.

As the children strove to find their sea legs the next morning, a leader appeared in the *Toronto Herald*, a newspaper of robust opinions and only a passing interest in the facts. The proprietor himself had penned the article, as he did from time to time, and the editor knew better than to change a word of it. The title left little to the imagination:

THE SCUM ON THE TIDE:
PLEASE GOD, DELIVER CANADA
FROM BRITISH CHILDREN

FIVE

'It did not start with children. Indeed, any involvement with that species was the last thing on my mind when I set off on life's journey. I am not maternal by nature.' Alice Hamilton told her story whenever she could find someone to listen, knowing that each time she did, charitable donations might wend their way to her door, or a well-connected person might make her acquaintance. It was time well spent.

She doubted that she had ever been a child herself, in the true sense of the word, more an adult-in-waiting. Being the youngest of many, and several years behind the nearest, she had largely been left to her own devices, bereft of company: a deficit that had suited her well. Almost an outsider, she watched the ups and downs of family life and, in the gaps between the action, reflected on what she had observed. She saw the respect that strangers gave to her father as a man of business and noted that her mother received rather less as a woman of the home. She found anomalies in the way that boys and girls were addressed, and in the subject matter discussed, and wondered why that should be so. She witnessed her father pay for his sons to be educated, but not his daughters, and even as a child she could not see the fairness or the logic in that.

So, while the sons had been dispatched to a middling public school, which guaranteed them a tolerable career, the daughters fell under the tutelage of Alice's mother, and their grounding was in the skills they would need to be a good wife in an equivalent family. This was not to Alice's taste. She saw some merit in the organisational and management aspects of the job, but she did not take to sewing or to the piano, and her small talk left a lot to be desired. Instead, she was in thrall to the array of books in her father's library. She devoured this resource, immersing herself in works of philosophy and science, politics and economics, intent on giving herself the education she had been denied.

When she reached an age when she could come and go as she pleased, albeit with some barbed comment from a parent in her ears, Alice began to look more outward. I will need a religion, she thought. Sufficiently robust to save my soul, but not so intrusive that it will unduly restrict my earthly business.

Thus far, she had paid lip service to her parents' Anglican faith, but now she cast her net far and wide, teasing a communion of priests and ministers with her potential commitment. 'I am looking for a spiritual home,' she announced on entering a Catholic church. But not this one, she had decided when she left less than an hour later. She did not need a go-between to intercede with any God. She was quite capable of doing it herself. In addition, the incense had brought on what might have been an allergic reaction.

Next, she encountered Methodism. She approved of its emphasis on charity and plain dressing, but was less keen on the teetotalism, having already developed a taste for sherry. She did not return. Baptists and Quakers came and went without approval, before Alice set sail for the extremes of evangelism, finding it to be populated by a bewildering array of factions.

'I cannot tell the difference between them, yet they all seem to hate each other,' she mused.

She worked her way systematically through each. 'I like the certainty of your beliefs and the passion with which you express them,' she told the leader of one congregation. 'And I am happy to live within the meaning of the Bible, as you insist, but it is not always clear what the Holy Book is trying to say. What if I disagree with your interpretation?'

'Then you are not for us, madam.'

And Alice was gone almost before the words had left his lips.

'It is a sin for women to be in authority over men,' another leader informed her.

And she left with even greater speed.

'I do not understand why you have embarked on this quest when there is already a perfectly serviceable religion at your disposal,' her mother remarked one day.

'The Anglican faith is too comfortable. It tries to be all things to all men, rarely women, of course, but ends up being neither one thing nor the other. It does not suit my temperament.'

Her mother could not understand how 'comfortable' could be viewed negatively.

After much inspection and enquiry, Alice concluded that she did not fit in anywhere precisely, and she was determined only to accept an exact match. 'It is not right to compromise on a matter of such importance,' she reasoned. 'To anyone that asks, I shall describe myself as an evangelist of an unspecified nature, and I shall deal with God on an individual basis. It does not require the involvement of a third party.'

So, religion was an item that she could now tick off her list. But there was a large and threatening cloud on the horizon. One by one, Alice's sisters had reached an age at which they could marry, and they duly obliged, entering into a variety of practical arrangements that served them well enough. But Alice remained aloof from this procession, neither displaying nor attracting any serious interest, and she was even unmoved by the appearance of nieces and nephews. If her father arranged for a young gentleman to call, he would either see her scuttling down the street as he arrived or, if she had not been pre-warned, his visit would play second fiddle to whichever book she was engaged with at the time. Her parents tiptoed around the matter until it could no longer be avoided.

'She will need a husband whether she wants one or not, that is the way of the world,' her father fretted. 'But what can we do? I have nearly exhausted my supply of eligible sons, and there is a dearth of older men with a vacancy.'

'Sadly, no one wants to watch a woman read.' Her mother sighed.

'It is our duty to set her straight, for her own good.'

'As you wish, but I fear she will not be told.'

So, one day her parents invited Alice into the parlour and sat her down. Outside it was dark and cheerless, and the rain beat down against the windows. Inside, all appeared to be snug: a fire crackled in the hearth and chairs were arranged so that all could benefit from it. But that was the extent of the welcome. Alice had known that a confrontation was looming, and she was bristling for a fight. She folded her arms in defiance, as if daring the conversation to take place.

Her father bit his lip. 'I will cut to the chase,' he began. 'Mankind is a social animal. Everyone knows that. We have not evolved to be alone—'

'And most will find at least some comfort in having a companion,' her mother interrupted rather desperately. 'Someone to escort us through the travails of life, to soften the blows that otherwise rain down upon us…'

'Quite...'

'Even if that someone is not of your choosing.'

Alice cast her eyes to the heavens. 'But marriage is not companionship. If it was, then I would be less opposed to it,' she replied, her voice betraying the impatience she always felt when others could not see what was so obvious to her. 'With the law as it stands, it is tantamount to ownership, and I do not wish to become the property of any man. I intend to be remembered for something worthwhile, beyond the mere production of children.'

'It is a laudable aim, but not inconsistent with marriage,' Alice's mother argued. 'You have met Lady Pevensey, my erstwhile bridge partner. She is involved in a number of worthy causes and still seems able to satisfy Lord Edgar.'

'A somewhat demanding man, in my experience,' her father added ruefully.

'And I have many similar acquaintances for whom philanthropy and matrimony go hand in hand.'

Alice shrieked with laughter – an outburst born of ridicule, not amusement. 'Your Lady Pevensey succeeds despite, not because of, her husband,' she scoffed. 'Her Ladyship inherited a multitude of interests from her late father, which she might have used for her own benefit had she been allowed, but instead her consort has proceeded to gamble them away. I have no need of such assistance.'

'Not all men are as unfamiliar with skill and luck as Lord Edgar.'

'Will you not reconsider?'

'Can we not persuade you?'

'The institution has served us well, has it not, my dear?'

Her father gazed expectantly at his wife, and Alice noted that she hesitated a little before she nodded.

There was a lull in proceedings while the maid brought

in afternoon tea. As a statement of intent, Alice made sure she took the first cup, contrary to protocol. She paced up and down the room in frustration, resulting in some spillage, and the maid trailed behind her mopping up.

'And what will you put in place of wedlock?' her father asked.

Alice's mother took her hand.

'We will not always be here to support you,' she said quietly.

'We had rather expected you would be gone by now.'

Alice's mother looked daggers at her husband, but their daughter was too absorbed in her own script to notice. 'I shall find a worthwhile trade or profession and earn my own living, and if such employment does not exist, I shall create it.'

The father spluttered, distributing little pieces of cake beyond their intended orbit.

'As you know, if I were to take a husband, any income I generate would become his own property, not mine, even though he would be wholly undeserving of it. That is the law.'

'If he permitted you to work at all…'

'But as a single woman, I can retain whatever I earn for my own use.'

'Yes, I can see the logic in what you say.' Alice's mother seemed as surprised as any by her sudden and enthusiastic endorsement. Her husband grimaced; they would have words later. Alice smiled and took some time to consider her next move. Might she be winning the argument, at least with one participant? And was now the right time to ask the question? It was a risk. It might not go well, but unless she tried, she would never know. And what did she have to lose? She diluted her natural belligerence and adopted a conciliatory tone that was unfamiliar to her and not entirely genuine.

'However, I have made enquiries,' she began hesitantly. 'Exhaustively so, and it transpires that a young woman such as I, with no independent means, might struggle…'

'To be taken seriously?' Suddenly her father seemed to smell victory.

'Yes, and—'

'Might find that a man would rather employ another man?'

'Sadly, yes—'

'And discover that your longed-for trade or profession does not exist?'

'Shamefully, there is little precedent for what I seek.'

'None, I would say.'

Alice stared into the fire that by now was in want of a log. 'Will you help me?' she whispered, each word having to be wrenched from her mouth, barely audible above the sound of swallowed pride. 'Either with finance or influence in finding suitable employment. You are well known among those I seek to impress.' Then her voice hardened a little. 'I have not previously asked much of you.' She looked anxiously over at her father, but he could not return the courtesy.

'I have paid generous dowries for your sisters,' he mumbled, poking the fire to avoid eye contact. 'And clearly one would be available to accompany you, should you choose to avail yourself of it.'

'No! No! No! That money would be set aside for my daily upkeep during the marriage, not for investment in an enterprise, as I would wish it to be.' Alice's voice had risen an octave.

'You would gain an indirect benefit from it, having a roof over your head and a place in society from which you can plan your adventures. And your husband might even be persuaded to support those ambitions…'

'But Papa…'

'Or, failing that, you will surely be in demand as a paid companion or even as a governess, given the extent of your learning. That should be adequate compensation.'

Alice's anger finally boiled over. 'That is nowhere near enough for me. And why would you think that it should be?' she snapped. 'I can quote Hume and Descartes, and I am familiar with the works of Adam Smith. My copy of the *On the Origin of Species* is well thumbed, as is my King James Bible. I have read Homer and Aristotle in the original Greek and understood much of what they say. And yet you want me to drink tea for a living? Or waste my time and knowledge on inbreds?'

Her father slowly raised his gaze from the fire. 'That is all I can offer.'

Unaccustomed tears welling in her eyes, Alice stormed from the room. 'I am so disappointed in you,' she shouted over her shoulder.

'We only want what is best,' her father called after her. 'One day you will see that.'

But Alice was not listening. She stomped into her room and slammed the door. 'Why can't he accept me for who I am?' she muttered to herself, pacing the floor and kicking out at anything that got in her way. Just as importantly, in her eyes she had shown herself to be weak and had been shamed because of it; that would not happen again.

Meanwhile, downstairs, her father was justifying his position. 'Well, that was a performance. But I am sure she will come round.'

'I can sympathise with the girl. I once had dreams of my own.'

'Really? I did not know that.'

*

But Alice did not come round. It became a point of principle for both sides and stubbornness prevailed; she was her father's daughter. And apart from the occasional loaded remark, the matter was not spoken of again. The years slipped by and there Alice remained, ensconced in her beloved library, making plans that never came to fruition and forever scratching at the door like a dog trying to get out, howling at the waste of a life. Then when she reached her thirtieth year, suddenly her father died, and for a time she was assailed with regret. Surely there were words that each deserved to hear, had they felt able to say them. Perhaps feelings could have been expressed that might have been reciprocated. Maybe they could have arrived at an understanding if they had but tried. Alice's melancholy deepened.

On the surface, life carried on as before. Then one day her mother called Alice into the parlour. A fire whispered in the grate and a pot of tea sat invitingly on the table. Alice noted her mother's expression. She was struggling to contain a smile, as if bursting to tell a secret. 'Your father's estate has now been distributed, and I find myself a wealthy widow,' she began.

Alice did not see what business it was of hers; she had not inherited a penny.

'And I wish you to have a sizeable part of my share.'

Alice's teacup rattled in its saucer as she shook with surprise and excitement. Surely, she must have misheard. 'But, Mama, what of yourself?'

'I am unlikely to spend all that he left me, and I can always remarry if I am desperate enough. Your brothers have their careers, and your sisters can rely on their husbands. You are the one that needs it.'

Alice was speechless, save for a succession of squeaks and squeals that were most unlike her. A thousand ideas ran through her head, as they had so many times before, but now suddenly all were possible.

'Then perhaps you can enjoy the life that I was not allowed to have.' There was a tinge of regret behind her mother's smile.

Alice had never been overly affectionate, even as a child, but now she leapt on her mother and hugged her with all the force she could muster. And there were tears and laughter and her mother felt quite swamped by the torrent of plans that came her way. She had forgotten that her daughter could be happy.

'Please don't think badly of him,' she said in a quieter moment. 'He was a man of his time. But now the time is yours, make the most of it.'

Alice did not need a second invitation. Where once she had been captive, now she was free to fly. 'And even the most benighted man will have to take me seriously as a woman of business,' she crowed.

And so it proved. Various enterprises and endeavours followed, some successful, others less so, but all entered into with the utmost vigour. There was a labour of love, an agency to find worthwhile employment for women such as herself, with Alice scouring London for men that could be persuaded, or if necessary intimidated, into training her charges in the gentler professions and, having found them, haranguing other men to give these women a chance. Once that business was established and even generating a small profit, she placed it in safe hands and cast around for other ventures. 'I wish to be remembered for achieving something worthwhile,' she reminded herself. 'To leave a legacy that might prove an inspiration to others.' But where to look? She was too impatient for science, and what if experiments did not align with her expectations? That would displease her greatly. Politics involved being nice to people that you did not like, and nasty to people that you did. She was a reader, not a writer; an insufficient experience of life dictated that (perhaps later, she thought).

Alice finally settled on philanthropy, which had several advantages: it seemed to play to her organisational and promotional strengths, particularly the latter; depending on one's interest, it was possible to make a real difference to wretched lives; and it was pleasingly visible. She first became interested in the plight of paupers and was shocked at what she found in the nation's workhouses, their conditions not being dissimilar to its prisons. This pointed her in the direction of lost and desperate children, of whom there were so many. 'Their condition should touch the hardest of hearts,' she observed, 'And yet they are barely catered for.' But children were not her natural constituency, and she thought long and hard before deciding upon this direction. 'I shall not find them a burden,' she eventually decided. 'I shall have staff for all that.'

So, with her usual zeal Alice set out to save as many as she could. She established a home in her name in which they could be housed, but what then to do with them? A visit to Canada provided the answer: children, who could be made useful about the home or the farm, would be most welcome there.

And a year later the first SAD child set foot on Canadian soil.

SIX

Whenever she sailed to Canada, Alice Hamilton would always seek out persons of influence to whom she could tell her story and who might subsequently be persuaded to contribute towards her work. It also helped to pass the time – sometimes agreeably, sometimes not. Such a course was not without risk; the sight of a woman approaching a man in determined fashion was open to misinterpretation. But overall it was worth the occasional embarrassment.

There were always those with important business in the Dominion, and this passage was no different. First Alice accosted a civil servant, who was running an errand for the British government; he was very keen to talk, expressing an unusual degree of interest in her work and questioning her almost to the point of inquisition. But it was soon clear that he had no money to give, so after that Alice avoided him, scurrying away if it seemed that their paths might cross. Other prey was more obliging: a British industrialist, who had some interests overseas and was keen to have more; a baronet returning to his colonial estates after a restorative sojourn in the mother country; and a Canadian entrepreneur, who had been touting for business in Europe and whose success had placed him in a generous mood. All found their wallets to be lighter after time spent in Alice's company.

The SAD children saw very little of Alice; even in the confined space of the ship, she contrived to avoid all childcare, leaving it to her helpers. Then, three days in, the *Parisian* was struck by a murderous storm, ferocious even by the standards of the Atlantic. It started as a small, black cloud in the distance, apparently innocuous, since the rest of the sky was set fair. But it soon chased down the ship, and within minutes you could not tell whether it was night or day. A westerly howled, sweeping grown men off their feet and sculpting waves that tossed the ship around as if it were a toy thrown between children. Great torrents of rain lashed down, each droplet a tiny cannonball, hitting the deck with such force that it seemed to rebound to the height from which it fell. On board, anything that was free to move, human or otherwise, could not help but do so, clattering into each other in a frenzy of breakage and bruising. And there was no escaping the cacophony: the complaint of tortured metal as the ship was forced into unnatural angles; the spectral howling of the wind as it poured through the structure of the vessel, finding cracks and chinks and vents of every size; the desperation of those who believed that their time had come.

Trembling helpers gathered the children in the ship's mess hall, where they huddled together, taking what comfort they could from each other. Some were wailing and whimpering, others were shocked into silence. Even Arthur Dilkes felt something that he thought might be nerves, perhaps even fear, although the situation was not so grave that he would let others see it.

'Storms always blow themselves out, you just have to hang on and wait,' he claimed with certainty, half-remembering something he had once heard.

But Sam Barney was in no mood for Arthur's dubious buoyancy, and he turned angrily on his friend. 'So much for your "good feeling" about this,' he sneered in between giant sobs. 'We're all going to die here. You happy now?'

'I ain't dying, don't know about you.'

'It's not in my hands, is it? Yours neither, and if you weren't so full of yourself you might see that.'

'If it's out of our hands, then why worry? If your time's up, it's up. If it's not, it's not.'

The pair were having to shout to be heard above the noise of the storm, but had it been quiet they would probably still have bellowed out of mutual frustration.

'Just think about it. Most ships don't sink when they hit a storm. If they did, no one would ever set foot on 'em.'

'But some go down.'

'And others don't.' Arthur could not help but deliver a final twist of the knife. 'You know, Sam Barney, if you're not careful you'll spend your life always being on the ship that sinks, whereas I'll be on the one that floats. That's the difference between us.'

And he contrived to move far enough away so that any further conversation was impossible, leaving Sam to stew in his resentment.

Further down the mess hall, Mary Oliver held Percy tightly to her, quietly murmuring words of hope and encouragement that she pretended to believe. However, Percy was already remarkably calm.

'The way I see it, sis, we can't lose.'

'How's that, my dear?'

'Well, either we'll live through this and that will be good. And if we don't, we'll be with Ma and Pa again in heaven. And that would be even better.'

Mary could not answer for a moment, marvelling at the

innocence and the bravery of his logic. While she had a strong preference for living, she did not want to undermine Percy's peace of mind by admitting it. 'Hadn't thought of it that way, but you're right. We've nothing to fear.'

'See, sis, I'm not as simple as you make out.'

'But we must keep close so that whatever our fate be, it befalls us both. We don't want one here and one there, do we?' Mary pointed to the heavens and redoubled her hold on Percy.

The children were joined in the mess hall by fellow steerage travellers, and even some from the cabins sought out company that they would normally shun. Few wanted to die alone.

Then, as the storm was at its height and with the end seemingly nigh, the door to the mess hall swung open and a middle-aged woman fell in. She righted herself, briefly staggered about, then felt the floor again until, at the second time of asking, she finally obtained a foothold in the room. Alice Hamilton weaved her way towards the mess hall table, climbed upon it so that she could be seen by all and, through a miracle of balance, set out to restore some order. Closing her eyes and clasping her hands together, she prayed for salvation. But she did not beg or plead with the Almighty, or prostrate herself at His feet, as many might have done. Instead she made a reasoned case, cogent in its argument and unanswerable in its reasoning, for why she and her children should survive. It was a matter of common sense, she thought, and any deity worth its salt was bound to see it.

'On behalf of these poor mites and those whose lives we briefly share, I seek mercy and crave forgiveness for our sins and omissions, which doubtless are many and various but surely undeserving of this extreme sanction.' There was even a note of disapproval in her voice. 'For many years I have been Your servant, rescuing innocents from the ravages of man and from their own deficiencies, setting them on the true path, while also making them productive here on Earth. This is valuable work and not to be dispensed with lightly. If we are to perish here, then not only would these hapless children be lost, but through my own demise any that would follow in their footsteps would also be abandoned. But if we can be delivered from this mortal danger, I pledge to You that I will redouble my efforts to save these unfortunates so that they might serve You and be of some benefit to their fellow man, which currently they are not...'

She was making Him an offer.

And after the prayers came the hymns to seal the deal.

'Eternal Father, strong to save...' sang the children, with particular emphasis on the refrain 'for those in peril on the sea'. At first, there was no change in their predicament and so they sang again, and yet again when the wind seemed to gather even greater force. Throughout, Alice remained steadfast.

'All will be well,' she repeated calmly but authoritatively.

Slowly the storm abated. The rain became a shower then a drizzle and finally a gentle spray, before subsiding entirely. The wind sped away to harass other souls; perhaps they would be more compliant and meekly succumb to their fate. And as the darkness lifted, the hymns were sung less in supplication and more in gratitude before the children erupted into joyous release as the first rays of the sun peeped through the thinning clouds.

'Told you, nothing to fret about.' Arthur Dilkes swaggered around the mess hall. Sam Barney turned away and did his best to ignore his friend. He almost wished that the ship had gone down, just to prove him wrong.

'So, we won't get to see Ma and Pa again.' Percy sighed.

'One day, I promise you. For now, they'll want us to make the most of being spared.' And Mary was soon organising him again as if nothing had happened.

In her cabin, Alice Hamilton plotted her next move. She had spotted a distant relative of the Queen who had sought refuge in the mess hall and who must have been impressed by her intercession. She spent the rest of the day refining her story for his benefit.

SEVEN

When the SS *Parisian* set its course for the Promised Land, some were not yet ready to leave their old life behind. Tear-stained and drained of spirit, Margaret Walsh sat alone in the first private space she could find, thinking of the father she might never see again. While other children gazed forward in anticipation, she was always looking back, her stinging eyes and aching heart anchored to a memory that was becoming more distant by the mile.

Just six years old (but nearly seven, as she would tell you), Margaret was the youngest to travel. She had not known the delights of Alice Hamilton's London home, nor had she trooped through its streets, nor experienced the clatter and hiss of the railway. Instead, she had been plucked from the Brownlow Hill workhouse in the city of Liverpool itself, joining the party on the quayside with minutes to spare. Her father, Michael, still languished in Brownlow Hill, and in her head, and particularly in her heart, Margaret remained there with him.

Kind-hearted Mary Oliver had noticed the girl, tucked away in a small cubby hole.

'Would you like some company?' she asked. 'I've a brother who is not much older than you.'

Percy bridled at the suggestion of equivalent age; he was at least two years to the good. But on the positive side, entertaining a juvenile would provide some respite from his sister's unwavering care and attention.

'I've been counting waves. Can you count?' he asked enthusiastically.

'Don't need no brother. I want my pa.' And Margaret turned her back on them.

'Just being friendly,' huffed Mary, and she did not trouble Margaret again.

Brownlow Hill was a pond in which Alice Hamilton was wont to cast her net, and some weeks earlier Michael Walsh had asked to see her when next she called.

'I want you to take my daughter to Canada,' he blurted out before they had even exchanged greetings.

Alice looked the man up and down. 'As you know, I am in that business, but it is important for me to understand your reasons,' she said quietly. 'It is unusual for adoption to be requested quite so forcibly by a loving parent, as you clearly are.'

'It's for the best. Can't see no other way out.' A deep sigh of sorrow and defeat. Michael Walsh was tired before his time, or so it seemed. He was perhaps thirty years of age, maybe less, but he had the appearance of an apology for forty-five and the air of someone north of sixty. He clearly spent little time in maintaining his appearance: a sunken face, the texture of glass paper, was framed by a straggle of hair and beard. He had a deep scar on one cheek and eyes that were coloured in by the darkness he had seen. As he spoke, Alice made some perfunctory notes and occasionally expressed an opinion that was not always appropriate.

'Second-generation Irish,' Michael began, as if there was no further need for explanation. 'Same old story. Loathed by the

Protestants that claim this place as their own, and us Catholics return the enmity with interest.'

Alice frowned; over time her views had hardened towards what she now termed 'popery'.

'We have our strongholds, and they have theirs,' he continued, his voice seemingly drenched in an accumulation of wrongs. 'Men fight to protect their hold over streets that only a lunatic would ever wish to own, and they deliver vengeance upon any stranger with a different address. I have done this myself in my younger days, but I am well past it now.'

That might explain the scar, thought Alice, and without realising it, edged her chair away.

'And even when it's calm there's the drip of insult and contempt, whipped up in print for those that can read and by firebrands for those that can only listen. They said we took their jobs and kept the wages low, and it's true they have little more than us, but what were we to do? Stay where we were and starve?'

'It is no sort of choice.'

'Anyhow, Pa struggled to find work on account of who we were, as many did, and we were frequent guests of the workhouse. I loathed every minute of it. Sure enough, it cares for the aged and infirm, folk that are seen as blameless for their condition. And it gives an education of sorts to children that would otherwise go without. But for the able-bodied of working age, the greatest fear is to be without employment. For then you are the undeserving poor and in Brownlow Hill you get your just desserts.' Michael was building up a head of steam. 'It is not so much the rations that you would not feed to a dog; nor the rat-infested dungeons that they call living quarters, where men and women rot away from the inside while still alive; not even the mockery of what passes for work. The most grievous punishment of all is the separation. Whole families interned, with husbands parted from wives, sons from daughters, and all estranged from each other. It is cruel and unnatural in the extreme.'

'I know it only too well,' Alice agreed sadly. 'Only the truly desperate seek sanctuary within these walls.'

Michael took a swig from a bottle and wiped his mouth with a grubby sleeve. 'Just water,' he muttered with a hollow laugh before continuing. 'I had sisters, and they were their own company, but I was alone among the boys. That is no sort of life for a child, prey to all kinds of wickedness. You spend each day dreading the hour when the lights go out, for then you get the initiations and the beatings and the unwelcome attention. And if you have an accent or a religion they don't share, the staff treat you even worse than they do the others. As I got older, I fought back, but always at a cost in blood and retribution from those in charge, who all had their favourites, and it was never me.'

'I hear many similar stories, and it only stiffens my resolve to save those that can be saved.'

'The worst time was when the big fire took away twenty children or more. I was a distance from the inferno and ran outside to be safe, and those of us with similar luck helped to ferry water from the standpipes to the fire. And the parents were howling from their separate places, not knowing whether their child still lived and not able to comfort those that had. And even now I hear the screams of the dying as the flames cut off their every exit. It was a foretaste of Hell itself.'

Michael stared into the courtyard below. Alice allowed him a moment but, as always, was conscious of time.

'Pray continue,' she said.

Michael wiped his eyes and obliged. 'By some miracle I reached an age where I could step out into the world, and in time I took a wife, for I was in no hurry to inflict such a life upon another. And when I finally chose, she was a Protestant by faith, because in my arrogance I believed that by marrying outside my tribe I was revenging myself on those who had tormented me for my inheritance. We said we wed for love, but in truth it was to avoid a bastard child. As you might imagine, our union provoked disgust among the good Christians of both branches.'

'Such a marriage is an unnatural state, born of sin. Twice over.' Alice could not help herself.

'Yes, that was what we faced,' Michael snapped back. 'Sin and damnation.'

Alice edged her chair further away, this time more deliberately, but Michael's anger was soon redirected.

'Anyhow, in time we were blessed with Margaret, and we soldiered on. But I could only make a pittance from my labour, picking up work that no one else favoured and meeting the same welcome whenever I sought to improve my lot: "Help wanted, no Irish need apply". And we were always the target of the ignorant, with their bile and their malice. Some would even cross the road to make sure we heard 'em right, and they would leave their spit behind to make the point.'

'I would never countenance that.'

'Then one day the missus could take no more of it and out she walked. I cannot blame her, although I shall never forget the tears that Margaret shed for her. But things settled down, and the two years that I had Margaret to myself were the happiest of my life. She would put her hand in mine as we walked, and I liked that very much. I made up fanciful stories and she laughed more than I had a right to hear. I would sing her to sleep – poor child, for I don't have a voice. But money was ever harder to come by. She was too young to be left alone, and there was no one to safely leave her with, so I only took on work where she could be by my side, and some of those positions were no place for a young girl. The best was a cotton factory where I did odd jobs, and Margaret would earn pennies by crawling under the machines to rescue offcuts. But when another child was badly hurt doing the same, I could not risk her further and gave it up. And the next day I was pleading for entry to the place that had been the scourge of my own childhood.'

By now, Michael was slumped on his stool, his voice barely audible, his straggly hair obscuring his face as he gazed at the floor. 'I am an imperfect man, and I have said and done things that I bitterly regret, but I have never known such shame as knocking on that door. I had failed my child, and there is no greater sin. We were separated within minutes and have barely seen each other since. I catch glimpses of her through gates and fences, and if I can judge my walking speed there might be a brief overlap as we all move about. Sometimes they allow us to meet, and these times are precious, but they are cruelly short and rarer than a Protestant smile.'

Alice bit her lip at the jibe.

'Then one day I saw a bruise upon her arm, and she had no good reason for it. And the next time, there were more, and what looked like a burn, and I was desperate to find out why. "It's just the way things are," she told me. "One day they will tire of me and find another." But it is a father's duty to protect his child, and I cannot do that at a distance. And that is why I'm giving her to someone that can look out for her, even though it robs me of everything that is precious to me. She must have the best chance, and that is not with me and certainly not in this place.'

Alice sat awkwardly as Michael's tears flowed. She was keen to get down to details. 'It is likely that her new family will not be Catholic.'

'I have no interest in that. It is the same God, if there is one at all.'

Alice smiled at the thought of removing a child from 'popery'; that was a bonus. 'And because of her age, Margaret will not be put to work but will be properly adopted. She will have a mother and a new father and a different name.'

'That is what I want for her. In my heart, I will know that I am her true father. It is not a matter of what name you answer to.'

'Then I will take her, if she is willing to go.'

But Margaret was most unwilling. 'Don't you love me?' she asked her father over and again. 'What have I done wrong?'

Michael could not bear to hear her question his devotion. 'I do this out of love, my beautiful child. You deserve a life that I cannot give you, and there will be those that can.'

Often, she asked him, 'Have I disappointed you?'

And his heart would break each time. 'You could never disappoint me.'

And sometimes it was: 'Am I to blame for where we are?'

'You are the last person to be at fault.'

And once she asked: 'But who will want me?'

'You will not struggle to be matched up. Miss Hamilton will see to it.'

Indeed, Alice already had someone in mind.

And when Michael ran out of answers, he would say: 'One day you will understand and thank me.'

Michael continued to make his case, and eventually the bond between them was strong enough for Margaret to accept that it must be broken. When the day arrived, the two sat among the baggage on the quayside at Liverpool docks, with Michael full of last-minute instructions, holding his daughter's hands one last time. Alice waited impatiently at a discreet distance.

'You must behave for your new ma and pa and give them a chance to earn your love. They'll be good folk who'll deserve that, and I don't doubt they'll be pleased with you.'

Margaret sobbed her agreement.

'And promise me that you'll be happy. Then I shall be happy too.' Even though he knew that he could never be. 'And don't forget your old pa. Try to remember him as a good man in a bad place.'

'It's time we embarked, or they will sail without us.' Alice could wait no longer. In truth, they still had several minutes to board the ship, but she was averse to the indignity of running.

There was a final embrace, a desperate clinging on, at first impossible to separate, then they inched away, as they knew they must, the letting go so extended it could barely be felt. And then suddenly they were touching no more. Margaret walked slowly along the quayside, pausing to look back every few strides, desperate to stamp her father's appearance so clearly into her memory that he would still seem real even when he was no longer there. Michael stared, unblinking, at her silhouette until it had passed out of sight, and there he remained as the ship edged out of port and slipped over the horizon.

And so it was that some days later, tear-stained and drained of spirit, Margaret Walsh sat alone in the first private space she could find, thinking of the father she might never see again.

EIGHT

The SAD children would remember their passage to Canada forever. What tales they had to tell – stories that would bear repetition down the generations and become ever more heroic with each recital. Whenever the sea allowed it, the children chattered among themselves, committing the details to memory and rehearsing the narrative so they were prepared for an audience that might not have witnessed such wonders or experienced challenges on such a scale. 'Do you remember how…?' they would ask each other, and 'Were you frightened by…?' and 'Did you see…?'

The days of all who sailed were governed by the practicalities of onboard life. Each dawn was greeted by a barrage of insistent shouting as unwilling children were stirred from broken sleep, their bedding so close together that it was impossible to rise and exit without a friendly hand to assist. Then there was the long, long queue for the wash house, any sleepiness soon lost as bodies were exposed to water that Alice Hamilton described as 'invigorating', although her own private ablutions were enhanced by the use of a kettle. The children's screams could be heard throughout the ship as pitchers of water, freshly liberated from the sea, were poured unceremoniously over each, first to prepare the flesh for soap and then to remove its evidence. True to form, Arthur Dilkes devised a plan for avoiding the horror of the wash house. Taking advantage of the fact that some helpers were unfamiliar with the children, he persuaded Sam Barney to take a second shower on his behalf, first in his own name and then in Arthur's. The plan worked for a few days, until the discrepancy in hygiene became all too obvious and Arthur had to brave the pitcher along with everyone else.

Throughout the day, and more so during the night, it seemed, the constant motion of the vessel was a trial: up and down, side to side; nothing was ever still. Some took to it better than others and it inspired the children to invent simple games, with the winner being the last to move, or the one to carry something the length of the deck without spillage, or up some stairs and down again in the fastest time. But most days, heaps of heaving children lay like fish in a barrel around the ship's funnel, even in waves of moderate size, while below decks many knew the relief of making it to the bucket while others experienced the repercussions of not doing so. They witnessed the helpers, and even Alice Hamilton herself, suffer the same fate, and took some perverse pleasure from that, while marvelling at the crew, who seemed to be immune to the impact of nature on the digestive system. Mary Oliver could often be found cradling Percy as he moaned and proclaimed that his death was surely imminent, and then, miraculously recovered, it was his turn to do the cradling. It was even more remarkable that Mary let him do it, such was the state to which the sea had reduced her.

Then there was the all-pervading dampness of everything, no matter how well protected it seemed to be, aggravating the cold that sliced through skin and bone. The temperature only ever seemed to fall, never to rise. The children lamented the failure of their clothing to offer even a modicum of relief, but how could any covering be devised that might be adequate for the task? They huddled together ever more closely, sharing body heat with their neighbours and extracting what they could from their communal breath. Even Margaret Walsh emerged from her hidey-hole in search of the warmth of others.

And there was never any quiet, not even in the dead of night; the incessant rumble of the engines; the screech of circling birds foraging for scraps; the thump of wave after wave upon unbending steel until it seemed that the latter must surely fail, but somehow it held firm, although it complained mightily in doing so. Arthur Dilkes had no trouble sleeping through it, or so he claimed. 'Don't know what the fuss is about,' he would say, although Sam Barney noted several occasions when he would surreptitiously open one eye, quickly take in the surroundings and then close it again, professing to have been unconscious throughout.

There were three meals per day, their timing a movable feast to coincide with calmer waters, if any were imminent: endless rows of children, squashed onto long wooden benches the length of the mess hall, spooning tasteless gruel into their mouths, just the right side of inedible and intended to fill bellies that might recently have been emptied. It was impossible to say whether it was breakfast or dinner or supper, given that the content was so similar. Mugs and plates had minds of their own, sometimes requiring more hands than were available to restrain them. There was a constant echo of scraping and clatter, grumble and chatter. Then one day, a rebellion was hatched by Arthur Dilkes but constructed so that he would not himself take the blame. At the head of the table sat Alice Hamilton, enjoying rather different fare from her charges; there were some potatoes on her plate and perhaps a slice of salted beef, and one child swore he spied a vegetable, although others doubted that he would recognise such a thing. The children looked on jealously. First Arthur exchanged whispers with Sam and then others were included until the message had been passed the length of the mess hall. After several false starts, Sam nervously rose to his feet. An expectant hush descended.

'This gruel, ma'am.'

'Yes, boy, what of it?'

'Please, ma'am, can we have a bit less of it?'

'What did you say?'

'And perhaps a bit more of something different?'

'What?'

'Maybe what you're having.'

'You ungrateful wretch. The Good Lord provides for all based on individual need and what is deserved. There are many that would be grateful for what you receive. Sit down and give thanks!'

And from that moment, Sam's card was marked. The menu remained the same.

Alongside the physical afflictions came the first spasms of homesickness, endured even by those who had known no such place. Whatever their history, all that was familiar to them had been lost; it might not have been much, but it was theirs, and they had taken some comfort from it. There was the absence of friends and the futility of making new ones, at least for the time being, when they were soon to be parted. Many had siblings who were no longer at their side. Some had left parents behind, never to be seen again. In the depths of the night, the sound of sobbing echoed through steerage and beyond: first one, then a chorus and soon a choir, harmonies of sacrifice and loss set against the plaintive orchestration of ship and weather.

Then on the eighth day, the *Parisian* slipped into the relative calm of the Gulf of St Lawrence, its banks gradually tightening their grip as the vessel crept up the river to Quebec. On the next day, there was an early and abrupt awakening for the children as the ship sidled up to the quayside and lurched into position, like a drunk returning home in the early hours and trying in vain not to wake sleeping others.

Then, after so much confinement, there was a sudden frenzy of activity. First, the madcap rush to disembark, the children bouncing down the gangway in a tidal wave of enthusiasm and relief, ignoring the bellowed instructions from all sides to let the cabin people go first. On the quayside they formed a line, and official-looking men paced self-importantly up and down, eyeing up their prey with authority and suspicion in a ritual of inspection that would have been recognised the world over. Clearly satisfied, or as much as he would ever be, the most senior of them barked an order and each child stepped forward to be checked off against a list. There was paperwork, and some of it might have served a purpose, and then the stamping of landing cards. Finally, Alice was presented with an Admission Form for her signature, and she obliged with a flourish. Ever alert, Arthur Dilkes noticed money changing hands.

'It's to pay for your passage, nothing more,' Alice explained quickly on observing his interest. 'My time and energy are entirely free of charge.'

But Arthur saw that her face had reddened a little.

The children had arrived, but that was not an end to it, for they had still to endure the slow train to Kingston, where they would be quartered for a few days before being cast far and wide upon the Canadian soil. There were occasional stops to refuel and take on supplies, where they could watch citizens going about their business in an ordinary way, as they attended to the needs of the train; large men lumbering up and down with shovels, weathered women with baskets, some children helping the women. They did not look very different from British people – which, until recently, was precisely what many had been. The train shuffled through mile after mile of forest and woodland, the comforting greenery occasionally scarred by irregular clearings where a pioneer farmer had staked his claim and dotted with homesteads that one day might host an immigrant child – or, indeed, might already do so.

'I could be going there!' cried Percy. 'Or there!'

'We could be going there,' corrected Mary. 'Remember, we come as a pair. I have an agreement.'

Margaret Walsh barely looked out of the window. Her body was present, but her thoughts had still not left Liverpool.

At last, the train pulled into Kingston.

'Where's the band?' cried one child.

'And the crowd?' asked another.

'And the welcome?' sobbed a third.

'You said they'd put flags out,' Sam Barney goaded his friend.

Arthur was clearly displeased to be reminded.

The children congregated outside the station before unravelling their legs by walking the final mile of their odyssey, their wide eyes absorbing detail and mood through a veil of tiredness and misgiving. The Kingston air was less contaminated than most had breathed before, and the sun more dominant through not having to penetrate a blighted atmosphere, its glare magnified by the pristine limestone of the buildings. The streets were sparsely populated when compared to what they had known, although vibrant by Canadian standards, with a riot of accents floating on the breeze, slowly evolving towards a common speech to which the children would soon make their own contribution. But as the crocodile walked by, there was a sudden quiet, followed by long stares and occasional commentary that was rarely positive.

'We don't need no street Arabs – be gone with you,' a man shouted from a safe distance.

'Leave 'em be, they're just children,' scolded a woman.

'Not decent ones like ours. Don't want 'em here.'

'They'll be trouble, you mark my words,' an anonymous voice piped up.

'A stain on our town,' cried another.

Later, a lump of dried earth was thrown from a hidden vantage point, narrowly missing the children. Some rascals could be heard running away and giggling.

Alice Hamilton swung her umbrella with more venom and strode out. All the SAD children quickened their step. Mary grabbed Percy, enveloping him as much as she could, and henceforth they walked as if in a three-legged race. Sam stared quizzically at Arthur, who seemed to have misplaced some of his usual composure.

'Why are we here if that's what folk think of us?' Sam asked, but for once Arthur had no answer.

NINE

When the SAD children arrived at the Kingston distribution centre, a young girl was keeping watch from an upper window, anxiously peeping out from behind the curtains. At first, she was free to observe undetected, then a boy happened to look up and see her. He alerted another boy, and then another, and soon the party were all staring back at her. The wraith slid away, leaving the children unsettled, and their feverish imaginations ran wild. Was it a ghost that walked the house – perhaps of a child who had met a grisly end in that very building? Or perhaps it was an omen of future misfortune? Possibilities were discussed and theories formed, the more outlandish the better. The truth was rather more prosaic but still disturbing.

'She's been here a year, but we can't seem to shift her,' a helper explained. 'It's not that she likes it here, just that she don't like it nowhere else. She clings fiercely to the door if someone tries to take her. Even those desperate for servants would rather go without than take on one that might be trouble.'

And the children were temporarily quietened by the thought that a successful placement might not be automatic.

In the spring of the previous year, Alice Hamilton had been putting together her latest emigration party. The Bilston

Road workhouse in Wolverhampton was one of her regular suppliers. The master ran through a list of potential candidates, until he came to the girl in question. 'You might consider Lily Mudd. Not her real name, but as good as any we could find. Age uncertain, perhaps nine or ten years, but could be one or two either side. Came from nowhere, going nowhere – unless you take her.'

'And what is her story?'

'I'll tell it as far as I know, which is not much.'

Two years earlier, on a dismal February morning, a passing constable had become aware of a girl sitting in a doorway. He noted that she was sparsely dressed for the British winter. Staring vacantly into the middle distance, she cut a fragile and solitary figure, a point of stillness amid the bustle of the town. Recent rain had left the street awash with filth, as horse droppings mingled with the overflow from adjacent ditches that doubled as sewers, producing a cocktail of mud and partly dissolved excrement. This foul brew was sprayed outwards by the wheels of speeding carriages and did not discriminate upon whom it landed. The girl did not move when it was her turn to be splattered. Close by, street sellers shouted out as they competed for pennies, while noise emanated from a local tavern that was unusually boisterous given the hour, as the night shift invested their wages in a fleeting escape from the hand they had been dealt.

The girl seemed largely oblivious to her surroundings and to the passage of time, and passers-by mostly gave her a wide berth. It was not clear if she had been abandoned or strategically positioned, or whether she had made her own way to that spot for reasons unknown. Best to leave well alone.

The constable moved on, but he walked the same beat in the afternoon. The girl was still there; she did not appear to have moved. Behind a fixed expression, her eyes spoke of inner conflict, as if she could not decide whether it was preferable to remain as she was, or to ask for help.

'Your ma and pa around?' the constable enquired.

There was no answer.

'You can't stay here – there's all sorts of mayhem and mischief once the dark sets in. Where's your home?'

Still no response.

'Not got a home?'

No hint of a reply, or even a suggestion that she had heard him.

'Not acting lookout for thieving, are you?'

Stillness and silence.

The constable consulted his watch. 'I ain't got time for this. I'll take you to the workhouse. They can sort you out.' To his surprise, the girl obeyed without question, trudging mutely by his side through the sodden streets, her hands thrust into the pockets of a threadbare coat, the uppers of her shoes flapping through want of a connection to the sole. In time they reached the Bilston Road workhouse, and the relieving officer was sent for. He would decide whether the girl could be admitted. Soon a hefty man appeared, whose breath betrayed his recent acquaintance with a bottle.

The girl hid behind the constable.

'Now then, girl, what's your name?'

She produced a scrap of paper from her pocket and snaked a hand around the constable's legs to deliver it. The note had been written in a shaky fist. The relieving officer read it out. *'I can't look after my Lily no more. Please help her and treat her good. She has suffered, poor child.'*

'So, it's Lily, is it?'

The girl poked her head out from behind the constable's legs and nodded.

'What's your last name?'

Lily said nothing.

'And your age?'

The girl looked at him blankly. The relieving officer sighed and checked a ledger. 'We've some space, so we'll take you in and see if anyone comes to collect. And we'll give you an age and call you by a proper name for our records. It don't have to be the right one, it's just so we can claim your share of people's taxes.'

He thought for a moment. 'I shall call you Lily Mudd, as a polite way of saying what you're covered in.'

And two years later, as Alice Hamilton considered her suitability for emigration, Lily Mudd's real name was still a mystery.

'She is one that our taxpayers would like to see emigrated,' the master stressed, having concluded the story. 'There is no chance of a child like her leaving here before she is fully grown, and that is particularly costly.'

'So, she has no parents?'

'Someone wrote that note, but no-one has claimed her. By all accounts, she is a solitary child. I would say timid and shy, but that would only tell the half of it. She don't speak unless spoken to, and even then, don't expect much by way of conversation. Matron says she is well behaved, if she can be said to behave at all, although there was one incident where she might have shown a different side.' The receiving officer waited for Alice to catch up with her notetaking. 'Some girls picked on her and a couple of 'em got very ill soon after,' he continued. 'They swore it was down to the girl, but we couldn't prove nothing.'

'Illness in a workhouse is hardly proof of deliberate intent.'

'True enough,' admitted the receiving officer. 'Innocent until proven guilty, I suppose. Anyhow, in schooling she is not a cretin or an idiot; she can read and write to a good standard. She does as she is told, but little else. We do not know what sort of life she might have had before her arrival here, but it has likely made her who she is.'

'As it does with us all.' Alice closed her notebook. 'I will speak to her and assess whether she is emigration material. As you know, I will only take those that will most benefit from the opportunity.'

'Perhaps she will thrive in a new place. She shows little sign of thriving here.'

Lily was summoned and stood nervously by the door, turning a handkerchief over and over in her hands for comfort. Her cropped hair and workhouse uniform made her appear younger than perhaps she was, and she would have been taller had she not been hunched almost into a ball.

'Now my girl, you need to talk to this lady and say more than you've ever said to me. She won't bite you.'

Lily turned over her handkerchief even faster.

'Sit down, child. You have nothing to fear from me, and everything to gain.'

Lily perched uneasily on a stool, her gaze fixed on the floor. Over time, Alice had learned not to show her claws until she needed to, and gaining the trust of a child was one such occasion. Slowly she explained what might be required of the girl, and the benefits that would accrue in return. Eventually some words were prised out.

'I done a bit on the ward with the sick and the old people. Helping the nurse, fetching and carrying, mainly, but useful work, I'd say.'

Alice made a note of it. 'That is good experience, child. Carry on.'

'And I sit and hear them talk, which they like to do, and the nurse don't have the time to listen. I could do something like that, maybe?'

'There is always a call for that kind of thing.'

'But one week I had to help the Tramp Master, and I wasn't keen on that. Nasty men, the lot of 'em. Some women too, mind you.'

Alice recoiled at the thought of such work. 'Do not fret, child, I will place you in service with a family, but I cannot say where or who they might be or what they might need. It may be in a town or more likely in the country. You will doubtless encounter some men, for they are a necessary evil, but there are no vagrants among my clientele.'

By now Lily had raised her gaze from the floor. 'I might like a village or a farm, where it's quiet and there are no people, or not many. I've only lived in a town, and it's done me no good.' She paused for a moment. 'I don't like people much and some not at all. I like being alone. It's safer that way.'

'Might you have parents somewhere?' Alice asked. 'Or at least a mother? If you come with me, you would be saying goodbye to them forever.'

'Ma's probably somewhere about, but I don't want her, and she don't want me. Not since she got a new man.' There was bitterness in Lily's voice.

'Did your pa die?'

'No, she just fancied a new one. But he didn't take to me. Wanted me gone and made Ma write a note so this place would have me. And she was happy to oblige, or so it seemed.' Now Lily was close to tears. 'At first I wouldn't go, but after enough slaps from him I changed my mind.' Suddenly she laughed. 'Got my own back, though. Made him a stew and he were sick for a week.'

Alice looked quizzically at the girl.

'We had rats, you see.'

And Alice put two and two together. 'And your ma's old man – your first pa?'

'Gone, don't know where. But he were handy with his fists too.'

Alice's notes had now covered more than two pages.

'This is a very bad place.' Lily continued what might have been the longest conversation she had ever had. 'You can't be alone here. And the big girls can slap as hard as any man, and they have a liking for it too. There's no peace for those that are asking for it, like I seem to be, even though I'm not. I'll come with you. Can't be no worse.'

Alice reported back to the master. 'I think she will do well in the right placement. I will take her.'

But once in Canada, it was a different matter. At her first distribution, Lily was selected as a maidservant but simply refused to go, screaming the place down and resisting removal by any means, until the interested party tired of her and took another instead.

'Didn't like the look of them,' Lily explained. 'Had a bad feeling about it.'

At her second distribution, it was the same again, and so on throughout that summer. And each time Lily had a different excuse.

'It was the wrong sort of place.'

'Reminded me of someone I wish I hadn't known.'

'Brought back things I'd rather forget.'

But she would never say what she truly meant.

And so while many an orphan came and went, Lily stubbornly remained in the Kingston centre, often the only child to be there. She clearly did not mind being alone, spending much of her day peeping out from behind the curtain in the upper room, at times watching people go about their daily lives but largely, it seemed, in a world of her own. She spoke little, and no one knew what she was thinking.

She's stringing me along, Alice thought, none too pleased. All that screaming and shouting, and five minutes later she's as right as rain.

Against her better judgement, Alice arranged for Lily to be fed and housed over the winter, but her patience was wearing thin. And when the first distribution of the following summer went the same way as those the previous year, it was time to show her claws. She gave Lily an ultimatum.

'I have been patient,' Alice began, although you would not have known it from her voice. 'I have tried to understand and accommodate your preferences. But the trouble is that you appear to have no preferences at all, other than to remain here, eating up time and money. I cannot allow this to continue. Therefore, if you do not accept a placement by the end of the summer, I shall return you to England and you can take your chance there in the workhouse. And as you know very well, that is no place for a young girl.'

Having said her piece, Alice stamped out, leaving Lily in a state of unease, with much to think about and an unsavoury choice to make. Thereafter, she hid herself away even more than was usual, only sporadically present at mealtimes, and never outside of those occasions. And while a casual observer might have thought her a daydreamer, in truth her mind was a whirl of possibilities, all of them hateful. Time strode inexorably onwards, and all too soon she was peeping nervously from an upper window at the approaching immigration party, all too aware that her reckoning was but a few days away.

TEN

The SAD children had hardly set foot in the Kingston centre when the scattering began. Alice Hamilton was ever conscious that time was money and that she was deficient in both, and hence she was keen to shoo the children out of the door as soon as it was respectable to do so. For their part, eager employers did not wish to be kept waiting. Farmers from every corner of the land were desperate for a reliable and hard-working boy or, failing that, one that would at least earn his keep. Meanwhile, local women were always in need of maidservants, preferably those that would not prove a distraction for the menfolk of the house, which sadly was often the reason for the vacancy. Demand regularly exceeded supply.

At breakfast on the first morning, Alice made a brief announcement. 'You have already seen the girl at the window, and there has doubtless been gossip and chatter about her.'

Murmurings across the mess hall confirmed her suspicions.

'There is merely a delay in the girl's placement. That is all I have to say on the matter. It is unlikely that your paths will cross, as she keeps herself to herself.'

Unsurprisingly, the explanation was not sufficient to still the prattle.

'You might also encounter two young fellows that are not of your party. They are between placements and that is all you need to know.'

'Might not be all I need to know,' Arthur whispered to Sam. 'Let's go find 'em.'

Picking a time when the staff were fully occupied in the kitchens, the boys set out to explore the home. It was a tangle of a place, with stairways erupting when least expected and rising ever upwards until they surely must have reached the stars; corridors that seemed to lead everywhere and nowhere; a multitude of doors to open and apologies to make when privacy was disturbed and something inappropriate was seen. Eventually, the returnees were found in a small attic room. Arthur and Sam invited themselves in and sat on a bed. One boy seemed happy to talk, but the other turned away and began to sob.

'So, why are you here?' Arthur asked the one that seemed most likely to answer.

'Bit of a story.' The boy might have been eleven years old, or thereabouts, and wheezed noticeably when he spoke. 'First, I was sent some fifty mile away, but they said I weren't cut out for farming. Made up their minds real quick, though. Didn't give me much chance to prove 'em wrong. Said I was too small, but I ain't shrunk, so they should have known that afore they took me. Anyhow, they brought me back and got another and I expect they measured him proper afore they put him on the cart. "You can't stay here", says Miss Alice in a huff, and next she sent me off tree-felling. Even further away that was and to no one's surprise, I weren't cut out for that neither. I could have told her that and saved everyone the bother.'

'What about the boy there?'

'Leave him be. I don't know the ins and outs, and he don't like talking about it. Something bad, I think.'

'Do many get sent back?' There was a trace of nerves in Sam's voice.

'There's been a few but most stay put, so they must be doing good, I guess. Perhaps I've just been unlucky, but Miss Alice says that if the next place don't work out then I'm on a ship bound for England. I won't be sad if that happens.'

'Can't see us having any trouble,' was Arthur's conclusion. 'Not like those lads, anyhow. We're made for this.'

Sam was not so sure.

Every emigration party contained a smattering of children under the age of eight, and they were considered too young for employment; instead, they were to be formally adopted. The spiritual nourishment of meaningful work would have to wait for these mites.

Casting her net far and wide, Alice had identified more than enough families that were desperate for children they could call their own; she was always spoilt for choice. She pored over each character reference as if it was written in hieroglyphs, peering through the blandness and the vested interest for an accurate translation, reading more between the lines than on the lines themselves. Then she paid each a visit, interrogating the trembling unfortunates with forensic fervour, quietly tutting at the state of their premises and sucking in a breath when examining their finances. She could not afford to get this wrong. 'The older children are better able to fend for themselves,' she would always say. And for the families that she selected there was unbridled joy, searing disappointment for those she did not.

On the appointed day, a gaggle of nervous men and women approached the Kingston centre, ambushed by last-minute doubts as they waited to be introduced to potential offspring. Are we ready to be parents? Will she accept us? Do we deserve him? Can we compete with what they've known?

Then the staged meetings, the shy greetings, awkward pauses, soft voices, fumbling for the right words. The ice is broken, a toy presented, smiles and laughter, tears on both sides, a blur of memories. The first impressions: it's what we've prayed for, it won't be easy, what hidden scars will there be? Nearly there now, urgent questions, signing papers, impatient to be gone. And for the child: feeling wanted, missing home still, sad but happy, all too much to comprehend.

As part of this gathering, Margaret Walsh was formally adopted by John and Daisy Bradley, a childless couple who owned a general store on the outskirts of Kingston. They were hard-working, decent and well-liked, their store a place where people gathered for pleasure as well as shopped out of necessity. John Bradley was a man who thought before he spoke, sometimes for an extended period, although Margaret was to find that it did not always guarantee that his eventual output would make any sense. He had a raucous laugh, regularly used, and would often find things amusing that others did not. Daisy was a whirlwind of talk and action. She spoke more words in a minute than Margaret had ever heard, and repeated the feat hour after hour, day after day.

'You'll be going to the local school – would you like that? I expect you've done a bit of reading and writing where you've been… The teacher is a good person, strict but with a kind heart… You'll have to help around the home… washing, cleaning, that sort of thing. Can you sew? I'll teach you… And cooking? I don't imagine you've done much of that… You'll be a bit useful in the store, fetching and carrying and the like. It'll help you to make friends. Do you talk much? Are you nervous? What food do you like? Oh dear, all these questions…'

A greater contrast to Brownlow Hill could not be imagined. Margaret had a room of her own, with a table and chair for her personal use, and her eyes lit up when she saw that; here she could think private thoughts and listen to the birdsong that charmed the air around her. There was a window and something worth looking at, a large red maple that had survived the advancing neighbourhood. Margaret would stare at it for hours, in awe of its beauty, marvelling at the infinity of its colours and textures. The room had shelves and drawers where she could arrange possessions, and there was a promise that she might soon acquire some. There was only one bed in the room, and its mattress had no obvious legacy from a previous occupant. Food was served that she did not have to queue for and where she could imagine why someone had taken the trouble to cook it. She was given clothes that were not identical to those worn by every other child.

Michael Walsh would certainly have approved of the arrangement.

The Bradleys did their anxious best and tried not to expect too much too soon but could not help but fret. Margaret generally preferred her own company, sitting by the open window in her room, her thoughts a continent away.

'She's very quiet,' John would often say.

'Everyone's quiet compared to you.'

'You're one to talk! Quite literally, as it happens.'

But behind the staged composure, they speculated regularly about what was going through Margaret's mind. Often, they would ask each other questions and try to find rational answers, but without ever quite dispelling their sense of insecurity.

'I wish she would play like the other children.'

'She's had no practice. She doesn't know how.'

'I've never heard her cry – is that a good sign?'

'I expect she learned not to.'

'I would be so much happier if she spoke more.'

'Perhaps she's not used to having anything to say.'

And in the moments when Margaret's head was fully in

Canada, she had equivalent thoughts about her new family. Pa said they'd be good folk, and it seems they are, she decided. Pa said to give them a chance, she remembered, and she tried to obey his wishes. Pa said I should be happy.

But that was easier said than done.

ELEVEN

One by one the boys were summoned to speak with – or, rather, listen to – Alice Hamilton. After a few minutes each emerged from her private office with a motivational speech ringing in their ears and a rudimentary knowledge of their placement. With so many to see, she spoke quickly, almost in a gabble, describing work that was as foreign to them as the strange land in which they stood, mentioning locations that might as well have been on the moon, quoting distances that meant nothing to them, and naming people who could have been anyone. It was not 'take it or leave it', as the latter was not an option. When they left her sanctum, every boy put on a brave face. Some shed tears in private.

Eventually, it was Percy Oliver's turn.

'Remember, I have an agreement with Miss Alice, so you make sure she abides by it,' Mary nagged him. 'It is the only reason we are here.'

Three years ago, Mary had stood shivering outside Alice Hamilton's Home for the Salvation and Advancement of Destitute Children, clutching Percy's hand and nervous of the welcome they might receive. She was soon able to put her fears to one side. The door was quickly opened and, much to her delight, their presence was neither resisted nor even questioned. First, they were taken to the kitchen, where the cook found some bread and cheese that tasted like a banquet to their impoverished palate, the bread being fresh and accommodating to the teeth, and there being no need to scrape the cheese. Then the matron of the home laid down some rules and sternly described her expectations of how children should conduct themselves, but Mary felt confident that even Percy at his cheekiest would broadly comply. A bed was found for each. There was a temporary stand-off when Mary insisted that they should be placed side by side, but after a brief introduction to relevant aspects of human behaviour, embellished by some overly graphic examples, she accepted the need for boys to be housed separately from girls. She felt some embarrassment in being forced to undergo a hygiene inspection, as strangers cast their eyes over her naked flesh and formed an opinion, but it was a small price to pay.

'We have fallen on our feet,' she pronounced, and Percy's mouth was too full of Cheddar for him to disagree.

As time passed, Mary found her life to be pleasingly uneventful, which was confirmed by Percy's regular complaints of boredom. The helpers were kind or at worst neutral, and even Alice Hamilton was not overly intimidating to a girl who had already encountered her share of characters. She acquired some friends, and a typical day allowed her some time to spend with them, while those who were less congenial simply left her alone. There was work to be done, cooking and cleaning and the like, but there was nothing that was unfamiliar to her and, wonderfully, there were always others to help. Her singing was tolerated and there were times when others joined in, although the matron had a tin ear when it came to music and she did not disguise her irritation. Mary missed her father greatly and mourned the image of a mother she could barely remember, but her brother remained with her and that made her richer than many. She would happily have remained in the home for the rest of her childhood, and possibly even for her entire adult life.

But Canada was a cloud on the horizon. Mary was aware of the throughput of children, as familiar faces came and went, and before long Alice began speaking to her about moving on. 'You are the ideal emigrant,' she said in a flattering tone that did not come naturally. 'Robust in mind and body, unafraid of hard work and older than your years, as so many of my children are. Try to imagine how well a spell in domestic service will equip you for your life to come. What a wonderful opportunity it is.' And she painted the usual picture of God-fearing folk living at one with nature.

But Mary was not interested. She was safe and happy as a SAD child and, most importantly, had Percy's wellbeing to think of, so why change anything? She said no and continued to say it. But as the home became ever more crowded with a relentless stream of needy children, these conversations became increasingly robust and eventually quite dogmatic, with Alice describing her as 'selfish' and 'ungrateful', often to her face, then campaigning to turn others against her. Mary sadly accepted that three years of calm would have to come to an end. But she had conditions that must be met, and as always, Percy was her prime concern. It was almost as if she was back in the street markets she had known, haggling with a trader, and she proceeded with caution. But everything about the home suggested that Alice Hamilton could be trusted, and Mary was eventually persuaded.

'I will go if Percy comes with me and we are in the same place, with the same family,' she insisted. 'Will you promise?'

And Alice Hamilton said whatever needed to be said to clinch the deal.

TWELVE

At nine years of age, Percy Oliver was considered ready for work, and he was happy to oblige. But now he found himself in Alice Hamilton's private office wearing a confused expression. Alice had just informed him that he was to be placed with a farmer near the settlement of Croydon. Wherever that is, he thought.

'And my sister, Mary, she'll be with me, won't she? We'll be together, won't us? We were told that afore we came here.'

'The man wants a boy to help about the place. He has no need of a girl,' Alice stated matter-of-factly, not looking up from her papers. 'Your sister will be elsewhere. Now go back to the others and be grateful for this opportunity.'

Percy stood silent for a moment, eyes welling up. 'But missus, we has an agreement. My sis says so.'

Alice looked up. 'We have no such thing,' she snapped. 'Nor have I with any child. I cannot favour one over another, or each of you will expect the same and then where will we be? "Oh, I don't fancy this" or "I don't want that". You'll take what you're given and like it.'

And before Percy could speak further, Alice resumed her interest in the papers on her desk. 'You are dismissed. And a word of thanks would not go amiss.'

Percy sidled sheepishly from the room and ran to find his sister. Soon screams of panic and disbelief were heard, followed by frantic footsteps as Mary sought out her nemesis. Alice had left her sanctuary and was bustling about the home, casting orders in every direction and not waiting to see if they had been understood.

'I have to find places for fifty boys. Given the choice, they would want a hundred different things,' she shouted over her shoulder. 'And it's the same for the girls. You should all count your blessings.'

She bustled some more, Mary in her wake.

'Previously I have tried to accommodate individual wishes, but the children took advantage of my kind heart most grievously. I have learned my lesson.'

Perhaps Alice had a certain girl in mind.

'You promised me, miss – you did, don't deny it. You promised we'd be together.'

'I would never promise something that I could not guarantee to deliver. You must have misunderstood.'

'It was clear as day, miss. You don't pull the wool over my eyes. Not that easy.'

Word had quickly spread of Mary's challenge to Alice Hamilton's authority, and a small crowd had gathered to witness the entertainment.

'It is a fact that most employers only want one child,' Alice continued, her voice harsher and more impatient by the sentence. 'Some will take two with a bit of persuasion, but not this time.'

'But he's so young, he needs me to care for him. I promised on my life that I would. He's never known a mother and can barely remember a father. I'm Big Sister. I'm all he has.'

'He's nine years old, girl, not a babe in arms. He's going to a good home, as will you within the week. And you can be sure his new people will want to treat him well. They will need him to work hard for them, if for no other reason. You must see the sense in that.'

Mary was in no mood to see the sense in anything. 'And will you make sure he's all right? Check up on him regular?"

'I am certain to be alerted if there are any concerns. Not that I would expect any.'

'And will I be living nearby? You will be sat in England for much of the time, and I'll need to be happy with his present state. How close will I be?'

'It depends on which family takes you. It could be near, it could be far, I cannot say.'

Alice knew it was likely to be far.

By now Mary's usual politeness and deference had abandoned her entirely. 'Miss, you lied to me, a brazen lie. Percy and I have already lost so much, and now you take away the one thing we have left – each other. We are not children to you, miss, just chattels to be disposed of. You don't care what becomes of us.'

There was a gasp from the audience. Even Mary was shocked by what she had said. Alice slowly turned to face her accuser. The stakes were high, her credibility was on the line. 'And who was it that gave you both a roof over your heads when you had none? And fed and clothed you for so many years? And who now gives you the chance to be more than just workhouse fodder? Oh, I care, Mary Oliver, I care very much. But I live in a world that is far from perfect. I deal in what is possible. I make the best of a bad job. I cannot conjure up employers that want a certain thing, I have to play the hand I am dealt. I wish things were different. I take no pleasure in separating you from your brother, but at least you can look forward to the future. One day you will both reach your majority and then you will be free to do as you please. It might seem like a long road, but time passes quickly, I promise you. Life is soon taken away. Make the most of it.'

For a second Alice touched Mary's arm with something close to affection, before making a bolt for her private office. Mary followed but was too late. When she reached the door, she could hear a key being hurriedly turned in the lock. The crowd was just a few steps behind, egging her on to pummel the door or at least engage in some shouting, but Mary saw that she was beaten. She trailed sadly away and spent the rest of the day on emergency tuition, schooling Percy in the ways of the world, as she had experienced them, and passing on the wisdom of her thirteen years. Their last precious afternoon quickly slipped away as they enjoyed each other's company, which they might previously have taken for granted. Things were said that needed to be said, to the extent that a child's tongue had the right words to say them. And when bedtime came around, lights were turned out on more than just bricks and mortar.

'You must be brave' were Mary's last words as she bade her brother goodnight for the last time.

'I shall be all right, sis. I'm more worried about you.'

The next day, Percy's farmer arrived to claim the child. He seemed a decent enough man, Alice thought, although it was impossible to tell with any certainty. Time would be the judge of that. To avoid any unpleasantness, she had arranged a distraction for Mary in the depths of the home, as far away from the street as possible, yet Mary heard some boisterous talk between unfamiliar men, which aroused her suspicions, then Percy's plaintive wail confirmed them. She ran to the door, leaving the matron and two maidservants floundering in her wake. Percy was reluctantly boarding a wagon, repeatedly looking back at the home and crying for his sister. Mary chased the wagon down the road, catching it within a few strides and clamping herself to its rear, locating holds where none truly existed, not caring if she fell beneath its wheels. The wagon temporarily shuddered to a halt and clumsy hands loosened Mary's grip, peeling her away and roughly restraining her to prevent a repeat. They moved off a second time, and Percy's yowls of grief slowly faded as the wagon put distance between itself and the home. For a moment there was silence. Then Mary knelt in the dirt and sobbed her heart out.

THIRTEEN

'Is this him?'

Ezra Wright was collecting Sam Barney from the Kingston Home. He spoke as if he was picking up a parcel or some other item of property, which in essence he was.

'He's a good, strong boy. I think you'll be very pleased,' Alice Hamilton gushed, anxious to complete the deal.

'He'll be back on your doorstep if I'm not.'

Sam stretched out his hand in welcome, as he had been taught, but his new employer was not of a mind to take it; a handshake had to be earned. Curt of speech and bleak of mood, an aura of sobriety hung about Ezra Wright like a burial shroud, a man almost literally weighed down by the gravity of life. He was clean shaven, and his lack of facial covering merely added to the severity of his appearance. Sam thought it unlikely that a smile had ever graced his features, or a joke passed his lips. Almost as wide as he was tall, the weight itself might have made the farmer physically imposing but the impact was lessened by its distribution. Sam soon came to recognise that Ezra Wright was a man of the Bible, with an outlook that was distinctly Old Testament rather than New; in his world, eyes would be exchanged for eyes and cheeks would not be turned. Sam also found that Ezra Wright had high expectations of others and did not like to be disappointed, although he often was, and he did not learn from this.

Sam watched and listened to the negotiations around his services, his heart sinking faster than the sun in winter. Even before this encounter, his morale had been low. His great friend, Arthur Dilkes, had left the home the previous day and a gloom had descended upon him that was noticeable to all.

'He's normally a bright young thing,' observed the matron. 'But all he's done since that other boy left is mope around like a whipped puppy.'

Sam had not taken it well when told that the pair would be placed a distance apart.

'You need to grow up, child,' snorted Alice Hamilton, who was allergic to both snivelling and to being questioned. 'Where's your pioneer spirit? Do you imagine that the men and women who built this country would have whined and blubbered when things didn't quite go their way? No, they would have relished the challenge.'

Sam's mood did not improve when he saw that Arthur was his usual cheerful and confident self. Their final exchange was far from satisfactory.

'I never wanted to come here,' Sam muttered. 'I always had a bad feeling about it, but you wouldn't listen.'

Arthur's patience had been wearing thin for some time. 'You could have stayed in London. No one made you to follow me.'

'You said you'd talk to Miss Alice. That you'd ask for us to be together.'

'I did speak to her.'

But Sam could not be sure what had actually been said.

'Look, give it a chance,' Arthur urged breezily. 'Things might be different from before, but we're still on the up. And you might get that family you want so bad. Less chance of that if there's two of us.'

'Guess so, but…'

'And what's the alternative, eh? What else are we good for?'

'We could have gone back on the streets. We were doing all right.'

Arthur broke off from packing his trunk. 'You know that was never a choice. It would have caught up with us in the end, even with my brains behind it.' His attempt at a joke fell flat. 'And when it went wrong, as it surely would, you'd end up doing a stretch or on the wrong end of a beating or worse. And it's a downhill slide from there. No, I'm glad to be out of it.' Arthur turned his attention back to his packing. 'Look, it'll be hard work and not what we're used to, but it's a chance to earn an honest crust. To learn a trade. To set ourselves up for life.'

Sam stared sullenly at his friend. 'Would you still have come if you'd known we'd be split up?'

'Expect so.' Arthur did not even need to think before answering. 'Look, it was handy for us to be together, and good fun too mostly, but now it feels right to go our different ways. We can stand on our own two feet.'

'Easy for you to say.'

It was nearly time for Arthur to leave.

'Might we meet up, do you think?' Sam asked, guessing what the answer would be.

'She said it were about seventy miles between us. That's not walking distance.'

'There's letters…'

'I'm not one for writing, and I've not seen that in you neither.' Arthur closed his trunk. 'Tell you what, we'll have a glorious reunion in a few years when we're of an age. Then we'll have some stories to tell.' He headed off for the railway station without a backward glance. It was some time before Sam entered his thoughts again.

---
*

Ezra Wright read through Sam's employment contract word by word, frowning and huffing and tutting over its provisions. And then he read it again. 'I can't afford a working man, so a child will have to do,' he muttered. 'He'll get his keep, but I don't see the need for schooling, not for the likes of him. And we'll see about wages. There may be some if he proves worthy.'

Alice pretended that she did not hear any of this, and finally Ezra Wright put his name to the document with as little enthusiasm as he could muster.

Soon man and boy were heading out into the country. Few words were spoken, and the atmosphere hung heavy, although Sam contrived to prise out some details on family. There was a Mrs Wright, of whom Ezra Wright spoke with great admiration and with a reverence that bordered on abject terror. There were four daughters of varying ages, and an elder son, who had once laboured on the farm but who had escaped to seek his fortune in Toronto.

'That's why we need a SAD boy,' Wright grumbled.

Time passed tortuously, but eventually they approached their destination. Ezra Wright was a settler of long standing, and his homestead was clearly recognisable as a farm if one was familiar with such a landscape. An obedient track strode between fields that were neat and ordered, occupied either by animals at pasture or crops that were soon for harvest. A central yard was dominated by a solid timber house, flanked by cavernous barns on either side and peppered with smaller constructions that quartered a regiment of poultry. The total acreage was just under two hundred, enough to be self-sufficient and to make a bit extra.

'Long journey, sir,' ventured Sam.

'Ten mile or so. Near enough to take you back if we need to.'

On arrival, Mrs Wright was standing at the door, arms tightly folded lest her appearance be construed as a warm welcome. The younger daughters displayed some curiosity from a distance, but the older girls were above that sort of thing and hid themselves away. Mrs Wright was taller than her husband and probably younger than her demeanour implied, with long fingers and a pinched face that looked as if it had seen too many things of which she disapproved. A smile briefly played on her lips but soon thought better of it and moved on in search of somewhere it would feel more comfortable. After brief introductions, it was down to business. Ezra Wright slid into the background, poised to interject, if needed.

'These are the rules of the house, so listen', Mrs Wright began. 'You'll be first to rise in the morning, so you be quiet going about your work. We're up early enough without you waking us afore time.'

Mr Wright grunted in agreement.

'At breakfast and at sundry times of the day you will join us in prayer.'

An even louder grunt of approval.

'When in the house, your place is downstairs, or in the cellar if you choose. Do not trespass upstairs – that is where we sleep and go about our private business.'

A collection of grunts.

'You're to bed down here.' Mrs Wright pointed at a straw-covered cot, little more than a large box, in the corner of the downstairs room. A blanket was neatly folded on top.

'Is there no bedroom for me?' Sam asked in a subdued voice.

'We have none that are spare. If you were expecting a

mansion, then you will be sorely disappointed. The youngest share, but the eldest are of an age where they need seclusion for the things that girls do. You'll have to learn to sleep while Mr Wright and I are still about of an evening.'

The grunting stopped and Ezra Wright pitched in. 'I'll wager someone like you could sleep almost anywhere. You must have laid your head down in all sorts of dark and sinful places.'

While that was true, Sam's new sleeping quarters were still a disappointment to him.

'I'll hear no talk of wagering, Mr Wright, that is the work of the devil.' Mrs Wright was always very clear on what she would and wouldn't listen to. 'And there's no space for that thing – it'll have to go in the barn.' She jabbed a finger at Sam's trunk.

The grunting resumed.

'You're to keep yourself clean. There's a trough here you can use. When the snow's bad, we will permit you to carry out your ablutions inside, at times to be agreed.' Mrs Wright refolded her arms, which had rebelliously adopted a less formal posture. 'And keep well away from my girls. You know what I mean.'

Sam was old enough to have some idea of what she meant.

'And if we catch you stealing or we find you slacking or if there's any ungodly behaviour then you'll be sent on your way, but not before Mr Wright has taught you some discipline.'

And then she was gone, and Sam could hear her shouting inside the house.

Ezra Wright picked up one end of the trunk, motioned Sam to assist, and they set off towards the barn.

'You pay careful heed to what she says or there'll be trouble,' he warned.

That night, as Sam lay in his cot, drifting in and out of sleep, he suffered a recurrent dream where he was drowning in the clear sight of his new employers, but they ignored him, other than to angrily demand that he got on with his work. The feeling of helplessness and despondency stayed with him all the next day and for some time thereafter.

FOURTEEN

Those SAD boys whose placement was too distant for them to be collected were escorted to the railway station at Kingston, where they reacquainted themselves with the meandering discomfort of Canadian trains. They travelled alone or in small groups, with no clear idea of where they were going, each wearing a prominent name tag so that the guard would know at what settlement to eject them. And there they would wait until claimed by their new employer, perhaps for many hours and occasionally overnight when there had been a misunderstanding over the delivery date.

As the trains clattered along from one tiny outpost to the next, even the most optimistic child would admit to feeling anxious and very alone. Fellow passengers often stared or gave them a wide berth or said something that was uncalled for, while some were curious and asked questions, to which the boys might not always have answers; it was unsettling to think that perhaps they should know more about their past and future lives. Some passengers were kind and shared food and drink, and that raised their spirits, the boys having invariably consumed their own provisions within minutes of leaving Kingston. All realised, if they hadn't before, that they stood out and would have to get used to it.

Arthur Dilkes sat outside the waiting room at Belleville station, enjoying the sunshine and the solitude – and, perhaps for the final time, the luxury of having nothing to do. He took in the sounds of industry: the pounding of metal on metal that rang out from the engine sheds beside the track, as new gladiators were born to transport future generations and old warriors were patched up for one last hurrah. He watched the station staff scurrying about with flags and whistles, bearing the luggage of the well-to-do, weaving in and out of smoke and steam in the furtherance of punctuality. It was always good to see others work.

Arthur glanced down at his trunk, less pristine now but increasing in value with each dent and scrape, relics of exploits they had shared and survived. Suddenly that was important. He was stepping into the unknown and felt a flutter of uncertainty that was as foreign to him as the view from the train. On the London streets, he had been in control of his own destiny – or at least, he had believed himself to be. He had a sense of who could be trusted and who was treacherous, and he was rarely wrong. He was skilled at forging alliances that bought him both protection and opportunity. Native wit and a velvet tongue helped him avoid or, if necessary, talk his way out of trouble. He knew every nook and cranny: the best places to shelter, the safest path from A to B and, in extremis, where the boltholes were. Always confident, he was never short of a plan or the inklings of one. But this was unfamiliar territory: wide-open spaces that he could not hope to know and surrounded by people that he did not yet understand. And his life was about to be controlled by another, and that was not a natural state of affairs.

'Nothing to be scared of. I've upped sticks before, I can do it again,' Arthur told himself sternly. 'However it turns out, I'll make it my own. That's always been my way.'

And to take his mind off unwelcome thoughts, he rehearsed some questions that he could ask his employer so that the final miles might not be too silent. As always, he was one step ahead.

As Arthur waited, a train pulled into the station from the direction of Quebec and an assortment of men and women emerged onto the street. Some headed straight for conveyances that anticipated their arrival, while others set off on foot; none paid him any attention. Then, emanating from the trackside, Arthur could hear the unmistakable sound of children being organised: a high-pitched babble of chatter, punctured with shards of screams and laughter, and intermittently quietened by the raised voices of elders at the end of their tether. Several minutes passed before a gaggle of children in uniforms, perhaps fifty strong, cascaded out into the street. A middle-aged woman proudly strode out at their head, waving a parasol in time to an imaginary beat. Arthur caught her eye.

'Ah, one of Alice Hamilton's boys, if I'm not mistaken,' the woman observed tartly, recognising the trunk. 'God help you, boy, is all I can say.'

If one moved about the towns and cities in an Ontario summer, one would often encounter a man or woman herding a party of British children; in some places, they were as common as the midges that blighted the season, and to some they were about as welcome. This woman was Clara Openshaw, and she had been emigrating juveniles for almost as long as Alice Hamilton. Indeed, when she had taken a sherry or two, she had been known to claim that she was the first to do so, and Alice had been pleased to put her right on more than one occasion. Now, having made her observation, Miss Openshaw strode off to deliver her latest batch to the distribution centre she had founded in the centre of the town.

'I guess if I don't like this placement, then perhaps she can find one for me,' mused Arthur, ever the pragmatist.

Soon his reverie was disturbed by a cacophony of creaks and rattles approaching from a distance. A rudimentary wagon appeared out of the shadows, drawn by two large Clydesdales that, judging by their progress, had seen better days and a great many of them. The wagon slowly manoeuvred towards Arthur. As it approached, the outline of the driver became apparent, hunched over the reins in a seat that was far too small for the occupant. A wide-brimmed hat covered his upper face, and the lower part was shrouded in an impenetrable black beard, so that his features remained something of a mystery even once he was earthbound and close at hand.

'You Arthur Dilkes?'

'Yes, sir.'

'Robert Gait. You're to come with me.' Gait's voice seemed to spring from the bowels of the earth, such was its depth and resonance, accommodated within an accent that owed little or nothing to the city. It was calm and measured, as if expecting an audience to listen, not raucous and impatient through always having to shout to be heard and then only having seconds to say what needed to be said. It was a voice that took its time and was worth waiting for.

'Pleased to meet you, sir.'

'Likewise, I'm sure.' Gait looked Arthur up and down as if inspecting potential livestock. 'I'll be honest with you. I wanted a country boy, but they didn't have none,' he grunted, taking hold of Arthur's trunk and swinging it easily onto the back of the wagon. 'Nothing personal, but city boys are unsuited to this sort of life. Too much mouth and not enough muscle.'

It was not a good start, but the status of the trunk at least confirmed there would be no immediate dismissal.

'I'm tougher than I look.' Arthur pulled himself up to his less than impressive height by way of evidence. 'Where I'm from, you had to have something about you, or you wouldn't last long. And I ain't scared of hard work.'

'Better not be.'

Arthur climbed up onto the cart, which groaned in protest. 'But I'll come clean, mister, I don't know nothing about the land. Miss Alice said she'd make us into farmers afore we left, but she never did. I've not grown nothing or fed nothing, and I don't know one end of a cow from the other.'

There was a snort that was almost a chuckle from the vicinity of the beard. 'If you're trustworthy and willing to learn, I'll teach you. If you're idle and dishonest, you'll be back on that train.'

'That's fair, mister.'

There was a clumsy silence, as first one started to speak then the other, before thinking better of it. The cart juddered and slowly moved off.

'Have we much of a journey?' Arthur ventured something neutral to restart the conversation.

'Just outside of Stirling, if that means anything to you. Probably not, and I wouldn't blame you. It's not much of a place. It's around fifteen miles, but it will feel a lot more on this contraption. And you'll struggle to sit for a couple of days afterwards.'

Remembering his rehearsed questions, Arthur set about discovering what sort of man his employer might be, but he soon ran up against the brick wall that was Robert Gait.

'I'm not one for talking much,' Gait pronounced after just a short interrogation. 'Some folks like it, but to me it's mostly a waste of time and breath. You will know what you need to know in good time.'

'At least tell me how you make a crust off your land. I'll need to know that soon enough.'

Gait paused while he guided the wagon over a particularly

demanding piece of terrain. 'Bit of a chatterbox, aren't we? As you wish. The government here gave us a decent patch to work on, but we have to clear it afore it's any good to us. We've done over a few acres and planted a first crop this spring. Animals are next, then more clearing. Mind you, last winter was hard – no decent shelter and we had to come back to town for the worst of it. Now we've built a shanty which should last until we can make a proper home.' Gait took a drink from a jug that was precariously attached to the wagon. Arthur followed suit.

'It's a hard life, but it's better than what we left behind.' Gait's voice deepened even further, if that was possible. 'What I have here is mine and no one can take it off me. And I won't let nothing get in the way of us making something from it.'

Gait's whole being tensed, his beard thrusting outwards in defiance. Arthur made a note not to get in the way of this ambition. Gait soon lightened the mood. 'Thinking ahead, if you do all right with me, you might get some land yourself when you're older.'

'Is that so?' Arthur's eyes opened wide, and the glimmer of a plan began to form.

'Not from me, of course, but the government's got more than it knows what to do with. Still giving it away and no sign of that stopping.'

Finally, Arthur asked the question that he had most wanted to ask. Gait took a moment to answer, clearly struggling with the words and the fact that he had to say them. 'It's just me and the wife. We did have a young 'un, but he passed three years ago.'

They fell silent as the wagon slowly plodded on towards the shanty. As they got close, Gait broke the silence. 'All this talk of me and mine – I doubt you've had it easy. You can tell us someday if you want. There's too many children like you, from what I see and hear. I'll give you a decent chance. Everyone deserves that.'

FIFTEEN

While the SAD boys were scattered far and wide, like seeds in the wind, the girls were all to be placed in and around Kingston.

'You can inspect and select your servant girl in person,' applicants were advised, and Alice Hamilton hired a meeting hall for that very purpose.

There were some mutterings among the older girls about the nature of the auction, it being rather too reminiscent of transactions they had witnessed in a previous life.

'They are all respectable folk that's coming,' Alice assured them. 'Shopkeepers, tradespeople, businessmen, perhaps a lawyer or two, some that work the land. Wherever you end up, you've nothing to fear. It's all above board.' But she could see that some of the girls remained wary. 'And your employer, whoever they may be, will put their name to a very legal contract,' she persevered. 'Although, of course, I cannot guarantee they'll stick by it' she could have added but chose not to.

It was a sunny August morning and around forty girls were being marched to the meeting hall. It was important to make a good impression, and every aspect of their appearance had to pass an inspection by the matron of the distribution centre: faces washed ('don't you cry now and spoil it'); hands spotless; hair combed and tied or plaited; Sunday best apparel; instructions on how to stay neat and tidy ('once you're there, try not to move about'). Some strode confidently towards their new life, maybe too innocent to be afraid, or perhaps whatever was to come could not be worse than what had gone before. Others dawdled behind, last-minute nerves or perhaps something deeper, maybe a sixth sense that held them back or a guardian angel that sought to intervene, but ultimately to no avail. The girls' trunks trundled along behind, underscoring the finality of the occasion.

It was quite an event. Prospective employers began to arrive, the women a swirl of elegant parasols and stand-out hats, the men solemn and businesslike. Most trailed children in their wake, some on their best behaviour, others not. The SAD girls stood at uniform intervals around the perimeter of the room, bobbing up and down like apples in a barrel as they curtsied to all and sundry, and obeying orders to smile prettily at all times. Staff were on hand to highlight strengths, hide weaknesses and serve refreshments, while Alice Hamilton fluttered from one party to the next, ingratiating herself through flattery and a feigned interest in their busy lives. The buzzards circled slowly around the room, studiously eyeing up their prey and ready to swoop when a particular girl took their fancy.

Questions came thick and fast.

'How old is this one?'

'Can she sew?'

'Are her parents in prison?'

'Does she know how to cook?'

'Any experience with young children?'

'Can we be sure she is not diseased?'

'Has she shown any interest in boys?'

'Will she know her place?'

There were some attempts at communication with the merchandise: 'Now, my girl, tell us what you can do.'

'How did you come to be an orphan?'

'Why are you here?'

'Speak up, girl.'

Opinions were sought from interested others: 'What do you think, my dear, will she do?'

'Might you like her, children?'

'She seems trustworthy, do you agree?'

Excuses were made for moving on to the next: 'I'm sorry, but I was looking for an older girl.'

'I cannot see how she has the strength for the work.'

'She looks like a simpleton.'

And when all was satisfactory: 'We'll take this one.'

No one asked the girl's opinion.

Once chosen, the newly employed maidservant would stand to one side while formalities were concluded, staring blankly into the middle distance while she was discussed as if she wasn't there.

'I wonder what she is thinking,' ventured one employer.

It was best she did not know.

Having been passed over by many, Mary Oliver was eventually placed with one of Kingston's celebrated families, the Hoggards. Dr Hoggard was a man of gravitas and local importance, as he was quick to confirm. But he was late arriving, and when he finally swept in very few girls were unclaimed. Even so, he hesitated and temporised, leaning first one way then another, strolling up and down the room, taking mental notes and then retracing his steps when they slipped his mind, stroking his chin and issuing grunts of displeasure and uncertainty. Throughout this performance, Dorothy Hoggard, his wife, struggled to control an indeterminate number of infants, the probable cause of their lateness. Her eyes begged him to quickly reach a verdict.

The good doctor's gaze finally alighted on Mary, albeit with an all too obvious reluctance. On cue, she spotted a child of Percy's age and burst into tears.

'Dear me, we can't have one that cries,' he remarked witheringly. 'We have quite enough of our own.'

'She's just lost her little brother, so to speak, but she'll soon be over it,' Alice quickly explained. 'And it does show she has the experience of caring for a young one,' she concluded at the end of her tale.

'I suppose so.'

Meanwhile, Dorothy Hoggard chased a toddler across the room.

'I have never been convinced that we need a servant girl, but my wife insists.'

Dorothy Hoggard wiped the nose of one child, who immediately sneezed in her face by way of thanks.

'I mean, what is the point of having children if the mother does not see to them herself?'

Dorothy Hoggard watched as one of her daughters was sick in a corner.

'But, as we're here, we might as well take one.'

Dorothy Hoggard broke up a fight between two offspring, sustaining a bruised leg and minor scratches.

'You know, I really cannot choose between this girl and the one over there,' the doctor mused.

'Anyone, we'll take anyone,' screamed his wife, and the decision was made.

To Mary, it mattered little which family might engage her services, or which child was to be foisted upon her if it could not be the one whose presence she craved. She was immediately put in charge of the entire brood while Dorothy Hoggard took some respite from her maternal responsibilities, and the good doctor tetchily queried every clause in the contract.

'They're all little characters, aren't they?' Mary offered, in an attempt to say something positive to break the ice.

'That's one word for them,' Dorothy Hoggard sighed.

There were two girls left unclaimed at the end of the proceedings, one whose bladder had given way in the excitement, the other a sickly child that, with hindsight, might have been left in England. They returned to the home in tears, their trunks trailing sadly behind them. But Alice Hamilton was on the case and had already dusted off some previous applicants. 'Don't fret, girls, we might be able to place you further afield, sight unseen as it were.'

If not, it would be a swift return to the old country. No children would be overwintering at the centre this year.

It was bedlam outside the meeting hall, as families made off with their new charges. One by one, nervous girls were loaded onto carriages and chauffeured away into the unknown, their ears ringing with the sound of quick-fire introductions and more orders than they could possibly remember. Some would find homes where, with luck, they might aspire to be more than just a servant. Others would only ever be drudges. Just minutes in, all would already have formed an opinion as to what their fate might be.

'On the whole, a successful day,' Alice decided, as she enjoyed the peace and quiet that had suddenly descended upon the distribution centre.

*

To avoid any unseemly outbursts or any disruption of the proceedings, Lily Mudd had been dealt with before the main event.

'You must accept this placement, or I will book your passage home before the day is out. And then it will be the workhouse for you,' Alice reminded her. 'You shall be in the countryside, as you once said you favoured, which I hope will make your decision easier. On the debit side, there are rather more men than you might find ideal, although two-thirds of them are still boys, more or less, so perhaps things are not quite as masculine as they might seem.'

'Didn't you have no ladies, miss?'

'None that were prepared to consider you, given your past – how shall I put this … shenanigans. Word travels fast and wide.'

'And this man, he don't mind?'

'I doubt he moves in circles where he would hear.'

Lily sat in a corner, deep in thought, while Alice paced the floor impatiently.

'I don't want the workhouse, miss. That's a bad place for the likes of me.'

'It is indeed a bad place.'

'Not much of a choice then, is it, miss?'

'No, it isn't.'

SIXTEEN

In the depths of Hastings County, amid a series of tumbledown buildings, on a smallholding of dubious worth, there lived a widower and his twin sons. Since arrangements had been made by letter, and not in person, Alice Hamilton was shocked to see the state of what arrived to collect Lily Mudd, whom she had contracted to this household. A rickety cart squeaked and wobbled through the streets of Kingston, tottering to a standstill outside the distribution centre, its driver looking even more neglected than the animals that pulled for him. Alice squirmed as passers-by turned their heads to look; he was not a good advertisement for her work.

An absolute shambles of a man, she thought, observing the rips and tears in his coat and trousers, and the ratty beard that seemed to have arisen from inaccuracy and forgetfulness rather than deliberate growth. That's what happens when a man loses the civilising influence of a good woman.

The farmer lifted himself down with some difficulty. He seemed unsteady on his feet as he weaved his way towards Alice. His sons lolled about at the back of the cart, a study in boredom and insolence, but ready to pounce should anything deserve their derision.

Alice summoned Lily to meet her new employer. Stifled sniggers could be heard from the boys. When Lily laid eyes upon the farmer and heard the braying of his sons, she hung back nervously at Alice's side, clutching her arm.

'You ever been on a farm, girl?' the farmer slurred belligerently by way of greeting.

Lily shook her head.

'Then you're in for an eye-opener, ain't she, boys?'

'Yes, Pa,' they chorused.

'So, don't expect no comforts nor any fancy ways. Nature ain't like that and neither are we. Ain't that right, boys?'

'Yes, Pa.'

'And be warned, it's hard work for us and we won't take it kindly if we're not looked after proper, eh boys?'

'No, Pa.'

The sons were twelve years old, and it was only their pa who was allowed to call them 'boys'. Otherwise, they considered themselves men in every respect. They had long since left behind the smidgen of schooling they felt necessary and now worked full time on the farm, fiercely competing against each other in matters of strength and stamina. But they cowered before their pa, an overbearing man with a fearsome temper and a tendency to use his hands to express it.

Lily edged further away from the farmer and hid behind Alice.

'Come on, girl, get yourself on the cart or we won't be home by sundown, and I shall be thirsty afore then.' The farmer liked a drink, an activity which occupied his non-working hours, and which swallowed up much of the meagre profit from his land. When that time of day arrived, he would slump in his chair, only leaving it to replenish his supply, while the devil settled in to keep him company for the evening. He was quick to chastise even when sober, but when he'd consumed a jug or two, his assaults were more sustained and required less excuse, and the sons bore many a scar from his excess.

'You recently lost your wife, I believe,' Alice gingerly enquired, searching for a more likeable side to the man. 'That must have been a great sadness for you all.' She gave a sympathetic smile.

'Lost is a good word for it,' the farmer sneered, and Alice watched as a surge of memories and emotions played out across his grizzled face. But his mind was clearly not sufficiently organised to place them in any logical order, and it troubled Alice that she could not tell what he truly felt.

The boys' mother had been the main recipient of the farmer's cruelty. It had not always been that way. Indeed, when first married they were broadly happy, and the twins soon appeared on the back of it. But the pressure of scratching a living from the land took a toll on the farmer's fragile temperament. The first punch was a shock to them both, and neither knew how to react. But when the world did not end, the beatings became progressively easier to administer until he barely noticed what he was doing.

'Who else would put up with the likes of you?' he would shout as his fist came down. When they were young, the boys were on their mother's side, helping to wipe away the blood and bathe her bruises, soothing her broken spirit with their tears. And she would willingly take her punishment if her children were spared. But as they moved into adolescence, the boys grew to admire their father's obvious strength and learned to despise their mother's perceived weakness. Then there was nothing left for her, and she began to look for a way out. And her husband knew it.

'Aye, she was lost to us long before she met her end. Ain't that so, boys?' A grim smile adorned his face, where sadness and grief might have been expected.

'Yes, Pa.' The boys seemed equally relaxed about her passing.

Alice looked down at Lily and saw the fear in her eyes. 'I think perhaps we need to reconsider this placement—' she began, but the farmer cut her short.

'Now don't you go letting me down, missus. You don't want to be getting a name for that, do you? Won't do you and your business no good at all.'

'But on reflection I don't think this girl is suitable…'

The farmer moved within touching distance of Alice, and she took an involuntary step back.

'In that case, perhaps I'll stick around for your main event. See if I can find me a better one. And as a bonus I'll get to be sociable with all those good folk that usually cross the street to avoid me. I can have a nice little chat with 'em.'

Alice shuddered at the thought of it.

'We'll enjoy that, won't we, boys?'

'Yes, Pa!'

'And the fact you're getting rid of her separate from the rest means there's something wrong with her, ain't that right? Your good folk won't touch her. But you're in luck with me. Much less fussy. Don't have no choice with that.'

Alice felt she had been backed into a corner. 'Very well…'

'It's a deal, then.'

The farmer was struggling to load Lily's trunk, expletives raining down on the street like hailstones. 'Get off your lazy backsides and help me,' he bellowed at his sons, and they leapt to his aid before his fists got twitchy.

Reluctantly prompted by Alice, Lily walked unsteadily towards the cart, silently repeating over and over, 'I mustn't let them see I'm scared. I mustn't let them see I'm scared.' After a moment to pluck up her courage, she climbed into the back, scrambling over the smirking sons in search of a private space.

'I am here if you should ever need me,' Alice called out, making sure the farmer heard.

But any response was lost in the rattle and creak of the cart as it set off for Hastings County.

SEVENTEEN

When Robert Gait met Arthur Dilkes, he had promised him a fair chance, and he was as good as his word. In return, Arthur displayed an enthusiasm for work that perhaps surprised even himself, and an aptitude for farming that was a revelation to all. What he lacked in strength he made up for in resolve and a knack for solving problems that stumped his less cerebral employers, although there were occasions when he thought he knew better and then discovered that perhaps he didn't.

'I see you've moved the horses from their paddock,' Robert Gait observed one day as he tucked into his breakfast, looking through the window with a quizzical eye.

'We have the most to do with them, so I thought it best if they were nearest.'

'I can see the sense in that,' Gait continued. 'Trouble is, there's one side of that enclosure that's just hedgerow, not fence.'

'There's no gaps in it,' Arthur remarked drily, not bothering to look up.

'That was true yesterday, but not today.'

Arthur ran to the window and saw that the enclosure was devoid of horse.

'They'll eat most greenery, and a juicy bit of young hedgerow will do them just fine. And they don't need much of a gap to push through.'

Arthur stared at the emptiness, reddening with embarrassment.

'You might like to find them and fetch them in.'

And Arthur spent the rest of the morning doing just that.

'Sometimes I do things for a reason,' Gait innocently remarked, his beard protecting a smirk of satisfaction.

There had been an early opportunity for Arthur to prove his mettle. He had been sent to the local settlement on an errand to acquire provisions and soon happened upon the general store, a ramshackle affair that saw no reason to better itself, given its captive audience. Arthur diligently rooted around, mentally ticking off the items on his list, mindful that the storekeeper's wary gaze was following his every move. Arthur presented the goods for payment, handed over some precious paper and waited for change. A small number of coins appeared in return.

Arthur looked down at the counter.

'Hey, mister, you still owe me.'

The storekeeper was surly at the best of times, with a reputation as someone not to be trifled with, a man unused to challenge from the likes of the boy that stood before him. He leaned towards Arthur until their faces were a distance apart that would be considered intimate in different circumstances.

'So, you reckon you're a better counter than I am? A boy like you?'

'Mister, I've done enough counting to know you still owe me.'

Their faces were now almost touching.

'I think you had better leave before I get fired up.'

Arthur's experience of fleecing London shopkeepers in a similar way was standing him in good stead. Instead of folding, he doubled his stake. 'And some of them are old British coins. They're not used no more.'

By now there were other people in the store, keenly listening in while ostensibly waiting their turn; without looking, Arthur could feel their impatience and prejudice. The boy should accept the verdict of his elders and betters and be thankful. Particularly a boy such as that. But Arthur would not budge. Slowly he recited the value of each item purchased, adding them together as he did so, and through the miracle of mathematics was able to prove that he had been short-changed. He also separated out the coins that would have some worth in London but not in Canada. Still, the storekeeper did not move to rectify the shortfall.

'Shall I stand outside and warn folk about you stealing their hard-earned cash? I'll warrant it's a regular trick of yours.' Arthur looked round at the listeners. 'You be sure to count your change too.'

With a curse the storekeeper slammed some additional coins down on the counter. Arthur made great play of counting them up. 'Aren't you going to apologise for your mistake, mister?'

'I don't apologise to no street Arab. Now get out.'

And Arthur thought it wise to stop when he was winning.

'You did well,' Robert Gait growled, with more than a hint of pride, but no real surprise, when told of Arthur's adventure.

'I don't let no one take advantage of me if I can help it. I learned that long ago. Besides, if I come home with the wrong money, you'll think I'm thieving.'

On the next occasion that provisions were required, Gait made sure he accompanied Arthur to the store. This time it was he that stood close to the storekeeper, pointing out the error of his ways in simple but graphic terms. By the time he had finished, a belated apology was forthcoming.

EIGHTEEN

Mary Oliver's placement in one of the more elegant suburbs of Kingston was not for the faint-hearted. The Hoggard household was in a permanent state of bedlam. There were children of seven, six, and three years of age, with five-year-old twins sandwiched in between: all at a stage of maximum hindrance, and each one of a disposition to make the most of it. The expectation of infant mortality, and its failure to materialise, had given rise to what Dorothy Hoggard regarded as too much of a good thing, and consequently she viewed any further approaches by her husband with extreme alarm, which might have explained some of his absences from the house. The menagerie was completed by three dogs, bred as hunting accessories, and a feral cat that would adopt a veneer of domesticity when it required feeding.

Given her state of mind, Mary would have found any placement difficult, but life with the Hoggards was a particular challenge. Wherever she looked, at whatever time of day, there was always at least one infant in view, but never the child she wanted to see. And they all suffered in comparison with her sainted brother. The distance to Percy's placement was around forty miles but it might as well have been a thousand, such was the impracticality of meeting face to face. They exchanged letters, and Mary wrote as if he was sitting quietly beside her: pages of tittle-tattle interrupted by quasi-maternal instructions on behaviour, cleanliness and eating habits. In his shorter and far less frequent replies, Percy professed to be happy but didn't give much detail, and she could never be entirely sure of the veracity of his words, given that the adults of his placement were likely to have helped him with the drafting. Overall, Mary lived in the doldrums, and her sobbing added to the cacophony in the house. Dorothy Hoggard was not sympathetic.

'Crying like a newborn from dusk to dawn,' she exaggerated to her husband, who was vaguely aware of some disturbance. 'I am desperate for someone dependable to help me maintain order in the house, a trustworthy menial. But this is like having another child, and I do not want or need another child. I am already overburdened with them.'

In a rare attempt to help, that evening Dr Hoggard slipped a sedative into Mary's drink. It had the desired outcome, in that she was quiet throughout the night, but with the side effect that she was late to rise the next day, leading to a collapse in the house's fragile ecosystem.

'You did what?' screamed Dorothy Hoggard when her husband mentioned in passing what he had done. 'I had five children forced upon me for several hours while madam slept, and it was all your doing?'

'There is no pleasing you.' Dr Hoggard stormed off, and within seconds his study door slammed. He did, however, think better of repeating the treatment and, slowly, Mary learned to suffer in silence.

On a good day, Mary was able to impose a degree of organisation upon the children, and it was only the noise that was out of control. There might even have been a room that was fit to receive visitors, and time to attend to them if they called. On other days, there would be simultaneous mayhem in several places, with Mary rushing from one to another putting out fires, literally on one occasion, assessing breakages, resolving arguments, redirecting activity and changing clothes faster than they could be washed. Meanwhile, the animals came and went as they pleased and in whatever state they happened to find themselves.

The good doctor floated, untroubled, above the chaos of the house. When not healing the sick, he would ride out with the Kingston Hunt Club, a body of men dedicated to inflicting loss on the local caribou population in the name of sport. Or he would undertake solo expeditions to stalk rabbits, and Mary would be charged with converting the outcome into something edible. When confined to barracks, he could generally be found in his study, the sole bastion of tranquillity on the premises. It was not clear what activities he pursued in there, but he insisted on privacy and only the dogs were permitted entry.

Dorothy Hoggard found it an intolerable strain to maintain the serenity that her status in local society demanded, while living in what she considered to be a madhouse, and her mood ranged from abject resignation to a state best described as 'beside herself'. It was always the case that at times of maximum pandemonium the wife of a local magistrate might call, or a prominent lawyer might recognise her in the street, and her face – permanently on the edge of mania – would instantly transform itself into a false but welcoming smile, while both parties pretended that nothing untoward was occurring in the background. Through her husband's membership of the Grand Lodge of Canada, she was charged with entertaining the grandees of the town at regular intervals, and with accompanying the doctor as he was similarly entertained elsewhere. Once the gentlemen retired from the table, conversation was competitive and searching, and the ladies judged each other ferociously on all manner of things. When it was Dorothy Hoggard's turn to be dissected, the conversation invariably turned to children. She held Mary responsible for the inevitable embarrassment.

'I cannot abide people thinking that I have spawned a tribe of barbarians.' She sniffed in Mary's direction. 'My children's behaviour must be exemplary, in public at least, and preferably in private too.'

Matters came to a head one evening. Mary was scampering from one emergency to the next when Dorothy Hoggard swept in, exuding panic and bother from every pore.

'You have failed to clean the doctor's boots or to mend the tear in his coat,' she wailed. 'And there is no meal on the table, or even any evidence that one might be forthcoming. In fact, the unruly state of the kitchen would suggest that we are still consuming your previous offering.'

Thus far, the evening was not untypical. Mary drew a deep breath and embarked upon a futile defence. 'I'm sorry, ma'am, but first one child needed me to watch over them as they played, and then another demanded my attention. I cannot take my eye off them as the house is too full of danger for young souls…'

Three children ran in and out of the kitchen, two hunting dogs in pursuit, chasing a stick that one child held to tempt them. Mary maintained her flow as she dealt with a broken jug. 'And then the twins came in, covered in mud like you would not believe, and in need of urgent repair before the whole house was filthy…'

From the depths of the dining room, Dr Hoggard could be heard bellowing for his supper.

'There's always something, ma'am, always something…'

'We employed you to deal with these somethings.'

'There are just too many of them, ma'am.'

Dorothy Hoggard snorted with derision. 'So, what can be done?'

For some time Mary had been building up the courage to say this. 'If you could just take them for an hour or two each day, ma'am, then things would be better, I promise.'

'What? Am I expected to do everything myself? A woman in my position?'

'Then perhaps Dr Hoggard would like to spend time with his children.'

His wife laughed bitterly at the absurdity of the suggestion. 'I think that is very unlikely, and it will not bode well if you were to ask him.'

'But, ma'am, they are unrelenting and do not allow me time to attend to other duties.'

'They see that you are weak, and they play upon it. You must instil some discipline. This is not good enough and it cannot continue.' By now, Dorothy Hoggard had worked herself into such a state that there could only be one release from it. 'Pass me the strap,' she ordered.

'Ma'am?'

'It is clear that you are in need of motivation.'

'But ma'am…'

'Now!'

Mary could see that disobedience would only escalate matters further. She sullenly fetched a leather belt from a drawer and reluctantly handed it over. 'Ma'am, I believe this to be most unfair…'

'Quiet!' Visibly shaking, Dorothy Hoggard took the strap to Mary's hand, although she had to wait until Mary had tied a child's shoe buckle and wiped another child's dirty mouth before she could apply it.

Gradually, over time, the belt became Dorothy Hoggard's first port of call, with its wielder permanently stretched upon the tautest of wires and needing little encouragement to snap. At first the strap would fall just once or twice to make the point, but soon the count increased, and its application became more stringent. And in time more than a hand would be exposed to its rigour.

'Let that be a lesson to you,' she would always say at its conclusion.

But the children would never give Mary the chance to learn that lesson.

NINETEEN

Lily Mudd thought she might be around eleven years old when she arrived in the wilds of Hastings County to take up her maidservant duties.

Never one to talk unless it was unavoidable, she had barely spoken since her arrival, obeying orders without question and accepting censure with a faint smile of contrition, no matter how unjustified the criticism. Don't provoke 'em, she thought. Don't give 'em an excuse. She treated half-hearted attempts at conversation with suspicion and tried unsuccessfully to ignore the ribaldry and masculine banter that soiled the air around her. She arranged her duties so that she could be alone whenever possible: when the others were indoors, she busied herself collecting eggs or tidying the yard and took her time about it; when they left for the fields, she started on her chores inside. And she was not above fighting back when the opportunity presented itself.

From the first day, the farmer's sons had delighted in tormenting Lily, whether through talk that scared and offended her, or pranks that might have been humorous in different hands or with contrary intent. And on each occasion, the would-be men became braver, as they saw it, or more childish and loathsome, as it seemed to her. On this particular day, the boys decided that Lily must visit the pond, and in she went, with a tree branch being robustly applied to prevent her getting out. Her screams of outrage mingled with the boys' laughter.

Then suddenly there was a full-throated roar from across the yard. 'You leave her be! She's got work to do. And so have you.' As the farmer lurched towards them, the boys cowered, their arms covering their faces, allowing Lily to extricate herself from the pond.

'I'm not paying for her to be your plaything!' their father bellowed, and his sons felt the weight of his fists.

With vengeance at the top of her agenda, Lily simmered in hatred and humiliation throughout the day until she came up with a plan. Prior to cooking supper, she rummaged around the chicken coops on the pretence of searching for eggs, but she was actually collecting a very different output. When the hour arrived, she plated up the stew away from the table and furtively mixed her extra ingredient into the helpings destined for the two boys, keeping untainted portions to one side for her own consumption and to reward the farmer for his intervention.

'Hey, girl, what have you put in this stew?' exclaimed one boy, as his stomach rebelled.

'Bits of chicken,' Lily answered truthfully.

'It tastes vile, Pa!' The other boy retched.

'Mine is fine. Be quiet and eat.'

It's never a good idea to rile the cook, Lily thought, for once satisfied with her day's work. And thereafter, if she was threatened or mocked or even just inconvenienced, then all manner of things might appear in that evening's supper, but never in sufficient quantity to be suspected or identified. Lily knew, and that was enough for her.

One evening the farmer was particularly morose, slumped in his drinking chair and scowling into the fire. Requests for him to sing sometimes diverted his attention: if they were successful, he would rise to his feet in serenade, his voice betraying an enthusiasm that was not matched by any innate ability – not that anyone was going to point that out. But tonight he was beyond distraction. Sensing their father's mood, his sons had abandoned the house on the pretence of important work outside, but Lily had washing and sewing to attend to and had no such freedom. It seemed that there were dark thoughts swirling around the farmer's mind, and that he wished to unburden himself but did not know how. He gave several grunts, which might have been a foretaste of something more coherent, only for him to think better of it and retreat into his liquid cocoon. Finally, he took courage. 'You know something? I hates this place,' he mumbled, emptying another jug and letting it hang limp from his hand, allowing the dregs to dribble onto the floor by his side.

Lily stopped in her tracks.

'Do you hear? I hates this place, and I always have.' His voice was simultaneously threatening and pitiful. 'Don't know what to say, do you? Probably "so do I", but you dare not say so.'

The farmer was correct.

'And it's all because of my pa, may he rot in his grave. Stubborn as you like, would never listen to reason. "I am a farmer's son and that's what you'll be, it's all we know" he would say. But mining has always been where the money's at in these parts. Never in farming. Only mugs like him, and now me, tend the land to feed those that have more sense.'

Lily maintained a watchful silence, unsure where this revelation might lead.

'You listen, my girl, and you take note of how unfair life can be. There's no skill in digging out what's already there, like them miners do; you just need a shovel and a bit of muscle. But they get all the rewards. Whereas us farmers create something from nothing, in the crops we grow and the livestock we nurture. There's real skill in that. But what's in it for us? Little money and no respect.' The farmer placed particular emphasis on the final word. 'I seen that from an early age. So, when they found gold around Madoc, I thought, here's our chance. I said to Pa that we should give up this place and go prospecting, but he wouldn't budge. Obstinate, contrary old man. "This is my land and it'll be yours after me" he said, and he made me swear I'd keep it alive when he was gone. So here I am, day after day, year after year, working this patch of nothing until my hands bleed, barely making enough to survive, while thousands arrive from all over and make their fortunes just by sifting a pan or wielding a pickaxe. And it's too late now – all the best pitches are taken. It's always too late.'

Still Lily made no attempt to reply, but that did not seem to matter. The farmer had never once averted his gaze from the fire. 'I go into town and see them spending, drink in their hands and women on their arms, waving their money about and looking down their noses at me like I'm something they trod in. Never thinking about who grows the grain that makes their beer and whisky, or who tends the animals they feast on. And there's me, clutching a single dollar and fretting how best it could be spent. Why couldn't I have some of that?'

His eyes closed for a moment, and it seemed he might be done, but no. 'I could have found a better wife if I'd had the money. One that didn't provoke and judge and criticise and complain and only see the bad in me. And then have the nerve to cast me aside. Served her right in the end, though, didn't it?'

Now Lily was listening very closely.

'I had to lock her up or she would have been gone. She said as much. I'd let her out to do her work, but only when I could keep an eye on her. We still had to eat, didn't we? Then after a while it all blew over, or so I thought. She seemed changed

– more like she used to be, like she wouldn't run off no more. So I thought, why not? Perhaps we could have got back to something decent. But the she-devil tricked me and as soon as I unlocked the door, she was off.'

Indeed, one spring day his wife had quietly left the house and made her way through the woods to the Moira River, which flowed through the county on its way to the Bay of Quinte, but at twice its usual speed due to the run-off from the winter snows. Later that day her body was washed up several miles downstream. It was impossible to tell what damage had been caused by the rocks and what might have preceded her entry into the water. Official records stated that she had accidentally met her end, perhaps through slipping on the bank, or maybe it was a case of over-ambitious bathing. But this did not prevent local tongues from wagging, suggesting that she had finally secured her own release. Some even speculated that the farmer might have had a hand in it.

'As I said, served her right in the end.' The farmer rose from his seat to refill his jug. 'I only tell you this because you're not really here.' Suitably replenished, he resumed his vigil in front of the fire.

Lily sped through her chores, setting aside those that could wait until tomorrow, and she left the farmer in his drinking chair in deep, indecipherable conversation with himself. She hurried to her bed but lay awake for hours, thoughts dancing around her head until her brain was in knots. Might he also lock her away when it suited him? She was in possession of knowledge, and that was a dangerous thing. She was safer without. But it might also be a hold over him. Perhaps it might give her some protection.

The next morning the farmer urgently sought her out. 'Now, you forget about what I said last night or there will be trouble for you,' he spat, his face a picture of bother and menace, the evidence of his consumption still obvious on his breath. 'I wasn't myself and the drink has a mind of its own. It was all nonsense.'

The farmer could recall little of what he'd said. He just had a vague feeling that, whatever it was, it should not have been spoken of. Lily said nothing but remembered everything, and she observed that the farmer did not. She locked that away.

Then out of the blue, the farmer raised his hand and caught Lily's cheek. 'As a reminder of what I've just told you to do.'

It was the first blow – and now that boundary had been crossed, Lily knew it would not be the last.

'You'd better be scared of me. My boys are,' the farmer boasted before walking off to start another miserable day.

That evening his supper tasted most unpleasant, but he said nothing.

TWENTY

It was the summer of 1884, and Alice Hamilton was packing a trunk in preparation for her return journey to England. She had recently completed a distribution of children, and a further shipment was scheduled quite soon. As she arranged some undergarments, she was disturbed by a visitor.

'You will remember me, I hope.'

Alice quickly shut the trunk. The man's face was familiar, and she soon recognised him as the civil servant that she had once buttonholed on a voyage to Canada. However, she had misplaced his name, and she had to pretend she had not until he confirmed that it was George Moore, chief inspector of Her Majesty's Local Government Board.

'I last saw you loading a quantity of exhausted children onto a train,' he began by way of small talk.

Alice was rarely interested in the niceties of a conversation, and certainly not when she had a deadline to meet. 'I am rather busy, so perhaps you could come to the point of your visit.'

Moore sat himself down, as a statement that he would not be hurried. Alice pointedly remained standing.

'As you know, the Board is responsible for the welfare of workhouse children and remain so even if the child has been emigrated.'

'I am aware of its interference from time to time.'

Moore raised his eyebrows, clearly registering the jibe, but did not react. 'Each year we receive complaints from various sources concerning the activities of child emigration agencies, and the volume of these grievances is increasing.'

'I am aware that there are some charlatans in the business, and that is unfortunate, but you'll find no objections to my enterprise.'

'You would be surprised, Miss Hamilton.'

And indeed she was. Of course, there had been some incidents that were to be regretted, but it was unrealistic to expect that things would always run smoothly. And some people would never be satisfied, no matter what she did or didn't do. But to make a complaint? Who would show such ingratitude?

Moore took some pleasure from Alice's obvious disarray and continued. 'Given the potential for embarrassment, the Board has instructed me to investigate the trade, to understand how it operates and to check on the state of the children that have passed through. Hence my presence in Canada.'

'You will find nothing untoward with my children,' Alice blustered, suddenly less confident but determined not to show it.

'Then you will no doubt be pleased to have this confirmed.' Moore allowed himself a fleeting smile, bordering on a smirk.

Alice snorted when she saw it. 'And what might be the result of your endeavours?'

'For many years, you and others like you have gone about your business largely unsupervised. I shall be recommending whether such laxity should be allowed to continue.'

'And if I do not co-operate in this time-wasting exercise?'

'You will no longer be allowed to emigrate workhouse children.' Moore ignored Alice's spluttering and protestations.

'I shall need the names of the children that have passed through your Kingston place, say in the last three years…'

'But…'

'And notice of where they might currently be found…'

'You cannot—'

'I shall return tomorrow morning to collect the details.' With that, he took his leave. Alice was too furious even to wish him farewell, and she stamped about her office for some time rehearsing things she wished she had thought to say, either by way of argument or simply as scathing abuse. But when she calmed down a little, she felt she had no choice but to comply, and so she abandoned her packing to immerse herself in paper and journals. It was long into the night before she was able to consider the task complete, or at least sufficiently advanced to be accepted as such. George Moore was not in her good books.

'Poking his nose in where it is not welcome,' she snarled to one of her staff. 'No doubt desperate to find fault to justify his trifling existence. I cannot abide a man who gets in the way.' And throughout the search she could be heard muttering words such as 'disruptive', 'unhelpful' and 'self-important'.

She might have added 'persistent', as persistent he undoubtedly was. Moore did not expect a welcome from the various emigration agencies, and he let their displeasure wash over him. Having acquired what he needed, however reluctantly given, he spent the Canadian summer and beyond touring the regions to which children had been scattered, observing how they lived and worked, listening to their stories, and making detailed notes of all he saw and heard. He became a regular feature on the nation's railways as he trundled, in a state of permanent discomfort, from settlement to settlement, ever conscious of the limited time at his disposal. And for the many placements where the railway feared to tread, he was conveyed even more disagreeably by horse and trap, driving up to fifty miles a day through untamed country until there was no part of his body that was at ease with itself. But not once was he discouraged; indeed, the more he heard, the more determined he was to see the job through.

He filled one notebook, then another and yet another. By the time the first snows arrived, his work was done.

TWENTY-ONE

Robert and Amelia Gait were hewn from the same stone then sculpted by a single hand. Robert Gait was driven to extremes of endeavour by the ever-present spectre of defeat. It sat on his shoulder, mocking his efforts and constantly reminding him of what failure would mean, goading him on when he might otherwise have surrendered. Although marginally softer around the edges, his wife Amelia was as indestructible as her husband and was capable of shifts that would put the strongest man to shame. But among their single-minded purpose and unwavering stubbornness, there was a child-shaped hole in their lives that they could never quite consign to history, no matter how hard they tried.

The Gaits did not waste words, and when they spoke it was from a common creed. If ever they were assailed by doubt or tempted by visions of an easier life as hired hands, Robert Gait would repeat this mantra: 'I'll die a free man before I prostrate myself before another.'

And they would clear their minds and persevere.

Day by day they slowly transformed the land, bending it to their will and extracting tribute from its subjugation in ever increasing quantities, for sale or barter or to keep their bellies full enough to power the next day's toil. When things went well there was back-slapping all round, which Arthur found even more rewarding, due to its delivery from sources that were not effusive by nature. When events conspired against them, they all rolled up their sleeves and rectified matters without apportioning blame. Every flourish of Gait's axe was a statement of intent, every thrust of his spade a riposte to those that would otherwise exploit him. It was work that required imagination as well as muscle: surveying a spinney and picturing a field of grain in its stead; inspecting a thicket and imagining cattle grazing productively there; being able to see the food for the trees.

One day Arthur had been helping Gait with a stump that was proving particularly stubborn. Hour after hour they hacked away, their faces red enough to burst, a delta of sweat irrigating the land on which they stood. But Gait would not rest until the job was done. Since their first meeting, Arthur had been intrigued about what made Gait the man he was. He had not encountered his like before: someone who didn't trumpet their achievements, even though they seemed worthy of frequent mention; a man who thought beyond today and just surviving it; an enigma, maybe, or perhaps the mystery was simply that there was no mystery at all.

'A story as old as time,' Gait muttered, as he swung again with full force. 'Injustice and exploitation and the poor consigned to an early grave because of it.'

'I'm listening.'

Gait briefly leaned on his pickaxe and thought for a moment. Arthur could almost hear him debating whether it might be more trouble to refuse than to reveal. He seemed to conclude that it was. 'There was this rich landowner, made his fortune in textiles and then thought he'd play at being squire of the manor, so people might think it was good money he'd inherited and not bad, that he'd stolen from the pockets of ordinary folk.'

His pickaxe came down with force, as if aiming for the rich man's skull. 'All the folk around us depended on him, labouring on his farm, slaving all hours. Then when the markets turned grim, the workers paid the price. Wages cut to the bone. Men cast off as if they were a piece of dirt being wiped off a boot. Families thrown out of their homes with no thought of where they might go. Children, babies even, left without a roof over their heads.'

Another swing at the rich man's head. 'Then there was a meeting and a man offering a passage to Canada, pledging this and claiming that. The Promised Land, no less, or so they said. Of course, he would say that, but I signed up for it anyway. And I'm glad I did. As I've said before, what's here is mine. No one will benefit from our toil and then throw us away like scraps from his table when he fancies it. Never again.'

Eventually the stump was tamed, and they walked home in triumph.

'Brave of you to leave so much behind,' Arthur remarked admiringly as they reached the yard.

'Desperation makes heroes of us all. I imagine you know all about that.' Gait reached into a water barrel and drew a bucketful for his ablutions. 'But that's quite enough talking for one day.'

And he set about making himself fragrant enough to be allowed inside.

TWENTY-TWO

'I'm not sure about Canada, miss,' Sam Barney had told Alice Hamilton when first she enquired about the possibility. 'I think I'd rather stay here, if you don't mind.'

'Can you remember having parents, boy?' she had replied.

'I think about them most days, miss.'

'And would you like the chance to again be part of a family?'

'More than anything, miss.'

'Then Canada is just the thing for you.'

In selling the idea of emigration to orphan children, Alice often dangled the carrot that, once placed, they might in time be seen more as a son or daughter than an employee. Naturally, this was an attractive thought to children who had lost so much, and it was particularly appealing to Sam, who was less insular and more fragile than many of his fellows. Sadly, Alice often neglected to mention that this happy outcome was the exception and not the rule.

It was not long before the formidable Mrs Wright made it very clear to Sam that theirs was purely a commercial arrangement. 'You are here to work, and I wish you would remember it,' she snapped, when he spoke to her in a manner that she thought dangerously informal.

'And I'm willing to do so. But I am also a child, in years anyhow.'

'We do not see you as a child, and the sooner you get that out of your head, the better for all of us.'

'Is there no chance that one day you might like me?' A tear appeared on Sam's cheek, swiftly followed by another.

'Liking has nothing to do with it.' Mrs Wright turned away so that she did not have to witness his tears. 'We have an agreement. You have your bed and board, and we will pay you some wages if you are diligent enough. That should be enough for you.'

'But missus, I was told to expect better than that.'

'If Miss Hamilton has lied to you, then you must take it up with her.'

'But I would be so much happier—'

'It states nowhere that we have to make you happy.'

And the matter was not discussed again.

At first, Sam did not blame the Wrights for the vacuum at the heart of where their attachment might otherwise have been, except perhaps on days when the emptiness was particularly profound. They looked after their own, and it was nobody's fault that he did not fall within that category. In some respects, it was not a bad life. He was worked hard, but not unfairly so. He was adequately clothed and fed, and wages at the agreed rate were regularly sent to Alice Hamilton for safekeeping. When censure was delivered or chastisement administered, Sam generally accepted it as deserved. It was true that he was only spoken to when there was a purpose to it. And gratitude for his efforts was a rare commodity, with silence being the best he could generally hope for. But all in all, had he been a grown man, he would have thought little of his situation. Of course he was not a grown man, and he thought about it a great deal.

It was in the minutiae of family life that Sam's condition was most deficient. He found himself alone in a crowd of people. Instead of warmth, there was icy coldness; in place of intimacy, there was distance. He was unheard and invisible. He ate separately, albeit from the same menu, as would a common labourer. When the Wrights enquired as to his wellbeing it was never out of concern, only to check his availability for work. He was clothed functionally and without any regard to his appearance; he had no 'Sunday best', as he had no occasions to attend that would warrant its wearing. The one speck of comfort was that he was excluded from the weekly pilgrimage to hear Ezra Wright preach; he heard enough of it on other days.

And he missed Arthur very much.

Had it not been for John Wright's regular warnings, the daughters of the house might have been allowed to provide Sam with meaningful company. John was the son who had left the farm for Toronto. Sam had replaced him in terms of workload, if not in parental affection. As a regular reader of the *Toronto Herald*, the junior Wright was familiar with its tirades against immigrant children and their perceived shortfalls in morality and behaviour. And as a concerned and dutiful son, whenever such a column appeared, he would carefully cut it out of the newspaper and post it to his mother, often with additional commentary of his own. Then Mrs Wright would show the piece to the family at large and inform them what opinion they should hold.

'Sam Barney is a gutter child,' she was keen to impress upon her daughters. 'He might appear harmless, even personable after a fashion, but one day his true nature will inevitably emerge, and I don't have to explain what that might entail.'

Indeed, no further explanation was required. The girls had each been named after a Biblical virtue, and with that came great responsibility: any behaviour that was not in keeping would have been akin to blasphemy, and Mrs Wright made it clear that disobedience of parental instruction was the greatest sin of all. Prudence was the eldest girl, and Charity was not too far behind in years, with Sam sandwiched in between them in terms of age. Faith and Hope followed at a respectful distance.

But despite, or perhaps because of their mother's warning, as time passed the elder daughters would occasionally sneak a glance or snatch a word with their forbidden fruit, and when nothing untoward resulted from it, they might sneak or snatch another.

'Oh dear, I've dropped my handkerchief in the pigpen,' Prudence cried out one day, and she whispered a 'thank you' after Sam retrieved it, adding a smile that might have encouraged further dialogue. But Sam was conditioned to expect the worst and doubted that he had seen or heard correctly. He sloped away before any trouble ensued.

On another occasion Sam found Prudence and Charity giggling, and they seemed to be pointing in his direction.

Must be laughing at something behind me, he thought sadly. Best not say anything.

It was several months before Sam discovered Mrs Wright's first name, and then only by accident. Ezra Wright would only refer to his wife as 'my dear', at least in public, and any neighbours who visited observed the appropriate formalities. Then one day a letter arrived addressed to Patience Wright – a hugely inappropriate epithet for a woman who was always in a hurry and who expected others to have similar intent. It gave Sam a happier day than he had known for some time. He chuckled away as he went about his duties, scarcely able to resist a smile in her usually fearsome presence.

I think he must be simple, she thought when she observed Sam's unruly grin. Or else he's up to something. She resolved to double her watchfulness.

Singing was a regular feature of family life – hymns mainly, and perhaps a chorus or two from an operetta if Patience Wright approved of the moral of the story. At such times, the family would stand in a circle, their faces almost transcendent with joy as they lifted their gaze to the heavens, their soaring harmonies charming the air around them. No individual voice could be identified, save the rumbling bass of Ezra Wright, yet each was integral to the whole, the family speaking as one. Sitting to one side in mute admiration, Sam witnessed the unity of purpose and listened with increasing jealousy as their feelings were expressed through a melody that was beyond mere words.

If I show them that I can sing, then perhaps they'll want to include me, he thought. Surely, they will. It's not as if they'd have to talk to me.

Sam had never had much time for hymns, so he would have to sing what he knew. He remembered the carousing that issued forth from London taverns as men tumbled out, under the influence of more than just music. And he recalled the ballads that street sellers would perform to make light of a difficult day. He could recite the words to a number of such ditties, although he did not always know what they meant. So, the next day, as he went about his work, Sam sang as many as he could remember, all delivered with great enthusiasm, if not total accuracy.

He crooned 'Goodnight, Ladies' as he mucked out the horses. Later, the poultry enjoyed 'Have I Got a Surprise for You,' and the pigs were treated to an encore. Sam was about to begin a eulogy to 'The Clergyman's Daughter' when Patience Wright stormed across the yard.

'How dare you let such filth spill from your mouth?' she screeched, her face pinched out of all recognition. 'This is the devil's music, and I'll not tolerate it.'

Sam's heart sank, his raucous mood crushed in an instant. 'I was hoping you might let me sing with you, if you heard me,' he whimpered. 'And these tunes are all I know, but I'm very keen to learn.'

'Singing is something we do as a family. We don't want no outsiders.' Patience Wright turned to stamp back to the homestead. 'The Lord gives a voice to those that will use it in His praise. He has not given *you* a voice!' She scoffed at the mere thought.

And thenceforth, whenever the family wished to sing, Sam was dispatched to the outer reaches of the farm, lest the urge to join in proved too strong. And there he would sit, straining his ears towards the angelic chorus, each note a dagger to the heart, yet he could not resist torturing himself with its beauty. And when the air fell silent, he would sadly make his way homewards, from one wilderness to another.

TWENTY-THREE

A concerned citizen of Kingston, a Mrs Dando, called at Alice Hamilton's Kingston centre one summer's morning, asking to speak to whoever was in charge. Alice herself was present, having recently returned from a tour of neighbouring settlements, where she had been whipping up interest among potential employers. She had been looking forward to a period of quiet, but that prospect faded as a clearly troubled woman was shown into her office.

'It's about one of your girls, name of Mary Oliver,' Mrs Dando began, speaking at a gallop until Alice coaxed her into slowing down to a walking pace. 'The poor child is in a terrible state – she's been treated outrageously by those she was serving. She's had such a harsh beating that she can hardly stand.'

Mrs Dando was persuaded to take a seat and relaxed still further when a cup of tea arrived. She could not remember when she last drank from bone china, if she ever had, and was momentarily distracted.

'Please proceed, Mrs Dando, and take your time,' Alice encouraged her, although, as always, she hoped that the woman would reach the point quite quickly.

Mrs Dando was pleased to accept a second cup, and then she felt able to start. 'We found your girl wandering the streets by our house, barefoot and crying, and bleeding from so many places that you couldn't tell where one wound stopped and another one started. Says she fled to escape even more punishment, and I believe her.'

'Please remind me of the family with whom she is placed.'

'Dr Hoggard and his wife.'

This was not good news. Acquiring someone as celebrated as the doctor had been quite a coup, and Alice had hoped he might encourage others of his ilk to consider her children when short of servants.

'Are you saying that the doctor himself inflicted the wounds you describe? That scarcely seems believable, since he purports to be a healer.'

'It's his wife, ma'am. She's the one that carries the clout in that house in every respect, at least as far as the children are concerned.'

'And is the girl still with you?'

'She is, ma'am. I've cleaned her up a bit, but we can't keep her. Folk will talk and then there'll be trouble for us. Anyhow, we've not the room for another.'

It was clear that something untoward had occurred. Alice summoned her carriage and accompanied Mrs Dando back to her home in another part of the town. It was a small brick house, adjacent to the old marine barracks and some distance – in every respect – from the grander architecture enjoyed by the Hoggards and other notables. On hearing their approach, Mary hid behind the bulbous figure of Mr Dando until she was certain that the visitor bore her no harm. When she saw who it was, she ran towards Alice and enveloped her in her arms, clinging tight, even though she flinched in pain.

'I'm so glad to see you, miss,' she sobbed, her words muffled by Alice's shoulder. 'Things have been very bad for me, and perhaps now they will be better.'

As a matter of principle, Alice did not encourage hugs, and hence rarely received one, but she found this more pleasant than she would have predicted, and she was quick to respond and slow to release. And so they stood, an incongruous pair, Mary already at an age where she towered over her protector, and Alice unsure what to do next. Eventually they extricated themselves.

'My dear girl, let me examine your injuries.'

At first Mary recoiled, embarrassed to be found in such a state. She backed into a corner and curled herself up into something small and secret. 'It's not right you should see me like this.'

'We must decide if you need a doctor. Not the one you've just left, I might add.'

Mary relented and they settled in the parlour, while Mrs Dando shooed away her own brood, who had come to investigate.

'That is a nasty wound across the bridge of your nose,' Alice noted. 'And I imagine it is responsible for the blackening of your eyes.'

'I'm not looking my best, am I, miss? Boys will run away from me even more.'

'That is no great loss.'

Mary winced as Alice examined the cut on her wrist.

'That must have come from a heavy blow, as it has pierced nearly to the bone.'

'That's the one that hurts the most, miss.'

'And there are two bruises on that arm, and on the other is a contusion as big as the palm of my hand.' Alice tutted loudly as she documented the outcome, while Mary's confidence grew.

'And just look at my legs,' Mary cried, no longer embarrassed to show them. 'They're a mess too.'

They were a mass of abrasions right down to the heels.

'And are there any injuries other than what I can see?'

'No, miss, but that's enough, isn't it?'

'More than enough.'

Mrs Dando brought in refreshments in cups that were noticeably less grand, and undoubtedly less hygienic, than those from which she had recently drunk. Alice pulled a face that she hoped her host would not see.

'Now tell me how you came by these terrible injuries.'

'Please, miss, when I came here, I wrote it all down in case I should forget anything.' Mary delved into a pocket and handed Alice a rather crumpled piece of paper. 'It took me most of a day, miss, and I had several goes at it. I thought it was important.'

'Will you read it for me?'

Mary was happy to oblige, her voice conveying the sense of injustice that she felt. *'I was wheeling the youngest child up and down the hall in a toy carriage. She is about three years old and most difficult to control at the best of times.'*

'A right little madam, she is,' Mary confided, and they laughed. *'The child was standing up as I pushed and I told her to sit down, but she would not do it. The Hoggards' cat was in the carriage with her and suddenly it jumped out, and when the child leaned over to catch it, she also fell out. She was not much hurt, although you would not know it from the noise. I took the child up to the mistress and tried to explain, but she got angry and took a stick out of the drawer and beat me with it.'*

Mary's eyes filled with tears as she recalled the moment. As she read, she could almost feel the blows once more raining down upon her. *'It was about as sturdy as a leg of a chair, about two feet long and perhaps half an inch thick.* I don't know why she would have such a thing so handy,' Mary sobbed. 'Perhaps she was expecting or even wanting to have a chance to use it.'

Alice nodded but somewhat distantly.

'She struck me across the face on both sides and on the top of the head. Also on the arms, three or four times on each. And on the legs, I don't know how often. After the beating she told me to lie down, as she was going to whip me again, but instead I ran out of the house, fearing for my life. I walked about for most of the day, keeping to the quiet streets in case they were searching for me. Then I met this kind lady and came home with her.'

Mrs Dando blushed a little. Mary waited anxiously for Alice's response, but it was some time before she spoke.

'This puts me in a very difficult position.'

Mary panicked. 'Please don't send me back there, miss, 'cos I won't go. I often let her take the strap to me, and that was bad enough, but I can't suffer a beating like this again. The mistress is a mad woman much of the time, and even when she's not she's on the verge of being so. Next time she'll kill me, I swear it.'

'Of course you will not be going back.'

Mary was not greatly reassured. 'So, can we set the police on them? I want them punished.'

'It is not that simple.'

'It's as clear as day in my eyes.'

Alice looked at the bruised and bloodied girl before her and sighed. 'I must do what is best for all my children, which means that I must weigh up the alternatives. If we alert the police and secure a hearing in court, it may lead to you gaining some revenge, and it might protect future children from such treatment, but only if we win. If we lose, it will make matters worse. And the notoriety of the case will make it difficult to place others, whether we win or lose.'

But Mary was in no mood to be sacrificed for the greater good, if indeed it was that. 'I should have stood up for myself afore now, and if I had none of this would have happened.' She scowled. 'If you abandon me now, I will make sure the world knows it, and what will your precious patrons think of that?'

Alice stared warily at Mary.

'I will travel back to England to be heard if I have to.'

In her years under Alice Hamilton's care, Mary had formed an opinion of what sort of woman she was, and what was important to her, and her threat hit home.

Alice identified the lesser of two evils. 'Very well, I shall report this to the authorities and see where that takes us.'

'Do what you like, but please don't involve us in this,' Mrs Dando whimpered. 'We don't have friendly relations with the doctor and Mrs Dorothy, and they already have bad feelings towards us. We had a serious falling-out a while back. I won't go into detail.'

'If it comes before a court, we will need you as a witness.'

Mrs Dando sighed from the depths of her soul. 'I'll see if I have the courage at the time, ma'am. But we don't want to provoke them. Things are unpleasant enough between us as it is.'

'What they've done to me is sinful and they should be taught a lesson,' Mary hissed.

'I doubt I've got the strength to be the teacher, miss.'

Alice helped Mary into the carriage, and they returned to the distribution centre. Mary's initial elation at seeing Alice had dissipated, and she sat, unsmiling, as she pondered her predicament and Alice's reaction to it. Out of the blue, she sprang a question on Alice. 'Tell me, miss, did you check they were decent folk before you let them take me?'

Not for the first time that day, Alice reddened with embarrassment. 'They are a much-respected family in the town,' she said, flustered.

'But did you make sure? The town don't live with 'em.' Mary did not need an answer; she could see that Alice had not.

'Do you blame me for what you have suffered?'

'Part of me does, miss, I cannot lie.'

Just before they reached the distribution centre, Mary piped up again. 'Miss, if you're going to be helping me, there is something else we need to settle. When I last saw you, we did not part on good terms, what with you separating me from my brother, Percy. I expect you remember it.'

'I recall there was a misunderstanding.'

'You broke your word, miss, far as I'm concerned. And what's worse is you made me break a sacred promise to my dead Pa. I know you think different, but you did. If we're to fight these people, I need to trust you. Can I trust you?'

Alice looked most affronted. 'Of course. I am most pained that you should doubt me.'

'I really hope so, miss. I meant what I said earlier.'

That evening Alice wrote a stiff letter to the Hoggards, outlining her disgust at Mary's treatment and requesting delivery of her belongings. A carriage subsequently arrived at the home bearing a trunk into which had been stuffed various items of clothing, which may or may not have represented the sum of Mary's possessions. It was accompanied by a short missive that was at the hostile end of glacial.

'Let battle commence,' Alice made a point of saying.

But Mary was not wholly convinced, and she resolved to keep her eyes open and her wits about her.

TWENTY-FOUR

While Margaret Walsh generally preferred her own company to that of others, whenever the opportunity arose, she gladly spent time in the Bradleys' general store. It was a place of intrigue and delight, guaranteed to lift her mood. The timbered floor complained under the weight of every imaginable appliance, their historic comings and goings leaving gullies, indentations, and a forest of splinters; it was not a place to go barefoot. Sacks of flour and potatoes, apples and grain were randomly scattered about, watched over by the seed for next year's harvest. When the store was quiet, Margaret liked to skip between the various obstacles – a test of skill and balance and the ability to brake quickly if a customer called. Three of the walls were bedecked with strangely shaped receptacles containing an assortment of treasures, while a selection of guns decorated the fourth. In the yard was a pile of wood, chopped and ready for use by those without the strength or courage to wield an axe.

As she sat among the merchandise, Margaret was captivated by the novelty of the conversations that swirled around her, mostly trivial in content but no less interesting for that. Inmates of Brownlow Hill were largely forbidden to speak and, in any event, would have little to talk about, each day being the same and identical for all. Margaret had not the confidence nor the inclination to join in, but she was more than happy to listen.

'This your new girl, then?' customers asked on first acquaintance, and some would add, 'Seems very interested in other folk's business.'

'She'll soon learn to ignore you, like we all do,' Daisy Bradley would joke in reply and unruly laughter would erupt from John's direction.

Margaret had been living with the Bradleys for nearly two years when a letter arrived that was addressed to her. Its journey had been long and devious, starting in a remote location in England and treading a tortuous path to Canada via Alice Hamilton and various associates of hers. Daisy had ultimately taken delivery and rightly guessed from the hesitant handwriting who the author might be.

'It's her father, I'm sure of it,' she whispered – unnecessarily, since Margaret was in school, at least half a mile distant.

'I'm her father, aren't I?' John was not a man for whispering.

'You know what I mean. Oh John, what might it say?'

'Only way to find out is to let her open it.'

'But what if it unsettles her, brings back memories of home? What if he's out to cause trouble?'

'Look, he wanted her to have a better life, and that's what she's got. It's not like he's round the corner, always popping in, is it? Just give it to her and see what she makes of it.' And for once John had the final word.

Once the store was closed and before the distraction of the evening meal, Daisy handed the letter over without comment to Margaret, who stared wide-eyed at the unexpected arrival, turning it over in her hands and looking at it from every angle, barely convinced that it was real. Suspiciously at first, then with increasingly urgent fingers, she began to reveal its contents, gasping and giggling and looking at Daisy as if asking for permission to continue. Once the letter was liberated, her gaze moved quickly over the irregular handwriting, too excited to settle on a single word to see what it might be.

'I shall read this in my room.' She sprinted up the stairs, and the scrape of her chair could be heard.

Daisy and John stared after her. 'What do we do now?'

'We wait.'

And it was a very nervous wait.

The best part of an hour later, Margaret clomped back down again. 'I can't make out bits of it and I don't know what some of it means. Please will you tell me what it says?'

Daisy almost snatched the paper from Margaret's hand. She started with suspicion but soon relaxed into the innocence of the words. Margaret listened with a beaming smile across her face; she could hear her father's voice in every sentence, as if he were reading it himself.

'My dear Margaret, I hope you've had enough schooling so you can make sense of this, although my writing is tricky, and you might need your new folks to lend a hand. I met a man who has helped me a bit with what to say and how to say it. I'm sorry if it don't come out right, but it's all written with the deepest affection so please don't think bad of me. I have missed you greatly. There's not much to life with just having me to think of. But it gives me strength to know you are well cared for, far better than I ever could. I left Brownlow Hill soon after you did and put that foul place behind me entirely. Ain't never going back there. Now I'm treading the roads and picking up work where I can, looking for somewhere I might settle. It's handy that I can carry everything I own and quite easily too. I often think of our time in

that vile shelter. No place for a child, nor a man nor woman neither. The only good part of any day was seeing you: if I could just catch a glimpse, it would keep me going. And you're still at the front of my thoughts as I walk and sweat and walk some more. It helps me get by. My health is mostly all right, apart from the aches and pains you would expect from this sort of life. I am hoping you are happy in your new home. Your folks are lucky to have you, and I'm sure you're blessed to have them. If you would like to write me a letter, then it would give me great joy to read it but see what your folks say. They may think better of it. Until I have a fixed abode, you could send it to Miss Hamilton, and I will ask from time to time whether she has heard anything. I will find a way, don't you worry. I shall always be your loving Pa.'

There were tears and cuddles when Daisy had finished. Then Margaret asked for the letter to be read again. For the remainder of the day she was even quieter than usual, exhausted by the emotion of it all.

'You must write back soon,' Daisy encouraged her.

'I need to think what to say.'

'Would you like some help?'

Margaret was very definite. 'No, it should be my words.'

Later, John could see that his wife was upset. 'Don't fret, my love. Children that age are always wanting to do things themselves. I know I did.'

'But I can never tell what she's thinking, and it worries me.'

'His letter was nothing to be concerned about, was it? Let's see what she says in return. I'll wager it's harmless too.'

For the next three days, Margaret thought about what to write. At times a big grin would light up her face, as a treasured memory resurfaced, and then the sadness of not being able to share it would overwhelm her. Finally she was ready. Daisy found an envelope and some writing paper; Margaret's existing supply had long ago been covered with doodles and drawings of her red maple.

'You had better give me plenty, as I am bound to get it wrong.' Margaret sat at the table in her room and put pen to paper. And as she had predicted, she did indeed get it wrong and had to start again, crumpling the discarded sheet into a ball and throwing it to the floor in frustration. The second attempt met the same fate, as did the third, and each time the crumpling became fiercer, and the resultant ball was thrown with greater force. Eventually, she filled two complete pages with large print and that would have to do.

Dear Pa,
I liked your letter very much and I'm very happy you wrote me. My new ma and pa helped me read it, as your writing looks like a beetle has crawled over the paper.

He won't mind that, he was always poking fun at me, Margaret thought.

My new folks have a general store, it sells anything you might want and more besides. They say I'll be able to help when I get older. For now, I do some washing and cleaning and you'll be surprised to learn I'm happy doing it, not like the workhouse where we all hated our chores, and everything seemed so dirty because no one tried very hard. I go to the school in the town, and I don't mind being there although I'd rather be somewhere else. At first, I couldn't read and write as good as the others and

I didn't know much else so I got teased and the teacher would get cross with me when I couldn't do something. I'm better at it now and so I get left alone a bit more. Some people here don't like children like me that have just arrived. They think we're not as good as their own and that we're lazy and filthy and got sickness they could catch. We get called some names by grown-up folks as well as by children. I won't repeat what they are. Ma and Pa get very cross and tell them not to be so cruel and that what they say isn't true, but they still think it, I'm sure. Don't get me wrong, I am content here and Ma and Pa have made me very welcome. I am their only child, which suits me well, but I think they might be a bit sad there's no more. I would be even happier if you could be here too, but I know you can't, and at least your words can. Write to me again. I am giving you a big hug in my head.

Your loving daughter, Margaret

Her task complete, she eased the letter into the envelope, taking care not to scrunch it out of shape. Then she sealed it and took it downstairs to be posted.

'Oh, we won't have the chance to read what you have said,' cried Daisy without thinking.

Margaret frowned. 'Why would you want to read it? It's from me to him. I didn't need no help with it.'

Daisy knew she had said the wrong thing. 'I just thought it would be nice…' she stammered, making things worse.

'I let you read what he wrote me. Ain't I allowed nothing private?' Margaret was angry now.

'I'll make sure it's posted,' John cut in. He took the envelope and Margaret clumped back upstairs. But some suspicions had been laid in her mind, and the next day she checked that he had done as he had promised.

And so the letter set out on its intrepid journey, first to Alice Hamilton's representatives, then to the lady herself, and finally on to Michael Walsh when he was sufficiently stationary to be confident of receiving it. Meanwhile, Margaret waited impatiently for further correspondence, questioning its whereabouts almost daily and being repeatedly assured that any delay reflected the haphazard lines of communication, not any absence of intent.

'Why is she so desperate to hear from him?' Daisy stewed over it. 'What are we doing wrong?'

John was unusually abrupt. 'He's her father, so of course she wants him to write. It doesn't mean she thinks any less of us. You must stop this, Daisy, or you'll drive her away.'

'You know why I'm like this. I cannot help myself.'

Several months passed before the now familiar handwriting made a further appearance. Margaret first took it to her room unopened but soon emerged. 'I need your help again,' she said, holding out the letter, and Daisy was careful not to make a big thing out of taking it.

'My dear Margaret, I cried tears of joy when I finally got your letter,' it read. *'Miss Hamilton has proved reliable as a post office, but now I have a proper address, as you will see, and you can use that if you want to. I've got the beetle helping me with my writing again.'*

Daisy looked quizzically at John, but Margaret just giggled, her whole face lighting up.

'I have found myself in a town that answers to the name

of Middlesborough, although I cannot see what it's in the middle of. It's nowhere you would know, but it's serving me well. Someone said there was a call for steel and that it was solid work to get into if you can, as most things in England are built of it, and other places too. Anyway, much of what's needed is made where I am now, or so they say, and the bosses were wanting men, so I changed the direction of my walking and joined up and I've been here for some time now. As usual, I started off doing the dirty work that no one else wanted, but I've learned some of what needs to be done, and I feel I might have a trade behind me if I keep at it. It's hard work and you can get hurt bad if you get it wrong, but it's keeping me off the roads and for now I'm glad to be standing still. I have a room in a house with several others. I suppose it's all right, although the rats are better company than the men.'

The letter continued in a similar vein, asking the sort of questions in which an absent parent would have an interest, and which Margaret was able to address in her next reply.

We go to church each Sunday and give thanks for our good life. I pray for you, and Ma and Pa of course. You wouldn't recognise me when I'm all dressed up, I look a proper girl… I can now help in the store and even get to deal with some customers, although I can see some don't trust me yet. Maybe because I'm still young enough for school, or more likely because I am an immigrant child, I don't know which… I can sew a little, although I'm not sure it looks very good. Ma wears it anyway, but maybe just to keep me happy… I am learning to cook, and they've not had to get the doctor yet… With all this learning, Pa says I'll make a good wife one day, although he chuckles when he says it. I say, 'Why would I want to be anyone's wife?' and Ma laughs at that.'

Again Margaret handed over a sealed envelope to be posted, and this time Daisy over-compensated in her obliging. Margaret added further suspicions to her pile but kept them to herself for now.

Another letter from the beetle was more reflective.

'The other day I was thinking of your first ma, as I do quite regular.'

Daisy stopped reading for a moment, but Margaret seemed keen to hear, so she carried on.

'I hope you don't blame her for walking off. She was brave to marry me, and braver still to jump when she wouldn't know where she'd land. And she will be most sad not to have you with her, I'm sure of it. But she must have thought it safer that you were with me, and she was probably right. It's a difficult business, life…'

As usual, Margaret was quick to reply, but this time when she brought the letter downstairs it was not in its envelope. 'I want you to see this one.'

Daisy nervously took the paper and began to read out loud.

I do think of first Ma a little, but I don't remember her much. She was right that I was safe with you. Even when we were apart in that evil place, I still felt you were beside me, and that gave me courage. It still does... I hope first Ma is not too sad, and I wish her well. I know it's not because she didn't like me or anything like that ... and I am very lucky with what I have now. New Ma is everything I could want, and new Pa too. And to top it off, it gives me joy that old Pa is with me through your writing and in your heart, if not in person.'

Margaret looked pointedly at Daisy. 'Perhaps now you can trust me.'

Daisy turned puce with embarrassment, while Margaret drove the point home. 'It was someone special I was writing to, not just anyone, so I wanted it to be from me alone. I didn't mean to hurt you, and I don't understand why it did. It never crossed my mind what you might think.'

'But you never talk to us – not about things that really matter, so we could not be sure that you were happy here. Perhaps I saw it as a way of finding out.' It was something that Daisy had wanted to say for some time.

Suddenly Margaret was on the back foot, and it seemed an age before she answered. 'It worries me, talking,' she said quietly. 'What if you don't like what I say? Where else would I go?'

'What could you possibly say—'

'Besides, there's no need for talk when things are clear as day. I have everything I could ever want. Except one thing, a really big thing. And now I have that too, I don't want to let go of it.'

'We would never ask you to. We're not monsters.'

'I know that. I just got scared.'

And that was quite enough talking for Margaret. She gave

John and Daisy a massive hug and hurried upstairs to her room, where she sat in her chair and thought some more.

'You see, I told you. Nothing to worry about.' John would always underline instances when he was proved right and Daisy wrong. It did not happen often enough for Daisy to tire of it.

And so the correspondence continued, becoming more regular now that Michael Walsh was tethered to a single place. He kept the beetle busy, as Margaret put it. Whenever he had something to say, and sometimes when he had nothing, he could always afford the cost of the mail ship and, if necessary, would go without a meal to make sure of it. The time soon came when Margaret could read his letters without any assistance from her new ma and pa, and sometimes she would make them public and at other times they remained private, depending on her mood.

When it was the latter, Daisy put on a brave face and tried to think positive thoughts. But she did not find it easy, and she continued to bend John's ear about how she felt.

TWENTY-FIVE

The Canadian winter led Arthur Dilkes to reappraise times in London when he had believed himself to be cold; this was on an entirely different scale. Come late November, the heavens opened and remained so for many months. Just when you thought the skies must surely be empty, they found a further supply. A cloak of sparkling white covered the Earth, not soot grey as Arthur was accustomed to, but dazzling in its purity. And when the sun appeared, you had to shield your eyes, such was its reflection. The wind whipped down from the north, sculpting a gallery of forbidding shapes that were there one moment and gone the next – perhaps the ghosts of victims of previous winters, or a premonition of those yet to fall. Landmarks disappeared and memories were all too fallible in locating trusted pathways. You could never rely on your tracks to find your way home. Nothing was quite as it seemed.

And yet people were expected to be out and about. Arthur soon found that his clothes were more suitable for English climes, and Amelia Gait was forced to cannibalise them and improvise to create something more effective. Using sacking and bedding as well as more conventional materials, she produced a series of outfits that were more scarecrow than labourer, but they served their purpose, and Arthur wore them twenty-four hours a day, only peeling them off for calls of nature and the most cursory attempts at hygiene. Arthur was familiar with a toboggan from a previous life and was overjoyed to find one in a barn. He made sure that every slope would know its markings and revelled in the feeling of days gone by. But snowshoes were a mystery, and he visited many a drift in trying to master them, with Robert Gait roaring with such mirth that it almost parted his beard and brought his mouth into view.

Once the remorseless cold abated, springtime ushered in a landscape that was no less challenging: the quagmire that emerged as the snows melted and the rains fell; the mud so deep it would wrench boots from feet as you walked; the threat of trench foot from perpetual immersion in the mire; wheel tracks and hoofprints that were carved deep into the sludge, then baked into permanent features by the July sun, making the journey to town a succession of jolts and bruises; and the unfading daylight of summer, when one working day would end and the next start seemingly without any interlude, in contrast to the almost total darkness of winter when sleep was restored.

It had been a day of great celebration when the homestead could finally be occupied, and the shanty abandoned to its fate as a storeroom. It was a statement of permanence. A town dweller, particularly one of substance, would have found the new accommodation to be rather modest, but it was a palace compared to what had gone before. Constructed of wood that was as solid and unyielding as its inhabitants, the homestead offered space and privacy, with separate rooms for functions that once were shared and enclosures where more than one person could stand at any moment. And its greatest glory: once summer passed, it would boast a temperature that allowed you to believe that you were inside, not still out.

'I can see me bathing more often in winter, now I can't

blame the lake for being frozen,' Gait joked. 'I shall be so fragrant you will hardly know me.'

'The dogs will think you're an intruder if they don't recognise your scent,' Amelia laughed. 'Even I can track you from a distance.'

That first evening, Robert Gait broke out some whisky to mark the occasion.

'Tonight we shall raise a toast in each and every room,' he announced, jug in hand, dragging his wife to her feet. 'And the boy can have his share, just this once.'

First it was the cooking space.

'Here's to the future feasts that we will enjoy.'

'And who's going to be preparing them, Robert Gait?'

'A joint toast, then. To Mrs Gait and her miracle stove.'

A glass was downed, and they moved on to what would be the inner sanctum.

'I toast the bed wherein we shall lie, and perhaps something more than that, Mrs Gait, if you would be so kind.'

'Behave yourself, Robert Gait, or sleeping is all you'll know. There are young ears here.'

A further glass was downed, and they set sail again, a little more unsteady than before. Guards were lowered by the warmth and intimacy of the whisky, and Amelia noted that Arthur was unusually quiet. 'Are you all right?'

'Been thinking about something.'

'Always a dangerous sign,' joked Robert Gait, who was almost giddy by his own standards.

'Don't discourage the boy, let him speak.'

They stood in what might have been the parlour or even the sitting room in more polite circles, but to the Gaits it was simply the living space. After a toast to its comfort and worth, they took advantage of its seating. Arthur was bribed by further whisky to overcome his reluctance to share his thoughts.

'The other day, when I was in town, I overheard someone complaining about us pauper children, so I kept quiet and listened,' he eventually mumbled. 'It was the usual hogwash about our parentage and how bad they were, even though they'd never met 'em. You know, "they're all drunks and thieves" and the like. And how us children were bound to turn out just like them. That it weren't our fault and we couldn't do nothing about it, because it's in our blood. I've heard others say it before, of course, but this time it got me thinking.'

Amelia took Arthur's hand, and he surprised himself by returning the squeeze.

'A lot of nonsense gets talked, and those that know the least are always the loudest, ain't that right, Mr Gait?'

Robert Gait was only half listening. 'You point them out to me, and I'll have words.'

'Not everything is sorted out by the threat of your fists, Mr Gait.'

'Most things are.'

Amelia glared at her husband, and he pretended not to notice, which was his usual tactic.

His face reddening with a combination of whisky and embarrassment, Arthur stumbled on. 'But what if I do turn out like Ma and Pa? What if they are in my blood and I can't get rid of 'em?'

'Would that be a bad thing? You've never spoken of 'em.'

Arthur was in unfamiliar territory. This was not something he had ever revealed, not even to Sam Barney in all the time they had spent together. While he felt uncomfortable – and that was unfamiliar too – something told him to push on. 'I don't like to talk about it. It's hard enough having them in my head, without them being in my mouth as well.' There was a long pause and a deep sigh. 'We never saw much of Pa. He put food on the table, but that was it. Ma would bellyache that he just wanted a quiet life, and off he'd go drinking with his cronies to prove the point. Then one day, without so much as a goodbye, he marches down to the army barracks in town and joins up, and that's the last we saw of him. So, that's what he thought of us. May he rot in Hell.'

'And your mother?'

The anger in Arthur's voice died away. 'Ma was difficult and got more so as time went on. It didn't help that Pa was never there, and when he was, they just fought. Never a kind word. Sad, really. I think they quite liked each other once.'

Amelia Gait was listening intently, but her husband was more interested in the jug of whisky and his own thoughts.

'Sometimes she would see things that weren't there. Really strange things that you wouldn't even dream of. Then she was being followed, or so she thought. People were always out to do her harm, she said. But they weren't. She got upset when people laughed at her. She didn't make that up, and I got in more than one scrap because of it. I was forever having to rescue her from some fix or other. She was rude to someone, or started shouting for no reason, or sometimes she was even a bit physical or threatening. In a shop, on the street, outside the public house where Pa was drinking. You never knew what would happen next. You had to think quick. Make up a story, invent an excuse, find some way of turning it into a joke.'

Arthur allowed himself a faint smile of appreciation for his own cleverness. 'Then she started thieving. Not things we needed, nothing useful; I could have understood that. Just thieving for the sake of it.' He saw Amelia raise an eyebrow. 'Look, when Sam and I stole, we did it to live. That's different.'

'I'm not judging you. I was never in your position.'

There was an awkward silence. Robert Gait had heard around half of what had been said and had paid heed to perhaps a quarter of it. Clearly there was something on his mind. Now he lifted himself to his feet. 'Shall we move on?'

And they shuffled off to toast the washroom.

'I'm still listening,' Amelia encouraged Arthur, as they admired the wooden tub that would service both skin and fabric. The whisky was doing its job of loosening Arthur's tongue: words tumbled out ever faster as he unburdened himself of the history that had been weighing him down, even though he had never admitted it was doing so.

'The strange thing was, Ma still had work all this time and that's what did for her in the end. She cleaned for some toff at the top of the town, been with him for years. So long as his house was spotless, he wasn't bothered about the rest. And she would scrub away like her life depended on it, which suited him well.'

Ma's employer had indeed been patient and prepared to overlook her unconventional ways. But then, as Arthur explained, he began to notice gaps appearing on the shelves of his library. He set a trap, and Ma was caught red-handed with an Alfred Tennyson volume concealed in her skirts, and a subsequent search of their lodgings revealed a large hoard that did not belong there. The books were not stolen to provide learning or enjoyment or moral sustenance, as Ma was unable to read. Neither were they put to any practical use in the home, perhaps in lieu of furniture or to seal off a draught. Instead, they sat in random order in a dark and filthy corner, Plato rubbing shoulders with *Vanity Fair* and Jane Austen scandalously astride Charles Darwin, each one under silent attack from damp and mould.

'Ma couldn't explain herself, and so she was committed to Maidstone Prison. Not even I could talk her out of that.' Arthur wiped an unwelcome tear from his eye. 'Mind you, she didn't enjoy their hospitality for long.'

Ma's increasingly erratic behaviour led to an alienist being summoned from the nearby lunatic asylum to assess her sanity. In his expert opinion, he felt that all parties would be best served if Ma were to be transferred to his asylum and detained there indefinitely, and so money changed hands, and she made the short trip across town. It was not obvious whether she noticed any change in her incarceration.

'There's many that's had folks do far worse than mine, and I've met a fair number of them. Ma wasn't bad, she was ill, not right in the head. They said she had some fancy name of a thing, but she was just mad really. In the end she didn't know who I was, and that makes me sad.'

By now, Robert Gait was toasting individual items of crockery.

'So when these folk say I'll end up like Ma and Pa, because it's in my blood, in my case that means I'll either be a selfish bastard of a man or mad as a hatter. Or both.'

By now Arthur's strutting cockiness had deserted him, leaving behind an unrecognisable fragility.

'I can see why that might alarm you, but—'

'Perhaps I'm already like Pa, or on the road to being him. I left Ma behind in the madhouse, didn't I? Made sure I looked after myself and let others make their own way, or not at all. And that's been the story ever since.'

'What else could you have done? You were a child.'

'It ain't about age. Poor Sam Barney deserved better of me, and I were older then. We were bound together for a time, and now we're not. I don't even think of him much. I'll be a hole in his life, for sure, but he's not in mine, and he should be.' Suddenly Arthur felt that he had said enough. He had always believed that baring one's soul was a sign of weakness, and here he was doing just that. Amelia sensed that there was no more to come and did not push him further. Robert Gait had staggered off while Arthur was speaking, and they went to find him. He sat by the window of a small space at the back of the homestead, currently free from clutter but built in hope that one day it might be different.

'This shall be the child's room,' he said quietly, raising a glass to a perfect future.

Amelia squeezed Robert's arm and gently eased him away. 'The boy don't want to hear none of that.'

By now they were all at the maudlin end of the jug, and it was time to call it a night. The next day Arthur was back to his jaunty self, superficially at least, firing off suggestions and ordering others about as he usually did. Robert Gait was rather more lethargic, and even less inclined to be told where he was going wrong. No one mentioned the previous evening, although beneath his nonchalant exterior Arthur had things on his mind. Before he had turned in the previous night, there was one last thing he had wanted to say to the Gaits. *Of course, if the two of you were in my blood, I'd not be so worried.*

But he had only said it to himself. And he regretted that he had not been braver.

TWENTY-SIX

She was now two years into her placement with the farmer, and Lily continued to be plagued by his sons.

Ever alert to the need for his underlings to be working, even if he was not disposed to it himself, the farmer made it very clear that no one should be distracted from their labours. So the boys reserved their pursuits for times when he was away for a predictable period. On such days, Lily knew what to expect. Unable to lock her room or otherwise prevent entry, she would run out into the countryside, desperate for a place of safety. But they always found her. The boys considered it sport to give her a head start, knowing they were much faster and better climbers, to add to their advantage in strength and number. Once they caught her, it would be trial by earth or water or whatever they had planned for that day. Lily screamed incessantly, ignoring the fists that tried to quiet her – not because she expected any intervention, but because to remain silent might have indicated compliance. It was a scrap of pride she could cling to.

Afterwards, the sons took pains to minimise any evidence of their exploits. Things that had been knocked over in the chase were righted; stray shoes were reintroduced to cold and bloodied feet; telltale breakages were hidden from the farmer's gaze. Bruises on either party were not thought a giveaway, as they could be blamed on the farmer himself. Lily always tried to exact a measure of revenge, and she had extended her repertoire of undetected reprisals: items might go missing or maybe a frog might find its way into a bed; perhaps the farmer's beer might be depleted, with blame falling on his sons. It was a miserable existence for all.

A less obtuse man than the farmer would soon have noticed that something was amiss. He did not question why his sons' allotted tasks and Lily's chores were behind schedule only on days when he was engaged elsewhere, assuming it to be simple laziness. Punishment for this perceived laxity would depend on his mood. Increasingly confident, the boys would openly taunt Lily. This should have alerted anyone listening in, but the farmer seemed to regard it as natural behaviour for growing boys, perhaps recognising his younger self in his sons. Lily stopped taking her meals at the table, but the farmer was pleased not to have her there and did not question her. Lily knew he would never believe her if she tried to tell him; the boys would have to be caught in the act.

*

Some two miles from Lily's placement, a pleasant walk through the woods on a summer's day, there was a school, which Lily should have attended until she reached the age at which children were thought to be educated. Initially she had looked forward to this distraction: her time in the workhouse had given her some knowledge of the basics and a desire to become more conversant with them. The school also had the perceived advantage of being away from her tormentors. But it did not provide the respite from farm life that she expected. Indeed, in time she was relieved that the farmer rarely gave permission for her to attend – although, noting her reluctance, he had occasionally forced her to go out of spite. On her rare appearances, no one seemed to notice the bruising on her arms and legs, or if they did then they were not prepared to speak up or act upon it. It was not that sort of place.

Unlike the pampered city dwellers, the extent of a rural child's education was determined by their usefulness elsewhere, and so Lily's class was often sparsely attended. On a typical day there would be a sprinkling of girls and two boys considered too feeble to be anything other than a hindrance at home. From the start, Lily's proficiency in reading and writing stood out, proof that she had been institutionalised for an extended period and had not experienced the sporadic tuition that her classmates would have received at an equivalent age. This made her fair game. Certain ringleaders orchestrated the torment, and the sheep followed. There were pranks and tricks that were merely more childish versions of what she experienced on the farm, while the verbal abuse was as hurtful and inventive as only children can devise.

'Lily's got the pox,' chanted the feeble boys, parroting what their parents often said about the SAD children. 'Keep away from her or you'll catch it too.' And all the children would run away as if Lily was toxic.

Then the girls would chant 'Your mother was a whore', with most unsure what that might involve, but thinking it must be true because their fathers had said it.

Lily's appearance also placed a target on her back. She soon outgrew the clothes in which she had arrived, and the farmer spent the bare minimum on replacing them. 'Rags and tatters' they would call her, or just 'Rags', and Lily would tremble with embarrassment – and cold.

'Rags stole her coat from a beggar' was one child's offering. How the others laughed as Lily's face turned crimson with rage.

Another child gave Lily a potato sack as a pretend supplement to her wardrobe. Then, having first been singled out for being ahead of her peers, Lily's enforced truancy soon meant that she fell behind, leaving herself susceptible to a new stream of childish invective.

'Stupid, stupid, stupid' rejoiced the girls who had overtaken her. And the teacher added Lily to the group in the 'dullard corner'. Lily did not appear to react to any of these provocations, but neither did she forget. Her day would come.

She had been attending school randomly for around two years when the teacher approached her one morning. 'How old are you, Lily Mudd?'

'Don't know for sure, miss. Perhaps about thirteen years. Possibly.'

The teacher looked her up and down. 'I'd say you were too old for school. Look at the height of you.'

In charge of the cooking, Lily could surreptitiously feed herself enough to grow and now stood tall, albeit fragile and spindly. 'Have you learned enough once you reach a certain height, miss?' she asked innocently. 'And do you need to be a certain weight, because I might not be that?'

The teacher frowned. 'Enough of your cheek. We will make this your last day. You've hardly been here, anyway, so it will be no loss to you.'

'As you wish. Can't say I'll miss it.' And Lily decided to skip lessons and spend the day in preparation for her leaving.

After school broke up in the afternoon, she spotted the feeble boys approaching her. While they still had the opportunity, they were intent on placing a motley collection of insects down the back of Lily's dress, a manoeuvre they had executed many times before with little resistance. But instead of trying to escape, Lily stood her ground. 'Where are you going with them?' she growled.

The boys stopped in their tracks. This was not the usual script.

'Let me see 'em close up.'

One feeble boy slowly opened his hand to reveal a writhing mass of bugs and vermin. Lily looked at them for a second then grabbed the boy's hair, forcing his head downwards, while simultaneously seizing his wrist and yanking it upwards so that hand and mouth met halfway. The boy cried out, but that allowed Lily to force the critters inside, far more than he could easily spit out. The second feeble boy fled, dropping his cargo of insects, which Lily quickly bent down and retrieved.

'Swallow!' she ordered. 'Or there'll be more coming in.'

The first boy did as he was told.

Then it was the turn of the ringleaders. They had heard it was Lily's last day and were eager for their final sport, but she was ready for them. Lily made as if to run, and they were quick to follow, but she led them to a place where she had previously hidden a bucket of water. It was straight from the river and ferociously cold, even in the summer sunshine, and the first ringleader's screams made pleasurable listening when it cascaded over her. Next to the bucket Lily had positioned some rotting food that she had found close by – a witch's brew of foul-smelling scraps that even a starving rat would have thought twice about engaging with. Lily threw the contents over the head of the second ringleader and vigorously rubbed it in; the smell would cling on for several days. The third ringleader ran off before she could discover her fate, and a week had passed before she slunk back into class, just in case Lily had not finished with her. And all of this was accompanied by some choice words and phrases that comprised most of Lily's Canadian education to date.

Observing this, the sheep briefly changed their allegiance, baaing their encouragement as Lily took her revenge, before suddenly realising that their new princess would not be there tomorrow, but their old queens would be. They dispersed in confusion.

When she had finished, Lily washed her hands in a nearby stream and slowly walked back through the woods, her elation draining away the closer she got to the farm. It was back to the lion's den.

TWENTY-SEVEN

It was another two years before an opportunity arose for Lily to rid herself of the attentions of the farmer's sons. With the farmer increasingly disinterested in his work, his absences were few and far between, restricting the boys' activities, much to Lily's relief. But now it was summer again, and surely it was only a matter of time before they could resume their torment. And so it proved.

One day the farmer was expected to be absent for several hours, sourcing supplies from the store in Stirling, then viewing some sows that a neighbour was looking to sell. His sons had known about this for several days, and Lily had overheard them plotting, supposedly in secret, but they could not help but raise their voices in anticipation. The sons were sixteen years old now, Lily probably fifteen or thereabouts, and this time they had a new plan: the final part in their schooling in what they thought it meant to be a man.

As soon as the farmer hitched up his wagon and rattled away, Lily was off. Flying breathless through the woods, she ran parallel to the track the farmer travelled, but with enough trees in the way so that she was invisible to him. Meanwhile, the boys were in hot pursuit: there would be no head start today. The farmer's wagon was slow, and Lily had soon overtaken it, but as the sons closed in on her, she cut across the woods towards the track. The sons followed, whooping and hollering in their excitement, forgetting that their father was nearby, their voices drowning out the clatter of his wagon so that even a man lost in self-pity was bound to notice. And he did. Alerted by the commotion, and thinking that an animal might be in distress, the farmer applied his whip and the horse responded. Further on, Lily spilled out onto the track just as the boys caught up with her, first tackling her to the ground then pinning her to it, laughing and falling over each other in their eagerness. The farmer was still out of sight, due to a bend in the road, as his sons set to work. Lily howled as she had never done before, partly out of fear and revulsion, but also to distract them so they would not hear their father's imminent arrival.

'What is this?' And there he was.

His eyes wide with disbelief, the farmer surveyed the scene, taking in his sons' panic and humiliation: flesh exposed that a father should not see, not at their age; their scrabbling for lost garments, tumbling over each other as they fought for a shirt, a tug-of-war for a pair of breeches; their awareness that retribution was only seconds away; and their knowledge of what it would entail.

But the farmer's wrath fell first on Lily. She had expected this; there was a natural order to such things. He strode across the track, grabbed her by the arm and roughly pulled her to her feet. 'Get back to the farm and wait for me in your room!' he thundered, his face an inch from hers. But however brutish and malodourous his presence, it was still an improvement on what had preceded it. 'You little slut, I'll deal with you later!'

Lily ran back towards the farm, but she waited just around the bend, still within earshot. She could hear the familiar sound of fist on flesh as the farmer turned on his sons. The young men huddled together, fending off the attack with raised arms and desperate words.

'Pa, we're just messing around. Having a bit of fun.'

'First time we've done it, Pa. Honest!'

'Anyhow, she don't mind, Pa, you can see that.'

The farmer shook his head. 'She seemed to be minding just then. That much noise from a girl you wouldn't normally know was there.'

'We weren't too rough with her. Just having a laugh.'

'Little boys, pretending to be men,' the farmer sneered. 'There's two of you and she's still fighting back. I'll show you what being a man is.' After a few more swings, he needed to catch his breath. 'And what if she reports you? I wouldn't blame her. Have you thought of that? I don't care what folk think of you, but I'd be tarred with the same brush, and I ain't having that. And I can't afford to have you sent away, otherwise who'd do the work around here? I can't pay no one, as you well know.'

'Who's she going to tell? She never says nothing to no one.'

'And if she does, it will be our word against hers.'

'Leading us on, she was. It's her fault, not ours.'

The blows resumed. 'And the worst of it is that you should have been in the fields, earning your keep. Little wonder we're so behind with the harvest.'

'We're sorry, Pa.'

'Forgive us, Pa.'

There was a last flurry of blows, then silence. The farmer needed to think.

Lily heard every word from her hiding place, silently egging him on to beat some contrition out of his vile progeny. She ached for them to feel the pain and the indignity that had been inflicted on her. But then she heard: 'Look, I'll back you up if she says anything, and I'll put the fear of God into her to make sure she don't.'

'Thanks, Pa!'

'We'll work extra hard, Pa!'

'Too right you will. I'd happily see you sent down for what you've done, but I can't stomach the disgrace of others knowing it. You'll earn your luck, I promise you.'

There was to be no justice. Lily knew what she had to do. She ran back to the homestead, followed ten minutes later by the returning wagon. Then she heard the farmer stomping across the yard. But when he barrelled into her room, she was waiting for him.

TWENTY-EIGHT

The farmer kicked in the door to Lily's room. He did not need to; he could simply have raised the latch, as his sons had done all too frequently, but he wanted to make a point. Now he paced the floor, first one way then another, a spring coiled ever tighter and on the verge of release. His face was a collage of red and purple blotches, since his heart was as deficient in circulation as it was in human kindness. His breathing was laboured from effort and bile. When eventually he spoke, he wheezed through his few surviving teeth.

'Don't you go provoking my boys, taking advantage of their natural urges and inclinations,' he spat. 'If I didn't need you to work, you'd be gone today with a whip across your back.'

But for the first time Lily felt no fear. 'It weren't down to me, mister, and you know it weren't,' she sneered, moving towards the farmer. In his surprise, he took a step back, then another.

Lily laughed and followed his retreat. 'Them boys got more muscle than brains, and still it takes 'em both to quieten one girl, so they clearly ain't got much of either. Plain ugly inside and out, they are. Ugly and stupid. Why would I want anything to do with that? It's bad enough having to look at 'em.'

'You watch what you say, girl.'

'Trouble is, they think they can have whatever takes their fancy. They get that from their father, from what I've seen.'

'I've heard enough!' The farmer raised his hand, but instead of quaking subserviently as she might previously have done, Lily stood her ground and stared him squarely in the eye. Then he saw the iron cooking pot in her hand.

'You might beat me bad, mister, but in return you'll take some damage from a girl, and how will you explain that? Eh?' Lily took a swing at the farmer, but the pot weighed heavy in her hand and by the time it had completed its arc, he had scurried behind the bed, placing it between himself and his assailant.

'Perhaps I ain't as scared as you think, and if I ain't scared, then that filth you call sons might also see you ain't nothing to be frightened of.' Lily rounded the bed and took another swing, but she found the farmer to be more athletic than she had expected.

'And if people ain't scared of you, you'll have to earn your precious respect, not beat it out of them.' Lily swung again, but this time the farmer was too quick for her, grabbing the pot and wresting it from her grasp. He threw it to the floor with a flourish and raised his fist – his weapon of choice.

But Lily still had her trump card to play. 'And don't forget I remember every word you said that drunken night, even if you don't, and I tell you there's plenty you don't want other folk knowing."

The farmers hand dangled in mid-air.

'That poor wife of yours – locking her away and no doubt giving her a good beating. Strikes me the law might be interested in that, what with her ending up dead.' Lily paused for that to sink in. 'And you following her to the river. All it needed was a push…'

Lily was bluffing now but was encouraged by the panic on the farmer's face.

'I never said that!'

'You don't know what you said. Or what people will believe. And I'll wager they'll believe almost anything of you.'

Lily had no ammunition left, and now she waited for a reaction. The farmer stared at Lily, and she glared back at him. The farmer blinked first. 'You're talking nonsense. You don't know what happened. You're just making up words and pretending I said 'em. You'll soon learn to stop doing that, my girl.' The farmer was flailing around for meaningful threats, edging out of the room as he spoke. 'And don't go thinking you can make trouble for them boys. You'll have me to answer to if you try.'

He turned and stumbled down the stairs, crossing the kitchen at pace and throwing open the door.

'Then you'd best treat me good,' Lily shouted at his back, laughing almost hysterically in celebration and relief. She watched the farmer lumber across the yard at a fraction of the speed of his previous crossing, hands thrust in pockets, shoulders slumped, weighed down by the shame of being bested by a girl. And as she gazed at him, Lily felt something foreign to her, almost unrecognisable: pride in herself. He had tasted some of his own medicine, even if she had been unable to connect with the cooking pot. Fire had been met with fire. Not a 'behind your back' kind of revenge, but full-on resistance. She was shaking with the emotion of the encounter – triumph, yes, but apprehension too, a more familiar feeling. What had she just done? There could be no backing down; she would have to follow through with it, wherever that would take her.

Despite his embarrassment, the farmer was never a man to speak quietly when he could shout, and from a distance Lily overheard him bringing his boys into line.

'Now you stay well clear of the little trollop, or there'll be a reckoning to be had,' he warned, hiding his indignity beneath an extra-large dollop of bluster. 'I don't want you giving her nothing she can twist and turn against us. When it's quietened down, we'll send her back and get another.'

'What did you say to her, Pa?'

'Did you put the fear of God in her like you promised?'

'Go on, Pa, tell us.'

'Never mind what I said or did. You keep well away, and it'll all blow over.'

'But will she tell on us, Pa?'

'Did you shut her filthy mouth, Pa?'

'She ain't going to talk, and even if she does no magistrate will believe her – not a girl like that. But we don't want no trouble or getting into any sort of disrepute. A bad name always sticks, even if the law takes no action. So, be gentle with her for the time being, just in case. Better still, keep your distance.'

'Yes, Pa.'

'Whatever you say, Pa.'

Lily took note and resolved to make the most of her new situation.

From then on, each morning she was sure to make enough noise on rising to wake those who would rather have slept, and she feigned deafness to any request for quiet.

'Don't let it rattle you, boys,' the farmer would say before returning to his bed.

Undisturbed by any pretence of supervision, Lily now carried out her work to suit herself, and at an increasingly leisurely pace. If she did not fancy a job, it remained undone, and there was no one to insist on it.

'Careful, Pa, just let her be,' the boys would counsel if his temper flickered into life.

Lily no longer felt the need to sabotage meals in secret. Instead, her cooking became openly unappetising and insufficient to fuel a hard day's labour: perhaps a plate of gristle and bone or a slop of something whose provenance was unclear, but about which you would not wish to enquire. And when serving, Lily would slam plates down on the table so that their contents spilled onto its grubby surface. Rather than complain, the menfolk bit their lips and dutifully gave thanks.

'Boys, get yourselves some bread and cheese when she's gone,' their father would whisper.

Days passed, then weeks, and no one raised a hand against her, nor was she dealt any harsh words; very few words at all were said. The farmer took his drinking chair into the barn so that she rarely saw him, and he looked away when she did. The boys would hurriedly leave the room whenever she entered, and she took pleasure in moving them around the homestead, never letting them settle.

Then one day, Lily was ladling hot broth onto plates at the table and by a genuine accident contrived to pour some molten broth into the lap of one of the boys.

'Clumsy little whore,' screamed the victim, leaping to his feet and rubbing the affected area in a most unseemly manner.

'She did that on purpose, I reckon,' his twin weighed in.

'Steady on, boys.'

It was the first real test of their changed circumstances as the twins squared up to Lily, with the farmer in the unnatural role of peacekeeper. With no hint of an apology, Lily glowered at the boys, daring them to step over the boundary, although the injured party might have struggled to step over anything for the time being.

'We're sick of this, Pa. It ain't fair.'

'She just does as she pleases.'

'Can we teach her a lesson, Pa?'

'No, and that's an end to it.' Their father was firm.

'But Pa…'

'It was an accident.'

And the boys knew what the outcome would be if they persisted.

'A tough man like you shouldn't be fretting over a bit of heat,' Lily jeered in the victim's direction. 'Anyhow, you've got no use for that thing these days.'

Later, as she lay in bed, Lily looked back on the exchange with satisfaction. But she knew her immunity could not last indefinitely. She had to make the most of it. So, she wrote a letter to Alice Hamilton and addressed it to the Kingston centre, where Lily felt Alice was sure to be – if not now, then soon. She described her ordeal in large writing and small detail, using up most of her paper. She felt immeasurably better when she had finished. The next day, she slipped away from the farm and made her way to the settlement of Stirling, leaving the letter with the local postmaster, and paying for the postage with some money she had found in a drawer. Her errand complete, she returned to the farm and waited, confident that salvation was at hand.

TWENTY-NINE

The investigation into the alleged assault on Mary Oliver trundled on for many months, the wheels of justice grinding almost imperceptibly and without any enthusiasm. The various parties were interviewed, and notes were taken, but nothing seemed to happen as a result of it.

Mary became increasingly impatient. 'It's because she's one of their own kind,' she complained. 'If I was the accused, they would have jailed me by now.'

Alice Hamilton found it hard to disagree.

But the Hoggards were taking the proceedings very seriously indeed. Dr Hoggard even offered to mind the children while his wife attended the police station, although she returned home to find that they had been locked in a room for the duration of her absence, and it was her job to clear up the mess. Given the family's prominence, the case aroused considerable local interest, and the good doctor spent this currency wisely, using his surgeries and consultations to drum up support for his beleaguered wife and to spread malicious lies about Mary. And because of their provenance, these fabrications were readily believed, and the doctor did not discourage those who took matters into their own hands.

The intimidation began not long after the case was opened. First it took the form of raised voices, threatening and vile words, and not just from a distance but sometimes face to face. Scribbled threats, mostly anonymous, were pushed under the door of the distribution centre in the dead of night, while one was tied to a stone and delivered through Mrs Dando's kitchen window. Those who employed an immigrant child and found them to be satisfactory, perhaps even worthy of affection and praise, kept a very low profile.

One afternoon, Mary followed Alice's advice to get some fresh air and was walking the local streets. Suddenly, she became aware that a man was following her. She increased her pace, but he matched her stride and more, gaining ground on her and shouting obscenities at her when he was within range. She ran, but he ran too. She cried for help, but there was no one to intervene. In desperation, Mary stopped to confront the man. It's what he'll least expect, she thought, and that might throw him. What have I got to lose?

The man drew level but continued on his way without stopping. 'See how easy it is,' he sneered as he passed. 'Let that be a warning to you.'

After this, Mary refused to step outside or even to sit by a window, if it could be seen from the street. And as her courage seeped away, she watched Alice Hamilton become increasingly combative and wondered why that should be so.

'Perhaps we should just forget this and let the Hoggards be,' Mary would say. 'I clearly cannot win, and I might lose a great deal more than I have already.'

'We must keep going,' Alice would reply. 'This is a matter of principle.'

It wasn't that way when first I tried to persuade you, Mary recalled, but said nothing.

And on receipt of a particularly offensive note, Alice would trumpet 'I will not be beaten!'

It won't be you that's beaten. I'm the one they'll go for,

Mary thought ruefully. Carrying on must be what suits her best. I doubt it's me she's thinking of.

Eventually the authorities decided that charges should be brought, if only to provide a mechanism for proving that Dorothy Hoggard was innocent. The case was brought before the Kingston magistrate, a man of notoriously harsh judgement, whose knowledge of the law was second only to his propensity to depart from it when it suited him.

'He has a particular aversion to immigrant children,' the prosecuting lawyer informed Alice, and she thought it best not to pass on this information to Mary.

There was a frisson of excitement in the courthouse as proceedings commenced, and its benches were full. Mary fidgeted in the accuser's chair, the eyes of the room burning into her flesh. By design, the whispered conversations were loud enough for her to hear, each barb stinging as it landed.

'You can tell she's a troublemaker, just look at her.'

'Who does she think she is, filthy little madam?'

'She deserved whatever she got, and more besides.'

Mary looked anxiously around the courtroom. She had never felt more alone. She stared at Dorothy Hoggard, sitting in the space reserved for the defendant, contempt chiselled into her features. Mary quickly averted her gaze. Dr Hoggard was just a few seats away, offering words of encouragement to his wife and graciously acknowledging supporters in the crowd. Occasionally he pointed in Mary's direction, and seconds later those around him would laugh more raucously than his wit deserved.

'I'm scared, miss, I don't feel safe here,' Mary whispered. 'All I can see is people who hate me. And there's no sign of Mrs Dando.'

Alice took Mary's hand in hers. It was some comfort to both of them that they were equally clammy.

Alice was first to take the witness stand. She described Mary's wounds in detail; given the delay in bringing the matter to court, they had mostly healed.

'And did a doctor confirm them at the time?' the prosecuting lawyer asked.

'We could hardly ask the accused's husband,' Alice replied, to much merriment on the benches. 'And there was some reluctance on the part of other local practitioners to see Mary, but a physician from Belleville was persuaded to conduct an inspection.'

'The court should note the medical support for Miss Hamilton's assessment of the girl's injuries,' proffered the prosecuting lawyer,

'The court will note whatever it chooses,' thundered the magistrate.

On seeing his face, puce with anger and disgust, Mary's heart sank yet further.

The defence lawyer rose to cross-examine Alice, and there was a burble of excitement. The entertainment was about to begin.

'Miss Hamilton, in taking this child under your wing, and subsequently inflicting her upon our innocent land, I assume you were aware of her beginnings...'

'Of course. I—'

'The undesirables from whom she was spawned, whose moral turpitude she will one day inherit...'

'I beg your—'

'The constant exposure to sin and corruption in her formative years that is already manifest in her carelessness and ingratitude, and in her absence of remorse.' The lawyer paused, and there was a flutter of appreciation from the benches.

'Miss Hamilton, how do you answer this?'

'I'm sorry, but I did not hear a recognisable question.'

'I clearly heard him ask you to comment on the girl's parentage,' growled the magistrate.

Alice cast him a withering look. 'Like all our girls, Mary Oliver has endured a troubled life, although her mother was respectable and her father a hard-working man, by all accounts. But I cannot see the relevance of her history, whatever it may be. This trial concerns the great wrong that has been done to the child here in Canada, in this very town, and that is all that matters.'

There was a bellow of rage from the magistrate. 'I will decide on what is and what is not relevant to this trial! Sir, you may proceed as you see fit.'

Happy to oblige, the defence lawyer continued in similar vein, disparaging child immigrants and their origins with impressive, almost poetic, savagery, undermining their character and truthfulness, and making the case for their automatic guilt in any situation.

He speaks as if *I'm* on trial, Mary thought. Then she looked around at the courtroom faces and she could see that she was.

Next Mrs Dando was due to give evidence, but she did not answer the call. After a third stone had found a window, she tired of clearing up broken glass and resolved to heed the messages that were attached to the missiles.

'It is no loss to these proceedings,' the defence lawyer claimed. 'She is an embittered woman who sought only to revenge herself on the good doctor through a cowardly attack upon his sainted wife.'

'Noted,' snarled the magistrate, signalling for the prosecuting lawyer to sit down.

Mary took the stand and looked out upon a sea of hostile faces. 'It's me that's in the right,' she told herself. 'Just keep calm and say your piece.' But her body ignored what her mind was telling her, and she shook and trembled as if afflicted by a palsy.

In her evidence, Mary soon arrived at the crux of the matter. 'I always had the children to look after and entertain, which kept me away from my other work, and that would bode ill for me. The mistress would shout and scream whenever anything wasn't perfect, which was all the time, and then she would take to her bed, but not before hitting me. I would sometimes ask her for help, but she just shooed me away, and the doctor was locked away in his study when not working himself.'

The magistrate muttered ominously under his breath and scribbled furiously.

Oh, what have I said? Mary thought. Then she told her story about the child and the cat, and how the cat's exit from the carriage was injury-free but the child's less so. Finally, and tearfully, she described the ferocious beating she subsequently received.

The defence lawyer was soon cross-examining her. 'You say that having to watch over the children, a perfectly reasonable instruction to my mind, kept you from your other tasks.'

'Often, yes. Most days, to be frank.'

The defence lawyer smiled unnervingly. 'And you were chastised for your failure to complete these other tasks.'

'As I said, but never as much as I was on this occasion.'

The defence lawyer turned to the courtroom, triumph etched on his face. 'So, you would clearly have borne some malice towards the children?'

Mary could see she had fallen into a trap, but what else could she have said? 'No, sir, I—'

'And why should the lady of the house take on work that she is paying you to perform?' The defence lawyer was unrelenting.

'Sir, I was just—'

'And is it a crime for a man to spend time in his study?'

'Depends on what he's doing, I suppose, sir.'

The courtroom erupted in laughter.

'Silence!' bellowed the magistrate, adding a further scribbled note.

The defence lawyer moved in for the kill. 'And as for your insinuations about the good lady's state of mind…'

At this point, the magistrate suddenly rose from his seat. 'Enough! It seems to me that this whole case has been dreamed up, a malicious invention on the part of this girl, aided and abetted by sundry others. Indeed, I struggle to understand how this has even come before me, so obvious is the conspiracy of falsehood and deceit against the accused.'

There was uproar in the court, and it was some time before order was restored. Mary heard the clerk whisper in the magistrate's ear that his verdict might be a little premature, as there was further evidence to be presented, and the magistrate grudgingly sat down again. The prosecuting lawyer complained loudly that it was pointless to continue and withdrew in high dudgeon; it took Alice at her most persuasive to coax him back.

Throughout, Mary stood shaking in the witness stand, muttering to herself, 'This can't be right, this can't be right.'

When the rumpus had subsided, the magistrate glared at Mary. 'Return to your seat, girl, you have said quite enough. Let us hear from Mrs Hoggard and finally bring an end to this nonsense.'

Dorothy Hoggard was soon holding forth. 'I was not in favour of hiring an immigrant girl, having some inkling of what they might be like.' She sniffed. 'I would have preferred a servant from better stock, but my husband said immigrant girls were cheap, and now I can see why. Indeed, had I known the true nature of this young madam, she would not have set foot in my house, and would certainly not have been entrusted with my children.'

'And what is your recollection of the day in question?'

'I was in my bed, sick with a fever, barely able to raise a glass to my lips, when my daughter was brought to me. I asked how she fell, and my beloved child said the servant girl had pushed her off the carriage—'

'That's a lie!' Mary could not help herself.

'Quiet!'

'I feared this madam had killed her or at least hurt her very badly. But I did not flog the girl, as claimed. Instead I took a strap and gave it to her over the hands, as was my practice. I positively say I did not touch her face. Indeed, I did not chastise her as severely as I would my own child under the same circumstances. With my sickness, I had not the strength to do so, even if I had wanted.'

'So, how did the girl come by these injuries?'

'If she truly had injuries beyond those I have admitted to, and there is little trace of them now, she could have found some way to inflict them on herself. Simply to cause trouble.'

With all the evidence heard, the prosecuting lawyer went through the motions of addressing the court. 'The defence has brought no evidence to tarnish the reputation of Miss Hamilton, who has provided a compelling account of the injuries suffered, supported by the testimony of a respected doctor. Accusations and innuendo concerning the character of the girl are wholly unsubstantiated. In short, there is no reason to believe that these witnesses are fabricating or embellishing their evidence.'

Mary could see that the magistrate was not listening.

'Mrs Hoggard has admitted that she beat the girl on this occasion, as she often did, and no evidence has been produced as to how her injuries might otherwise have been inflicted. As the law stands, a parent can only chastise a child in a reasonable and moderate manner, and an employer is even more restricted. The assault on this girl is clearly neither reasonable nor moderate.'

The defending lawyer took a different view. 'The charge hangs on the slender thread of the girl's evidence. It is one word against another. On the one hand, a bastion of the community, here accused of an act of brutality that is wholly at odds with her husband's calling and her own sweet nature. On the other, the alleged victim, a girl dredged from the river of filth that flows through London, an example of what the British themselves call "gutter children", generously employed and boarded under the roof of a munificent family but betraying their benevolence through brazenly endangering a young child. Who should we believe?'

Believe me, Mary screamed silently. *Please believe me.*

'And the injuries themselves, corroborated by a quack from Belleville, and witnessed only by a vengeful harridan who cannot even be bothered to testify, and a woman whose standing cannot be seen as independent. Were the injuries real? Exaggerated, I'll wager, if they existed at all.'

Mary saw the magistrate nod his approval.

'But even if Mrs Hoggard had inflicted all the injuries that are claimed, which she is clear she did not, the chastisement would have been wholly warranted, given the serious nature of the offence perpetrated against her precious child, and it would have been no more than a loving and responsible parent would administer for a lesser transgression.'

The magistrate delivered his verdict almost instantaneously. 'My fellow magistrates and I see far too many instances of immigrant children biting the public-spirited hands that have reached out to feed them. You cannot believe what these children say, and nor can you trust those that are supposedly in charge of them, given their vested interest. There is always some motive behind their deception, even if it is not always obvious what that might be. This case is typical, and I have no hesitation in dismissing it. Mrs Hoggard, you may return home with no blemish upon your character. Mary Oliver, you need to reflect on what you have said and done.'

Given the magistrate's earlier outburst, there was no drama in the announcement. The courtroom emptied quickly, amid a buzz of gossip and congratulation. Even Mary was numb, almost as if events were happening to someone else. Dorothy Hoggard had some final words for her as she passed, but Mary rose to her feet in challenge and her abuser moved on more quickly than she had intended. Mary turned round to see Alice deep in thought.

She'll only be concerned with her business and how this might harm it, Mary brooded, and her mood darkened still further.

It was a dispiriting journey back to the distribution centre.

'How can they say those things about me?' Mary kept asking. 'How can the law mean so little?'

Alice did not have an answer for her. 'We must decide what to do with you,' she said cryptically.

'All I want is to be with my brother.'

'Sadly, that is not possible.'

'Then I don't care what happens to me.'

Some weeks later, Percy Oliver sat in the kitchen of his placement, resting his weary body after another strenuous day in the fields. The farmer was reading an out-of-date copy of the *Toronto Herald* and commenting on items that took his interest.

'This one sounds like a right so-and-so,' he muttered. 'Immigrant girl – nearly killed a child in her care and then had the nerve to complain about her treatment.'

The farmer's wife kicked her husband under the table.

'Course, as you know we're not against immigrant children. Not like some,' she cut in, with Percy in mind.

The farmer was about to expand on the girl's story, but he noticed her name and quickly changed the subject.

And as Percy was not one for reading newspapers, he was none the wiser about the identity of the girl. Nor was he overly curious about why Mary had not written for so long: it meant he did not feel obliged to write back. And it never occurred to him to put two and two together.

THIRTY

It was Sam Barney's fourth summer with the Wrights, but he was just as much an outsider as when he'd first set foot on the premises. He still lived a parallel existence, occupying the same physical space as the incumbents but otherwise trapped in an alternative dimension. It was an arrangement of convenience. From the Wrights' perspective, someone had to be there, and it just happened to be Sam, while he dared not leave them in case things were even worse elsewhere. He had heard tales of other immigrant children that implied that he might not be too badly off.

I'm sure I once knew a Mary Oliver, he thought as he listened to Patience Wright read out the *Toronto Herald*'s report of the court case. I'd better just do my work and stay out of trouble, or that could be me, he decided.

That summer, excitement was in the air – or as close to that mood as the Wrights would ever venture. The eldest daughter, Prudence, now sixteen years of age, suddenly found herself betrothed to the son of a fellow churchgoer that Ezra Wright had been stalking for some time. The marriage, and its consummation, would have to wait a year or two, but at least the foundation had been laid. Prudence was as surprised as anyone by the news.

'He's certainly no oil painting,' Ezra Wright mused. 'And from what I've seen, there might be a shortage of stimulating conversation. But I suppose she's always got her sewing.'

'A woman does not enter into marriage to be entertained,' his wife scolded. 'Nor to have something pleasing to look at. The Good Lord created nature for that purpose. Matrimony is a sacred duty, not some kind of distraction or amusement. And as for passion, that is the work of Satan himself.'

In that respect, Patience Wright could never be accused of consorting with the devil.

A gathering was arranged to celebrate the betrothal; to call it a party would have exaggerated its bonhomie. Prominent local churchgoers were invited, alongside more secular others with whom the Wrights felt obliged to maintain good business relations. In preparing a suitable arena for discourse and ceremony, if not outright jollity, Sam had emptied the various outbuildings of their usual inhabitants, bribing the chickens to relocate with a generous trail of feed, and removing as much evidence of their occupation as he could. A pig had been selected to play a more central role in proceedings than it would have wished for, and Patience Wright had spent the intervening days preparing it for its big moment. The yard was tidied and its clutter discreetly camouflaged, creating a further setting to which revellers could spill over or escape.

The day was sufficiently auspicious for the Wrights' son, John, to grace it with his presence, travelling by train and wagon from his Toronto home where, by his own admission, he was making exemplary progress in a business that sold insurance. He did not possess an agricultural physique, being insubstantial in height and build, and this had likely contributed towards his migration. But he had inherited his mother's pinched face, and he used it to good effect when displeased, which was much of the time – another trait acquired from her extensive repertoire.

On his rare visits, he contrived to ensure that Sam was always in hearing when he shared the latest bile being directed towards immigrant children by the *Toronto Herald*. And as he revelled in the shock and laughter that his interventions generated, John Wright would stare accusingly in Sam's direction, daring him to respond.

On this day, the prodigal son was holding forth about the *Herald*'s latest revelations.

'Apparently, these miscreants inherit all manner of disease from those that sire them – usually out of wedlock, of course.' He moved even closer to Sam so that he could not fail to hear. *'They may appear to be harmless in their infancy or even into early adulthood,'* he read. *'But these children are a serious threat to the health of the nation.'*

John Wright put down his newspaper for a moment. 'Hey, boy, what do you say to that?'

Sam ignored the bait.

'I hear they're all riddled with syphilis,' Ezra Wright intervened enthusiastically.

'Mr Wright, it's not Christian to mention such things.'

'With respect, Mrs Wright, not saying the word don't make it go away.'

'Pa is right.' John Wright stirred the pot. 'It says here, and I quote, that *immigrant children invariably originate from the unbridled promiscuity of the lower classes, men and women who have little else in life to divert or entertain them, and no moral compass to direct their actions. Inevitably their offspring will inherit a syphilitic taint from these wastrels, which later manifests itself once they reach a certain age.* Written by a doctor, no less.'

'I stand corrected,' Patience Wright conceded, a rare event.

'So you keep a close eye on that lad over there.'

And they all glared at Sam, who suddenly found an excuse to be elsewhere.

Later he received his orders for the day.

'You're to see to the horses as folk arrive and hitch them up again when they leave. You can help yourself to food and drink when others have had their fill but otherwise don't trouble our guests.'

Sam trudged off, feeling even more sorry for himself than usual.

Carriages began to arrive around noon, and the mumblings of awkward conversation gradually increased in volume as the afternoon progressed. Huddles of men put the world to rights or bemoaned the price of everything: always too high for things they bought and too low for things they sold. Meanwhile, a cluster of women discussed matters of a more personal nature, primarily concerning those who were not present to defend themselves. Children were both seen and heard. There was beer and cider, but not in sufficient quantities to loosen tongues or incite any indiscretion; Patience Wright had strong views on the consumption of alcohol.

'It is the devil's brew, the root cause of profanity, the enabler of lechery, the harbinger of depravity and lust, the source of all evil,' she informed her guests. 'Now tell me, would anyone like another drink?'

Prayers were said and hymns were sung. There were speeches from the two fathers and a contribution from the groom-to-be. The womenfolk looked on with fixed smiles, loyally hiding any embarrassment at content or delivery. A toast was proposed and executed, and everyone agreed that it was a very fine match.

Sam was hiding away some distance from the frolics when Charity Wright found him. He was staring intently into the forest, and he took some time to realise that she was there. Now fifteen years old, he had grown tall, and the relentless toil had made him physically strong, although he was increasingly brittle inside, his morale chipped away by his master's indifference and the sharpness of his mistress's tongue. He would have been considered a handsome young man by anyone motivated to hold an opinion, but to his knowledge there had yet to be anyone so inclined, and that was part of the problem.

Thus far Sam had traded no more than half a dozen sentences with Charity, and even they had been the blandest of exchanges, hardly worthy of being called a conversation. He had seen her smile on many occasions, but never at or because of him. Not once had he felt able to make her laugh or blush, as boys of his age would seek to do with just the slightest prompting, and which girls of her age would pretend not to welcome but secretly enjoy.

Today, it might have been her sister's betrothal that had awakened her interest, or the fact that her watchful parents were distracted by their hosting duties. It was certainly not the beer or cider, as that was strictly out of bounds for both. But here they were, talking quite normally and regretting that they had not done it sooner.

'Ma always says not to speak to you.'

'You'd best be off, then. You don't want to get on the wrong side of her.'

'I thought it was about time. It's not right that you're always on your own. I wouldn't want it.'

Charity sat beside Sam, seemingly half his size, but exuding a confidence that more than compensated for it. Her cinnamon brown hair was usually tied back when she was out and about, but today it was hanging loose in celebratory ringlets. Her matching eyes peered out at the world with fierce intensity and just a hint of rebellion, her fingers forever moving unruly strands of hair that blocked her view. She was wearing her only party dress, cut out and sewn under the guidance of her mother, and hence not entirely as she would have wanted it.

'They don't give me nothing decent to wear,' Sam grumbled. 'I know it would be a waste, as I'm not asked anywhere or invited to anything, but it would be good to know I could dress up if I needed it.'

'Believe me, you're missing out on nothing, including today. That's why I'm here.'

'Not the thought of my company, then?'

Sam could see that Charity immediately regretted her words. He smiled to confirm that he had not taken offence. 'Don't worry, I know what you mean. But I'd like to be thought of as someone who might be invited to something. To have people who might want me there, wherever it was. To have the choice whether to say yes or no.'

They sat in silence for a moment, each searching for a conversational route down which they could safely travel.

'I heard how my brother was speaking earlier,' Charity started uncertainly. 'He's just trying to cause trouble, always has done, but Ma and Pa hang on every word he says. It can't be easy listening to all his nonsense and have them agree with it.'

'One day you might find your brother with a pitchfork up his backside and then let's see how he sits down in his fancy office.'

Charity gasped in mock indignation before her luminous smile took over. 'It's embarrassing for me and Pru when they go on so. I hear them pray to have the money for a "good Canadian man" as they call it, but God doesn't seem to be listening, so here you are still.'

'That's the rub, ain't it? They don't want me here, but they can't afford better. Or what they see as better. And it would be the same most other places, as far as I can see. Your folks are no different.' Sam hesitated. It was a risk giving too much away to a girl he hardly knew, but something told him to plough on. He might not get a better chance. 'You might laugh at this, but the hardest thing is hearing you all sing. Together as a family, like it should be. That's when I feel the most unwelcome.'

'I could sing for you.'

'One day, maybe. When no one else is about. And perhaps I could join in?'

Charity laughed. 'You'll have to learn some better tunes. Ma told us about your last offerings.'

'Or I could teach you "The Clergyman's Daughter" It's a fine story, if a little rustic in places.'

The breeze carried some music over from the barn, and occasional yelps and squawks of enjoyment could be heard, suggesting that there might be dancing.

'Pru isn't happy about the betrothal,' Charity confided. 'She's still just a girl, really, even though she plays at being grown-up. And she hardly knows him. We see him at church, and he seems nice enough, but not the sort to spend the rest of your life with.'

'That'll be you soon.'

'Better not be.'

'Another two years, you wait and see.'

Sam could see the horror on Charity's face. She knew it was probably true.

'And I wager they'll find someone singular for you. It'll likely be a bald-headed, squinty-eyed preacher with the breath of a dog and the brains of a sheep – or, even worse, a Frenchman.' It was the first time Sam had teased a girl.

As they laughed, Charity was startled by the sudden presence of her sister Hope, who had mastered the art of moving about very quietly and appearing at inconvenient times. 'Ma says we need to help clear up, and I ain't doing it all,' she announced, speaking to Charity but looking archly at Sam while she said them.

Charity skittered to her feet. 'How long you been there?'

'Just now.' The reply was pitched to create the maximum uncertainty.

Chivvying Hope along in front of her, Charity hastened back to the yard, but she turned discreetly to Sam as she passed. 'It's good to finally meet you,' she whispered.

'Likewise.'

THIRTY-ONE

Arthur Dilkes had never been much interested in writing for the sake of it, nor had he possessed the skills to do so until very recently, but here he was drafting a letter to Alice Hamilton. It was not a reply to anything previous, nor was Arthur requesting a favour or asking permission for something, but he felt an obligation to write it. Before each SAD child was placed, Alice Hamilton made it clear that she expected to hear their news from time to time, particularly if it was good, and a wad of writing paper was stuffed into each child's trunk, so they had no excuse. Such letters, appropriately edited, would help prove to patrons that their money had been well spent. By the spring of 1885 Arthur felt he could put it off no longer and devoted a winter's day to his duty, gratefully putting down his pen just as the light faded. Robert and Amelia Gait, hardly paragons of literacy themselves, made some corrections in grammar and punctuation before it was sent, but the content spoke for itself.

Dear Miss Hamilton
I thought I would write, as you might be interested in how my time here has gone so far. You always said we

should try if we could, so here I go. It might even be worth printing this in one of your journals, if you think the letter makes some sort of sense.

Alice smiled to herself. A child's redemption story often loosened the purse strings of a reader.

It's four years now since I made the acquaintance of this place. Seems so long ago I can hardly remember what went before. I knew less than nothing to start with, but I've learned a bit since then. Mister and Missus are good people who have helped me a lot. Mister trusts me to do things and do them well, and I try my best to oblige. I wasn't here long before he sent me off into town on my own, in charge of a wagon, no less. That was a big adventure, and I was pleased when I got safely there and back again. That set me up for doing other things, and now I can take on most that's needed. In the fields, I do all the easier stuff with the walking plough and it's more or less straight when I've finished. And I had a go on the riding plough and Mister weren't too unhappy with how it turned out. Or if he was, he didn't say and that's not like him.

In the last two years we have cleared more land, and I have had the axe in my hand more often than not, either that or digging out the stumps of the trees that I felled. That is hard slog, I can tell you, just to get the land fit to take a plough over. Then there's the animals always needing something, like mucking out the pigs or feeding the chickens and collecting the eggs they kindly give us. Then there's the horses, we must look after them proper or we can't do half the jobs we need to.

I helped Mister and Missus build their new homestead too, and very grand it is. I made sure I got a good room out of it. I showed myself I can handle a hammer and saw, and to my surprise, I've got a bit of patience to get things just right. I might build something for myself one day, you never know.

I have a few more years here, if they can put up with me, which they say they will. Then maybe I can get some land of my own if the government is still offering it – take advantage of what I've learned and reap the benefits myself. That's what Mister has taught me. Working the land is difficult and every bit of me aches a lot of the time, but it's a much better life than where I came from.

I hope other boys and girls have been as lucky as I have.

Alice read the letter through twice, such was her satisfaction with it, before placing it in a pile of similar others.

That will do very nicely, she thought.

THIRTY-TWO

'I think it might be my birthday,' Sam Barney said when he and Charity were talking one day. 'I once saw a bit of paper, and I think it had this date on it. But I guess days and years might be different in England, so maybe not.'

'Let's say it is.'

Charity slipped into the kitchen and found some fruitcake that might not be missed, and they made off to the woods where they could eat in secret. By now, their skulking around had become a regular feature. They took any chance they could to talk, ever watchful, always keeping to the shadows and out of sight. On this day, Ezra and Patience Wright were in town haranguing storekeepers, while the sisters were engaged with school or chores. All was quiet and peaceful.

'I should be harrowing the big field, but it can wait.'

'I should be sweeping the floors, but they'll only get filthy again.'

And so they celebrated Sam's new landmark, and soon there were telltale crumbs littering the ground where they sat. Amid the teasing and the small talk, they spoke of family and loss and what the future might hold.

'I remember one birthday of mine,' Sam said. 'I'd not really had one before, we hadn't the money for it, but this was different. Ma had not long died, and I think Pa wanted to make it a bit special for me – I guess because I was missing her so bad. Anyhow, we were out and about, can't remember where or why, and we walked past this stall with all manner of cakes for sale. Suddenly, Pa stopped and asked me to choose one. Well, I was so surprised it took me an age to pick the best, but finally I did, and he bought it, and one for himself. I didn't ask how he paid for them. It was nothing particular, just a fancy of a thing, but it tasted like what the Queen might have for her tea. And we sat by the river eating our cakes, watching the great ships sail up and down, and making up stories about where they'd come from or were going to'. A rare serenity had settled over Sam's face. 'Course, it weren't many birthdays before Pa had gone too, but at least I have the memory of one happy day.'

'And what do you think of this birthday?'

'I've had cake and company, and that's good enough for me.'

Charity seemed less content with her ma and pa. At times there was genuine anger in her voice. 'They just want to marry me off and that will be the end of my life,' she protested. 'I watch them talking to people and I can see the cogs in their brains turning. "Are they suitable?" they're thinking, whatever that means, and "What are their prospects?" They're speaking to the father but never take their eyes off the son. I wouldn't mind so much if they were good-looking, but they're always rancid.'

'So, you'd be happier if they looked like me?'

'You have a high opinion of yourself, Sam Barney!' She punched him playfully.

'If your ma found she had me as son-in-law, I think she might explode.'

And they could easily agree on that.

'Look, your ma and pa are difficult people. Heaven knows

I've felt the force of that. But it's better for you that they're still here than not.'

'I suppose so.'

A sudden chill descended, and Sam's contentment melted away. 'It only takes a few words, and they don't have to be unkindly meant. They just remind me of what others have and I've lost.' He fiddled with the cloth that had wrapped the cake, folding it one way and then another, struggling to find the words to express what he was thinking. 'I have this regular thought that helps me, or daydream if you wish. In my head I see myself returning to the yard after my work and there's my folks, waiting for me, just as I remember them. And it's the most wonderful feeling you can imagine. There's hugs and tears and promises that we'll always be together from that moment on.' A tear trickled down his cheek, and he angrily swiped it away. 'Of course, the disappointment digs deep when I get back and they're not there. My heart sinks and I'm not the same for the rest of the day. But it's still better than thinking it can never happen. There's always tomorrow.'

Charity took Sam's hand, and for a spell they were lost in their respective worlds. And then they heard Charity's sisters nearby, and it was time to return to reality.

While Sam was sometimes keen to share his innermost thoughts, often he was a closed book. The trick was to wait for him to make the first move. One day, they sat on the lower boughs of a tree, hidden to all but the most observant and with a view that would likely give them some warning of discovery. Sam was unusually subdued and monosyllabic, and Charity bided her time, restricting herself to banalities until he was ready.

'I dreamed of my ma last night.'

Charity was unsure whether this was a good or a bad thing, so said nothing.

'Dreams are evil things. It could have let me visit some of the good times we had, and there were plenty of them, but no. It was the day she died. It always is when I dream of her. And it's as real as being there.'

Charity could see that Sam was close to tears and was embarrassed because of it.

'You've never spoken of your ma.'

'You can see what it does to me.'

'I'd like to hear. If you can bear it.'

Sam had waited ten years or more to tell the story but had never known anyone who might listen; Arthur had not been one for dwelling on the past. But now, at last, he had a willing audience; he just needed to find the words.

'She was a quiet, gentle soul,' he began uncertainly. 'Not one to talk much, even when surrounded by her own, happy just to care for those she loved. I would spend my time watching her go about her business, cleaning or cooking or whatever, neither of us saying much. We didn't need to.' Sam smiled at the memory. 'I might have been five years or so, and I had never known her be anything but sick. Or if the scourge gave her a moment's peace it would always come back stronger. In those last weeks, she couldn't move from her bed. Her lovely face was disfigured with pain until I could barely recognise her, and her clothes dripped with night sweats as if she had just come in from heavy rain.'

At first the words landed carefully, as if crossing unfamiliar terrain, then they became more surefooted and in time they careered forward, with barely a gap between one leaving his mouth and the next arriving.

'She knew her time had come and didn't want me to see the horror of it. So Pa arranged for neighbours to take me foraging for coal.'

Charity looked blankly at him.

'You never foraged for coal? Collecting lumps of it that have fallen from a cart as it went over bumps in the roads? All right, sometimes we encouraged it to fall.'

'You forget how different we are.'

Sam laughed. 'Just as well. I can't see you grubbing around in the dirt. Anyhow, usually I was well keen on it, but here it was just a trick to get me gone. So, I clung to Ma's blankets with all my might and grabbed her arms and legs and wouldn't let go. I thought, if I hold on tight, perhaps I can keep her in this world just a little longer.'

Charity's ears pricked up. She thought she had heard a noise. Perhaps it was innocent, maybe not. She shot off nervous glances in every direction, hoping Sam wouldn't notice that her attention was suddenly less than total. She could not ask him to stop.

'My poor frail mother – my hand could pass around her limbs and touch on the other side, and me just a little 'un. My grabbing must have hurt her bad, being as she was, but I was desperate, and I don't think she wanted me to let go. Not in her heart, I could tell. But Pa used all his muscle to drag me from the bed, and I lost my grip. I have never cried so much, and I doubt I ever will again.'

It was definite now. Charity could hear voices – Faith and Hope, distant still but getting closer.

Sam remained oblivious. 'Then Pa led me away and before I knew it, I was out foraging and you can't cry in front of strangers, so I had to be quiet. But there was such an ache in the pit of my stomach that I could hardly stoop to pick up anything. And the guilt I felt when my attention was briefly drawn to the job in hand, rather than thinking of her. I can't tell you how long we were out, but it must have been quite a time. And when I got home, she was gone.'

The sisters were very close now. Discovery was imminent.

Charity could almost hear her mother's screech and feel the thwack of her father's belt.

'And that was it – my dream. It lasted the whole night, it seemed. There I was, crawling and scrambling towards her with all my strength, but each time I looked up I was further away than before. Watching her slowly disappear into the darkness until there was no one there. And the next time it will be just the same. It's always the same, because that's how it was.'

Charity could no longer pretend she was listening. She leapt down from the tree and beckoned for Sam to do the same. They ran through the woods and made their way back to the homestead by a circuitous route, eventually entering from opposite sides of the yard.

As they parted, Sam grabbed Charity's arm. 'You've seen me as no one else has. I hope I can trust you.'

'You can trust me.' But in truth, she might only have heard half of it.

*

Summer quickly became autumn, which in turn soon surrendered to the inevitable. First the days shortened and then the snows arrived, forcing everyone indoors, where it was a challenge to find a space that was not occupied by another. Secrecy was at a premium and contact between Sam and Charity was ever more furtive and fleeting. Of necessity, theirs would mostly be a warm-weather friendship.

But that Christmas, while others were briefly engaged elsewhere, Charity gave Sam the first seasonal gift that he could remember – a kiss planted firmly and willingly on his cheek, and another on his lips. There might have been more to come, but they heard Patience Wright approaching, squawking about something, and the moment was lost. Still, a gift was a gift, and Sam experienced a rapture he had rarely known.

Unsurprisingly, Christmas Day was special in the Wright household, and for one day only they extended a measure of goodwill to their employee, although peace was still in short supply. There was church in the morning. For the first time, Sam was invited to attend. There, he spent the best part of two hours not knowing whether to sit or stand or kneel, speaking when he should have remained silent, and ignorant of what to say when expected to contribute. Ezra Wright stood on his hind legs and preached until it seemed that next Christmas was quite close, and it was only the discomfort of the seating that kept people awake. But amid all this, Sam saw his chance to make a point. The Christmas Day service was replete with opportunities for singing, and Sam stood beside the family, next to Patience Wright. Although she had shuffled along the pew as far as she could go, it was still no distance at all. She could not help but listen to him. And with Sam putting his heart and soul into each refrain, surely the midwinter had never been bleaker nor had the faithful come more joyously.

I think I've proved I can sing with the best of them, Sam thought confidently. Now they can see what they're missing.

But it was as well that he did not mention his thoughts to others, as it might have soured the festive mood.

'He sounds like our cows when they're in calf,' Patience Wright scoffed under her breath. 'And to think he asked to sing with us.'

When they returned to the homestead, Sam was allowed to share in the Christmas goose but not in the conviviality that followed. He was back at work by the time that games were played and more secular songs were sung.

'The animals still need tending, even on such a day,'

Patience Wright informed him as she measured out thimblefuls of gin for the family.

And Sam sadly donned his snowshoes and his tatty winter coat and grudgingly left the festivities behind. As he trudged from barn to shed and back again, he could hear sweet music emanating from the homestead, and he tried to sing along under his breath.

By the time he had finished his chores, Christmas was effectively over.

THIRTY-THREE

Alice Hamilton returned to Canada in the spring of 1885, ostensibly to find employers for her new band of pioneers, but with a more pressing problem to resolve. After the damage inflicted at the hands of Dorothy Hoggard and her subsequent savaging by the magistrate, Mary Oliver was broken seemingly beyond repair. She had taken refuge in the Kingston distribution centre throughout the winter, when it was largely empty of other children, but since the emigration season was just over the horizon, Alice had to decide on Mary's future.

'You must see the girl,' said the matron on Alice's arrival.

They quietly opened the door to Mary's room. She sat on her bed, her arms round her knees, staring into space and sobbing as if possessed by the most desolate of spirits. She did not notice her visitors – or if she did, she gave no hint of it.

They closed the door again.

'She's like this most days and she's getting no better, miss. The opposite, if you ask me,' the matron explained. 'At other times she has fits of rage and we have to lock her in, or she would be a danger to herself and to others.'

On cue, they heard a crash and what sounded like a plate breaking from Mary's room.

'I'll wager that's her breakfast gone,' said the matron. 'And you should know that I've heard her say very bad things about you, miss – shocking things.'

'She would not be the first, or the last, I'm sure.' Alice knew that at least some of it was deserved. 'One thing is clear, she cannot stay beyond April. All our beds will be needed.'

'It's not just beds, miss. She cannot be left to her own devices – you don't know what she'll do. She demands so much of my attention, miss, and I cannot give it when our new shipments have arrived.'

Alice and the matron went back into the room. Mary was looking blankly out of the window and did not move. Alice touched her on her shoulder, and she recoiled. 'Come to send me back to that mad woman, have you?'

Alice shook her head.

'Then what do you want?'

'To help you.'

'Don't believe that.'

Whatever others thought of her behaviour, Mary regarded it as a logical response to her situation – perhaps the only one. When she looked in the mirror, she did not recognise the girl who returned the gaze. It was not so much the physical appearance, which was to be expected – an assembly of skin and bone that spoke of self-inflicted neglect; eyes puffed up and marbled with the darkest red, the residue from a never-ending swell of tears. She would not have believed that she could cry so much. But what lay behind her eyes hurt her most: defeat and surrender. Once she had been proud of her independence, a child navigating her way through a world where even an adult might struggle, surviving when others did not, flourishing compared to some. Now she was helpless, too scared even to step outside, disappearing in every conceivable way. Where was Big Sister now?

And when she looked at others, she mistrusted their motives: either they had connived in her debasement, or they were sure to have plans for more of the same. And as for Alice Hamilton, Mary sensed that she was no more than an inconvenience to her, someone to be rid of as soon as possible.

Alice sat down on the edge of the bed. Mary viewed her with deep suspicion.

'We must find somewhere you can be safe and happy.'

'Place me with my brother. That will do the trick.'

'Sadly, they have daughters aplenty and have no need of a maidservant.'

'Then somewhere nearby?'

'We have no one in that vicinity that wants a girl.'

'No one that wants me, more like, or perhaps no one that you trust me with.'

'It's not a question of me trusting you or not.' Mary could feel the impatience just beneath Alice's words. 'News travels fast and wide, and even those sympathetic to your plight would not wish to face the malice that your presence might provoke. It will be difficult enough to place our newcomers—'

'Never mind one who is seen to be trouble.' Mary finished the sentence for Alice, who might have phrased it differently but largely agreed with the sentiment.

'Might you benefit from returning to England?' interjected the matron.

Mary screamed and threw a cup to the floor.

'Not without her brother,' Alice hastily replied, nudging the matron into silence. 'What we need is a temporary arrangement. It is not long until you are a grown woman, and then you can make your own life. I aim to keep you safe until then.'

But Alice did not know how. She sat behind her desk and thought long into the night, guilt weighing upon her as if she herself had dealt the blows and delivered the injustice. Then she prayed. While in the throes of supplication, an idea emerged, and she was finally able to retire to her bed.

The next day, Alice sent word to Toronto. A week later, in receipt of a positive response, she summoned her carriage and drove the short distance to Kingston station. The mighty Grand Trunk Railway carried her on her way, riding the contours of Lake Ontario, each settlement that she trundled by reminding her of a SAD child, past or present: Whitby, where a boy had done well and now had land of his own nearby; a girl had been placed in Pickering, but only briefly, there having been an unsavoury incident; a child had disappeared from a position in Scarborough. Alice smiled at the successes and tried not to dwell upon the failures.

After disembarking in Toronto, Alice took a landau to the outer edge of the city and her ultimate destination, the city's lunatic asylum. Approached through acres of well-tended lawns and gardens, the roadway was bordered by colonnades of deferential trees, bowing in welcome in the Lake Ontario breeze. A central dome soared above the grand entrance hall, which was flanked by wings of stone and window, each extending a hundred yards or more, standing four storeys tall and hinting at further levels beneath. Functional rather than ornate, it was not a home for princes. Had such a structure stood in London, it might have housed a hive of public servants, its vastness reflecting the glory of a nation with so much to administer.

This might do very nicely, Alice thought, impressed by the sense of order and calm. She alighted at the entrance and knocked on the door. Soon a tall, spindly man appeared, formally dressed in jacket and cravat, his hand extended in welcome. His facial creases and receding hairline suggested he was around sixty, while the luxuriance of his sideburns more than compensated for any shortfall in coverage elsewhere. He announced himself as the medical director, and he was to be Alice's host for the day.

'Our institution is run on certain principles upon which I will not compromise,' he announced as they began their tour of the building. 'This is a sanctuary, where those in mental suffering can be removed from whatever so afflicts them in their daily lives and instead seek healing in a place of peace and tranquillity.'

'That is your reputation, and the reason I am here.'

The corridors were long, well-lit and unusually broad, so that patients and staff could converse at a respectful distance, should the need arise, and where no one might feel threatened by a chance encounter or the proximity of another. The ceilings were high and varnished a brilliant white, while the walls were hung with canvasses by artists who painted more for pleasure than for income. Each patient had their own cell, where they lodged in simplicity and comfort, with doors that were locked from the outside when this was felt necessary.

'Of course, residents from the wealthiest families have their own suite of rooms, but I assume that is of no interest to you.'

'You assume correctly, sir. I have not the means for that.'

The sound of a bell reverberated throughout the asylum.

'It is time for the men to have their spiritual instruction, and then the women will follow,' the director shouted above the din. 'And after that there will be exercise and then a meal. It is the same routine each day. Our patients need a rhythm to their lives, some consistency and predictability, so they can concentrate their energies on rehabilitation.'

They passed through a large room in which women were engaged in sewing with varying degrees of attention and proficiency. Alice could hear a woman singing, not unpleasantly, otherwise all was quiet.

'A healthy diet is key to a healthy mind,' he continued.

'Outdoor activity and the curative properties of fresh air are equally important, as is the dignity of meaningful activity. You will find patients engaged in all manner of constructive pursuits, both inside and out.' He pointed to a window, through which residents could be seen digging and sowing, weeding and watering, while others simply enjoyed the delights of nature.

'I have always been a great believer in meaningful activity,' Alice agreed enthusiastically. The director was indeed a kindred spirit.

'And we must always remember that this is a hospital, and those we care for are not prisoners.' The director might have seen some concern on Alice's face. He quickly added: 'Of course, they are not allowed to leave unless deemed cured or otherwise legally discharged. But under our regime we would expect eventual recovery to be very likely.'

The director's mood suddenly changed, and he seemed more exasperated than angry. 'At least, that is our intended purpose, and one we would achieve if left in peace. But my treatment methods are not cheap, and sadly, those that pay their taxes would rather we simply locked people away and forgot all about them. I am forever in argument with the powers that be.'

'I can sympathise with you. Politicians and civil servants are the bane of my life. People should stick to what they are good at.'

It was as if Alice and the director had been lifelong friends.

'Furthermore, we are distracted and overwhelmed by hordes of those that should not be here – men and women we cannot cure as, on arrival, they are already as sane as I am.' The director swung open a door with more force than was necessary to the consternation of the patients behind it, and he spent the next few moments calming them down again.

'The medical profession is wholly complicit in this,' he eventually continued. 'To many, committal here is seen solely as an efficient means of ridding the world of awkward people…'

Alice felt a twinge of embarrassment.

'It is a matter of convenience, not therapeutic necessity. Some of the habits claimed by relatives and practitioners as leading to mental illness are quite absurd and have no grounding in medical science. Individuals are committed here for "religious controversy" or "political excitement" – in other words because they disagreed with someone more important than themselves. Some are deposited here merely for choosing to live their lives harmlessly but differently. And by far the most common cause is "intemperance"; these people are not drunk, they are mad, apparently.'

They had moved on to the men's wing. There was more noise and less order and more staff scurrying around. They passed by patients who were stationary when required to move, and others who were moving when they should have been at rest. Some were merely comatose and there was less evidence of useful activity. The director was still in full flow.

'And if all this was not enough, we are overrun by criminal lunatics from the Provincial Penitentiary and the county jails, and increasingly by those villains who affect insanity as a means of evading punishment for their crimes. It is an outrage to cast them into the same house of refuge as the feeble and kind-hearted victims of ordinary madness. The time and effort needed to maintain a degree of separation would be far better spent elsewhere.'

There were yet more corridors, traversed at increasing pace to reflect the growing intensity of his monologue; further patients to see in different states of consciousness and calm; staff to observe going about their business; planned activities and unplanned interventions; stairs, more stairs and then even more.

Alice felt that things were taking longer than they should. 'May we talk about Mary Oliver?' she interrupted. 'Can you help her?'

As quickly as it had departed, the director's old self reappeared. 'I apologise, Miss Hamilton. It is such a joy to unburden oneself without being threatened with the need to seek alternative employment. You make a sound case for your girl. The grief suffered over many years, the loss of those dear to her, and now extreme violence against her person. Her descent into mania, or something like it, is understandable. I am happy to take her.'

They were nearing the end of the tour. Alice followed the director into his office and was handed the papers that, once signed, would commit Mary for an indefinite period. Alice hesitated for a moment.

'One final thing. I mentioned the girl's brother, who is some years away from his majority. When he achieves that landmark, can I be assured that she will be released into his care? If that is what he wishes, of course.'

'You have my word. I would be pleased for the girl.'

The director's parting shot was an attempt at reassurance. 'Take heart, Miss Hamilton, I believe the girl can be cured. A period spent in an atmosphere of decency and compassion will revitalise her. She may even be ready before her brother's majority.'

'I doubt that very much,' Alice thought, as she retraced her steps through the colonnades of trees and back to Kingston.

THIRTY-FOUR

'It is an absolute maze.'

Alice Hamilton was describing Toronto Lunatic Asylum to the matron.

'But might the girl be lost in such a place?'

'She is already lost. My hope is that she will be found again.'

Once more they opened the door to Mary's room. As always, she sat in mess and clutter, staring impassively through an unopened window at the life that passed her by. She was not pleased to see her visitors. In her eyes, it could only mean trouble.

'So, I am to be locked up as a lunatic,' she said, scowling, once the proposal had been explained to her. 'Nicely out of the way of your business. How convenient.' She continued to gaze blankly at the street; she would not let them get away with it that easily.

Alice tried to remain calm. 'It is not as bad as it sounds. There's plenty there that are like you, sane but troubled and in need of somewhere to hide. You will be safely out of sight of the world, who will quickly forget you…'

'As will you, no doubt.'

'And when you and your brother have reached your

majority, you can be handed over into his care and do as you please.'

Mary turned on Alice. 'I'll not be under his care, he'll be under mine, like it's always been.'

'If you wish to see it that way.'

Mary looked at Alice with deep suspicion. 'And they cannot keep me in there when that time comes?'

'The director and I have an arrangement.'

Mary was quiet for a moment, trying to make sense of the thousand voices that were shouting in her head. 'I will think about it.'

Alice could no longer hide her impatience. 'You may think if you wish, but you should know that you have very little choice. None, in fact.'

Alice swept from the room, leaving Mary to brood on her situation. But the more she dwelt on it, the more attractive the proposal began to appear to her fragile mind. Perhaps she might finally escape the terrors that continued to ravage her: the spectre of Dorothy Hoggard, seeking respite from a desperate life by blaming her ills upon another; the sound of a drawer being opened, then a swish through the air and finally the thwack of wood on trembling flesh; the contempt of the magistrate and the raucous celebration of those that witnessed it; the menace of strangers and the fear of stepping outside; the dread of a repeat should she try to resume her life.

'Enough is enough,' she decided and the next day she gave Alice an answer. 'I will trust you one last time, although the Lord only knows why I should.'

'It is for the best.'

'There is no such thing as "best". But it cannot be worse than being here.'

So, Alice signed the committal papers and dispatched them before Mary could change her mind.

A matter of days before she left the home, Mary approached Alice. 'I have written a letter to Percy,' she blurted, producing a folded paper from her sleeve. 'Read it and see what you think.'

Alice took the letter. It said:

My dear Percy,
You must have been wondering what on earth has become of me, although I doubt you have missed my nagging about what to wear and how to speak and to be sure you go to church regular. Anyhow, for some months now I have been in a new placement, which I am most pleased with. The children grew up in the old one and they didn't need me no more, so here I am.

I began as a maidservant but now I am almost a daughter to them. The mister of the house is a very important man in the town. People look up to him and when I am at his side, they look up to me as well. The missus is kindly and does much selfless work with those less fortunate than us. She is teaching me many useful skills about the house so that I may one day make someone a good wife. The children are angels and no trouble at all. At times, they remind me of you, bright and good-natured but not above some mischief.

But the big news is that they are all about to go travelling to a foreign place called Europe, perhaps for as much as a year or maybe even two, and I am to accompany them. It may mean that I will struggle to send or receive letters as we move about, so do not fret if you do not hear from me. You will be glad of the peace, no doubt. I will write again when I return.

Mary was clearly pleased with herself. 'I need an excuse to be silent. He cannot know what has happened to me. I cared for him. I protected him. I was Big Sister. He mustn't know that I am helpless. I still have some pride.'

And so, just three weeks after her initial visit, Alice repeated the journey to the Toronto Lunatic Asylum, this time with Mary at her side. As Kingston disappeared into the distance, Mary felt a weight being lifted from her shoulders and she even allowed herself the briefest of smiles. Perhaps she might now be able to forget.

A stiff breeze blew off Lake Ontario as they approached the asylum. Its avenue of trees was quite animated, seemingly waving more in warning than in welcome. There were fewer people in the grounds than Alice had remembered, and very few were in the uniform of a patient. Otherwise, all appeared to be as expected.

An unfamiliar man opened the door. He was fashionably dressed, his jacket and breeches clearly cut from an expensive cloth and tailored to disguise an over-generous figure. His waistcoat carried suggestions that he had been disturbed at his luncheon, and there was similar evidence upon his breath and in his beard. The man towered over Alice, which did not make him exceptional, and over Mary, which was less common. The austerity of his surroundings lent him a brooding presence that might not survive a change of venue. Mary quailed before him, taking several steps backwards. But before anyone could speak, a piercing scream rent the air, originating from the woman's wing and echoing down a deserted corridor until it reached the domed entrance, where it rattled around for a time before subsiding.

'Yes?' said the man, clearly unruffled by the disturbance.

'We are here to see the director,' Alice stated in her most formal voice. 'He will be expecting us.'

'I am the director. As of one week ago. And I am expecting you.'

Mary cast a terrified glance at Alice.

'I'm not sure about this, miss,' she whispered. 'Did you hear that scream?'

The director looked down on her with disdain. 'You will soon become accustomed to it.'

Alice quickly took him by the arm. 'May we talk in private?' she asked, marching him to his office and leaving Mary frightened and alone in the entrance hall.

'He picked one fight too many,' the new director remarked in an offhand manner when Alice asked about his predecessor. He popped a pastry into his mouth. 'Our taxpayers have limited resources but rather more influence. They wanted him gone and, what they want, they generally get. Things will be very different now, and not before time. The asylum will be run properly. Efficiently. Economically.'

Alice looked suspiciously at the man. 'I will need to consult with the girl. We had expectations for her treatment that might not now be realised.'

'She will receive whatever is appropriate for her condition. If you thought it the right place for her then, it is still right for her now.'

'Even so…'

'In any event, it is too late. The girl is committed. You signed the papers and payment for her confinement is due. Today.'

'But—'

'The committal was not conditional on the identity of the director.'

As he spoke, Alice heard Mary crying out. She hurried towards the entrance hall. Mary had a man on either side of her, each holding an arm.

'You may see her by arrangement,' the director advised Alice. 'But now it is time for you to leave. After you have paid, of course. We will see to her trunk.'

And Mary and her escorts quickly disappeared down one of the never-ending corridors, leaving Alice open-mouthed and impotent. The director stood with his hand outstretched, and Alice reluctantly handed over a wad of notes.

'An equivalent payment will be due each year.' And before Alice could complain that this was not her understanding, the director turned on his heel and returned to his office. Alice noticed that he transferred some of the notes to his pocket.

I have failed her again, she thought as she sadly made her way back to Kingston.

THIRTY-FIVE

It was a special day when Amelia Gait knew for certain that she was with child. Over the past weeks, she had kept the possibility to herself, and her husband wondered why she appeared distracted. But then the secret was out. Robert Gait was not a demonstrative man, but now he smiled, and for a time his approach to life was almost playful. The mother-to-be was euphoric in a matter-of-fact kind of way, more at home with the practicalities than the emotions. But the news also released a profound sadness that she had largely suppressed since their first child passed, and it was a time for tears as well as joy. And in the darkest moments of the night they would lie sleepless, tormented by the anguish of their previous loss and their fear of a repeat.

To his shame, but not his surprise, Arthur had mixed feelings about the news. He was cheerful enough in company and was happy to share Gait's celebratory whisky, but when alone he moped about the place and his brooding was obvious from a distance. While not the most empathetic of men, even Robert Gait could see that all was not well.

'Don't get me wrong, I'm made up for you,' Arthur mumbled when Gait cornered him.

'It don't seem like you are. Never seen you so miserable.'

'Look, mister, it's hard for me when it's right there in front of me.' It was most unlike Arthur to be unable to look Gait in the eye. 'That is one lucky child, having a proper ma and pa to its name. It makes me think how things might have been for me with the right folks, if I'd had what your child will have. Until I came here, I never knew what it could be like, and now I do.' He tried to pull himself together. 'Just feeling sorry for myself, I guess. It'll pass.'

Gait shifted uncomfortably. Clearly a response was expected of him. 'Look, there's no point fretting about what you haven't got. Just give thanks for what you have. You've done well for yourself here, fallen on your feet. Got a chance of a life that's as good as many will enjoy. Don't waste your energy dwelling on the past.'

While this might have made sense at another time, Arthur was in no mood to hear it. He grunted inconclusively.

'Jealousy is a killer. Don't let it take hold.' And with that, Gait strode away, confident that he had provided insight and motivation, and glad that he could now concentrate on doing something useful. Arthur sullenly went about his work and deliberately kept out of Gait's sight for the rest of the morning.

Later that afternoon, Gait stumbled upon Arthur in the paddock. 'You've done a good job with that fence,' he said cheerily, as if they were their first words of the day.

Arthur ignored the comment, which was most unlike him; he would usually revel in any praise that was on offer. Robert Gait sighed; they would have to have another conversation. 'Was there something else? I thought we were done.'

Arthur was almost as reluctant to speak. 'It's not easy to say…'

'Try, and let's finish with this.'

'I suppose … the new child … it brings home that I just work for you. I'm not family and never will be. That's hard for me.'

'And we're supposed to forego a child of our own just to make you feel better?'

Arthur looked away, clearly upset. Gait must have realised that he was being a bit harsh, and he softened his tone. 'Look, what you say is true, and I can see how you might feel uncomfortable, threatened even. But the child will make no difference to how we are with you.'

'You wouldn't be human if it made no difference. It's your flesh and blood.'

'You think it's going to leap from its cot, run straight out the door and grab the plough from your hand? We'll need you more, not less.'

'Suppose. For a time, anyhow.'

Frustration was creeping into Gait's voice. There was work to be done, and this was wasting precious time. 'Look, we still want you here, if that's what you're angling for me to say.'

'Perhaps.'

'You have my word.'

'You sure?'

'In the name of – there's no talking to you when you're like this.' Gait stomped off. 'I thought you were stronger than that,' he called out over his shoulder. 'Where's your confidence gone? It's not hard to find as a rule.'

And later the sound of his pickaxe was particularly strident.

Rudely awakened from his malaise, over the next few days Arthur gave himself a good talking to. He had learned some things about Robert Gait that he filed away for future reference, under 'disappointing' and 'cannot always be trusted'. More importantly, he did not recognise the self-pitying figure that was now grumping about the place. This wasn't the boy who had led London a merry dance, the lad who always found a way.

I'm turning into Sam Barney, he thought, and shivered.

Gait observed the change in Arthur's mood and assumed that his various interventions had done the trick. He told Amelia about his achievement. 'I had words with him, and you can see how he is now. And you say I can't talk to folk.'

But Amelia kept her own watch, just to be sure.

Later that year Amelia gave birth to a boy, and he thrived as his predecessor had not. Throughout the homestead there was noise and clutter and endless diversions from the job in hand. But there was also joy and fulfilment and more talk of the future, which was suddenly less finite. Arthur saw the love his parents bestowed on the infant and could not help but feel deep piercings of jealousy. He heard plans being discussed that did not involve him. He watched as lives were made complete, but not his. Still, he kept up the pretence of being unconcerned.

And outside his head and heart, there were big differences in Arthur's life and work, there being less of the former and rather more of the latter. 'I need you to take this on for me,' Gait would often say, or 'I can't help you with that today' or 'You'll need to do this yourself'. And sometimes supper was not ready when his appetite demanded it. Or clothing might go a time without repair. And there was little sleep to be had, so of a summer's night Arthur would often bed down in a corner of the shanty, in search of physical if not mental peace, reliving the time it had just been the three of them.

So successful were the new living arrangements that another child, also a boy, arrived before anyone could blink. And the newborn unsettled Arthur to an even greater degree than had the first. The enhanced privacy of the homestead was clearly being utilised to the full, and it was possible, perhaps even likely, that there would be multiple Gaits arriving in the coming years. But the usable acreage of the farm was insubstantial and even if extended beyond its boundary, there was a limit to the hands required to work it and the mouths that it could feed. One day the cuckoo would be ejected from the nest. He needed to make plans.

Robert Gait's mantra of self-reliance had embedded itself deep within Arthur's core, being much in accord with his own philosophy and experience. He could imagine himself shouting it from the hilltops, much as Gait did quite regularly: 'I'll die a free man before I prostrate myself before another', or words to that effect.

Although unsure what response he might receive, Arthur convinced himself that the new arrival gave him a clear excuse to broach the subject, and there was no time like the present. Gait was chopping wood in the yard.

'I want to start thinking about getting my own place,' Arthur began nervously, hoping for a reaction that might help him to construct a cogent thread. But Gait was as inscrutable as ever.

Chop. Chop.

'I hear the government is giving more land away.' Arthur floundered on. 'Much like they did here, but this time out west. Winnipeg and beyond.'

Still no reply.

'I might put my name down and see what comes of it.'

Gait raised a shaggy eyebrow, and the all-encompassing beard twitched open. 'But you're still no more than a boy.'

Chop.

'Aren't you getting ahead of yourself?'

A particularly hefty chop.

'And why would you want to leave us? This is your home. You helped build it.'

Arthur spotted an opportunity. 'But why should I work for another if it can be avoided? Even if that other is you and the missus? You've drummed it into me, forever talking about having no one to push you around and take advantage of all your hard work. And I can see you're right.'

Robert Gait leaned on his axe for a moment. Arthur was pleased that he had made him think.

'Yes, I have always said that. And meant it with all my heart. However grim life is, and you know as well as I that it can be very grim indeed, you've got to look after yourself and your own. You can't trust no one else.'

The chopping resumed.

'But that's the rub. I'm not your own.' Arthur's voice trailed off; he was finding it hard to admit the obvious. 'No matter how decent you and the missus are to me, and you have been very decent, you have your own sons now. The older they get, the longer I'm here, the more of an outsider I'll be. One day you will want my room for the eldest and then you'll just be my boss, nothing more.'

'I'm your boss now, always have been.'

'It hasn't felt like that.'

Robert Gait rested his axe against the wall of the old shanty. 'I have some idea of what you mean, and I might feel the same if I'd had the life you've had. Yes, they're giving land away out west, but you have to be at least eighteen before they will even think about giving you anything but a telling-off for wasting their time.'

Arthur's heart sank; he was still eighteen months short of that mark.

'And you'll never clear the land on your own, so you'll need to employ some labour – a hired hand or at the very least, a child like you were.'

'You didn't have no help until I turned up, and you did all right without it.'

'I had the missus and she's worth two men, as you know. Anyhow, you'll need money for a host of things. Just have a look round here, then add up what all of it might cost. We've been putting wages away for you, as per our agreement, and the

SAD people should have 'em safely. But you'll need a lot more besides that.'

Now there was desperation in Arthur's voice. 'I can't get at them wages 'til I'm twenty-one, and that is such a distance away. There'll be no land to give out by then.'

'You've got time aplenty. There's enough land for a million like you, and they're not going to stop handing it out, not in my lifetime. Do you know how big this place is? And there's always holdings that come up for sale from those that have tried and failed, and that might give you a better chance, as some of it might already be cleared. But heed the warning: for every one of us that makes a living, there's another that packs it in, and you'll find them labouring for a pittance or scraping the barrel in one of our foul cities. If you work the land, it's a precarious life.'

'If you work the streets as a child, it's a precarious life.'

'You've got me there.' Robert Gait resumed his assault on the firewood and seemed to consider the matter closed.

Arthur looked despairingly at him. 'So, will you help me towards it? Getting my own place?'

'Do you mean now?'

'Please, mister.'

Gait laughed. And then he saw that it was a serious request, and he stumbled about for a non-committal answer. 'Right now I can't do nothing other than carry on paying wages in return for your services. Perhaps I can help when the time comes, perhaps not, we'll have to see. No point in thinking about it now. Not for a long time.'

'But I need to have it sorted in my head, to have a plan. I always have a plan.'

'I can't make promises. A lot can happen between now and then.'

'I thought you might want to recognise how I've helped

you these last few years.' As soon as the words passed his lips, Arthur knew that he had poked the beast too far.

Gait took a moment to compose himself, and when he replied it was with enough hostility for Arthur to take a step back in self-preservation. 'Look, there are two sides to this bargain, and we've always stuck by ours. If you don't like what I'm saying, we can always send you back and get another.'

'I'm sorry, I…'

'And in the meantime, if you want my assistance, you can help yourself by making sure you deserve it.' Gait picked up his axe and turned his back on Arthur. 'I thought you'd got over all this,' he said as he smote the final log and strode off to the homestead.

It was some time before Arthur felt able to join him for supper.

THIRTY-SIX

Throughout the autumn and into the winter, Lily Mudd waited for Alice Hamilton to respond to her letter. Her dream was that Alice would appear in person and whisk her to safety while delivering vengeance of Old Testament proportions upon the farmer and his sons. Having witnessed Alice berate assorted tradesmen and officials to within an inch of their lives, Lily could readily picture her as an avenging angel, with her stern features, caustic tongue and 'don't you dare' demeanour making her more than a match for any man.

So, when the sun rose each morning, Lily climbed optimistically from her bed, expecting that it might be today when her saviour would arrive. And when the day reached its end, she felt a sense of disappointment, almost betrayal, that she remained in jeopardy and unavenged. Hadn't Alice said that Lily was to contact her if she needed help? So, where was she? As she knelt by her bed, Lily's prayers reflected a growing impatience and shrinking confidence. She wrote a second time, again risking discovery by stealing the cost of the postage, and she was much relieved when the sons took a beating for it instead. But the second letter disappeared into the same void as the first and there seemed no point in penning a third. Each night she slept a little less easily.

Meanwhile, the farmer kept a close eye on his sons'

behaviour and rarely left them unchaperoned, while the sons monitored their father's reaction to drink and were quick to restrain him if there was even the slightest movement of his fist in Lily's direction. The stand-off continued into the autumn and beyond: on one side, a girl in possession of secrets; on the other, the fear that those secrets would be told. The winter snow added claustrophobia to the mix by forcing the combatants into suffocating proximity: endless days of treading on eggshells, drowning in a sea of mutual hatred.

But as time passed without retribution, or any sign that it might be imminent, Lily saw her hold over the farmer and his sons diminish. Each day, the farmer became more attentive towards her work, and eventually he demanded a return to previous standards. Although he had not yet resorted to enforcement, Lily felt obliged to comply.

Meanwhile, the sons were regaining their courage. 'We haven't forgotten you,' they sneered, tentatively at first, testing the waters, then with greater menace as each day passed.

'And I haven't forgotten you, or what you did,' Lily would respond with a resolve that was ebbing away.

'Told you she wouldn't say nothing,' the boys bragged to the farmer, and he began to believe them.

One cold February morning, Lily was serving porridge for the farmer and his sons. Aware of her weakened position and not wishing to challenge or antagonise, she had reverted to taking care over the preparation of meals; hence, there were no unlikely ingredients in the mix, and the oats were cooked with the intention of them being digested. There was a poisonous atmosphere around the table, but that was how it mostly was. The menfolk ate silently, scowling at Lily, while she busied herself, hoping not to catch their eye.

'Bring me some milk, girl,' the farmer called out, crashing his mug down for effect.

Lily picked up the jug, which, unusually, was full to the brim, courtesy of the handful of scrawny cattle that had survived the farmer's attentions. They produced just about enough for the family's needs and no more, so their output was precious, and fresh milk in the morning was a treat.

'And be careful with it.'

The jug was heavy, and Lily struggled to carry it over the uneven floor, stumbling more than once. First one splash hit the ground, then another, and a third was lost on the table as she tried to pour.

'You clumsy girl, you know how valuable that is!' And the farmer lashed out. His flailing fist, hardly even clenched, caught Lily on the shoulder. She locked eyes with him, determined not to show any fear, and he stared back.

Nothing was said, and the house was quiet for the rest of the day. Then, in the absence of any repercussions, the farmer hit Lily again, harder this time and deliberately, and again there were no consequences.

Hell had reopened its gates.

'But don't you go near that little slut,' he warned his sons. 'It's still too risky. And I need you to be working.'

'But Pa, you're having your fun, can't we have some too?'

'I ain't having fun, just keeping her in line.'

'Please, Pa…'

'You do as I say.'

And his sons knew better than to argue further.

Seemingly resigned to her fate, Lily went through the motions of what passed for a life. Some days as the sun rose, the weight of her thoughts and an overwhelming lethargy in her limbs would seek to shackle her to the bed. I don't have the strength for this, not for one day longer, she would think. But somehow, she did.

At times she would revisit the distant past. This is all I've ever known, just different shades of it. I must have been born bad, she thought.

There was submission: 'I don't care no more. Let 'em do as they will.'

And defiance: 'They've done their worst, and I'm still here. What more can they do?'

And sometimes she seethed with murderous intent: 'I'd swing for it, but I swear it would be worth it. I've no sort of life to lose, anyway. It would be a kindness, and at least I'd have the last laugh.'

But always the same emptiness and despair: 'I can't even bear to be alone no more.'

She reserved her deepest anger for Alice Hamilton, more even than for the farmer and his sons, although she had boundless contempt for them. 'Them's just savages, they don't know no better. But she has no excuse.'

By the spring, Lily had lost all hope. There would be no rescue and no avenging angel. And there was no one else she could tell, no other saviour-in-waiting. If Alice Hamilton was unable or unwilling to intervene, then why would a neighbour, that she hardly knew? Particularly given the farmer's well-earned reputation.

*

Then one day, just as the May sunshine was driving away the last evidence of winter, Lily left the farm and did not come back. No one saw or heard her go. When examined, her meagre belongings seemed intact and in place. The farmer paced the floor. Had she gone in search of people to tell? Was this the day their secrets would be out? He backed his sons against a wall. 'You've not been up to any of that business again?' he thundered, to desperate denials.

'Or is it one beating too many, like it was for Ma?' one son added in an act of bravery and foolishness that he instantly regretted.

The farmer organised a search for Lily. Neighbours were asked, the police were informed, news spread. A handkerchief that might have been Lily's was found on the bank of the Moira River, which again was flowing full and fast. But otherwise there was no trace of her.

'Probably just run off, like a lot of these guttersnipes,' a police officer advised, keen to return to more pressing duties. 'Looking for something better, I'll warrant. The trouble with these ragamuffins is they don't know when they're well off. She'll fetch up somewhere else when she's hungry. Then we'll bring her back.'

But Lily did not fetch up. And, as before, local tongues began to wag. Had she gone the same way as the farmer's wife? Surely, it was too much of a coincidence. Might it even be…

THIRTY-SEVEN

It had been more than a year since George Moore had traversed Canada collecting the stories of immigrant children. There had since been an ominous silence. Alice Hamilton dared not hope that she had heard the last of him; she would not have recognised the phrase 'got away with it'. She continued her work at full pace, shuttling back and forth between England and Canada, recruiting, delivering and distributing further shipments. Now it was the summer of 1886, and another busy season was upon her. It was business as usual.

Then one day a letter arrived, under the seal of the Local Government Board, and Alice read it with great irritation and some concern. 'How dare he summon me to a meeting? Who does he think he is?' She sniffed and placed the letter in a pile where it was unlikely to ever see the light of day.

A week later, a second missive arrived. More urgent and less polite, it met with a similar fate. 'I have better things to do than pander to that man's vanity,' Alice fumed. In her heart she knew the matter would not go away, but in ignoring the letters she at least felt that she was making a point.

A further week passed, and Moore's patience was exhausted. A different tack was required. Abandoning protocol, for which he was usually a stickler, he resorted to the informality of arriving, uninvited, on his prey's doorstep. He was rewarded when a startled Alice Hamilton opened the door, not wholly dressed for visitors.

'Miss Hamilton, I insist that I speak with you.'

Struggling to regain her composure, Alice hastily rearranged her garments as she spoke. 'If you must, Mr Moore. But be advised that I am extremely busy and have little time for this.'

'You have received my letters, I assume, but have not felt the need to reply.'

'Sadly, the hours that God allots to each day are never wholly sufficient for what needs to be done.' Observing Moore's distinctly unhappy expression, Alice sensed it would be diplomatic to offer him some hospitality. She let him in and watched anxiously as he carefully picked his way around the piles of books that littered the hallway, an obstacle course that threatened his balance more than once. Alice had inherited the bulk of her father's library, and there was space for little else. Shelves lined every room, but they were insufficient for the task, and the surplus spilled out onto every available surface.

'I have read most of them,' she boasted. Now he will know that I am an educated woman and not to be trifled with, she thought. 'And I have recently installed a room for bathing inside the house itself,' she enthused, feeling a need to score as many points as she could. 'It is my little luxury. Do you have such a place?'

'Unfortunately not.'

Alice made a face to imply that it was obvious that Moore lacked such a facility.

Soon they were ensconced in the parlour with a pot of tea, with Alice dressed more appropriately and with her hair attended to.

'I need to appraise you of the results of my investigation,' Moore began.

'You have taken your time about it.' Alice snorted. 'Which suggests that it cannot be seen as important.'

'On the contrary, government is incapable of doing anything in a hurry, or even at a normal pace, as I am sure you have observed, but you shouldn't read anything into that. There is interest at a high level.'

Alice sat, teacup poised in hand, feigning indifference but hanging on every word.

'I must stress that I have not singled you out.'

Alice felt very much singled out.

'And to get a full picture, I did not just seek out the workhouse children, but also those that were rescued directly from the streets. I know you are involved with all.'

'In Canada no distinction is drawn between them.'

'Indeed. So, aside from a sample of your children, I also visited some placed by Clara Openshaw, who feeds solely off the workhouse, as you know. Also Edward Joyce, who takes children from the streets of Edinburgh, and William Irving, who does the same in Bristol, and, most importantly, James Berkeley, who acquires waifs and strays wherever he can find them. And I contrived to corner John Nicklet, a most secretive man, whose children appear as if from nowhere and just as suddenly vanish again.'

'You have been busy.'

Moore ignored her sarcasm. 'Of course, I was only able to meet a very small proportion of those that have been emigrated...'

'So, your findings are worthless then.'

'But I have no reason to believe that my sample is unrepresentative.' Moore took a deep breath; he had known this would not be easy. 'To begin positively,' he said brightly.

'The outcome for the very young children who are formally adopted may be spoken of with unqualified approval. I visited several, and without exception their condition was most satisfactory. However, scarcely one-tenth of emigrant children are disposed of in this way.'

'Still, a significant number in absolute terms.'

Moore stared wearily at Alice, but he did not respond. 'Before these fortunate children are placed, extensive investigations are carried out, which undoubtedly contributes to their success,' he continued. 'However, this contrasts with the disposal of the older children, where there is little or no scrutiny of the homes to which they have been allocated, and no checks made into the suitability of the individuals that live there. They make an application, arrive at a certain place at a particular time and take the child away. Few, if any, questions are asked.'

Alice bristled at the suggestion of neglect. 'I have always found that a reference from a local clergyman or from some other worthy is sufficient.'

'But surely one must question the accuracy of such opinions when the provider will wish to exist peacefully thereafter alongside the subject of their assessment. The more wayward the individual, the less likely it is that truth will be spoken.'

Alice grunted. If asked, she would always give an honest opinion, whatever the consequences, and had no time for those weaker than herself.

'And even if we ignore the danger into which a child might be placed, if better enquiry was made as to the needs and character of the applicants, the early and frequent change of placement might be avoided. As you know, many a child is quickly returned, often for reasons that should have been known before they were packed off…'

'It is like a marriage,' Alice interrupted, keen that Moore

should not be allowed to develop a compelling argument. 'No matter how careful you are in selection, you only truly find out if you are compatible when you share a roof. At least, I am told that's how it is.'

'... And some simply run away, often vanishing entirely and permanently from view, despite the reward that employers sometimes offer for their return.'

'I accept that a more robust process might cut out some wastage.'

'Surely, a child disappearing off the face of the earth is more than just "wastage"?' Moore's voice was increasing in urgency and volume, and Alice regretted the unfortunate phrase. She could sense that his concern was genuine and not just an exercise in covering his back.

'And the want of sufficient care in selecting placements is greatly aggravated by the almost total absence of proper supervision thereafter,' he declared forcefully, replacing his teacup with a clatter. 'Unless there are unfavourable reports, it is assumed that the child is doing well, if any thought is given to them at all. However, I encountered many instances where that was not the case.'

Alice shuffled uneasily in her chair. Is he about to point the finger? she wondered. Does he have any specific evidence against me? There were certain names that she definitely did not wish to be mentioned.

'Furthermore, even in the rare instances where a child's placement has been visited, this is more akin to a social call than a robust and impartial assessment. I could not, for example, find a single instance of enquiry into their accommodation. Yet I encountered many cases that were most troubling – a small boy sleeping in a dark recess without any ventilation, essentially a cupboard; a girl of twelve in a room away from that of her mistress, without door fastening, and close by the rooms of two men; and several children who were sleeping in a stable or a barn.'

'Were any of these my children?'

'No, but—'

'As I thought.' She gave a sigh of relief.

'Although there were several of your arrangements that were far from ideal,' Moore stressed – a little defensively, Alice thought.

'It is not a perfect world. And you should see the conditions in which they were originally found.'

Moore battled on. 'My point is that you would not know whether their circumstances were acceptable or not. It is a scandal waiting to happen.' He then turned to some instances of egregious treatment elsewhere. 'A master had horse-whipped a girl of thirteen… I found the marks of a flogging on a boy's shoulders… A girl's hand was bruised from repeated application of a strap…'

Alice winced as he read out each entry. But at least he would not have stumbled across Mary Oliver, whose name, as well some problematic others, had mysteriously not found its way onto her list of children. How could I be blamed for what happened to her? Alice had justified the omission at the time.

'And I heard stories of far worse.' Moore persisted. 'There have been some prosecutions, but it is difficult to find a magistrate that will support the abused child against the perpetrator.'

Alice knew that only too well; she blushed a little at the memory.

Suddenly, Moore relaxed a little in tone and posture. 'However, to complete my account I must say that I also encountered many children who spoke of their contentment, even happiness. They were placed with good people and were well looked after. In some cases, they were treated more like a family member than an employee.'

'And I can give you further evidence of that happy state.' Alice rummaged around on her desk and produced a clip of papers. 'Letters from some of my children, expressing how content and grateful they are.'

The clip included that penned by Arthur Dilkes. Moore skimmed through some of the letters, which had clearly been selected for their positivity. His mood had lightened somewhat, but Alice knew that the most difficult part of the conversation was yet to come. To curry favour, she made another pot of tea, and this time it was accompanied by a slice of Madeira cake.

'And where do we go from here?' she asked, just as Moore took a large bite.

'I am not seeking to curtail your trade,' he spluttered amid a shower of crumbs. 'There are many benefits in migrating a certain class of child. We live in troubled times, and the misery and destitution that we see all too often might one day lead to civil disorder, if not outright insurrection. These children would only add to the conflagration, and emigration is an important safety valve until matters improve.'

'And, of course, it should also lead to a better life for the child,' Alice reminded him.

'Yes, that goes without saying.'

'Then, if it is so valuable, leave me in peace to get on with it.'

Moore adopted a conciliatory tone. 'At this stage, I am merely encouraging you to exercise greater care in the placement of your children, in line with what we have discussed.'

'At this stage?'

'The Board does not wish to enforce a set of rules nor to bar individuals from their trade, but…'

The threat was left unsaid. Alice felt it was time to mount a counterattack. 'Sir, I am an alchemist. I take those that are surplus to requirements in England and transform them into what Canada most needs. This is not the work of an afternoon, as must be obvious from your investigations, yet you fail to recognise the constraints on what can be done in the time available. You ask the impossible.'

'On the contrary, it should not be too onerous keeping track of the whereabouts of these children,' Moore hit back. 'They should be where you put them, and if they are not, you should be expected to find them. And having some idea of the suitability of their recipients does not seem too much to ask, nor from time-to-time checking that all is well, when you have said yourself that you cannot know in advance how things might turn out.'

The exchange continued for some time, both sparring vigorously from their fixed positions, until they had fought themselves to a standstill. During a short silence, Alice debated whether she should place discretion before valour and opted for the latter, as she generally did.

'Sir, my children are well chosen and, I believe, allocated with sufficient care,' she concluded. 'I do what I can to ensure that all is in order, both before and after placement, but there is only so much I can achieve. As I said, it is an imperfect world, and no amount of bureaucracy will render it less so. If others are lax and wantonly send children into danger, then by all means bring down your sword upon them. But I shall not be changing my methods. Good day to you, sir.'

Alice rose from her chair and made her way to the door. Moore was more reluctant to rise but could not insist that he remain, and he bid Alice a perfunctory farewell.

'We shall meet again soon,' he predicted.

*

Just a few days later, Canadian newspapers carried the tragic story of the death of Simeon Harding, a thirteen-year-old child who had been emigrated by Alice Hamilton from the Shrewsbury workhouse the previous year. His employer was in police custody on a charge of manslaughter. The British press picked up the story and roared their disapproval that such a fate had befallen one of their own in a foreign land, when there would have been little interest had it happened in England. Meanwhile the *Toronto Herald* paraded him through their pages for several days as further evidence for banning child immigration entirely.

And as he had foretold, Alice once again found George Moore on her doorstep.

THIRTY-EIGHT

For a second time, George Moore perched on a chair in Alice Hamilton's parlour, nursing a cup of tea. This visit coming so soon after the previous occasion, there was a danger that people might talk. He sat somewhat awkwardly as he watched Alice dry her tears; he had not expected this emotion from her.

'I have some records of Simeon Harding in my office here, but most will be in Kingston.' She sniffed. 'I have no recollection of the boy. I see so many…' Her voice trailed off and it was some moments before she could speak.

'You will need to travel soon to Canada,' Moore advised. 'There is an official investigation into the death, as well as the prosecution of the farmer. As you know, the topic of immigrant children is controversial at the best of times.'

'I am scheduled to sail within a matter of days.'

Moore referred to some hastily scribbled notes. 'I only know what has been reported,' he said. 'But I understand that the farmer was a solitary man, who struggled to extract a sufficient living from his land, and in trying to motivate the boy to greater efforts, he took the handle of an axe to him, perhaps on a number of occasions. Then at some later time, the boy was found to be dead. The farmer is claiming that the discipline he administered should not have been sufficient to kill a healthy child, and that his death must be due to some unidentified medical cause.'

Alice perked up a little. 'And how likely do you feel that to be? '

'It is possible. A neighbour apparently described the boy, and I quote, as "unusually short-sighted and of weak intellect, as well as being uncertain of speech and infirm in the leg". But if that is an accurate description, we should first ask why he was ever a candidate for emigration and then, to make matters worse, why he was placed in an employment for which he was clearly unsuitable.'

Alice's demeanour changed the instant she felt the need to defend herself. Now she sat fully upright, her piercing eyes chiselling away at Moore. 'If you are questioning his suitability for emigration, you might ask the medical examiner at the Port of Quebec, who clearly found him fit to work.'

'I have already done so, and part of the fault will lie there.'

Moore dangled his teacup as a hint and Alice reluctantly replenished it. Moore had not finished yet. 'You previously implied that you have made some, albeit not many visits to placements. Might Simeon Harding have been one of them?'

'I have no recollection of it. And if his reported location is correct, it is a hundred miles or more from my centre at Kingston, and in the opposite direction to my return journey to England. You can probably guess my answer.'

Moore could not help but stick the knife in. 'Perhaps you can now see how a regular inspection might identify children in peril before it is too late?'

Alice huffed but did not reply, and Moore did not immediately push the point. Some minutes later he was bidding farewell to Alice at her front door when he unleashed his thunderbolt. 'I forgot to say,' he lied. 'The Simeon Harding episode has tipped the Board over the edge. They have decided that no further workhouse children will be emigrated until a rigorous inspection regime is in place to ensure their welfare, and they have instructed the Canadian government to implement this. They are the people the Board trusts the most out of the various parties involved, although even there, confidence is in short supply. You can still ship your waifs and strays. For now, at least.'

And then he was gone.

Alice sat in her favourite chair, deep in thought and damp of eye. While not a maternal figure, and often contrary to appearances, she did care for each child in her own way. And if she sometimes viewed them as a commodity, they were a precious one. Alice thought of the promises that would have been made to Simeon Harding in advance of his boarding that ship, and how badly they had been broken. She tried to imagine how he must have felt, betrayed and abandoned. She had known fatalities before among her children, through accident or misadventure, and that was bad enough. And there was another death that might have been by a child's own hand, although nothing was ever proved. But Simeon Harding was the first to perish through the act of another. At least, it was the first of which she was aware.

And so Alice cried for Simeon Harding. But she also shed tears for herself. 'This will do untold damage to my enterprise,' she muttered, pouring herself a large sherry. 'Attracting patrons and raising money will be more difficult. Reputation is everything in my line of work, when there are so many others vying for support.' She treated herself to some Turkish delight, to which she was partial. 'And if that wasn't enough, now we have the workhouse business.' She took another piece and perked up a little. At least my other children are unaffected, and they make up the majority of my clientele, she thought.

Alice found her glass to be empty, but that was soon rectified. 'But even if the current furore blows over and workhouses are reinstated, I'll wager the likes of George Moore will forever be on my shoulder with his "you must do this" and "you cannot do that". How can I work efficiently with that sort of interference?' Her anger at the thought of it made her feel even better.

Finally, Alice moved from chair to bed, but sleep eluded her. The next morning, she packed a trunk, and within days she was bound for Canada once more.

THIRTY-NINE

Ever since her discovery of Sam and Charity's communion, Hope Wright had been spying on her sister, applying a level of diligence and perseverance that she had not previously displayed, and a measure of cunning that was less foreign to her. Given the teachings that had been drummed into the Wright children from birth, her actions might have been driven by a Christian concern for the welfare of Charity's soul. Or perhaps it was a piece of mischief more redolent of the devil and his works. Or maybe she was just bored and thought it might add some colour to her dreary life.

Over the course of her snooping, Hope witnessed many of the pair's clandestine meetings, stalking her prey at a distance and maintaining a silence that she found difficult at other times. She had observed the change in her sister's demeanour: suddenly less child, more adult; one minute radiant, the next prone to melancholy; increasingly secretive yet hinting at unknown wonders that she ached to share. Similarly, the gutter child was displaying a repertoire of emotions that went beyond his previous shades of miserable; her parents might have noticed, had they paid him any attention.

Then Hope found a letter, in Charity's hand. Just a few sentences – nothing that would have been viewed as indiscreet or incriminating to a rational eye. And there was no proof that it would ever have been handed over to the addressee. But its writing was an act of rebellion. Whatever her motive may have been, Hope ensured that the offending missive was soon in her mother's hands. Her screech of outrage could be heard a distance away, dispersing a gathering of crows in an adjacent field and sending chickens scuttling into the safety of their barn.

'Get your father!' Patience Wright shrieked, and Hope ran to find him.

But Ezra Wright was already on his way, having heard an echo of his wife's fury in a far-off place. Minutes later, Sam was intrigued, then perturbed, to see the frenzied pair hustling towards him, bellowing incoherent abuse as they ran. Once within range, Patience Wright waved the letter aggressively in his face to accompany the cacophony. Hope Wright sat on a hay bale to enjoy the spectacle.

'We spoke friendly just a few times, nothing more.' Sam nervously tried to calm the storm. 'No harm in that.'

'There's every harm in it – a boy like you getting your claws into our daughter.' Patience Wright paced around Sam as if marking out her territory.

'Forcing yourself upon her with your lustful ways.' Ezra Wright was more stationary, but equally inflamed, jabbing his finger into Sam's chest to underline the gravity of his offending. 'Tempting her with sweet words and hard luck stories.'

'Taking advantage of her innocence and good nature.'

'Luring her into writing all sorts of nonsense that should never enter a young girl's head.'

'And no doubt encouraging her with dangerous blether of your own.'

This was already Sam's longest conversation with the Wrights, or so it seemed, and it was far from over. He stared uncomprehendingly at his accusers, but with a feeling in the pit of his stomach that this would not end well.

'And we must pray there's been no indulgence in the sins of the flesh.' And there it was – Ezra Wright's biggest fear.

'Mr Wright, I'll not hear talk of fornication. Not in connection with our daughter.' Patience Wright was almost sick at the thought of it.

Sam's retorts were ever more desperate. 'There's been none of that, I swear it, nor anything else bad. I just needed a friend, someone to talk to. Everyone needs a friend, don't they? No harm in that. Look, I ain't seen no letter and I ain't written one neither. You know I can't write much beyond my own name.'

'Satan will always find a way.'

Sam looked towards the homestead, but Charity's only thought was self-preservation. Perched on the edge of her bed, trembling like a sapling in a thunderstorm, she could hear every word through the open window of her room. She knew she must keep quiet, stay put and yield to whatever parental retribution was forthcoming. That way, she might live to fight another day.

Sam turned back to face his tormentors. Their hate-filled eyes bored into his very soul, almost choking him with the force of their indignation. Still, he tried to reason with them. 'But what if she did want to talk to me? What's wrong with that? I'm just a normal lad, I ain't no monster.'

'We won't have our daughters wasting their lives on a gutter child…'

'… We're not ignorant people…'

'… We read the newspapers…'

'… We hear people talk…'

'… We know how this would have ended…'

'… One day your inheritance will catch up with you…'

'… It's in your blood, it will follow you to the ends of the earth…'

'… We must do what is best for our children…'

'… We must do what is best for our family.'

The Wrights competed furiously with each other for verbal space, their voices rising in pitch and volume, each interjection more feverish than the last. Finally they were spent, for a moment at least. Sam had done his best to decipher the bile that was aimed in his direction. He found himself shaking as he returned fire. 'You think I don't know how important family is? You don't have to convince an orphan boy about that.' He was not far from tears. 'Look, she felt sorry for me, that's all. She's not a halfwit – what else would she want with the likes of me?'

'But what if you were forced to marry, if you get my drift?'

'There you go again with your fornication, Mr Wright. Enough of it.'

Sam ignored Ezra Wright's preoccupation. Now a genuine anger was building inside him; they could insult him as much as they liked, but not his parents. 'Look, it's not my fault where I come from. I didn't ask to be born a pauper. I didn't make London what it is…'

'But you cannot escape it.'

'And my ma and pa were good people, not like some. Just poor, that's all. Worked hard when they could and when they couldn't they—'

'Went thieving…'

'Scraped by,' Sam insisted. 'They were not so very different from you.'

'How dare you compare us—'

Suddenly, Sam began to laugh, and the Wrights were momentarily silenced. He could see that logic and common sense had no place here. It was time they knew exactly what he felt.

'You're right. That was unfair,' he admitted. 'They were so much better than you.'

There were gasps of astonishment from Patience and Ezra Wright and suppressed giggles from Hope, for whom this was entertainment beyond her wildest dreams.

Fuelled by years of loneliness and rejection, Sam went on the attack. 'Just think of how you are with me. When I was shipped out to this godforsaken country, they promised me a proper family where I could be someone's son. Like I used to be. And have a sort of mother, like I used to have. And perhaps a father. And friends, to replace those I'd lost. I'd have to work, but that was fine, I don't mind that—'

'It was a business arrangement, nothing more,' Patience Wright snapped. 'That's all we signed for. We made that very clear to your Miss Hamilton. And to you.'

'The very first thing I said was that we wanted a working man but couldn't afford one,' her husband growled. 'I remember it clearly.'

Sam carried on undeterred. 'And they put me here, when I was still a child, in years anyway, but I was expected to do a man's job and be satisfied with being treated like one…'

'We made no promises beyond feeding and housing you and paying some wages, all of which we have done.'

'Yes, you've done all that. And I have worked hard, tried my best, and done quite well, I think.'

'We have no complaints on that score.'

'But you could have made me more welcome. That wouldn't have hurt you. Think what it's like not to hear a kind word, or see a smile aimed in your direction. Never to share a joke, or even a simple conversation. Not to be asked how you are and for there to be some interest in the answer.'

'Other labourers we've known don't need that.'

'But they were grown men!'

Suddenly, Patience Wright gave an ear-splitting squeal of frustration, barely human in its tone and frequency. She had said and heard enough. 'We are being led down a winding path away from the main issue. You will remember the instruction we gave you when first you came here? That you were to keep well away from our girls. You have blatantly disregarded this. And in doing so, you have endangered our family.' Patience Wright pulled herself up to her full height as she passed sentence, her arms folded so tightly they almost squeezed the breath from her body.

'Go on, discipline the boy.'

Sam looked round in desperation. 'Charity!' he called out. 'Tell 'em how it was.' There was no reply. 'I trusted you. Even told you about ma.' He thought he might have heard some sobbing, but nothing that would help him. 'Don't that mean something?'

Patience Wright was beside herself. 'I said, discipline the boy!'

But Sam stood his ground. He was no longer a boy, at least not in physique. Taller and quicker, and with youth on his side, he would be most people's favourite against Ezra Wright. His opponent was equally aware of the balance of power, and hesitated.

'Now!' Patience Wright screamed, her face pinching with malice and loathing until it was little more than a rasher of skin and bone.

Ezra Wright's decision was made for him. Sam might inflict some physical damage, but that could be repaired, whereas his wife's fury knew no bounds, nor was it constrained by any finite timescale; empires could rise and fall, and her anger would dissipate not one jot. Sam raised his fists in readiness. Wright slowly took off his thick coat and edged forward, launching a tentative assault, which Sam repelled with ease. Punches were thrown but few landed, and those that did caused little damage.

'Do I have to do it myself?'

Goaded into action, Wright gave up on using his fists and

looked round for a weapon. He picked up a lump of wood in the approximate shape of a club, a remnant from the making of a fence post and, taking heart and strength from its solidity, he moved in for the kill. As Sam took a step back, Patience Wright caught him a glancing blow to the head with a milking stool, sending him to the ground. The lump of wood came down on his back as he tried to rise. He was now at their mercy, and several further blows broke his spirit.

Ezra Wright stood over Sam, club at the ready, while his wife strode over to the stable. Soon she emerged brandishing a horsewhip. She handed it to her husband.

'This is God's work,' he intoned. 'Accept your punishment like a man.'

As Wright took the whip to him, Sam curled up in the dirt, arms protecting his face and leaving his back and limbs to bear the brunt of the assault. And in that moment a small voice spoke in his head, with clarity for the first time, but he recognised that it had long been striving to be heard. Perhaps not so much a voice, as it did not speak with volume – it was more an instinct, or an awareness of his true self – but it was simpler to give it a name. *Let them do as they wish*, it ordered him. *You are worthless, just as they say. If you were not so, they would want you to be their son. You had ideas above your station. You deserve this.* And Sam could see the sense in what the voice said. He surrendered to his fate; in the end he almost craved it.

The whip was not administered with full vigour, and the chastisement was soon over, its primary purpose being not to hurt but to shame. The Almighty might not have approved of permanent damage. And throughout the assault Patience Wright capered about in evangelical fervour.

'We must preserve the sanctity of family life,' she roared. 'We must shield our children from the evils of this world. You will learn from this and one day you will thank us for it.'

'The Lord protects those that protect themselves,' added her husband between lashes, although he did not quote the scripture that confirmed this.

And when sufficient punishment had been meted out, Ezra and Patience Wright knelt and prayed. 'We beseech you to forgive our errant daughter for her transgressions … restore her innocence that has so cruelly been impaired … and we pray that with your guidance she will henceforth exercise more discernment in her affections.'

Sam lay motionless, apart from the tears of pain and humiliation that coursed down his cheeks. In time, his body would heal, but he would not forget this day. The voice in his head was pleased. *Now you can truly wallow in your misfortune.* It laughed. *Before, you were only playing at it.* Sam listened to the voice and recognised the opportunity.

Ezra Wright hobbled into the farmhouse, exhausted by his righteous labours and carrying the scars of battle. A few minutes later he returned to the yard and stood over Sam, still prostrate where he had fallen.

Wright threw some coins in the dirt. 'The balance of what we owe you,' he spat. 'Now, get off my farm and don't ever come back.'

The Wrights retreated inside the farmhouse and slammed the door. Now it was Charity's turn to receive her dues, and her cries rang out as the strap descended on her outstretched hand.

When Patience Wright later emerged to feed the chickens, Sam was gone.

'Next time we'll get an ugly boy,' she mused, adding it to her list of chores.

FORTY

Now approaching twelve years of age, Margaret Walsh was cocooned in the embrace of a loving family, her life enriched yet further by old Pa's regular letters. She had completed her schooling, and had been pleased to put behind her the offhand treatment by her teacher, the sporadic name-calling by the children and the feeling of never quite fitting in. Now she earned her keep by cleaning for a neighbour and taking in washing from 'the Palace', as she called it, as well as working shifts in the family store.

The Palace was home to one of the elders of the Bank of Toronto, and he was the nearest thing to royalty in the town of Kingston. As she washed and scrubbed and laid washing out to dry, Margaret encountered a very different suite of clothes from the plain and workmanlike wardrobe that was the Bradleys' preference. Some outfits were contrived to intimidate in business, others to dazzle local society when at play, and even the more casual items were grand beyond her own experience. The children's clothes were merely smaller versions of the adult wear and seemed most impractical for a juvenile lifestyle. All this finery told a tale of wealth and influence, although Margaret was amused that even such luminaries wore undergarments that were recognisable as belonging to the same species.

Daisy was intent on teaching Margaret how to run the store. 'In case anything should ever befall us,' she would say, as Margaret clasped her hands over her ears and John protested about not tempting fate.

It was a statement of continuity and inheritance, and Margaret appreciated it for what it was.

Daisy was the driving force in the business, ordering stock, negotiating prices and managing the finances. Each night she would sit with a ledger and pen, counting the dollars and not disturbing her bed until each cent had been found. John knew his place: fetching, carrying and being sociable with the customers.

'Your ma lets me stack things. Other than that, I'm not to be trusted,' he once told Margaret, who thought it best not to mention the pile of boxes that had toppled over that morning.

Margaret threw herself into her role as storekeeper, learning through trial and error and the occasional 'quiet word' to Daisy from a customer who was less than satisfied. She grasped how to engage clientele in conversation without being overly intrusive and came to understand what information could be passed on to third parties without breaking a trust. She became quite a saleswoman ('Are you sure you only want one of these?') although occasionally too honest ('I wouldn't have that, it looks broke to me') and sometimes her background betrayed her, finding things exotic that others regarded as mundane ('It's only a salmon' she was once advised, somewhat disdainfully). Most customers were polite, and many were friendly, particularly those who knew John and Daisy best. A small number experienced some discomfort in her presence, but did their best to hide it, and only one or two walked out when they saw who would be serving them. Margaret learned to live with it, as she had at school.

Away from the store, she remained a solitary child, never happier than when she was reading, sewing or lost in thought. For the most part, you would not have known she was there, apart from the brief time when she tried to learn the fiddle, and then her presence was all too obvious. While she was happy to join in with gossip and nonsense, she still gave few clues as to her true feelings, and new Ma and Pa were never entirely sure what they might be. Whenever Daisy sought to pry, as she did from time to time, Margaret quickly retreated into her shell, and the exchange would be over.

One spring day, when her duties were complete, a letter arrived for Margaret. The beetle had been active again. As she had always done, Margaret took the letter to her room, and she was now practised at deciphering her father's somewhat erratic handwriting, so she did not need outside help to read it. There was a different tenor to this letter; Michael Walsh was not his usual self. After the usual hellos and enquiries about health and happiness, his mood darkened.

> *Things are not so good. The steelworks want less men now – they're not hiring new ones and are getting rid of some already here. And cutting back on wages for those that stay and expecting more hours in return. They say other places are making their own these days, so want less of ours... I expect my time will come soon, there's others that know more about the job than I do, and some have been here since it opened...*

The gloom descended further.

> *And there's no jobs to be had apart from steel, not round here, and any place is a bad place to be if you don't have*

work. We've bitter experience of that, my lovely. I can't go back to that again, not now I've known something better. I've not been feeling myself – I can barely drag myself from my bed some days, weighed down by it all. You can see there's less money in the town ... more men hanging around, drinking away what little they have, and beggars on every corner. Less money in my pocket too, just barely getting by these days...

And then the revelation.

I hear people talking – someone said they just built a steelworks in Canada and they're looking for skilled men to run it. Judging by where I write to, it's not too far from your place, and they reckon there'll soon be others. Some of the men said they might try their luck over there, and you know what, I might join them. What do you think to that? There's nothing to keep me here.

Margaret was trembling as she finished reading the letter, sporting the widest smile in Kingston, and with happy tears damping her cheeks. 'I can't believe it. Old Pa might come to live just down the road!' She read the letter again and again, as if doubting her own eyes, and there it was every time. But she could not tell new Ma and Pa – not yet. It would lead to misunderstandings and difficult conversations. Best to leave those for later, when everything was certain, and he was on his way. In the days after this, Daisy could see that Margaret was strangely buoyant and even more reluctant to talk, but she had learned not to prod her as to the reason.

Each year the Bradleys would mark the anniversary of Margaret's arrival into the family. It was typically a low-key affair, with Margaret insisting that it should be just the three of them.

'I don't know anyone else I would want to be there' she had often said, and everyone was very happy with that. On these days, the store would close early and there would be games and cake and dressing-up. Then Daisy might play the battered piano that sat in the corner of the parlour, and they would all be grateful that Margaret no longer owned a fiddle. And part way through, John would rise to his feet and insist on making a speech, with his audience cringing in mock, and sometimes real, embarrassment.

'It is now six years since this troublesome girl came into our lives,' he began this year's monologue, dodging a folded-up napkin with practised ease. 'And I can safely say that I have never been able to find anything about the house since then…'

'You never look properly!' heckled Margaret.

'It's always been that way,' added Daisy with feeling.

'And I am forever falling over things that she leaves lying about…'

'That's because you never wear your spectacles!' his audience chorused.

The speech carried on in similar vein until John put on a serious and quite emotional face. 'And so we remember that happy day when our family was made whole. I propose a toast to Margaret.'

'To Margaret!'

'To me!'

And they all clinked teacups.

Later that day, Daisy cooked a special meal which they enjoyed greatly, and then they played a few hands of whist, with John cheating outrageously while lamely protesting his innocence. There was laughter and kindness and love in abundance.

'It's a shame your old pa can't be here to see this,' Daisy declared, caught up in the moment.

It was a thing someone might say when they were confident that it could never happen.

'Well, next year he might be.' Margaret had not intended to let the news slip out, but slip out it did. And now she had to give the whole story. She nervously retrieved the letter from her room and read it out. She could guess what would come next.

'Why keep it a secret?' Daisy asked pointedly.

It was exactly the conversation that Margaret had wished to avoid. 'I thought you might worry and not be happy for me. I didn't want the joy taken away.'

'You once expected us to trust you, and we did. Why won't you trust us?'

'I'm not sure you've ever trusted me. Not where old Pa is concerned.' Margaret looked pointedly at Daisy, whose reddened face betrayed her guilt.

Now it was Daisy' turn to be reluctant to speak her mind, and instead she dived for cover under the practicalities of the situation. 'You shouldn't get your hopes up too soon…'

Any sense of celebration had disappeared from the room.

'It's a big step from him just chatting to some men, probably with a drink in his hand, to standing on a boat, having said goodbye to everything. I would hate for you to be disappointed.'

'I know how big a step it is. That was me all those years ago.'

'But it's not as simple as just turning up with a ticket and a trunk, as you did. He'll have all sorts to arrange and people to square…'

'I'm not stupid!'

'And a passage costs money. It doesn't sound as if he has the means to pay…'

Margaret gave up trying to interrupt and sat with a face of thunder.

'And the immigration people don't have to let him in. If things in England are as bad as he says, they'll be spoilt for choice, and they might have too many already…'

John stood behind Margaret, waving frantically for Daisy to stop.

'It could be years before he arrives, if he ever does…'

'Sounds to me like you don't want him here.'

For the first time, Margaret felt genuine anger towards new Ma and Pa. 'This was why I didn't tell you.' She was almost shouting. 'I might get to see my dear pa again – just imagine what that would mean to me. But you're inventing all these difficulties and making out he wouldn't be wanted here, when he's as good as any. And he won't be saying goodbye to things because he has more here than he has in England, which is nothing…'

Daisy was about to respond, but John put his hand over her mouth. Better that Margaret should be uninterrupted.

'It seems it was fine when he was at the end of a letter, all those miles away. But now he's close, or might be, suddenly there's no welcome for him. Don't you start thinking of him as some folks think of me, as not being as good as them. He's a decent man, a kind man.'

'That's not what we meant at all.' John had contrived to arrange his thoughts into the words that perhaps should have been said first. 'I am sorry that it has all come out wrong so far,' he began, for once talking quietly, barely louder than a whisper. 'Without meaning to, we have hidden our true feelings behind some ridiculous detail that we don't know anything about, and we did so because it is too difficult to find the right thing to say. But I will try.'

Margaret sat quiet as his words tumbled out, stony-faced but listening.

'Of course we see how wonderful it would be for you if old Pa were here, and nothing would please us more than for you to be that happy.'

Margaret wondered whether it really was 'we' and 'us', and not just 'I'.

'But please try to understand. We've told you about how we so longed for a child, and they said it wasn't possible. Imagine how we felt. And then you came along, and you are everything to us, just as you are to old Pa.'

John flashed a glance at Margaret. Slowly her expression was softening.

'The way we see it, he gave you up when he had no life to speak of, but perhaps now he has one, and we don't know that he won't try to reclaim you.'

Daisy wiped away a tear. 'I'm just scared that we might lose you,' she sniffled. 'I couldn't bear that. We waited so long for you.'

By now Margaret was feeling twinges of embarrassment. She had not wanted to hurt them, and she looked for a way out of the conversation. 'But you're my ma and pa now, and I never want that to change,' she said in a voice she hoped was reassuring. 'Old Pa's not a man to cause trouble, he'll just be grateful that I'm cared for. And him being here won't mean I love you any less. Look, I've taken your name. I'm a Bradley now.'

'We know that in our heart of hearts, I'm sure. And of course we are very happy to welcome him to Canada. I might even make a speech.' Then John gave Margaret an enormous hug and she responded, slowly at first but eventually in kind, and then Daisy joined in. The celebration resumed, albeit with rather less abandon than before.

Later Margaret went to her room, much relieved. The conversation she had been dreading had not gone to plan, but it had turned out well in the end. And at least it was over. Now she could dream without fear.

Downstairs, Daisy stared nervously at John.

'What else could I say?' he mumbled.

But Margaret's dream was soon to fade. She answered old Pa's letter with pages of excitement about how good it would be to see him, and did he have a definite date for when it would be? What would he like to eat when he arrived? Would he spend Christmas with them, even if he had his own place somewhere else? And a hundred other questions. It was several weeks before she was able to intercept the postman and take a reply to her room, but its contents were not what she expected or wished for.

> *My dearest Margaret, I seem to have misled you badly, for which I am most sorry. When I last wrote I was just thinking out loud really – about Canada, I mean. And to be honest, I might have had a pot of ale or possibly two, which always sparks my imagination. Things are not good here, but I still have some work, and changing country would be a step into the unknown, although I've done that before and lived to tell the tale. And now it's out in the open, the more I turn it over in my head, the more sense it makes. So leave it with me and I will see what I can do. But I am not likely to be with you for Christmas, my lovely…*

Margaret threw the letter to the floor, stifling her tears lest she be heard, a deep void settling into the pit of her stomach where once there had been a tingle of anticipation. She was too embarrassed to admit, even to herself, that Daisy had been right in her misgivings, and so she kept this letter private: new

Ma and Pa were not even aware of its arrival. Margaret was very subdued for several weeks and spent even more time in her room. And each time a new letter arrived she approached it with trepidation, not wishing to be disappointed again, desperately trying, and failing, not to pin her hopes on comments such as 'things get worse here by the day' and 'I am still thinking about that thing…'. John and Daisy knew something was wrong, and Daisy worried, as she always did, but they felt unable to pry into what it might be.

'She will tell us in her own good time,' John said, although Daisy doubted it. But when Michael failed to appear, and there was no further mention of his coming, Margaret's source of discontent was clear. New Ma and Pa kept a diplomatic silence.

FORTY-ONE

It had taken Sam Barney the rest of the day to walk back to Alice Hamilton's Kingston centre. He had nowhere else to go. It was a miserable slog of bitterness and shame, fuelled by unbridled rage and abject self-pity. At first, he followed the main track, his battered body in need of the gentlest of surfaces. He had not been walking long when a cart approached from behind. For a moment the driver kept pace with him, perhaps with a view to offering a ride, but when he saw the bruising to Sam's face and the welts on his arms, and in particular the hostility of his expression, he took fright and hurried his horse along. From then on, Sam took to the forest where his progress might be more anonymous, even if it was at the cost of pain and speed.

The voice in Sam's head was now a constant companion, shaping and twisting his mind into a certain way of thinking. At times Sam would take heed and follow its advice, while at others he tried to shut it out. The inner struggle exhausted him as much as the journey.

You could just lie down here and never move again, the voice said. *Think how they would feel if they had caused your death.*

'They wouldn't give a damn,' Sam decided and limped on.

Come nightfall, he stood outside the doors to the centre, with liquid eyes and raging heart, debating whether the privations of a night on the street were preferable to the embarrassment of accepting shelter. Eventually his brooding and suspicious presence was noticed, and someone expendable was sent to investigate. With Sam not at his most communicative, it took some time to ascertain who he was and what he wanted, but eventually he was escorted inside to see Alice Hamilton, who happened to be in residence, having recently brought over a party of children. He found her sitting in faux splendour behind a desk that aspired to be oak, but which had fallen short in its ambition. A grandfather clock kept time somewhat haphazardly in a corner, while the walls were adorned with landscapes depicting agricultural serenity; there were no scenes of children being whipped.

Sam stood sullenly before Alice, shifting from one foot to the other to alleviate the pain of putting weight on tortured limbs, each movement exaggerated so that perhaps she might offer him a seat. But Alice was determined that the dirt and dried blood should have no contact with her furniture, nor was she keen for Sam to get comfortable and outstay his welcome, and so he remained standing. And it was fortunate that she did not recognise the boy who had complained about the food on his passage to Canada, otherwise she might have been even less accommodating.

I am in luck that all the children have been distributed, otherwise I would have some explaining to do, she thought, gazing upon the picture of misery before her.

But before she could ask how he happened to arrive in such a state, Sam piped up. 'So, what are you going to do about this, missus?'

Alice was not accustomed to being addressed so informally but let it pass.

'I lost my job for no reason. And then they beat me. That ain't right, is it?'

'Tell me exactly what happened and spare me no detail.'

Sometime later, when Sam was still in full flow, Alice regretted being so encouraging. He told his story in a piteous voice, but it was peppered with volatile interjections, and he broke off several times to wipe away tears. Some of his vitriol was reserved for Alice herself. 'You said they would treat me as family,' he snapped.

'I would not have been so definite. Some of my children do find themselves in that happy position, but others do not. It can be as much the fault of the child as the employer.'

'So, I'm to blame, am I?'

'I did not say that. Please continue.'

And when Sam described his friendship with Charity and the secret nature of it, Alice was not as supportive as he had hoped. 'So, your employers were not entirely unprovoked, it seems, given that you wilfully disobeyed an instruction.'

'Talking to a girl deserves a whipping, does it?'

'I agree that the punishment does not fit the crime. But I do not wish my children to get a reputation for indiscipline. It will make them more difficult to place.'

Eventually, Sam ran out of words. Light-headed with hunger and exhaustion, he had only one thing on his mind. 'What now, missus? How can we hurt them?'

Alice had been dreading this line of enquiry. 'You certainly deserve some redress, but I struggle to see how we might obtain it.' She sighed. 'We could try the courts, but I know from bitter experience that anything short of murder is seen as reasonable chastisement when it involves one of our children, and even that would mostly be excused.'

'So, you can't help me get some kind of revenge.'

'They'll not get another child from me.' It sounded feeble even as she said it.

'Is that it?' Sam looked disdainfully at Alice. 'That don't even inconvenience 'em. There are others that will gladly hand one over.'

'And I shall write them a strongly worded letter.'

'They'll quake in their boots!'

'And I will pass the Wrights' name to the Immigration Department. Perhaps they can blacklist them.' Alice sighed again. 'But I doubt they will.' She looked sadly at the defeated boy who stood before her. 'I'm afraid there's nothing else that can be done.'

A nurse bathed and dressed Sam's wounds, and the next morning a doctor was called. After a perfunctory examination he declared that there should be no scarring, at least none that would be visible.

Three days later a wagon drew up outside the centre and Sam's trunk was thrown from it. When he opened it, he found there was little inside. He had long outgrown the clothes with which he had originally been furnished, and their replacements, grudgingly provided by Patience Wright and often fashioned by her own fair hand out of inappropriate odds and ends, were ill-fitting, inadequate in number and often lacking in robustness and weatherproofing. The Sankey hymn book was still there, seemingly unused, as was the Bible, whose pages were similarly unturned. There was no sign of *The Pilgrim's Progress*.

Alice summoned Sam to discuss his future, and he stood before her, sullen and glowering.

'There is always demand, particularly for an older boy or the half-man that you are,' she began positively. 'People will always want strength and experience, and you have that in spades. It's probably best to look elsewhere in the province, a good distance away from your first placement. Tongues will no doubt be active locally.'

(As indeed they were, with Patience Wright scaling new heights of invective.)

'I suppose I have no choice.'

'You have no choice.'

'Then so be it. If someone is prepared to take the risk.'

And risk it was. Sam was in a poisonous mood, a potent mix of self-loathing and a thirst for vengeance. Them farmers, they think we're the scum of the earth, so I'll not disappoint them, he thought.

There was one more thing on Sam's mind, an itch he couldn't scratch, a slight he could not forgive. 'Heard anything about the boy, Arthur Dilkes?' His old comrade-in-arms had been much on his mind in recent days, the rainbow memories of their time together a vivid contrast to the current monochrome bleakness. 'Is he doing all right? I'll bet he ain't been beaten, has he? Too clever for that.'

Alice remembered the name and rummaged in a cupboard, emerging with a copy of the letter that Arthur had written to her the previous year. Sam looked blankly at the paper for a moment before passing it back to Alice to read for him. Its optimism cut him to the quick.

'He's got all the time in the world to write to you, but I don't deserve a word,' he choked.

'Did you write to him?'

'Those devils wouldn't let me have no implements for it. And I ain't got the education anyhow.' And the voice in Sam's head chirped up. *You see, he has no interest in you. You cannot trust him. Worse still, he is to blame for your suffering. Dragging you here to this godforsaken place. Forget him.*

A week later, Sam was back on the road. He was first sent to a farm that was considered a safe distance beyond the range of any gossip. His trunk was replenished, but not his appetite for taking orders, while his opinion of Canadian farmers was jaundiced beyond redemption. Within eight weeks he was back at the home, with an explanatory letter from the farmer burning a trail behind him.

He is no earthly use to me. I don't know where he's been

before, but they can't have put up with him. I expect they sent him away, and good riddance. I was expecting a boy that would make some sort of difference, and he does, but not in the direction you want. He is so terrible slow I cannot do anything with him. And unreliable too. And won't do as he's told. I cannot put any dependence on him.

The letter continued in similar vein for two pages.

By now Alice Hamilton was safely back in England but had left instructions for her staff in the event that Sam should return before she did so herself. And so other placements followed, each shorter than the last, Sam's length of stay being in perfect correlation to the savagery of the critique that accompanied his homecoming. Complaints included that he was 'dirty', 'disobedient', 'drunk', 'obstinate', 'untruthful', 'profane', 'unaccountably absent' and 'forward with the girls of the house'.

In frustration, one farmer took his whip to Sam. He immediately regretted it, although he did not wish to involve the courts.

At their wits' end, the staff of the home wrote to Alice to advise her that Sam was now in permanent residence, having exhausted all other avenues.

On her next trip to Canada she was quick to confront him. 'Let me hear the story of each placement, and perhaps we can learn from them,' she said despairingly.

But Sam's attempts to explain the frequency and severity of these breakdowns began with him uninterested in the exercise, becoming increasingly half-hearted until he could no longer be bothered to try. First it was: 'They looked on me as a servant.'

'That's more or less what you were paid to be,' Alice snapped.

And the next one: 'They treated me like dirt.'

'That is unfortunate, but if that is your reason for leaving then I fear you will struggle to hold down any employment.'

And the next: 'They spoke to me funny.'

'I believe they might originally have hailed from Scotland.'

Alice's attempt at a joke fell on stony ground.

And finally: 'They wanted someone bigger.'

'Bigger than you?' Alice asked in surprise.

'Or possibly smaller.'

'Why would they want someone smaller?'

'Maybe younger.'

'Someone who could do less work than you?'

'Then older.'

'When higher wages would be due on account of age?'

'Look, they wanted anyone but me, all right?'

Eventually, Alice was left with no alternative. 'There is nothing for you here. I must send you back to England.'

'Branded a failure, no doubt.'

Alice felt some sympathy for the lad. 'It has not all been of your own doing, and people will recognise that when they know the full story.'

'What if I don't want that? What's there for me back home? More of the same?'

'If you stay here, I can only see trouble ahead for you. The courts may be slow to help an innocent British child, but they are devilish quick to punish one that is seen to offend. And, rightly or wrongly, given the way you are with people, one day someone will make such an accusation against you that you'll likely see the inside of a Canadian prison.'

Sam thought for a moment. When he spoke, there was an air of resignation and finality in his voice. 'I'm past caring. Make your arrangements if you must.'

And Alice did.

But that night, when everyone was in bed, Sam crept though the home carrying a small hessian bag that contained a few essentials – mostly scraps of food that he had liberated from recent mealtimes, now misshapen and tarnished due to being secreted about his person until they could be transported more hygienically. He entered Alice's office and made straight for her desk. In his encounters with her, Sam had formed a view of what her desk might contain and, happily, one drawer yielded up a sum of money that had been intended for wages and provisions. He pocketed the treasure and, opening a window, escaped into the street and ran off.

The next morning, Alice noted the absence of boy and currency. She drew the inevitable conclusion but decided to take no action; that much she could do for him.

Then, two weeks later, an officer from the provincial police force called at the centre.

FORTY-TWO

The peace of a spring morning was fractured by a scream of intense pain and the squall of equine distress. Amelia Gait hurried from the kitchen, child in arms, to assess the damage. Arthur Dilkes lay in the dirt outside the stable, while a horse ran free around the yard, repeatedly charging in to threaten the helpless figure before veering away sharply at the last instant, only to repeat its orbit.

Fearing for her child if she stepped into the melee, Amelia hung back and took stock from the safety of the front porch.

'My leg – he kicked me. I'm hurt bad, missus.'

Amelia could see Arthur's bloodied leg, even from a distance, and knew the injury was grave. She waited until the horse was at the furthest point of its gallop and ran to fetch her husband from an adjacent field, where he was sowing the new year's grain crop. Robert Gait calmed the horse and secured it to a post before examining Arthur's leg.

'We must get him to the doc. I'll get the cart ready. Stay with him for now.'

Amelia knelt beside Arthur and cradled his head in her arms.

'I'm scared, missus,' he breathed. 'How is it? I dare not look closely.'

'You'll be proper cared for, we'll make sure of that. But it's best you don't look down for now.' Ignoring her own advice, Amelia found her gaze morbidly attracted to the damage, and she struggled not to retch at the gruesome violation. 'I cannot ride with you, I have the children, but I will make you as comfortable as I can.'

They slowly lifted Arthur onto the back of the cart, but it was not an easy transfer, and despite their attentiveness his damaged leg bumped over various obstacles, producing primal outbursts from its owner and leaving a trail of blood in its wake. Amelia propped him up and secured him as best she could against the motion of the cart, giving him a piece of rope on which to bite should the pain overcome him. Each jolt, of which were many on the rutted tracks, saw the rope in use, and the slow progress of the cart prolonged the agony. Yet Robert dared not ask the horse for speed, as further torment would result.

Dr Cranston heard the cart approaching from a distance and was waiting at his door. A cursory examination of the patient told him what he needed to know. 'The break is far from clean, and there is a good chance he might lose the leg,' he diagnosed. 'However, I am loathe to treat any SAD child for injuries such as this, and the hospital will feel the same. The expense is significant, and there is no certainty that I will be reimbursed. In my experience, the farmer will insist that the child must pay, but they have no money, as the emigration agent keeps hold of their wages, if any have been paid at all. In turn, the agent claims that the farmer should foot the bill instead. And there I am in the middle, trying to earn an honest living.'

'I'll make sure you get paid. You have my word,' Gait barked, taking steps towards the doctor. 'Now, treat the boy.'

Robert Gait was not a man whose word you doubted, at least not to his face. Cranston sighed deeply and went into his house, emerging with his medical bag after what seemed like an unwarranted delay. He plied Arthur with a potion that he claimed would alleviate the pain, but which failed miserably to do so, and reluctantly agreed to take him to the hospital at Belleville, around ten miles further down the track.

Manoeuvring Arthur from one transport to another was a delicate operation and not without mishap, heaping further suffering upon the patient. In theory, the doctor's carriage was a more comfortable ride, its suspension being superior to that of the cart, but the rugged track overwhelmed any respite. It was more than an hour before the carriage arrived at the hospital, after which there were further transfers until Arthur finally came to rest on the bed he would occupy for many weeks. Nurses fussed around him and a within an hour a doctor paid him a call.

'I will not immediately take the leg,' he advised cheerily. 'We will see if it can be set and persuaded to mend. But be warned: even if this is successful, your mobility might be permanently inhibited, perhaps quite severely. And if it doesn't mend...' The doctor saw no need to finish the sentence.

Arthur was uprooted yet again, this time to an operating room where ether was applied with a confidence that belied the inexactness of the science. The errant limb was arranged into a more traditional format and encased in lashings of plaster. Arthur awoke sometime later, his body anchored by the weight of the cast and his mind stilled by the various potions that had been administered.

Robert and Amelia Gait, accompanied and hindered by their two children, were quick to visit. Arthur cut a despondent figure, ashen-faced and a prisoner to dark thoughts. 'What if I lose the leg? Or can't walk proper on it?' he wailed. 'How will I make any sort of living? No one wants a cripple. Never mind having my own place and being my own master, like I dreamed of. How can I clear land and raise crops if I can't even move about the place?'

'It may not come to that,' Amelia tried to reassure him, but without much conviction. 'You see men return from all sorts of mishaps and still able to work.'

'More likely you see them begging on the street.'

'You've got too much time to think, and that's always dangerous,' Gait chimed in almost dismissively. 'Things get out of all proportion and every possibility seems a bad one. You've done that before about other things, and no good will come of it.'

Arthur looked sadly at his lower body and the structure that encased much of it. 'I don't think I'm out of proportion. Not this time.'

But Gait ploughed on. 'Just remember, you've been through far worse in your short life and come out laughing.'

'That were different – in the end it was always down to me. But here, I'm at the mercy of nature and doctors, and I can't say which I trust the least.'

The visit lapsed into silence. Arthur was in no mood for Gait's unthinking interjections and pretended to drop in and out of sleep when the exchanges became too vexing. Amelia was preoccupied with attending to the children, the elder of whom was intent on exploration while the younger had a regular need for food and changing. Never the greatest conversationalist, Gait himself seemed distracted and was less encouraging towards Arthur than he might have been.

'Will I be all right to come home to you?' Arthur enquired in a small, sad voice when no offer was forthcoming.

'Of course, to start with.'

'What about further down the line? What if I can't work enough for you? Or even not work at all?'

'We'll have to see. You know we can't have someone not pulling their weight.'

'Mr Gait, I need to speak with you,' Amelia interrupted. 'Let us stand outside for a moment.'

Gait knew better than to disobey his wife when she was wearing her serious face, and so they found a quiet spot where they might disagree without too much of an audience.

'Just listen to yourself, Robert Gait. There's that poor stricken lad, and all you can do is wash your hands of him.'

Gait stood sullenly, staring out of a window at nothing in particular. 'Of course I'm worried for the boy,' he growled. 'It is a grievous injury, and he is right to think he might not recover fully. And yes, that throws his ambitions into question. But what concerns me more is that I was obliged to give my word that the medics will be paid, and we have not the means to do so. You know how badly we are placed.'

Indeed, the previous year had delivered a poor harvest. The spring rains had been too plentiful, while the temperature gauge had not risen sufficiently quickly, and the yield and quality of the crop had suffered. Money was tight and provisions were low.

'It's not like it was when it was just the two of us. If we didn't eat today, we would still be here tomorrow. Now we have the boys, and I won't have them going without. I'll do whatever it takes.' Gait beat his fists together to emphasise the point.

'Likewise, but we can't—'

'And we are without his labour for this season, and possibly beyond. He might never work again. We cannot afford to hire a man, but if we don't then we shall have even less to sell. And on top of this, you expect us to support an invalid?'

'You must not disown him. It's like he's our boy too.'

'But he's not though, is he?'

Amelia Gait glared at her husband. 'You will look back on this moment and not be proud of yourself.'

Gait hemmed and hawed, but he knew that his wife was right. 'Look, we can have him for a stretch, I'm not that cruel, but there are only so many hours in the day and there is a limit to what the pair of us can do. There will come a time when enough is enough.'

'I know that, but he doesn't need to. Not yet.'

They returned to Arthur's bedside, where he was expecting the worst. 'I can tell what was said from your faces. I know you too well.'

Gait allowed Amelia to do all the talking.

'We need to think. About what's for the best,' she said.

'I've always done well by you. Worked hard. Helped you out.'

Gait was about to say 'and been paid for it' until he saw his wife's expression and thought better of it. 'We know that, and we'll do all we can to help you.'

But Arthur knew that it might not be enough.

And the Gaits doing all they could did not extend to visiting regularly, and when they did materialise, time was always pressing, and the conversation was superficial at best. Arthur knew that this did not bode well.

He wrote to Alice Hamilton from his hospital bed.

My leg is broken and badly splintered, and its future is uncertain… I have been in the hospital for three weeks and they say I will have to stay several more to see if it has healed and who knows how much longer if it has not… There are bills that are mounting up … the hospital mentions it often and I remember the doc that brought me here was talking about money, although I had other things on my mind at the time. Who will pay for this? You are holding wages for me that I am not yet old enough to take, and I'll need that money to start me off in life once my time with the mister is over, if I have

> *any sort of life after this. Please advise me what I should do.*

It was not uncommon for Alice to receive a letter of this nature. Farming was a dangerous game, particularly for those not born into it – sharp tools, applied with force, unpredictable animals and any number of things that might topple over onto an unsuspecting farmhand. She immediately wrote to the Gaits.

> *We have received a letter from this boy. It appears that he has met with an accident and that the damage occurred while engaged with his duties on the farm. Under these circumstances, you will, of course, be liable to pay all costs in connection with his treatment and maintenance at the hospital.*

Robert Gait was not impressed, and Amelia had to cover the ears of their older boy in case he remembered what he heard.

'It's like the doc said – there's always a row over money when a SAD boy gets hurt,' Gait protested, and he wrote back to Alice by return with a vehement denial of his liability, although the reply was somewhat less forceful, and rather more polite, once Amelia had seen a first draft.

Two weeks later, a further letter arrived from Alice Hamilton.

> *It is difficult for me to pronounce definitively without a more intimate knowledge of the circumstances. But unless it could be shown that the accident was a direct result of negligence or carelessness on the boy's part, I am strongly of the opinion that if the case went to court you would be held responsible for payment of the medical expenses, if nothing else.*

Further shielding of ears was required. Then Gait prepared the cart, and he set off for the hospital at Belleville, on this occasion with a motive that was more than just pastoral – and without the civilising influence of his wife.

When Gait got there, Arthur was not in the best of moods. 'I've not seen you for a while. Forgotten where I was?'

'There's not much time left in the day now we don't have no help.'

'I didn't choose to be here, you know.'

Gait could hold back no longer and thrust Alice's letters into Arthur's face. 'What have you been telling her, to make her say that I must pay? You know full well we don't have no spare money for this. We can barely feed ourselves, and on top of that we must make do without your labour, which will hit us even harder.'

'I just said what happened. I never asked you to pay. I don't know how this works.'

'Tell me again exactly how you ended up here.'

'I can't remember much about it. I went to get the horse, and next thing I know I'm on the ground with bits of my leg sticking through.'

'You must have done something to unnerve the animal. I need to be able to say it was your fault.'

Gait was at his most intimidating, and Arthur was in no position to resist. 'Look, mister, I don't want this to cause trouble between us. I'll still need a home when I get out of here. Anything else will have to wait. Say what you want, and I will back you up.'

The next day Gait wrote back to Alice in a more controlled fashion.

The colt that hurt him was never known to kick before, so it must be down to the boy. He says he was hurrying and may have touched the animal without it knowing he was there, so that is probably what set it off. I am not able to pay his bills, nor am I obliged to do so. Any fault lies with the boy… The money will have to come from his wages. It is a shame that it will damage his prospects, but it cannot be helped…

By the time Alice read this, she had received a further letter from Arthur that, by remarkable coincidence, repeated Gait's version of events almost word for word. She breathed a sigh of relief at the consistency of the evidence and drafted a letter to Robert Gait.

Whatever the rights and wrongs of the accident, the boy is very unwilling to enter into any dispute or cause any ill feeling regarding the expenses arising from his mishap. Accordingly, he has requested that all costs should be met from the wages that we hold in trust for him. He is now old enough to form an intelligent judgement, and I have no desire or intention to take any course which would be in opposition to his wishes. Therefore, I shall do as he says.

So, the matter was settled to everyone's satisfaction. Except Arthur, lying immobile in a state of atrophy, undisturbed save for basic nursing, and railing at the unfairness of a world in which each ray of hope merely served to illuminate the despair that would inevitably follow. Gone was the canny lad who ruled the roost, who was always in control, who was never without a plan. Self-pity had moved in, unpacked and made itself at home. And this time he could not talk himself out of it.

FORTY-THREE

Alice Hamilton had a long sea journey in which to collect her thoughts. Even when she had assembled them and put them in some sort of order, they brought her no comfort. She did not forage for patrons among the wealthy, as was her normal habit for passing the time. Her story had been undermined by recent events, even if she was in the mood to tell it, which she was not. Haunted by the ghost of Simeon Harding, Alice rarely left her cabin. When the storms hit, they were barely a distraction, the upheaval of the ship a mere trifle compared to the turbulence in her head.

On the quayside, Alice was met by an associate with news that she had been summoned to meet the Deputy Minister at the Department of Agriculture. She had encountered him before, as the individual responsible for ensuring that Canadian farms were fully staffed, and she had found him to be a man with whom she could do business. But on this occasion, she was not so sure. Would he try to blame her for Simeon Harding's death? Or perhaps for having emigrated an unsuitable child and then wantonly placing him in danger? And because of it, would he now say that her services were no longer required? Or worse still, might he attempt to set the law on her?

'Pull yourself together, woman,' she told herself. 'It was not you that wielded the axe handle.'

The associate handed over various papers that might be of use, and Alice made haste for the Ottawa train. Some hours later, she was shown in to see her host, and she made herself as comfortable as she could in the circumstances. Over the years, she had met a plethora of officials on both sides of the Atlantic, all of whom were quartered in what she considered to be unnecessary splendour, and the Deputy Minister was no exception. His office was of a size where it could have housed a pauper family and made them feel that they had improved their lot. And the desk behind which he sat was immeasurably larger than it needed to be, given that most of the paperwork was done elsewhere. But there were noticeable differences between Ottawa and London. In general, the room felt less steeped in history than its English equivalent, as one might expect from a country that was almost brand-new. And while a likeness of Queen Victoria dominated one wall, the remainder were adorned with serene landscapes and colourful studies rather than forbidding portraiture of predecessors, perhaps simply because there were no such individuals. Moreover, a general untidiness suggested that there were fewer underlings to maintain order, with such a class yet to evolve in the Dominion.

The Deputy Minister got straight down to business. 'I will not detain you long over the Harding boy,' he began, much to Alice's surprise. 'It will be dealt with by the courts, one way or another, and the government will keep a distance from it, as should you. Those opposed to immigration will seize on anything they can, and we might present an easy target for them.'

'I hope there will be justice for the boy. Each night I pray for his soul.'

'You're better off praying that we get the right judge.' The Deputy Minister took a long swig of his tea and pulled a face, quickly realising that it was lacking in whisky. He remedied this via a hip flask. 'I have seen reports that he was a sickly child and mentally deficient. Many have wondered why he was brought here. Can you explain?'

Alice had prepared her defence to some degree and presented it with her usual authority. 'It is true he had only one functioning eye, but that was plenty for the very basic work that should have been asked of him. You do not require perfect vision to lift a bale or haul a plough. Nor should such work have been beyond a simpleton, if that was his capacity. And while he was not the sturdiest, there was nothing to suggest he could not have survived the reasonable application of the axe handle.'

'So, you believe the farmer to have murdered the boy through overuse of the implement?'

'I am convinced of it.' Alice rummaged in a pocket and produced a crumpled document. 'I have also found a record of the farmer's application, and there is no mention of him being a solitary man, without even the support of a wife. I might have placed a more resilient boy there, had I known that he would be relied upon to such an extent.'

The Deputy Minister nodded but did not pass an opinion.

'Will I be needed to give evidence at the trial?' asked Alice a little nervously.

'I think not. We can take a written submission, but I suspect your presence might be counterproductive. While most of the jurors will be fair, there will inevitably be some who do not look kindly upon those responsible for immigrant children, and I would rather the case was decided on the facts and not biased by preconceptions.'

'But I would welcome the opportunity to clear my name, as it were.'

The Deputy Minister laughed, somewhat unkindly, Alice felt.

'Have you forgotten your previous appearance in one of our courts?' He smirked. 'That girl of yours, remember? No, I would stay well clear of it this time.'

Alice bristled at the suggestion that she was incapable, although it was tinged with some relief at not having to repeat the experience.

But before she could respond, the Deputy Minister had changed the subject. 'I am plagued by your wretched Local Government Board,' he announced angrily, suddenly thumping the desk in frustration.

This was a subject that Alice could happily talk about all day. 'It is not my Local Government Board, and so am I, if it is any consolation.'

'They are exercised about the death of the Harding boy, of course, and that has prompted their recent intervention. But it has been coming for some time. That chief inspector of theirs started it off, asking all those questions…'

'I know the man you mean. I had to sit through his conclusions.'

'And no doubt twisting what was said, particularly by the children…'

Alice was less sure of that.

'And now we are expected to inspect each workhouse child in their placement and confirm their wellbeing. Every year, mind you. And they will not allow any more of them to be emigrated until we surrender to this demand.'

'I was aware of that.' Alice plucked up the courage to voice what she knew would be an unpopular opinion. 'Perhaps that is where the responsibility should lie. I have been thinking about this. It is your country that benefits from the children. And if there is mistreatment, it is from your authorities that redress would be sought. There is a logic to what they ask.'

It was not what the Deputy Minister wanted to hear, and Alice could feel the convivial atmosphere dissipate.

'That is not how we see it,' he replied coldly. 'Such an imposition would be wholly disproportionate. Which is why I am meeting with all the emigration agents to ask if instead they would conduct inspections of their own children. It might be enough to appease your Board.'

Alice could not help but laugh. 'Deputy Minister, I have not the time nor resources to visit each one, and certainly not each year. I do not have battalions of functionaries at my disposal…'

'Perhaps we could make it a condition of us doing business with you.'

Alice ignored the threat. 'Sir, I have emigrated over two thousand children in my time. How would it be possible for one woman to do as you ask?'

'But if your government remains responsible for these workhouse children, as they claim, then so do the people who brought them here. Those who have profited from them.'

'I had always thought it was Canada that profited. Otherwise, why pay for their entry?' Alice was always sensitive to accusations that she benefited financially, and she could not hide her disdain for the comment. 'And to be clear, I make no gain from my activities in the way you insinuate. Any income I enjoy is ploughed back into my work. I live off my inheritance.'

The Deputy Minister could see that he had touched a nerve and backed off. 'Whatever the rights and wrongs, we have a decision to make. And while we do not want any interruption in the supply of children, that should not be at any cost. Perhaps our government can merely pretend to agree to carry out these inspections, then by the time anyone notices their absence, Canada might have all the children it needs.'

By this point the Deputy Minister was more thinking aloud than expecting a response. 'Or we could cover any labour shortfall with greater numbers of immigrant men and women, particularly those of foreign extraction. The British government won't like that, I'll warrant, and that might focus their thinking. Or perhaps agents such as yourself might increase the flow of the waifs and strays.'

'I am surprised that they are not also to be inspected,' Alice noted, well aware that George Moore had made sure he included them in his investigation. 'Why would the Board be so protective of the one and so careless of the other?'

'Apparently, those that have not enjoyed a workhouse stay are "beyond their remit", as they have said more than once.'

'But a child is a child.'

'Apparently not all are equal.'

Despite their failure to agree, recent events had prompted a change in Alice's thinking, although she did not mention this to the Deputy Minister; he was bound to want more than she was prepared to offer. That evening she sat in her room at a local inn and reached some conclusions. Whilst she found it preposterous to try to do as the Deputy Minister had asked, she could see some value in an inspection regime. And clearly the Canadians could not be trusted to deliver it. 'So, this year I will remain in Canada until just before the snows and visit as many of my placements as I can,' she decided. 'It is June now, and I have a good number of free weeks, although even that will be no more than a drop in the ocean. And I will have to rely on others to arrange my July and September sailings, but at least I will be here to receive them.' And to keep her spirits up, she kept reminding herself that there was only so much she could do.

The next day, Alice took the earliest train from Ottawa and arrived at her Kingston centre in the middle of the morning. After a reviving bath and light luncheon, she settled herself down in her office and was presented with a pile of correspondence that had accumulated since her most recent visit, together with certain items that had been overlooked in her rush to depart for England at the end of the previous season. In this second bundle were two letters from Lily Mudd, recounting her experiences in graphic detail and begging for help. Alice read the letters with a sinking heart and burgeoning guilt.

'Men are barbarians,' she cursed, hurrying to her rooms to prepare for travel.

FORTY-FOUR

And so Alice Hamilton rode to the rescue of Lily Mudd, the long-anticipated and much delayed avenging angel. Lily's placement was some twenty miles distant and unconnected to the railway, meaning a wearisome expedition by road and track. Quickly packing a small bag, just in case, Alice summoned her driver and departed immediately, rereading the child's letters time and again to make sure she had not mistaken their contents, her mood darkening with each perusal. It was tortuous progress, with every jolt and judder adding a physical bruise to match that already inflicted on her state of mind.

By late afternoon, the farmer espied a carriage slowly moving towards him, and he stood four-square in the middle of the yard awaiting its arrival. He watched as a diminutive and seemingly innocuous woman alighted with difficulty amid a certain loss of decorum, taking pleasure in not offering her any assistance, and finding humour in her struggle. The yard was more akin to a swamp after recent rain and the woman soon found that she was inappropriately dressed, her skirts trailing in the mire, her shoes unsuited to the mud and threatening to remain stationary while her feet moved on. This was topped off by a bonnet that flapped precariously in the stiff breeze.

The farmer remembered Alice Hamilton from their previous encounter, and he snarled in anticipation of renewing her acquaintance. Bristling with indignation and primed for a fight, he pulled his hat down over his eyes to contrive an aura of menace. If this was the reckoning, he did not feel immediately endangered. Indeed, he began to relish the confrontation. His sons gathered round for the sport.

'You want something?' he barked, looking belligerently down on Alice from his much greater height.

'And greetings to you, sir,' came the sardonic reply. 'I won't detain you. Lily Mudd, the girl I placed with you. I will speak with her. In private, if you please. And then I shall be taking her away.'

'She's not here. Gone some weeks ago. Don't know where. And I don't care, neither. Good riddance.'

'Am I supposed to believe that a young girl would just disappear of her own volition?'

'Search the place if you wish. You won't find her. Couldn't wait to see the back of her, could we, boys?'

'No, Pa.'

As she had feared, Alice was too late. The child was lost, maybe still in danger, conceivably beyond all hope. And she was partly to blame. Perhaps wholly to blame. No, the abusers were the architects of this tragedy, the perpetrators of this evil. But she was not without fault. First Simeon Harding and now this. A pattern was emerging. But Alice could not allow the farmer to see her disquiet. *Pull yourself together, woman. Don't give him any sense of victory.* She decided to do what she always did – attack. 'You should know that she has made some very serious accusations against you and your sons.'

The farmer had long planned for this conversation, rehearsing it in his head over and over, scripting the drama and honing the dialogue, and always arriving at a successful denouement. The scene had lived with him as he ploughed and chopped and milked and drank. And now, confident in his lines, he launched into an animated and suspiciously articulate defence.

'I don't take kindly, nor my sons neither, to being charged with such nonsense,' he bellowed with all the outrage he could muster. 'I never beat her, didn't even touch her, and you cannot prove I did. I might have shouted, and quite often too, and no doubt loud and clear, but who wouldn't? Such a lazy girl, I was just trying to get some work from her.' He paused for breath.

Alice was straining at the leash but allowed him to continue in his own time. Keep your powder dry, she told herself.

'Always complaining, she was,' the farmer ranted on. 'Thought we worked her too hard. Should have fed her more. Talked nicer to her, as if there's time for that when there's jobs to be done. Wanted wages on top of her board when there's not enough to go round as it is. And she was a liar too – you could never trust a word she said.'

Alice maintained an outward calm she did not feel.

'And she was a dirty little miss. Throwing herself at my boys. Lifting her dress and showing herself off. I seen it myself. And talking like you wouldn't hear in polite company. They're good boys, they wanted none of it, and this is her revenge for them not taking the bait. Isn't that right, boys?'

'Yes, Pa, that's right, Pa.'

Alice breathed deeply, and a smile briefly graced her lips. 'You seem very certain of your argument. An impressively detailed rebuttal.' She half turned, as if to leave, then quickly swung back. 'Which surprises me, since I have not told you what her accusations might be.'

The farmer was momentarily winded.

'So, I shall consider your outburst an admission of guilt, and we will see where the law takes us.'

The farmer stuttered and spluttered, and it was some time before anything resembling words emerged. Fists at the ready, he shoved his face a fraction from Alice's own, bending almost in half to do so and looming over her like a vulture that was about to feast. Foetid breath wheezed through his rotting teeth and a foul stench emanated from his clothes – and doubtless from what lay beneath.

But having once found herself intimidated by the man, with disastrous results, Alice was determined that this would not happen again. She stood her ground.

'You've got no witnesses to back up what you say,' he shouted, temporarily deafening Alice. 'It's her word against ours, and who do you think the court will believe? Not one of your spawn, for sure. They never do, I've read it in the papers. But it won't even get that far, will it? Because she ain't here, is she? And she ain't nowhere, as far as I know. So, there's nothing and no one for us to answer to.'

Alice knew that the farmer was probably correct in his assessment, given her experience of the local judiciary. And her patrons would not welcome the publicity of a trial, particularly yet another that was lost. On top of Mary Oliver and Simeon Harding, another damaged child might be beyond her powers of explanation. But she knew she had to keep the pressure on.

'I have these letters,' she proclaimed, stepping back, and removing them from a pocket. She brandished them heavenwards as if she were Moses, recently descended from a mountain. 'This is proof that at least some will believe.'

There was a moment of stillness and silence, save for the ambient lowing of cattle and the incongruous beauty of birdsong. Then suddenly the farmer lunged forward. In her haste to evade his advances, Alice slipped and sprawled helplessly in the mud like an insect that had been turned on its back.

The farmer grabbed the letters from her flailing grasp. 'You'll not be getting these back,' he trumpeted. 'They'll make a good fire while they last.'

'I have copies,' Alice cried, even though she did not.

The farmer laughed long and hard. 'Copies? Poor desperate woman,' he crowed. 'Can't you see? They'll be written in your hand. Where's the proof in that? You just made it up. All of it. To cover your tracks in selling us such a madam in the first place. Didn't she, boys?'

'Yes, Pa.'

Alice's driver was striding across the yard. 'I'll get 'em, ma'am,' he called out.

The farmer swore and walked slowly towards him, while his sons spread out and did the same. The driver was soon encircled.

'Think you can take us on, do you?' the farmer growled. 'Come on, boys, we need to show him that he's wrong.' And they did. With relish. Punches rained down on the driver and soon he was floundering in the mud alongside Alice.

'I think he's had enough, boys,' the farmer brayed.

'Are you sure, Pa?'

'Just a bit more, Pa?'

'No, leave him be. He's no threat to us. Nor she.'

The three of them backed off. Alice rose to her feet rather indelicately and helped up the carriage driver.

'There is a higher authority,' she wailed in desperation. 'This will be on your conscience for as long as you live. And when the curtain falls, you will stand in judgement before Almighty God, and I shall pray that He will sentence you to eternal torment in the sulphurous fires of Hell.'

The farmer laughed bitterly. 'Ah, your ever merciful God. If he wasn't so busy judging and sentencing, perhaps he might have time to make our lives a bit more bearable for the short time we have on this Earth. Working my fingers to the bone, every day the same, barely scraping a living and just an early grave to look forward to. If you want me to be in torment, then I'm already there.' He turned away and trudged back into the homestead, his sons following. 'And if there is a Hell, then no doubt we'll meet again. But not before, I trust'.

Alice stared at the retreating farmer until he had disappeared, then sadly trailed back across the mud to her carriage, her driver limping along beside her. The light was fading, and she would not reach Kingston by nightfall, but that was the least of her concerns; she often sought shelter in places that ladies of her standing would not typically countenance. She found an inn, and changed her clothing, and once she had restored respectability, she sought out a local police officer. As she feared, he was disinclined to take an interest.

'They said she was trouble when we went searching for her,' he muttered, barely looking up from his papers, which he shuffled about in a display of self-importance. 'Sounds like the sort of thing she'd do to create mischief. These young rascals are forever making claims about this and that, trying to get money out of it more often than not, and some pay up just to keep them quiet. Where's the proof of any harm? Just her ramblings in a letter that you've lost. Is that all you've got? Look, you can't go around making accusations that you can't back up with solid evidence.' The officer rose to his feet to signify that the conversation was over. 'If she turns up, we'll ask her and see what she says. That's the best I can do.'

'Useless man,' Alice snorted when she was outside. And her spirits fell yet further. But she had one more avenue that might deliver a measure of revenge, if not justice.

That evening, Alice took a meal at the inn and made sure she engaged in conversation with various local drinkers. Some had been involved in the search for Lily, and they were most interested to hear about the letters she had sent. And Alice obliged by giving lurid detail, even adding some embellishment with which a respectable woman would not generally have been familiar.

'So, she made these terrible accusations about the farmer and his sons and then she disappeared,' Alice remarked, as innocently as she could. 'That's a coincidence, isn't it?' And she followed it up with: 'Didn't something very similar happen to his wife?'

Alice watched the cogs turn in the minds of her listeners as they assessed these revelations in the context of what they already knew.

'I tell you, I would not be at all surprised,' someone said.

'That would be just like him,' pronounced another.

'I can see him doing it,' added a third.

Others had previously arrived at such a conclusion but now they had corroboration and there was a degree of 'I told you so'. And Alice could be confident that their reasonings would be circulated quickly and widely, and that rumour and conjecture would destroy the remnants of the farmer's reputation as efficiently as any conviction in a court, even if he did remain at liberty to witness it. Perhaps that made the punishment more severe.

And while he had never been sought-after company, the farmer did indeed find that people never treated him quite the same again. The men of the town seemed less inclined to talk to him, and no one was willing to share a beer. The women gave him a wide berth, often quite ostentatiously. Credit was no longer available at the local store.

He will die a lonely man, Alice consoled herself as she took her leave of the drinkers. And perhaps those boys of his will struggle to find wives.

Later that evening she fidgeted in a chair in her room at the inn. The adrenaline of the day had ebbed away, replaced by the large sherry she had taken upstairs to help her sleep. But far from soothing and relaxing, as was its purpose, it merely encouraged her mind to rove ever more desperately in all directions, picking over the bones of what had brought her to this place, seeking salvation as much for herself as for Lily Mudd.

'I should have left her in the workhouse' was her starting point. 'She was safe there, more or less. I could have taken another. Or not taken any.'

But after a moment's deliberation, a different argument emerged. 'No one with any sense of decency would ever leave a child in such a place if there was an alternative. A place she hated, she was clear about that. And what would have become of her when she reached her maturity? No, taking her was the best thing to do, and the kindest.'

She relived that first meeting: winning Lily's trust; the girl slowly coming out of her shell. 'She was happy to go or seemed to be. At least, until the day she arrived here. I don't know what changed.'

And once she was in Canada, Lily was given special treatment, there was no debate about that: the extended hospitality; how she was allowed to choose when others were not, a freedom that she abused or, at least, did not take advantage of. There was nothing wrong with some of the placements she turned down. Alice had sent other girls to those families and heard no tales of woe.

But then there was the farmer, his arrival branded on Alice's memory, hunched over the reins as he approached, his menace barely disguised. Alice sighed. Despite knowing in her heart that it was wrong, she had handed Lily over anyway. That monster of a man and his wicked sons – she should have sent them packing. But she had an agreement with the farmer, and he would have caused trouble if she had broken it, he said as much. Who knows what he would have done? Anything that endangered her work threatened her children, all of them – past, present and future. They must be protected at all costs. But Alice didn't even convince herself with that argument. No, she had displayed unforgiveable weakness. But even so, could she have done more?

A swig of sherry took her along one path. If she had visited regularly, or even just the once, she might have saved Lily. And that was terrible to admit. But another slurp brought a change in direction. Lily might not have been able to speak freely, so how would Alice have known that anything was amiss? That man would have kept Lily close for sure. And a further sip confused the matter even more. If that was so, then what was the point of visiting any of her children? If the only ones that can speak are those that have nothing to say.

And then there was the matter of Lily's letters. Alice did not recall seeing them, although perhaps she had. Maybe she had seen a child's writing and thought it couldn't be urgent. Just one of those scribbles telling her how wonderfully they were getting on. Rewarding to read but something that could wait.

Soon Alice was travelling a darker road. It is not as if we know that Lily is dead, she thought. There is no evidence to suggest it. And she tried to ignore whatever her intuition might be telling her. 'We all know it is not uncommon for an immigrant child to disappear,' she reassured herself. 'She might still turn up, plenty do, and then we can enjoy a true reckoning with that man.' She allowed herself to rehearse some vitriolic encounters and increasingly savage punishments, which she found herself enjoying perhaps a little too much. Then her thoughts veered back to Lily. If she remains absent, that does not necessarily mean…

Alice did not want to think about what that might imply.

She drifted into a fitful sleep and awoke early the next morning, still wedged into the chair. The artificial melancholy of the sherry had worn off and now she was in a more pragmatic mood.

'I have done all that I reasonably can for now,' she told herself. 'I will search for Lily in the coming weeks. And God willing, I shall find her.'

Alice returned to the Kingston centre with every intention of making extensive enquiries, but first a new party of children arrived and then she had to prepare for the visits she had promised, and they were followed by yet more arrivals. And before she knew it, it was November and Alice was staring at the waves through the porthole in her cabin.

Time passed, and Lily Mudd was still nowhere to be found. In truth, no one was looking for her.

FORTY-FIVE

Ten weeks after he was first carried into the hospital, a doctor cut away the plaster on Arthur Dilkes' leg with rather less ceremony than he might have expected. His cries echoed throughout the building, causing some alarm among the less trusting patients. He looked down in trepidation as the doctor stared and poked and prodded about with some theatricality. Arthur's leg bore little resemblance to a human limb. Once the congealed blood had been washed away, the skin was revealed to be alabaster white, perforated by a dark scar where the bone had once protruded. The muscles had wasted badly, and it was difficult to imagine that such a structure could ever again support a person's weight.

The doctor reached a conclusion. 'I think we can say that we have saved the leg, at least for now,' he confirmed, looking pleased with himself. 'Now let us see if you can stand unaided.'

Arthur struggled to his feet, but the weeks of inactivity had taken its toll on his strength, and the undamaged limb was unable to compensate for the weakness of the other. He slumped back on the bed in a cloud of curses. But fired by an urgent voice in his head, with its tales of injustice and betrayal, he persevered, and within the hour was able to remain upright and even make some awkward progress across the room.

'As I thought,' the doctor concluded when he returned. 'You can leave tomorrow but should assume you will not be of any use for many weeks, and seasons will pass before you can resume your duties in full. We have a stick that you can take, which may allow you to be more productive than you would otherwise be. But the leg has set not quite straight, and it will be an impediment to walking. Indeed, you might always be incapacitated to some degree. I shall draw up our account for payment,' he added unnecessarily and with some relish.

As the doctor moved on, nurses scurrying in his wake, Arthur could feel his spirits rising, cautiously at first but with a momentum that would soon banish the self-pity that had overwhelmed him. A great weight had been lifted from his soul, as real as the one removed from his leg. Suddenly, he could see a future of sorts. He spent the rest of the day on his feet, shuffling back and forth across his room until he was dizzy, intent on building back strength and sinew, and ignoring the protests of his tortured limb whenever weight was placed upon it.

The June sun illuminated his room late into the evening, a reminder that he should be out in the fields. Perhaps one day he would be, a possibility that had been unthinkable until now. It was something to aim at.

I'm becoming less like Sam Barney by the minute, he thought and laughed out loud for the first time in weeks.

FORTY-SIX

Alice Hamilton had sent a letter to Arthur Dilkes listing the various medical expenses that he had incurred, commenting on their reasonableness and the lack of any ability to challenge them, and confirming that all had been paid. Now very little remained of his deferred wages.

I have worked all these years for nothing except my keep, Arthur thought as he tore the letter into fragments. I'm no better off than if I'd stayed in Miss Alice's home in London. Worse off, in fact – I'd still have two proper legs if I were there. And he could not erase this cheery thought from his head for some weeks.

Robert Gait attended the hospital with his cart and drove Arthur back to the farm. The journey was less harrowing than he had endured in the opposite direction, although his leg was still tormented by the rutted track and it bobbed about almost independently, as if unconnected to anything that might control it. Conversation was limited to practicalities and logistics, as was Gait's wont, but there was an undercurrent of hostility on both sides.

'So, when will you be back working?'

'Not this side of winter. Not fully, anyhow. I'll do what I can, but the doctor says it won't be much.'

'You'll get your keep, but I can't pay wages if you don't work.' It was said with a hint of malice, but Arthur did not rise to the provocation.

'Do you think that's fair?' Gait persisted.

'Doesn't matter what I think.'

There was a silence while they both wallowed in mutual loathing.

'And the way things are, there's less of everything that you've got used to. For all of us, except the young'uns.'

'I've never needed much of anything.'

'Just as well.'

The cart eventually rattled into the yard, and the travellers were put out of their misery. Arthur eased himself down and, aided by his stick, moved slowly across the yard to the homestead, where Amelia welcomed him with a hug that enveloped him almost entirely.

'Busiest time of the year and he'll be no help at all,' Robert Gait grumbled as they went inside.

Arthur overheard, as he was meant to, and bit his lip. Then he set about proving him wrong. From that moment he volunteered for, grasped, appropriated and commandeered any job that was physically possible, and some that any reasonable person would have thought beyond him. He fetched and carried whatever was portable in one hand or slung over a shoulder or strapped to his back, while he took comfort from the stick in his other hand. He harvested eggs from the shed and fed the providers. He collected wood in small armfuls, the paucity of each payload being offset by the number of visits to the source. One day he took his courage in both hands and groomed the horse that had caused him such hardship, finding that he held no fear and bore no animosity towards the beast. He also helped Amelia in the homestead, and busied himself with washing and cleaning, cooking and minding the children, releasing her for other duties.

'That's not man's work,' Gait scoffed at him.

'A man's work is whatever needs to be done' was Arthur's retort, as he swept the floor around Gait's feet. 'As you'd expect a man to recognise.'

They had arguments aplenty that Arthur might have turned into something more physical had the odds not been stacked against him. Gait always expected more than Arthur could possibly deliver, and he expressed his disappointment with characteristic bluntness.

'It would be clear to a blind man what I can and cannot do, yet he abuses and humiliates me and blames me for the all the ills that beset him,' Arthur fumed at Amelia, who could be relied upon for a sympathetic ear. 'I am not at fault for the poor harvest. I didn't ask the horse to kick me.'

'He is not his usual self,' she offered in Gait's defence.

'The problem is, he is precisely his usual self.'

These were difficult times, as the money from the previous year's harvest gradually dwindled away to nothing. Amelia kept a close tally, but eventually their position would have been obvious even to those without her counting skills. There was food on the table, but precious little of it, and it was of limited nutrition. Dinner might consist of a few slops of a basic stew with a small wedge of bread to mop up the thinnest of gravies, and the menu for the next day would be very similar. Belts were tightened. Clothes were patched. Feet got wet if boots could not be mended. Livestock that were earmarked for longer-term purposes had to be sold or slaughtered. Gait even tried his hand at fishing but had neither the skill nor the patience to make it a regular source of sustenance.

'I saw him with his hand in the river trying to hit one with his fist,' Arthur reported back, and Amelia chuckled disloyally.

Their finances were made worse by the need for paid help to cover for the shortfall in Arthur's contribution. Gait hired a labourer from a local settlement but had been late in doing so and had to make do with what was left over. The man proved to be lazy and ineffective and was confident of getting away with it, knowing that whoever hired him must be desperate. The walk from his home and back again was almost the full extent of his daily activity, and he proved adept at finding fictional tasks in distant fields, away from the increasingly frustrated gaze of his employer. Arthur watched the man receive a wage he did not deserve and eventually came to the boil.

'I can do more on one leg than he can on both,' he challenged Gait.

'All right, show me you can, and I'll sack him.'

'If you pay me the wage he was getting.'

'If you prove to me that you've earned it.'

So Arthur threw away the stick, determined to make his point. At first, he walked slowly and with irregularity, but did so tirelessly, ignoring the pain. Over time he moved quicker, until he was close to his previous pace, albeit with an uneven stride, his errant leg having almost to be picked up and carried to enable it to keep up with the other. Gait watched him struggle, setting him tasks that he would inevitably fail and when he did so, would rail against him.

One day Amelia could take no more and sat her husband down in an unusually forceful manner. 'I am going to speak, and you will not interrupt me until I have finished,' she said in the voice she reserved for difficult moments. Gait recognised the tone and knew to listen. 'You treat that boy most unfairly, and I will not indulge it a moment longer. You berate and admonish him from dawn to dusk, yet look how hard he tries, hopping about on his one good leg. It's a miracle he can walk from one side of the yard to the other, yet he still puts in a harder day's labour than most could manage.'

Gait snorted and moved towards the whisky jar, but Amelia's glare told him to sit back down instead.

'Just compare him to that wastrel you hired, supposedly with all his faculties and limbs intact, some of which he clearly forgot to bring to his work.'

'I can't defend that good-for-nothing—'

'Look, I know how much you worry about our current predicament, and so do I, but we have been in worse trouble before and survived. You take the weight of the world on your shoulders and cut yourself off from those who can share it with you. Have you forgotten how much that boy helped us settle ourselves here? He ploughed the field that gave us grain for this bread. He carried the timbers for this very room and hammered them in. Without him, we would not be where we are.'

Amelia drew breath, awaiting a rebuttal, then pressed on when none arrived. 'There, I've said my piece. Now, be the man I thought I had married, and act on it.'

Gait sat quietly for a moment then took himself to the woods, where he remained for several hours. Amelia went about her chores, wondering what his reaction might be. And when he returned, he said nothing.

In the late afternoon, Gait was hammering in a new fence post and spotted Arthur hobbling wearily homewards. 'Come here, lad.'

Arthur limped pugnaciously across the yard, expecting yet another reprimand, but as he got closer it seemed as if Gait's mood was softer.

Thud. The hammer moved the post a fraction.

'I am a stupid man,' Gait began uncertainly, lining up another blow.

'I cannot disagree with that.'

'Don't make this more difficult for me.' Gait took two

further swings at the post while Arthur stood quietly and waited to see where the conversation would go.

'I know I have served you bad, and I am not proud of it, but I could not help myself. When I looked at you in your helpless state, all I could see was another claim on what little we had, more bills to pay, less money coming in. And it looked like there was no end to it. If you were a horse, I would have taken my gun to you.'

Thwack. The post was quickly disappearing into the earth in search of relief. Arthur leaned on another section of fence and waited for his turn.

'I've said it often enough. Protecting your own is all that matters, and nothing must get in the way of it. Nothing and no one. Fortunately, I have a wife who is rather less blinkered than I. She saw the need to remind me that you are one of our own. More or less. I should not have forgotten that.' Gait had stopped battering the post. Now it was his turn to listen.

Arthur thought for a moment. 'You have made things a misery for me, on top of everything else, and I don't believe I deserved it. I would have left you to rot if I had anywhere to go.' He trembled as he spoke. 'If you had been the one with a leg hanging off, I doubt I would have behaved as you did. But perhaps I might. You don't know 'til it happens.' He turned his back on Gait and made his way back to the homestead. 'I need to clear my head and think this through.' He locked himself in his room and was not seen again that day.

The next morning, Arthur sat at table for his breakfast in the usual way. He was halfway down his bowl before he spoke. 'About yesterday,' he began.

Gait put down his spoon to listen.

'The missus has always been good to me, and so were you for a decent time. I ain't forgotten that.' He broke off to attend to his bowl.

'What you said, I can see that's as near as you'll get to apologising.'

Another mouthful disappeared. 'And so you can take this as being as near as I get to accepting it.' The empty bowl clattered on the table. 'Let's get to it, there's work to be done.'

They shook hands, tentatively at first and then with more gusto, and over the next weeks and months they settled back into something resembling their previous relationship. The matter was not discussed again but was always there, its echoes never quite fading away, the improving fortunes of the farm helping to paper over the cracks. And while they were overtly polite and comradely, even cheery at times when the whisky flowed, it was not the same between them, and everyone recognised that without saying it.

FORTY-SEVEN

Alice Hamilton had kept a diary for many years, extracts of which she would publish from time to time. While her words had an inevitable ring of self-congratulation and she used some artistic licence with the facts, it was as much a fundraising exercise as a pitch for immortality. But in the wake of Simeon Harding's death and her other misfortunes it took on a deeper purpose, providing some reassurance for nervous patrons and, more importantly, for the author herself. Hence the 1886 version was rather more selective in its material and upbeat in its tone than the events of the year demanded.

> *This year the Almighty has again looked favourably upon my work, for which thanks and praise are due. Firstly, on the tenth of May, I dispatched eighty-five young souls, eagerly seeking refuge from the poverty that stalks our land and the Poor Law that fails to protect them. They sailed for Canada under the stewardship of trusted associates and were subsequently placed with an array of righteous and upstanding citizens. Meanwhile, I remained in England to arrange later shipments and attend to various matters of importance. Then, in early June I crossed the Atlantic myself – I will not say*

what drove me to this, she thought – and a further ninety-three blessed children followed on just a month later. After placing them with yet more virtuous souls, of whom there is a plentiful supply in that fair land, I embarked on visiting some of my previous successes. I started out in the neighbourhood of Brighton, Ontario, which lies at the furthest reaches of my territory, where I have around twenty little ones living within a comfortable radius of each other. There I enjoyed the hospitality of the local cleric, a man of a pleasingly low church, and some of the children came to tea with me – those that could be spared from their labours. Next, I journeyed to Trenton and saw a further six, or it might have been seven, from whence I went on to Wooler, then to Frankford and thence to Stirling. I have children in each of these places, and I visited nearly all of them.

There was no mention of Alice's vain attempt to find Lily Mudd, or several other children who also were not where she expected them to be. And there was certainly no reference to Simeon Harding. By now, his name had fallen out of the newspapers and slipped from people's minds, and Alice thought it best that it should remain that way.

Finally, I returned to Kingston, calling in on placements at Corbyville and Cannifton as I passed. I only wish I could include all my children in these visits, but it is precluded by the vastness of this great country and the primitive nature of its transportation system. But I have resolved that I shall visit others, should God permit me to return. Then, with my work finished in the Dominion for this year, I hastened to Quebec to take ship for England, with the Good Lord ensuring that we would outrun the winter storms. After some brief respite from my travails, and with the opportunity for reflection, it was again time to comb the streets of England and extract those mites that can be saved. Sadly, my work is never done.

And with that, she put down her pen.

'Damn their stubbornness,' she cursed, as she thought of the impasse between the British and Canadian governments that had placed the workhouses out of bounds. 'It is the children that will suffer, as always.'

She had considered sending a copy of her diary to the Deputy Minister in Canada, to show what could be achieved by just one determined woman but eventually decided not to do so. She could almost hear him say *Given how successful your visits seem to have been, you should repeat them every year and we can tell the Local Government Board that you have taken on the job for us.*

And so her diary was only published in Britain, where she hoped that George Moore might read it and be tempted to leave her alone.

*

It was the following January when Simeon Harding's employer finally stood in court, charged with his murder. The trial played out very much like that of Mary Oliver, and it was not long before the jury had returned a verdict of not guilty. Alice shed a tear when she read the report. There was some renewed interest in the case by the more popular newspapers, and a modicum of chatter in the capital's tea houses and gentlemen's clubs. And then everyone moved on to the next story.

FORTY-EIGHT

The police were investigating a spate of barn fires over a large and seemingly random area, but a common factor was emerging. The police officer had identified Alice Hamilton as someone who might know the whereabouts of a suspect.

The first incident had occurred on the property of Ezra and Patience Wright, and three others had swiftly followed. As there had been no attempt at theft from any of the premises, suspicions fell upon disgruntled former employees. Lists of names were compiled, but such was the arduous life and lowly status of a labourer, where much was expected but little given in return, that each farmer could point at several individuals who might have an axe to grind. But when the lists were compared, one name was a constant across them all.

'There was the Barney boy. Sam Barney, I think it was,' reported one of the farmers. 'Just the sort of thing he'd do, if you ask me.'

Another could not recall Sam's first name, but his surname rang some bells. A third, who had employed Sam for the briefest period, had no recollection of what he called him, but the physical description sounded familiar. Patience Wright was in no doubt as to the culprit and recalled Sam's name as easily as those of her own children, adding some pejorative embellishments for good measure.

'Is it likely to be him, from what you know of the boy?' the officer enquired of Alice. 'Seems likely, don't it? What with him being a gutter child.'

Alice bristled at the attack on her children. 'Just because a child is born of lowly stock, it does not necessarily mean that they harbour criminal intent…'

'It's a good indication, though, ain't it?'

'And while Sam Barney is indeed a troubled young man, he has good reason to be so, for in his dealings with these farmers there were heinous slights and provocations and, in one case, serious violence towards him.'

'So, it's him then.'

'I did not say that. I was merely making the point that the boy's life has been fraught with hardship and adversity from a very early age, and that continues to be the case.'

The police officer put on his most formal face. 'And so it is for lots of other folk, but they don't go around setting fire to things. If he's done the deed, then he'll be put away for it and never mind any excuses. Now, do you know his whereabouts?'

Alice could truthfully answer that she did not, but she neglected to mention that a sum of money that was not strictly his had accompanied him on his way.

'Then, what were his other employments? We can warn them to be on the lookout.'

There were two others, and Alice reluctantly provided details.

'And if he resurfaces back here, mind you tell us. Or there'll be trouble.'

Later that day, Alice wrote to the headquarters of the provincial police, complaining in stringent terms about the presumption of guilt applied to her children and to others like them. She did not receive a reply.

Sam's first target for retribution had been the Wrights, the original architects of his fall from grace. He walked through the night and arrived in their vicinity around dawn, hiding in the surrounding woodland until darkness, when he could enact his revenge. He made himself comfortable and invisible to the casual gaze, yet he was close enough to hear familiar voices as they went about their business, although in the case of Patience Wright he could have been at quite a distance for that to be true. The Wrights had acquired a new child labourer from a different source, and he was busying himself under the dour tutelage and screeching instruction with which Sam was all too familiar. It was clear that the Wrights had neither mellowed nor grown more welcoming since his departure, and he took some comfort from that. It also seemed that the boy had been chosen for his unprepossessing appearance.

'Can't see any of the girls talking to that,' Sam muttered to himself.

As the day strode purposefully towards its maturity and then slowly meandered towards its dotage, Sam was left alone with his thoughts. They were not good company. The gloom hovered above him like a thundercloud as he relived all that had brought him to this place, at this time, with these intentions. His life had been punctuated by one loss after another. First the death of his ma, then his pa – and, with their passing, the forfeiture of his home. Arthur was next, a brother in all but name, now estranged and despised. With Charity, there had been the potential for something more than friendship, before he was reminded of his place. Then, in quick succession, the remains of his self-respect were beaten out of him, any hope of gainful employment was squandered, and, as a finale, he was likely to be relieved of his liberty once his current initiative had played out. Things were always taken away from him, and whenever anything was added, it was only done to make its subsequent removal yet more painful.

Despite his mood, Sam had hoped to catch sight of Charity. When he heard her voice, he risked discovery by moving to within sight of the yard. She was prettier than he had remembered, and her words skipped lightly off her tongue, while her smile reflected an inner warmth that seemed to owe nothing to inheritance.

She's not her father's daughter, thought Sam approvingly. And particularly not her mother's.

Later that morning he saw her again, alone this time. He crept even closer until he was just one tree away from standing in plain sight, and suddenly he was back in a time of covert meetings and shared confidences, secret cake and a Christmas kiss. He had not planned it, but he found himself whispering her name. The third time he did so, Charity looked directly at him, but there was no smile or greeting or any sign that his presence was welcome. Instead, there was terror in her eyes and panic in her voice. 'You can't be here. Whatever possessed you to come back?'

Sam was shocked by her response. 'Things have been so bad for me, like you couldn't imagine,' he stuttered pathetically, making no effort to hide his disappointment. 'I just needed to see a friendly face. I ain't seen one in such a long time.'

'Are you mad? They'll not let you walk away a second time.'

'He'll know my fist proper if he tries anything like that again.'

Charity squealed in anger and frustration. 'It isn't just you, though, is it? What about me?' she hissed. 'You might be happy to risk a beating, but I'm not. I still have scars from the last one. If you won't leave for your own sake, then do it for mine.'

They were interrupted by a blast of discontent from the homestead. Something had irked Patience Wright, and she was not one to keep such things to herself.

'I'll not have you turning out like that other scoundrel!' she shrieked, and there was the sound of a slap. 'We were too soft on him, and we'll not make the same mistake with you.'

Charity rounded on Sam. 'I must go, and so must you. I won't say anything about this; they'll only claim I encouraged it, and I don't want to feel the strap again.'

And before he could respond, she was on her way.

'And don't come back. It's for the best, believe me.'

Perhaps she *was* her mother's daughter, Sam thought. A great weight descended upon him as he slunk back into the woods. But he remained within sight of the farm, with revenge now burnt even more deeply into his thoughts.

I could have told you that would happen, mocked the voice in his head. *When will you stop believing that there's good in anyone?*

Finally, the homestead slept, and Sam stole across the yard to the barn he had selected, deftly negotiating the rickety door and silencing its creaking hinges, which might otherwise have raised the alarm. He left it ajar to admit his accomplice – the light from a thousand stars that gazed down benevolently from the northern sky, illuminating his activity. The chickens slept and did not betray him; in return, he would see that they were safe.

Sam had known how to make fire since his London days. Quickly, he raised a small flame, setting it to good use in all four corners of the barn and laying a pathway between these extremities so that no part would feel left out. Then, when the blaze was firmly established, with urgent cries and whirling arms he directed the evacuation of the chickens, a tidal wave of squawk and feather that shattered the silence of the night beyond repair.

All pretence of secrecy abandoned, Sam disappeared into the woods at speed, swiftly putting distance between himself and potential capture. Had he stayed to watch his creation unfold, he would have seen the family emerge in varying states of confusion and undress, running back and forth across the yard as haphazardly as the flapping poultry, each shouting instructions to which no one was listening, and all the while the flames danced in celebration.

With a template established, one by one Sam burnt his way through the roll call of his previous employers, searching for inner peace through the purification by fire of past rejections and mistreatments, real or imagined. He made his way cautiously as he went about his work. The forest was a reliable ally in places where he might be recognised. Otherwise, he walked the roads, hitching lifts on passing wagons for which he invented a character and story that could explain his journey without suspicion being aroused. The food he scavenged from the home kept his hunger at bay until he was able to make an anonymous purchase with the stolen money. He found Canada to be an easy place in which to be faceless and lost.

After his first raging success, the remaining fires became increasingly functional, distinct from the emotive roar that had been the Wrights' inferno. And with each blaze came less satisfaction and a greater sense that perhaps this was not the answer. There was to be no redemption by heat and flame. Another disappointment to add to the burgeoning list.

Maybe it's time to stop, Sam thought as he trudged towards his latest appointment.

Just one more, encouraged the voice in his head, and Sam obeyed.

He approached the next farm in the sequence, a sprawling but well-established affair amid a clutch of similar others. He had worked there for about four weeks during a time when his mood would not allow him to lift a finger or to utter a sentence, this being the reason given for his relatively muted dismissal. In line with his established routine, he lay low during daylight, reminding himself of the layout of the farm and reacquainting himself with the personalities that lived there. At nightfall he approached his target. It was a ramshackle structure in which were stored certain rusting implements and a supply of fodder, hardly worthy of its description as a barn. But it would serve his purpose; this was a statement of principle, not a mission to impede or impoverish.

Sam gained entry and had begun his usual arrangement of hay and other combustibles to ensure a good spread, when suddenly there was a voice in the darkness.

'That's the most I've seen you move,' it snarled. 'If you'd worked that hard before, I might not have got rid of you.' The farmer stood in the doorway, shotgun cradled in his arms, squinting to get a better look at his prey. 'Police said you'd try, and now I've got you. Met your match this time.'

The farmer was boastful now, but as he turned his head to call for witnesses to his cunning, Sam hurled himself towards him, knocking him to the ground amid a flurry of breathless expletives. He sprinted for cover, while the farmer scrambled to his feet and raised his gun. It may have been a warning shot, or perhaps the farmer was less proficient than he thought himself to be, but Sam felt no thud of a bullet and kept on running, ducking low and weaving erratically across the yard to present a slippery target. The farmer's young sons appeared, with smaller shotguns of their own, firing indiscriminately and endangering their father more than their prey, while the lady of the house poked her head out of a window and let loose a blast of her own without reward.

Sam hurdled a fence, careered through a paddock and dived into the forest, crashing through undergrowth, bouncing off trees, tripping, falling, hitting the ground and immediately rebounding without losing momentum, acquiring a multitude of cuts and bruises that would not pain him until the adrenaline receded. When he could no longer hear any pursuers, he stopped and waited for daybreak. The forest wrapped its arms around him, making him feel safe, even wanted, and giving him the chance to think. By morning, he was ready for whatever was coming his way.

'I showed 'em, didn't I? Made 'em take heed,' he consoled himself. 'Now they might think twice before treating other lads the same as they did me. And others like 'em might take note.' *And all those folk that said you would never amount to much can be pleased you've proved 'em right,* the voice added unnecessarily.

As the first rays of morning kissed the top of the forest, Sam was on his way, making no attempt at concealment, walking proudly towards the rising sun. Part way across a clearing, a phalanx of men on horseback appeared: the farmer, two officers from the provincial police, and a selection of neighbours, along for the ride. Sam stopped as they circled around him. One of the officers rode forward. 'You'll not run any more, or you'll know my rifle.'

Sam looked the officer in the eye. 'I gave you the runaround, didn't I?'

'If it makes you happy to think that.'

'It was punishment for what they did to me.'

'Nothing like the punishment you'll be getting.' The officer dismounted and walked towards Sam. 'Now put your hands out for me.'

The voice was insistent in Sam's ear. *Go on, make a run for it. If a shot finds its mark, what does it matter? A fitting end to a wasted life. You won't be mourned, not by anyone. You won't even mourn yourself.*

'Come on, boy, I won't tell you again.' The officer took

aim. 'Makes no difference to me, boy. Just one less piece of vermin.'

And hearing that, Sam's mind was made up for him. 'I'll not give 'em the pleasure of seeing me fall,' he told the voice. 'Not yet anyhow.' And with his arms outstretched, he knelt in surrender.

FORTY-NINE

With Sam Barney's guilt a foregone conclusion, his trial did not detain its participants for long, and the magistrate was comfortably punctual for his lunchtime appointment. The involvement of an immigrant child triggered more publicity than such a case would normally merit, and the *Toronto Herald* was its usual self, devoting an entire page to a graphic exaggeration of events and treating its readers to a thoughtful analysis of how similar outrages could be prevented in future. It arrived at its customary conclusion.

Sam was sentenced to a three-year stretch inside 'the Big House', as Kingston Penitentiary was known to local folk, and he soon recognised the irony in its name. At just 2½ feet wide by 8 feet deep, and with a clearance of inches above his head when standing, his cell was more like a coffin. He was set to work in the carpentry shop, making cabinets and chairs to fulfil one of the many commercial contracts that the prison had negotiated with businesses beyond its walls. He proved skilful and learned quickly, and the opportunity to hit a nail very hard suited his mood, although it might not have been wise to give him access to sharp objects.

Away from the carpentry shop, Sam was soon marked out by his jailers as a troublemaker: sporadically insolent, often disobedient, occasionally threatening and permanently ill-humoured. They needed little excuse to put him in his place. He also fought with fellow prisoners over petty slights, contested victuals or inadvertent contact, and both formal and informal punishments were meted out. If Sam did not add a bruise or a cut before lockdown, he regarded it as a waste of a day.

One mealtime in the mess hall, Sam was walking towards a vacant seat at a bench, a mug of weak tea in one hand and a bowl of broth in the other, juggling a hunk of bread between the two. He did not see another inmate making for the same space – a muscle-bound gentleman serving time for beating a man to pulp. The inevitable collision led to the other prisoner's tea ending up on the floor, along with Sam's bread. They slammed what remained of their meals down on the table and faced each other like rutting stags.

'You done that deliberate,' snarled the other prisoner.

'What if I did?' growled Sam, even though he hadn't.

Protocol dictated the outcome. After some preliminary pushing and shoving, the men were soon rolling around on the floor, their uniforms mopping up the breaded tea and general filth, holding and kicking and punching, much to the raucous amusement of fellow diners. The other prisoner was first to rise. He picked up Sam's bowl of broth and poured it over Sam's head, so that chunks of unrecognisable meat and vegetable residue were deposited in his hair. Sam leapt to his feet and rejoined the fray, but now the jailers were upon them, and when the sixth man arrived, they were finally able to drag them apart. The head jailer considered the respective reputations of the serial troublemaker and the violent offender.

'You'll go hungry tonight. Now back to your cell,' he barked, allocating blame in just a single direction, and Sam was led away with the triumph of another and the mockery of all ringing in his ears.

He stewed all night, working himself into a lather of self-pity and plotting all manner of revenge, the grislier the better. Then the next day, he picked up a chisel in the carpentry shop and made to secrete it about his person, but he took little care about it and was apprehended. Perhaps that had been his intention.

Sam was marched to see the warden of the prison, but not before a detour to the jailer's room, where he was shown the error of his ways via the sole of the jailer's boot. Eventually, he stood in the warden's office, insolence personified, blood dripping onto a rug that in another place might have made the room almost seem cosy. Two jailers accompanied him to ensure his good behaviour, both keen to increase the damage to the flooring if given the chance.

'You are one of our more regular offenders,' noted the warden, grateful for the presence of the chaperones.

'I have taken the lash, twice I think, and a fair degree of punching and kicking has come my way from various of your men. And I'm quite familiar with bread and water. But I don't keep a tally.' There was almost a hint of pride in Sam's voice, and certainly no evidence of regret.

'Perhaps you should. You are fortunate to be incarcerated under the current regime, which takes a more enlightened view than its predecessors. The sweat box is no more, and beatings are much reduced.'

'Yes, it is quite the place to be these days. I might refuse to leave when my time is up.'

A jailer slapped the back of Sam's head for his impudence.

'I cannot find rhyme or reason in your behaviour,' the warden continued. 'You hit out at whoever happens to be in front of you, and you seem to be happy to take the consequences, whatever they might be.'

'I don't always know myself. Sometimes I am punishing the world for how it has treated me, and other times I am punishing myself for letting it happen. And often I can't tell which is which. Or it might be both.'

The warden took a deep breath. 'You will not want advice from me, but I will offer it, nonetheless. However much you rail against the unfairness of your life, and however right you are to do so, you must come to terms with your present situation. Don't let yourself be provoked, and don't incite others against you. Don't speak out of turn. Lie as low as you can. Become a master of the trade you've been given – it will make your stay more tolerable and perhaps give you a better chance when you are let out.'

'Easy for you to say, mister, not so easy to do.' Sam's belligerence had melted away and he spoke calmly, almost pitifully. 'I know what you say is right, but there is something in my head that talks louder. It takes over and won't let me be. It sees offence where there is none. Makes me angry when there is no need. Won't be told what to do. Must always make a point. Insists I stand up for myself, whatever the outcome. I wish that voice was quieter, I really do. It deafens me much of the time.'

'You must find some way of silencing it, or it will be the death of you.' The warden thought for a moment. 'I think a period in solitary confinement is a suitable punishment and might even serve you well. There will be no one to fight with other than yourself.'

'That's often all I need, mister.' And once Sam was settled in his isolation, the voice in his head reappeared. *You are never truly alone,* it comforted him. *I am always here with you.*

FIFTY

At least once a year, and more frequently when her schedule allowed, Alice Hamilton took the Grand Trunk Railway to Toronto and visited Mary Oliver in the asylum that was now her home.

'It is good for the girl's morale,' the director would say as he placed some notes in a cashbox and others in his pocket.

Mary was always pleased to see her visitor, although she sometimes wondered which one of them obtained the greater benefit from the meeting. If she thinks I'm doing well, it makes her feel less guilty, she thought, and for sport would often be mischievously vague in her answers.

At first, Mary's daily routine was little different to that promised by the previous director.

'I have learned to crochet, and I have grown some plants from seed,' Mary once proudly announced. 'And no one takes a strap to me if my work is not perfect or if I cannot achieve all that I set out to do. Can you imagine that? And no one minds if I sing, as long as it is not at a disagreeable hour.'

'And are you safe?'

'More or less, miss. There are some bad men in the basements, but they are locked away. I have witnessed one woman slapping another and I sometimes hear threats of dire consequences, but never aimed at me, and they generally come to naught anyhow. I keep myself out of trouble. Thankfully, there is no one here as mad as Mrs Hoggard.'

'You seem content.'

'You know me, miss. I've always been able to make myself comfortable in places like this.'

Alice prickled at the rather unflattering comparison with her London home but let it pass.

One summer's day in 1887, they were sitting on a bench in the garden, taking in the summer sunshine, as they liked to do. Alice had a surprise for Mary. 'I paid a visit to Percy last week,' she said almost matter-of-factly, and waited for the response.

Floods of tears. Squeals of joy. Unease and alarm. So many questions. 'Is he well cared for? Do his people like him? Does he eat well? Does he look like a man or is he still a boy?'

'See for yourself.' Triumphantly, Alice produced a monochrome photograph that she had arranged to be taken. It was a picture of a fine young man, now fifteen years of age, tall and strong, agriculturally dressed, and looking more than a little uncomfortable in the pose. Mary could not wrench her eyes away from the likeness.

'Another three years and his placement will be over,' Alice reminded her.

'Is that right? I have lost track of time. Every day, every year is the same here.'

'He asked if he could visit you, wherever you were, and it was not easy to find a reason why not.'

Mary was horrified at the thought. 'Does he know where I am, miss? Please say not.'

'No. I spun the tale that you were still travelling and only in sporadic contact.'

Mary resumed her study of the image, tracing her finger round its outline, smiling in wonderment. She would carry it with her always.

'He also asked for a photograph of you.' And before Mary could object, Alice outlined the arrangements. 'A man will be with us this afternoon and will employ his magic to create a likeness. Before you say it, I have brought some clothes for you to change into, nothing fancy, so Percy will not see you in uniform. And I can help with your hair.'

'But miss, then he'll know ... all about this...'

'We can say that the photograph was taken on your travels. This is a grandiose building, on the outside at least, and we can pretend it is a palace or opera house in some obscure European country.'

So, later that day the photographer set up his equipment on a grassy area with the grand entrance hall as a backdrop. At first unsure, but quickly growing in confidence, Mary was indeed a picture in her civilian clothes, with her hair combed and tied up, and with a smile, at first uncertain through lack of practice, but becoming more radiant as the day progressed. Quite the young woman. And then the spell was broken as, once more in her patient's uniform, she watched Alice and the photographer disappear down the road, before trailing sadly back to her cell. For the briefest of moments she had lived a normal life.

Meanwhile, Alice forwarded the photograph to Percy, who was delighted. He was always quick to show it off. 'That's my big sister,' he would say proudly as others feigned an interest.

But as time passed, Mary painted to Alice a darker picture of life in the asylum, and this was not out of mischief.

'Have you made any friends?' Alice would sometimes ask; Mary had previously described some conversations that were not unpleasant. But this day her reply was, 'Friends? What are they, miss?'

'Well ... er ... have you learned any further crafts?'

'Look, miss, this is not a place where young ladies study the niceties of how to how to charm a young gentleman. Quite the opposite. Here we learn how to be invisible to a gentleman of any age, or a woman for that matter, and particularly those in staff uniforms.'

'You have more experience of that than I do.'

'Thanks to you, miss, I do.'

There were times when Mary was prepared to go into more detail. 'We have been organised into working parties, those of us that still have some faculties, and now we grow or make items for sale to the people of Toronto. Of course, we see none of the income ourselves. And a stick, or some other implement, is sometimes used to encourage us to meet our quota, even on those who have little idea of what they are doing.'

'And have you…'

'Don't worry, miss, I have avoided it so far. I am one of the better ones. But it brings back memories, and none of them are good.'

On another occasion, she appeared quite scared. 'There is more screaming and crying among the women and the girls, more fighting and shouting among the men. It is so crowded, with all manner of sick and desperate people, and I'm sure there are less hands to control them.'

'The director is obsessed with money.' Alice had found this out, to her cost. 'He is charged with turning a profit, and he takes his slice of it too.'

'We are called lunatics and maniacs now, not patients. When not working, we are to be pacified and not cured, except the lucky few, those with rich families. Thanks to God, I am seen as one of the quiet ones, and I am allowed free use of my limbs and can go about my business relatively unhindered. The furious lunatics are mostly wrapped up in them jackets and they rarely see the light of day.'

On another visit, she told Alice, 'Some days I never leave my cell except to eat, and sometimes not even that. Don't want to see no one – it's the safest way, because if you see a person you might have to talk to them, and then you're at the front of their mind when bad thoughts arise. Best to keep quiet and hope no one notices you.'

'I should take you out of here.'

'No, miss, not until Percy is free of his commitments. There is nowhere for me to go, and I shall be on my own, which is not a good place for me still. It is not long now.'

The fabric of the asylum was deteriorating in sympathy with the treatment of its residents. To the visitor, the external architecture remained as impressive as ever, but internal shortcomings were all too obvious and there was little interest in rectifying them. A recurring problem with the drains caused an unsavoury bouquet to hover over certain parts of the building; damp was climbing from the ground and descending from the roof and would likely meet halfway before long; and dry rot had undermined the integrity of the flooring, which often yielded below to passing feet. Outside, the gardens gradually returned to nature, untended and unloved.

One day Alice was railing against the new regime. 'It is a disgrace, the way that everything has been left to rot, people and building alike,' she fumed. 'I will give that director a piece of my mind.'

'Please, no, miss. No good will come of it.'

'If we meekly accept the situation, things will only get worse.'

Mary sighed. Whatever she said, it would not dim the light of battle in Alice's eyes.

At the visit's end, Alice buttonholed the director in his office, where he was enjoying an array of cakes and fancies. He listened to her lengthy diatribe with an obvious lack of interest, fingers tapping on the desk, his gaze fixed upon a distant tree.

'I pay good money for the girl to be here, and I expect better,' Alice concluded with a flourish.

The director slowly rose to his feet with a wearied expression. 'And where else would she go?' he scoffed, holding the door open for Alice to leave. 'Remember, you committed her to this place, and here she stays. And how it is run is none of your business. My employers are happy and that is all that counts.'

There was a momentary stand-off, with the pair glaring at each other in silence, before Alice flounced out.

Not one to be fobbed off, on her return to Kingston, Alice penned a strongly worded letter to the mayor of Toronto.

The letter went unanswered.

On Alice's next visit to the asylum, they had hardly sat down before Mary made her displeasure known. 'Don't you say nothing to no one about anything ever again, it only makes trouble for me,' she pleaded, real anger in her voice. 'Things will never get any better here no matter how much you froth at the mouth. If you want to help, just keep quiet.'

Alice was unused to anyone talking to her in such a manner and was about to respond in kind, when she noticed the marks on Mary's arms. 'Are they—'

'I'm not telling.'

There was an awkward silence. But it was clear that Mary had more to say, and then she did.

'Perhaps it's best if you don't come back. Until it's time to take me away.'

Alice thought for a moment. 'Yes, perhaps it is best.' She thought again. 'I might send someone else instead – one of my staff, perhaps. If I can find the right person.'

'As you wish. Mind you, they'll have to keep their mouth shut.' Mary suddenly stood up. 'On second thoughts, don't trouble yourself.'

And she stomped back inside, leaving her visitor alone on a bench, staring at the wilderness that had once provided the asylum with vegetables.

It was the last time that Mary would see Alice Hamilton.

FIFTY-ONE

A letter arrived for Margaret, written in her father's inimitable hand.

I have some big news for you, which I hope will make you smile at long last. I can hardly believe that I am able to write it. And this time I am not giving you false hopes, for which I have been guilty in the past, so hear me out. The Canadian immigration agent came to Middlesborough the other day, particularly looking for steelmen. He travels around England picking up workers that they ain't got enough of, and it was our turn. He took up residence in a large room in the town hall, and lots of us men went along to hear what he had to say. 'It is a land of opportunity,' he claimed, more times than I could count, although as far as I could tell it was only the chance for us to carry on doing what we are doing here and perhaps getting paid a bit more for it. But, in all honesty, that would be enough, with so many being thrown out of work, and not just in the steelworks neither. Anyhow, as well as having a job to go to, he says they'll pay our passage and find us some temporary lodgings and even give us some loose change to get us started. After that we're on our own, which is fair enough. All in all, there were plenty of big words and solemn promises, and if only half of them is true it is a trip worth making. Several of the men signed up and I was one of them, and next week I shall be off to Liverpool to take up my berth for the crossing. It will feel strange being in that city again, if only for a few hours, and leaving it will be the best part. By the time you read this, I should be on the ocean.

At first, Margaret would not allow herself to believe what she had read. After all these years of disappointment, could she trust her own eyes? Or was she just seeing what she wanted to see? Slowly she convinced herself that it was real, and when she finally did, she whooped and danced and could barely keep her tongue still for the rest of the day. It was four long years since Michael had first implied that his presence might be imminent, and thereafter Margaret had tried to convince herself that it would never happen, although in her heart she always held out some hope, which made it feel worse. All of that was now forgotten in an outburst of pure joy. John and Daisy exchanged public smiles when they heard the news, and in private they crossed their fingers.

'Remember, that ship takes forever to cross the sea, and he'll need to go to his work first,' counselled Daisy. 'And even then, he will have much on his plate and many things on his mind. So, don't expect that he'll be on our doorstep the minute he lands. He will get to us in due course.' Then she added quickly, 'I'm only saying this so you aren't disappointed.'

And over the following days Margaret felt that she was

mostly saying 'Yes, Ma. No, Ma. Ma, I know that.' But through bitter experience, she knew now that Daisy would often talk sense at such times, so she did not suspect any ulterior motive.

'Just let the girl enjoy being excited,' John intervened, after a particularly intense bout of logic.

Whenever she was not busy with work or chores or family life, Margaret would stand on the street corner and wait for old Pa to arrive, straining her eyes into the distance so as not to miss him. She'd scrutinise every cart or carriage until she had verified the identity of the occupants. Having learned the timetable by heart, she would often walk to the railway to meet the incoming trains, only to trudge home in disappointment when no one but strangers alighted. At times Margaret worried that new Ma and Pa might be jealous of her attention towards old Pa, but they said nothing, and Margaret was not going to put thoughts in their minds or encourage a difficult conversation.

Eventually, even Daisy ran out of legitimate reasons for Michael's non-appearance. 'I cannot imagine where he is or what detains him. Poor Margaret cannot sit still for a moment.'

'There must be a solid reason. He is not a man who would trifle with her feelings, if I'm any judge.'

Then one morning the Kingston telegraph office delivered a telegram to the store.

'You must be people of importance,' joked the deliveryman, as he always did to recipients who clearly were not.

Daisy looked suspiciously at the envelope, inscrutable and ominous in its plainness, and waited for John to return from his errands before opening it. Margaret was dealing with a consignment of washing from the Palace and was happy to be disturbed. They gathered round as Daisy prised open the envelope and read the contents. *Michael Walsh with us. Very ill. Come quickly.*

The telegram was signed on behalf of the Hôtel-Dieu de Québec.

There was a moment of shock, then Margaret gave a howl of anguish. 'They think he'll die, don't they?' she wailed, her fingernails biting into Daisy's arm as she clung to her. 'Why else would they have said to come quickly? Might as well have said "before it's too late".'

Then guilt began to rage inside her. 'Something terrible has happened on the way, and he is only here because of me. He'd have been safe if he stayed in England, and at least I could have had his letters.'

John gently took her trembling hands. 'It might have been no different even if he'd stayed put. He's said before that he's not a well man, and then suddenly he's fit again next time he writes. Whatever it is, it comes and goes. It'll be the same this time, I'll warrant.'

'And it was his idea to journey here, so don't you go taking any blame,' Daisy added.

But Margaret was not listening. She had barely cried since she became a Bradley, not when she was cut or bruised through falling, nor when she was laid low by sickness or fever, and when others were not kind to her, she would shrug it off. But now she was inconsolable.

Daisy quickly took control. 'John, you must go with Margaret, and you must leave immediately. I will send a telegram to that place to tell them you are on your way – it's some kind of hospital, I think, run by nuns and the like; I'm sure I read something once. I will hold the fort here while you are gone. And, Margaret, I shall enjoy becoming acquainted with the Palace's undergarments.'

Within an hour they were packed and ready.

'Quebec? Heaven help us, they don't speak a proper language there.'

'I'm sure they'll feel the same about you, John. Now be on your way.'

And Margaret knew exactly when the next train was due.

FIFTY-TWO

George Moore had long since given up communicating with Alice Hamilton by letter. So, here he was again, knocking on her door and speculating about whether she would be properly attired. On this occasion, she was appropriately turned out and there was no embarrassment for the hostess, nor scope for an anecdote for the visitor.

As they manoeuvred around the opening pleasantries, Alice could see that Moore was not his usual self: he was remote, distracted, his eyes dimmed. He did not appear to be a man on a mission, which was most unlike him. She placed some biscuits within easy reach and listened.

'As you know, the Canadian government eventually agreed to annual inspections of the workhouse children, after years of excuse and prevarication.' There was an unfamiliar cynicism in his tone.

'And once more I was able to save children from those loathsome workhouses,' Alice chirped. Making a point was second nature to her.

'If you will. Anyway, nearly two years have passed since that agreement, and we have yet to receive a single inspection report. Not one. And neither is this likely to be rectified in the near future. It is almost as if they had no intention of ever complying and were merely seeking to delay the inevitable.'

Alice remembered her conversation with the Deputy Minister. 'I believe you have hit the nail on the head.'

Moore sighed and took a deep breath. 'Therefore, it is likely that we will once again place a moratorium on the emigration of workhouse children.'

Based on previous experience, Moore expected some choice words in reply, but Alice merely offered him another biscuit.

'Have you nothing to say?' he asked gingerly.

Alice smiled sweetly. 'While I have sympathy for the workhouse children, who will lose a great opportunity because of this decision, these days they are only a small part of what I do. I have adapted.'

Moore's relief was almost palpable. 'Do you still visit your children? It may give you more time for that.'

'I do what I can, and unlike the Local Government Board, I do not discriminate between those from the workhouse and the poor waifs that make up the balance of my activities. Each is equally deserving, to my mind.'

Moore leaned forward enthusiastically. 'I agree wholeheartedly. This is a serious bone of contention for me, and I do not pretend to agree with my lords and masters on this matter. Indeed, I have been disciplined more than once for making that plain. And if I hear the words "it is beyond our remit" once more, I shall not be responsible for my actions.'

Alice laughed heartily. Perhaps for the first time, she could see that Moore was a man after her own heart, just as much a rebel in his own – very different – way.

'It is time that I gave this up,' he suddenly said, his voice soaked in regret. 'I have indicated that I wish to retire, and no one has tried to change my mind. They will be pleased to see me gone, I imagine, but feel they cannot say so.'

Alice could not have foreseen her reaction. She was

surprised, yes, but saddened too. 'That would be a great shame. What will the children do without you?'

'They are desperate for a voice, and mine is no longer heeded. I am no further use to them.'

Alice looked at Moore and recognised how she might feel if she was having to abandon her life's work. She took his hand, and he did not resist. 'We have had our disagreements, but I have never doubted that you are trying to do the right thing.'

'I could say the same.'

Thereafter their talk was increasingly convivial. Alice unearthed some cake and dispensed more tea and suggested that they move to the ancient Chesterfield, where they could sit in greater comfort. Unusually, she found herself asking questions of a personal nature and, to her bewilderment, took pleasure in responding to equivalent enquiries. Private thoughts were exposed and confidences shared and, contrary to her innermost beliefs, Alice found it a perfectly natural thing to do. She could not recall a more enjoyable conversation. Then Moore remembered that he had to be elsewhere, and he took his leave, this time with Alice happily accompanying him to the door and beyond. As he walked away, she suddenly blurted, 'You may like to call again, even though we have no business to discuss.'

Moore turned back and smiled. 'Thank you. I would like that very much.'

FIFTY-THREE

Later that day, Alice Hamilton sat quietly at her desk with a cup of tea and a teacake for company. The news of George Moore's retirement had set her thinking.

She knew that she would not always be engaged in this work. That there would come a time, perhaps quite soon, when enough was enough. It was perhaps an obvious conclusion for a person of a certain age, but it was the first time she had articulated it. And it felt quite a step to say so, even if only to herself.

'Before the Lord takes me, I intend once again to spend time with my books,' she muttered to herself as she poured another cup. 'Scandalously, there are some that I have not read, and for too long I have been remiss in adding to my library.'

She thought some more and reached a conclusion. 'I have always said that I wish to be remembered for something worthwhile. Since I was a girl, that has been my goal. I want people to know what I have accomplished and how I went about it, so that people can see just how much a solitary woman can achieve. And perhaps others might be inspired by my example.'

Yet more tea followed. By the time the pot was dry, Alice had decided to embark upon a project, ambitious in the extreme, to collate the names and experiences of every child she had migrated over the years. She wanted to prove to herself as well as to the world that, all things considered, she had been a force for good. She had not forgotten Simeon Harding or Lily Mudd or Mary Oliver, or the others like them, but she needed confirmation that they were the exception, and not the rule.

Within a day she had a plan. She had designed a simple classification for different circumstances and outcomes, and each child was to be placed into one of those categories. Then she planned to write 'success', 'failure' or 'unknown' against each name. She knew she could easily make this judgement if she had the information and perhaps more so if it was lacking; that would be telling in itself.

It proved a Herculean task, and one she might not have started had she properly thought it through. She quickly found that she had not always been as meticulous in her record-keeping as she had in other aspects of her life. This laxity now came back to taunt her, inflicting unaccustomed anarchy upon her otherwise ordered existence. She knew that everything was there, somewhere, although its precise location and even whether it was in London or Kingston was open to conjecture.

Weeks turned into months, then years. So many lives had been transformed, for better or worse, and each year added to the tally. There were so many stories to tell. But slowly the project took shape. There were workhouse records, shipping lists and placement contracts to trawl through. The registers taken on each emigration morning were dusted off and added to the other comings and goings. Long-serving staff were interviewed for their memories, which often proved fragile and contradictory, and in the heat of questioning there might have been harsh words when an associate could not remember something that Alice herself could also not recall. She was not proud of that. She had filed away letters from children, generally positive and quite easily found, and correspondence from employers, more variable in tone and content, and less accessible. Very few complaints had survived Alice's fury at receiving them. And finally, there were the endless scraps of indecipherable scribbles to which her handwriting regressed when under pressure of time: she was sure they must contain treasure, but so often they flattered to deceive.

The task was all-consuming, and Alice liked that it was. It demonstrated to her that it was important. In the summers, she could only devote fleeting moments here and there to it, while in the winters, entire days or even weeks could be invested, but the project was always in her thoughts. And the closer it came to fruition, the more nervous Alice became about the conclusions she might draw from it. What would be her legacy? Would it confirm or disappoint? What would it tell her about herself?

FIFTY-FOUR

The ship carrying Michael Walsh and other hopefuls had docked two weeks previously in the city of Quebec. The journey was tolerable for those fortunate enough to have a cabin, boasting access to a private deck and the luxury of a porthole that could be opened. The ladies donned their best clothes for dinner and there was fresh air aplenty for the gentlemen to smoke in.

Sadly, the Canadian government's generosity only stretched to a passage in steerage for its immigrant labourers, and several hundred men, and not a few women, were packed into the hold like cattle and then largely forgotten. When conditions were fair, they would stand on deck in a huddle like a colony of penguins, partly to conserve heat and also because there was so little room to walk about. When the weather was foul, as it generally was, the ship's hatches were battened down, and its human cargo lay below for endless hours on wet, filthy bedding, breathing air that had already passed through multiple lungs, any goodness having been extracted and replaced by all manner of foreign bodies. It was fertile ground for an infection to take hold and spread, and one could never be certain whether a person's sickness was a reaction to the waves or had a deeper cause.

Michael Walsh lay on his mattress and tried to put all negative thoughts out of his mind. He had something to look forward to that would more than compensate for these privations. He closed his eyes and counted down the minutes.

But the man on the adjacent mattress was not in a good way, his breath rasping and irregular, interspersed with fits of coughing that threatened to tear his chest apart. His clothes were saturated in a sweat that was at odds with the freezing temperatures, and he moaned horribly in discomfort. Michael turned his back on his neighbour and tried not to think about what might be ailing him. As the ship approached Newfoundland, the noise from the man became more varied and intense before slowly fading to an unconscious rattle. After one last gasp, there was silence. The corpse lay there for several hours before it was picked up by crew members on their daily trawl and deposited in the bowels of the ship, where he had others for company. Whatever sickness it was, it did not keep itself to itself.

Finally, the weather turned, the hatches were opened, and the subterraneans poured out onto deck, blinking in the unaccustomed daylight and gulping down great draughts of fresh air. Michael found a space away from the crowd, intending to stay there day and night for the rest of the voyage, out of harm's way, he hoped. But it was too late, and within hours he was forced to take to his bed again.

When they docked, steerage slowly emptied and haggard men and women trudged down the gangway, where they were met by serious men in uniforms, who marched them away to be processed. The stricken were manhandled onto the quayside, where they were placed on stretchers, and those that had passed were separated from those that still held on. Survivors were transported by cart to the Hôtel-Dieu de Québec, conveniently situated and primed to receive those in desperate need. The hospital was under the command of the Augustine order, and its patients were cared for by the nursing sisters, whose responsibilities were both spiritual and temporal. It was as much a place of God as a home of medicine, which was opportune for those who were soon to meet their maker. A nurse identified Michael Walsh from the papers he held. He was given a bed, and a telegram was sent.

FIFTY-FIVE

John and Margaret had travelled through the night and were not at their sharpest on arrival in Quebec. Daisy had packed some provisions, but these had long been exhausted, and sleep had been elusive. Now the city stretched out before them as a mystery to be solved. Emerging bleary-eyed from the railway station, they procured some bread and apples and urgently sought out the Hôtel-Dieu de Québec.

They first made their way to the immigration office, where they were given vague directions in faltering English by an uninterested official who barely looked up. From there, they stumbled around the cobbled streets in search of further guidance, never more than a few hundred yards from their target, but somehow always managing to take a wrong turn or follow a false trail. And at each dead end, Margaret urged them on to ever greater speed, only too aware that time was running out. As a confident man, John thought he might know a few words of the French tongue, but it transpired that he did not, or at least he did not know any that were relevant to their situation, although he suspected that some listeners understood more than they were prepared to divulge.

Finally, they turned a corner and the Hôtel-Dieu de Québec stood majestically before them, mocking their travails, and dismissively asking 'what kept you?'. Its size alone should have made it unmissable, yet it had concealed itself for half a morning. Wings of imposing length and height straddled a central courtyard, interrupted frequently and with mathematical precision by identically fashioned windows and doors, offering entry to light and people. To one side was a walled garden around which a shaded cloister offered the promise of peace and prayer. Ominously, a cemetery was laid out by its side.

Walking unchallenged through the hospital, they threw themselves upon each passing sister, only to be met with blank stares and foreign words spoken brusquely in an unfamiliar accent. At last, they heard: 'We have a man of that name. Follow me.'

The nun did not break stride and John and Margaret had to run to catch up. She seemed to float above the floor as she moved, her tunic sweeping the stonework and trapping any echo of her progress. An aura of compassion surrounded her, tempered by the sharpness of someone who was not to be trifled with.

Clearly not a native French speaker, she answered their question before they could ask it. 'My calling is to serve God through nursing the sick and the destitute, to relieve their suffering and to mend their tired and broken bodies, if that be His Will. Many years ago, I left my home and followed the legion of poor Catholics that crossed the ocean in search of a life, knowing that their road would be hard, and that their needs would be great and not well served by others.'

The sister led them down a maze of corridors, casting words over her shoulder that John and Margaret could barely stay close enough to catch.

'Too often the ships that land here bring disease and death. The carts arrive laden with humanity, and no one outside this place cares much if they live or die. There will always be more to follow. If they live, the immigration men are on hand to check that they are fit for work and, if they are incapable of the toil for which they were recruited, they are sent straight back from whence they came. If they perish, the officials wash their hands of them, and sometimes we do not even have a name for those that have passed over. But at least God will know who they are.'

'Did Pa ask for me?' Margaret was barely able to contain herself.

'He has not spoken, at least not that can be understood. He had a letter in his coat, and that is how you were found. It was I who arranged for the telegram. No one should die alone if it can be helped.'

Margaret shivered at the nun's words. 'What ails him? Will he die?' she sobbed.

'He is in the heat of a fever mostly, but sometimes he wakes as cold as if his veins were packed with snow. His cough could wake the dead, and I have rarely seen a man work so hard to breathe and still live. But live he does, at least for now. A priest read him his last rites, but that was two days thence and yet he clings on. So, we cool his brow and put water to his lips, and we encourage him to take whatever simple food he can. That is all we can do. The rest is in God's hands.'

They entered a cavernous place. Sunshine streamed in, illuminating the room to the fullest extent of its vaulted ceiling, its radiance in stark contrast to the cargo of human misery arranged below. Regiments of the sick were laid out on either side, perhaps sixty men all told, with scarcely enough room to walk between them. Murmurs of pain were sporadically pierced by the cries of those nearing the end, summoning those they loved, and pleading for help and forgiveness, desperate to be heard one last time. Others lay immobile and suffered in silence. An assembly of nuns scurried back and forth, tending to their charges, exuding competence and duty. A priest wandered in and out, expecting business at any moment. At the far end of the room, Michael Walsh lay on a straw mattress, struggling for breath.

'Where is he, where is he?' Margaret ran down the walkway, sidestepping human and material obstructions as once she did in the Bradleys' store, ignoring the frowns of disapproval. And when she found him, she hurled herself on his bed before anyone could tell her not to.

Michael was barely recognisable to his daughter. Food had never been plentiful enough to bless him with unnecessary weight, but now he carried markedly less. His grey skin was stretched taut over protruding bones, as if grown for a smaller man. His beard was flecked with grey, and his hair was sparse and untended as the fields in winter. He had aged more than could be explained by the length of their separation. He tried to speak, but nothing emerged from his parched lips. Then suddenly Margaret felt the press of his hand on hers and saw the light return to his eyes.

'I thought I had lost you,' she cried, kissing his fevered brow. 'I have missed you so much. You must never leave me again.'

Another press of the hand, but weaker, reflecting the energy already expended.

'I have so much to tell you, but it can wait until you are strong enough to hear it.'

The next press of the hand was still more feeble.

John stood quietly to one side. After a respectful time, he felt an introduction was needed. 'Sir, in case it is not obvious, I'm … I'm…' And for a moment he could not think how to describe himself to Margaret's father.

'This is my new pa,' she interrupted, smiling as she looked up from the bed.

'Yes, her new pa.'

Old Pa gave her hand a final squeeze.

Soon the sister reappeared. 'You cannot stay longer today. Maybe you can visit again tomorrow, we'll see. There is a room here where you can sleep in return for a meaningful offering towards our work.'

But Margaret could not drag herself from the bed. She clung to old Pa.

'I will fetch you if there is any change,' the sister advised impatiently. 'Now be gone.'

John slowly eased Margaret away, and this time she reluctantly agreed to be moved. Over the following days, they sat patiently by Michael's bed for whatever time they were allowed. He was unable to speak with any sense or reason, and they said little themselves so as not to drain his energy, but their silent presence seemed to soothe and heal. Each day there were small improvements: the river of sweat abated first to a stream and then a trickle; his cough exercised him less and less until it became an infrequent visitor; he lay quieter and apparently in greater comfort.

While Michael slept, Margaret and John prayed in the hospital chapel. There was a constant stream of the faithful, petitioning for a miracle to save a loved one or, failing that, for a serene and guilt-free exit and eternal peace thereafter. John shuffled about uncomfortably, whether sitting or kneeling, intimidated by the intensity of his surroundings: the strange refractions of light as it passed through ornate windows; the extravagance of its trappings of gold and silver; the images of saints of whom he was ignorant, their gruesome suffering depicted in its full glory. It was a far cry from the welcoming simplicity of his own church. Margaret was more at ease, an innate Romanism coming to the fore that pushed aside, perhaps only temporarily, the enforced Protestantism that she had mostly known.

Then on the fifth day, in between gasps for breath, Michael spoke in words that could clearly be identified. 'You took your time coming.' A smile briefly played out across his ravaged face, accompanied by squeals of delight from his listeners.

In the days that followed, Margaret talked incessantly, summoning memories that had some meaning for one or both, often trivial, always important; invoking encounters that were retrospectively amusing or troubling; conjuring fragments that could be expanded into a saga with sufficient wit and embellishment; remembering and lamenting the absence of others, people they had known and, in the case of old Ma, had loved dearly; images frozen in time but still clearly visible from across the sea.

'And the time you chided me for fighting with that red-haired girl. Remember, I tore her dress and pulled her hair so hard I got a clump of it in my hand. And she was older. I think you was proud of me, even though you wouldn't say.' Margaret laughed at the thought. 'Wasn't me that started it,' she quickly clarified, catching sight of John's startled expression.

'I'm seeing a different child here. If only we'd known this…' And he tutted extravagantly, wearing an expression of mock seriousness that could safely be ignored.

'And that time I got in trouble with the matron at the workhouse, just because I broke some filthy jug, not on purpose neither, and she gave me the strap and sent me to bed with no supper. But you gave up your own and managed to get it to me, so I didn't go hungry.'

'Actually, I stole it from an old man, and I could run faster than he could.' His smile told Margaret that this might not be true.

'And when I got scared, which was often, with all those rough men and rougher women and so many devil children, I just had to wait until I saw you, and then you would comfort me, and they didn't look so mean no more. I always felt brave when you were with me, and it gave me strength until the next time…'

'You were always brave, whether I was with you or not. You proved that by coming here.'

From his position outside these shared memories, John initially found conversation difficult, and he sat in awkward silence for much of the time. Margaret saw this and, with her encouragement, John's confidence grew, and soon he was regaling Michael with stories of the chaos he claimed Margaret had brought to the house. 'There's so much noise now I cannot hear myself think.'

'You're the one with a foghorn for a voice,' Margaret retorted.

'And we can barely move about the place for the mess, and everywhere you look, half-eaten scraps of who knows what. It quite offends me. I am such a tidy soul.'

'That's not what Ma says when you're out of hearing.'

'Oh … what does she say?' John asked.

'I'm glad to see you two getting on,' Margaret said later to John. 'It's important to me.'

Some of Margaret's talk was all too familiar to Michael.

'Not everyone is pleased to see incomers like us, and some of them make that quite clear. You may find you don't always get a welcome.'

'I am well acquainted with being an outsider, and what that means.' Michael sighed.

'It's like people used to speak to us when they saw we was from the workhouse, or they found out where you were born. But I've heard all them words before and it doesn't bother me much.'

'Seems like our past follows us to the ends of the earth.'

Sometimes John would leave father and daughter alone so

that they could speak in private. It was as if they had never been parted.

'Tell me about new Ma and Pa,' Michael was quick to ask.

'They are generous and kind, and I want for nothing. They have never raised a hand against me, nor even their voices. They only want the best for me, and I have always felt loved, as a child should.'

Michael sensed there was more to come. Margaret whispered, even though there was no one to hear. 'But they are nervous of you, particularly Ma, and that has upset me at times.'

'I can understand how they must feel. I would be the same.'

'But I think we're over that now.'

'That is good. No one should make you choose. They have nothing to fear from me.'

And Margaret made sure to say, 'I have been very lucky, really. I hear of some that have not been so fortunate.'

It was not long before Michael's bed was needed by another traveller and, by happy coincidence, he was deemed to be sufficiently revived not to need it himself. But before they could leave, he had to attend the immigration office to determine if he could be permanently entered into Canada.

John had been investigating what questions must be answered and which boxes needed to be ticked. 'You must look as if you are in decent health and capable of work, either now or soon,' he advised. 'And there are things I can say that will help.'

Michael took advantage of the washing facilities, and John procured clothes that were both clean and serviceable. He trimmed Michael's beard, and the remains of his hair, so that he looked more human and might now pass for an asset, not a liability. John supported him to walk until they were in sight of the officials, when with great deliberation Michael strode out, as if in prime condition.

'You were brought here for a purpose,' recited the officer in charge. 'There's no place here for men that cannot work.'

'He will work when he has fully recovered his health,' John interrupted. 'He has family here and we will care for him until that time, which will be soon, as you can see from his vigour. He will pay his way in this country, or we will do it for him. Either way, he will not be a burden.'

'I have always worked when given the chance, and that is my reason for being here,' Michael added. 'I know only too well what happens when you don't have work. I nearly lost a child because of it.'

The officer looked Michael up and down with suspicion, weighing up the pros and the cons. Then he reluctantly picked up his pen and signed the papers.

After the formalities were complete, John found the telegraph office and sent a telegram to Daisy, so that once again the delivery man could tell her how important she must be.

FIFTY-SIX

Soon after he passed his twenty-first birthday, Arthur wrote to Alice Hamilton to enquire about his wages. After receiving a favourable response, he left for Kingston to collect them, retracing his steps from so many years ago, riding the train that had been the start of it all. Robert Gait accompanied him for moral and practical support, and in case there was a need for any shouting.

As the train jerked and clattered through the countryside in the autumn sunshine, conversation quickly withered away, and Arthur was free to let his mind roam. After so many years of backbreak and heartbreak, enmity and camaraderie, and perhaps too much whisky, it was bittersweet to finally see some tangible reward – sadly diminished as it was by his accident. Time had been up to its usual tricks, as days flew by at ferocious speed, yet his eventual goal never seemed to get any closer. And then suddenly here it was, almost out of nowhere.

It felt strange to see the Kingston centre as a grown man. It was smaller and less imposing than he had remembered, but even as a child he had strolled in with such confidence and made the place his own, as he always did. And in those few short days he had even found time to play a prank or two. He smiled at the memory of Alice's rage when she found a rather unflattering effigy of herself chalked on a wall. He thought it best not to remind her of this.

The men were shown into Alice's office. She seemed to have changed little, Arthur thought, still bustling and officious but with steel in her blood; he had always considered her to be old. They settled down for some stilted conversation before the main event.

'How have you found the boy?' Alice asked Robert Gait, as he sipped a beverage that he wished was stronger. 'And would you consider taking another?'

Arthur looked nervously at Gait, who winked back at him. He clearly had no intention of highlighting their various fallings-out. Since they had reconciled over Arthur's leg, the two of them had bumped along reasonably well, with just the occasional relapse, and neither wished to reopen old wounds.

'He's lasted the course, which is much to his credit, but I won't need no other as I've boys of my own now,' was Gait's response.

'And what about you?' Alice turned to Arthur. 'Is there anything you would like to add?'

Now it was Gait's turn to look nervous.

'You might remember that I wrote to you some time back, saying how I found it. Not much has changed since then.'

'Apart from that unfortunate episode with a horse.'

'Yes, apart from that.'

'Which hit your finances quite hard.'

Arthur could not help but look accusingly at Gait. 'I guess it couldn't be helped,' he muttered, not truly believing it.

Alice saw no reason to probe further, particularly as there was no repeat business at stake. She consulted a ledger and removed a clutch of notes from a cash box. She carefully counted Arthur's share, then she counted it again, only handing it over when she was completely sure of its value.

At last, Arthur felt the reassuring crinkle of banknotes in his hand. He feasted his eyes on them, taking in every feature of their design and mentally allocating each to a particular expenditure.

'Before you go, would you be prepared to make a contribution towards my work, so that other children might benefit as you have?'

Arthur stared blankly at Alice.

'Donate some of your money,' she clarified. 'To a cause you know to be worthy.'

Arthur looked at her outstretched hand, then at her expectant face; he had been ambushed. With a deep sigh, he reluctantly handed back one of the precious notes.

'And how about you, Mr Gait?'

But Robert Gait's expression told Alice all she needed to know.

After the men had gone, Alice sat back in her chair and congratulated herself on a job well done. She remembered Arthur as a rather arrogant boy, and cheeky with it, but he had turned out a fine young man. I imagine he soon had any nonsense knocked out of him, she thought. And she mentally filed Arthur away as one that could be proclaimed a triumph.

The next stop for Arthur was the Land Grant office, just a few streets away, where he joined a queue of robust men of varying nationality. At its head was an official who was clearly a stranger to manual labour himself, but no doubt he was able to recognise someone who was not. When their turn came, Robert swore to Arthur's age, in the absence of a birth certificate, and vouched for his agricultural competence, although this did not seem to be a major requirement. It was not a rigorous process. In return for a $10 fee, Arthur was granted an initial plot of one hundred and sixty acres, around ten miles to the west of Winnipeg, close to the Assiniboine River, and with a promise of further acreage if he proved himself capable. He was given a detailed map showing the boundary of his land, and a document that proved his ownership. He would take up his holding the following spring.

And that was it. Arthur had walked in a hired hand and strode out a farmer. It was as simple as that. Had it not been so momentous, it might almost have been an anti-climax.

In the months that followed, there was a maelstrom of preparation for the new settler. As excitement jostled with impatience and trepidation, there were times when Arthur wondered if being a free man was all it was claimed to be. Robert Gait produced a list of what Arthur would need to begin his adventure, and Amelia helped him to add up the costs. The list began:

- *A tough old horse for ploughing and a range of things for him to pull*
- *A good axe, or preferably two, with stones for sharpening them*
- *A solid spade*
- *A hammer for nails and another for fence posts*
- *A shotgun for hunting and to keep the vermin down*
- *Assorted knives for skinning your prey*
- *Clothes and bedding suitable for a place that will test your endurance*
- *A pot to cook with, otherwise a mug, a knife and a spoon will suffice for now*
- *A large chest that will keep things dry…*
- *A horse and cart – preferably one that ain't too rickety.*

It included a hundred other items and was accompanied by copious advice: 'Don't buy nothing new. There are always second-hand goods for sale, if you don't mind a dead man's handprint on them…' Robert Gait pointed at the table on which they ate. 'Shot himself by accident, they said. Got it dead cheap.'

Amelia Gait rolled her eyes.

'And don't waste time building somewhere fancy to live. Knock yourself up a sod house and learn to live in earth and grass like a rabbit. Mind you, afore long you'll be yearning for our old shanty…'

Arthur was struggling to keep up.

'And I've told you this a dozen times: find yourself a good woman. You'll have no chance to meet one natural, like, so you'll have to advertise. Lots of men do it and women expect it.'

'Say that she must have the strength of a bear, the stamina of a packhorse and the patience of a saint. That's what she'll need, in my experience,' Amelia added with a meaningful look at her husband.

'I have no idea what you mean.'

Once Amelia had added up the costs and compared the total to Arthur's savings, it was clear that there was a substantial shortfall.

'You will have to get a loan from the bank,' said Amelia. 'I can help you with that.'

Arthur was suspicious. 'Why would they give me money?'

'They'll be seeing a lot of hopefuls, all like you, with a bit of land and no means to do anything with it. They'll figure out that some will thrive, and the ones that do will pay for the ones that don't.'

'Don't seem very likely to me.'

'How do you think we got a start? We had less than nothing.'

So, Arthur scrubbed up as best he could, trimmed his hair and beard, dressed himself in his finest clothes and still hardly looked any different from a normal day. On this occasion, Amelia was his chaperone, having persuaded Robert Gait that his talent for speaking at volume would most likely be counterproductive. After a long wait on uncomfortable chairs, they were shown into the banker's office. He imperiously waved a hand as they entered, barely looking up. Arthur and Amelia sat as instructed.

'I have some money that I've been told I should leave with you for safekeeping,' Arthur began. Amelia had advised him to start with the good news.

The banker's eyes lit up, although they dimmed again when he saw the pitiful amount in Arthur's hand.

'But I will need some more from you so I can work my smallholding proper,' he continued nervously. 'I believe it's called a loan. Because that's what I shall be. Alone.' Arthur had thought that a joke might break the ice, but either it was familiar to the banker, or he was difficult to please.

He frowned. 'And why should I lend the bank's hard-earned cash to you?'

Arthur's heart sank, but it was just the start of the dance. Slowly, the banker extracted the information he required, scratching a quill across some paper to make the detail permanent and occasionally sighing at the inadequacy of Arthur's answers. Finally, he arrived at the decision he had probably made some time before. 'We will lend you what you need. You have as good a chance as any.'

After some rummaging about, the banker presented Arthur with a document for signature that appeared to be written in an entirely different language. He and Amelia read it through and were no wiser at the end than at the beginning.

'What it says, in a rather long-winded way, is that you will have to pay for the privilege of using our money, and if you fail to repay us in a timely manner, we shall take possession of your land,' the banker advised cheerfully.

Arthur stared at the document some more, but without further enlightenment. 'Should I sign this?' he whispered.

'You have no choice,' Amelia breathed, and the banker nodded.

And so Arthur added what passed for a signature on first one copy and then another, and he walked out of the bank with the promise of a future, albeit an uncertain one.

He was very quiet on the journey back to the farm.

'But you aren't going to fail, are you?' Amelia tried to reassure him. 'Think of all you've learned from us. Mr Gait has many failings, but he's a good teacher and he soon lets you know if you're not doing something right.'

'It's different when you're on your own, though, ain't it?'

'True. But just think of all you worked out for yourself, particularly back when you were so young. You've always found a way. And you always will.'

And when he thought about it some more, Arthur knew that she was right.

FIFTY-SEVEN

A train chugged slowly into Kingston on a Saturday afternoon and discharged its arrivals, with a farewell kiss of smoke and soot to send them on their way. John and Margaret Bradley trailed wearily home, but where two had set out, three now returned. Still weak from his illness, Michael Walsh stumbled over the rougher ground and needed frequent support, but there were always willing hands to oblige.

As they walked, John provided a running commentary on his hometown, dispensing more detail than Michael needed or could hope to remember, pointing out landmarks that might be useful in navigating its streets: 'If you start at City Hall you can find anywhere quite easily...' And historic locations of varying degrees of interest: 'That is the first iron bridge in the county...'

He also mischievously signposted the whereabouts of not-so-favourite customers: 'He owes us money and she's quite rude.'

'And the daughter tried to tease me in school,' Margaret chipped in. 'Mind you, she regretted it later.'

Then he highlighted places of personal significance. 'This is the school that Daisy and I attended...'

'Hard to believe he's had any schooling,' Margaret added, and old Pa chuckled so much he missed the next three items in the travelogue.

And then they were home, to the warmest of welcomes; radiant smiles and joyful tears; hearty yet tender embraces; expressions of gratitude and words of endearment. There was a room set aside for Michael, the first he could remember where he would not need to sleep with one eye open. Daisy fussed over him and made sure he was fed and watered and then fed again. A pot of beer was forthcoming, and a second followed soon afterwards. Margaret barely spoke, happy enough just to stare at the miracle of her father, sitting on a simple chair in a basic room. Soon tiredness overcame them all and the house was quiet from an early hour.

The next morning they attended church where the Bradleys, plus one, gave heartfelt thanks for an outcome that underlined their faith in a guiding hand. Margaret sat between old and new Pa to avoid any suggestions of favouritism, holding the arm of each as they walked down the aisle. John was comfortable in his place of worship, although Michael silently questioned the plainness of the church and the simplicity of the ceremony, wondering how any god could take their supplications seriously in the absence of the finery and drama to which he was accustomed. Where was the gilt and the guilt?

There was widespread interest in Michael's presence. As they were leaving, Daisy was proud to tell the story and make some introductions. Michael was more guarded in his answers. Looking back over his shoulder, he registered several animated conversations and some dubious glances in his direction. Margaret squeezed his hand; some things don't change, she thought.

The remainder of the Sabbath was devoted to making delicious plans for the future. There were no boundaries, nothing was out of the question, everything was possible. But John and Daisy were very clear on one thing. 'You must stay with us.'

Margaret jumped up and down, chanting, 'You must, you must, you must…'

John cleared his throat and put on his sensible face. 'Michael, you are here now, all legal and above board, but things are very different from when you signed up for this adventure. So, don't think you must devote yourself to making steel just because that's what you told some man all that time ago.'

'I feel I am obliged to. I made a promise and put my signature to it.'

'But your circumstances have changed beyond all recognition. Your strength is depleted, and the work may be beyond you even if you are willing to try. It is hard and dangerous, and however much they pay you it doesn't compensate for that.'

'And the steelworks are a great distance from here,' Daisy added. 'You would have to find lodgings nearby, and I'll warrant your wages would only pay for something akin to what you've previously known. You deserve better than that.'

'And your health demands it.'

'And we wouldn't see you from one week to the next, and I could not bear that,' Margaret pleaded.

'We have vouched for you so you can do as you please.'

'And if the steelworks want their money back, then so be it.'

Michael looked round at the eager faces. 'I admit, I did not consult a map before travelling and if I had, I doubt it would have helped. "Near" and "far" are quite different here. And you are right, making steel is work for a younger and fitter man than I now find myself. But I cannot be a burden to you, that would rip my heart out.'

'We are not wealthy, as you can see, but there's enough for one more.'

'Besides, there'll be work for you in Kingston, something that befits your health and vigour, so you can pay your share.'

Margaret watched with delight as new Ma and Pa set aside their worries and made her father welcome. And perhaps for the first time, she began to appreciate what it must have taken for them to do this.

The issue was soon settled. There was much laughter and a celebratory meal, and Margaret baked some cakes, a craft at which she was not yet wholly proficient.

'It's such a splendid day that I shall scarcely notice if I crack a tooth.' John only just dodged a ball of cake mixture that might have caused equivalent damage to his skull.

There was a small bottle of wine that had sat for many years in a rarely entered cupboard, lying in wait for a special occasion. The ladies of the house ensured that it was opened and enjoyed although, to her annoyance, Margaret's share was watered down a little. The men consumed beer in an increasingly rowdy manner until Daisy reminded John of his morning commitments, delicately at first and then with mounting irritation until his temporary deafness abated. Goodnights were said in the spirit of a new beginning.

It's a long time since I knew a proper home, Michael thought, as he settled contentedly into his bed.

Meanwhile Margaret looked up at the stars as she bade farewell to the happiest of days. Soon she was dreaming of bright tomorrows.

So far, so good, thought Daisy, and for once she was not disturbed by John's snoring.

The working week started just after dawn, with Sunday's excitement temporarily forgotten in the scurry and bustle of the new day. At first, sleepy eyes hardly noticed that Michael did not appear for breakfast.

'It's early, let him rest, poor man.'

'Give him another day at least before we send him out to work.'

Anxious to see old Pa before she left the house, Margaret eventually made a drink and took it to him. A minute later, she bolted back downstairs. 'I can't wake him. I can't wake him.'

Daisy bounded up to Michael's room. 'Fetch the doctor!' she hollered after the briefest of examinations.

Margaret was already on her way, running through streets that were slowly coming to life, competing with the early morning shufflers and sidestepping those with their minds still elsewhere, as was hers. She was lucky that the doctor believed in a leisurely routine, and he had yet to start his rounds. Her frantic knocking on his door brought forth a maid, whose frosty demeanour and general lethargy must have been shaped by an overexposure to desperate people. Margaret was left, fretting, in the hallway while the doctor was advised of her presence, and she could hear him slowly complete his breakfast, savouring each mouthful and slurping his beverage, while she paced the floor in panic. When he finally emerged, he seemed to take minutes to select a coat, and even longer a hat, before a mirror delayed him further. Once satisfied, he set off for the Bradley store with Margaret impatient beside him, accelerating several steps in front, then having to retreat to match his deliberate stride before repeating the cycle, not daring to chivvy him along in case he took umbrage and turned tail. Finally, the doctor arrived at the store and with a curt 'Wait here' he banished Margaret to the kitchen and climbed alone to Michael's room.

John and Daisy sat Margaret down and each took her hand. She was trembling and desperate, words stumbling over each other in a forlorn quest for reassurance. 'What's happening, Pa? Why is the doctor taking so long? He'll have some medicine, won't he? Something to wake him up?'

'I don't know what to say...'

'Ma, you saw him. He's all right, ain't he? Just a bit tired. That's understandable.'

But Daisy was sobbing and unable to answer.

'Don't tell me. Don't tell me.' But in her heart, Margaret already knew.

A few minutes, later careful footsteps could be heard on the narrow stairs, and the doctor poked his head into the kitchen. 'He is dead,' he declared in a matter-of-fact way.

Margaret screamed, a primal explosion of grief. 'No! No! No!'

She ran up to Michael's room and flung herself on the bed. Daisy followed in fruitless consolation, while John turned on the doctor. 'How can he be dead? He was fine yesterday.'

'You can see from the state of him. It is a miracle he has lasted this long.'

'I cannot believe it. What could possibly have seen him off so quick?'

The doctor was accustomed to being blamed, implicitly or otherwise, for a sudden demise. 'Could be one of a hundred things. Does it really matter?'

John ran up to Michael's room. The bed could hardly be seen. Margaret was draped over Michael's body, with Daisy clinging to her. John found a precarious space and they all lay together.

Margaret was quieter now, almost as lifeless as her father. 'I'm not leaving him,' she breathed over and over.

'My dear, you must…'

'This all happened because I left him.' She buried her face in Michael's silent chest, willing it to rise and fall. 'There, he breathed!'

'No, Margaret…'

'I'm sure of it. Listen.'

But there was nothing to be heard.

Some minutes later, there was an attention-seeking cough at the doorway. The doctor was waiting for payment.

'I will see to the formalities,' he said dispassionately as he pocketed his money.

In Michael's room, Margaret had hardly moved. 'I want to be alone with him,' she said, calmly at first and then more assertively when Daisy suggested that it might be better if they stayed. At last, she had him to herself. John and Daisy listened at the bottom of the stairs as Margaret talked quietly to her father as if he could still hear her: words of love and despair, helplessness and loss, the debris of a broken heart.

'What do I do now?' she was heard to say more than once.

And Daisy thought she made out 'Will you write to me? When you're settled.'

And when the undertaker arrived some hours later, he had to delicately remove Margaret from the room before he could deal with the body.

FIFTY-EIGHT

While he was waiting for his land to become available, Arthur Dilkes surprised Sam Barney by visiting him at the Big House. He thought long and hard before doing so. The fearless scamps from the London streets had trodden very different paths to manhood, and they would not meet as equals. In truth, they never had been on a par, but the gap between them now seemed as wide as the Atlantic, and then some more.

Yet, here they were, face to face after nearly ten years and enough mishaps to last a lifetime. The cell was barely big enough to hold the two of them, and their proximity added to the intensity of the occasion. Arthur had anticipated the arctic conditions and had worn so many extra layers that he took up more space than a man should, further restricting the room they had available. Sam sat huddled in a coat that he had hardly removed since the summer. They looked each other up and down with suspicion, trying to reconcile the children of the past with the men they had become.

There was little to remind Arthur of the cheery companion he had known from their rascal days, when Sam's innocent grin had been a winning counterpoint to Arthur's persuasive patter. Now his face was gaunt and frozen in a scowl, carved out by a prison diet and its frequent downgrading to bread and water, but also moulded by the fire that burnt inside him. His eyes were tired, his shoulders slumped, as if they bore the cares of the world, while his hair looked as if it had been hacked at by a knife – which, in truth, it had. He wore his bitterness like a cloak, and any positive thought that might briefly flicker in his brain had little chance of permanently escaping its smothering. The brawn he had accrued while working for Patience Wright had not wholly wasted away and, when allied to his imposing height, it confirmed that his propensity to fight was not merely an exercise in optimism. One cheek carried evidence of a recent skirmish, and he had dried blood on one hand. Arthur was on his guard, just in case…

Sam found Arthur to be much closer to the boy he remembered. Yes, he sported an adult frame and a complexion that spoke of prolonged exposure to weather, but that was true of many. And perhaps unconsciously, Arthur had spent more time on his appearance that day than he would normally, further underlining the imbalance between them. But Sam was mostly drawn to what lay beneath the façade: the confidence of the man, so familiar to him from their previous life and clearly retained and enhanced. It was most obvious in the way he conducted himself, looking people in the eye, speaking with authority and charm, always comfortable in his surroundings, no matter what he might have felt inside. It was almost pleasing to see that Arthur favoured one leg and walked with difficulty, this being the one area in which Sam could compete.

'Come to gloat, have you?"

It was not a good start.

'I saw old Miss Alice recently and she told me where you were and how you got here.' Arthur talked as he might to a child to gain their trust. 'I'm sorry to see you in such adversity, truly I am. I had hoped if we met again, it would be in happier circumstances.'

'You're all fixed up for life, I hear. Some good years with a proper family and now off you go.' Sam was reduced to a whisper as he struggled to control the voice in his head. 'I'll warrant I worked as hard as you did. I should have prospered and had a decent time of it. I deserved that much. But I didn't have the luck you had with your people. You were always blessed with luck. If she had swapped us around, I'll swear you'd be here, and I'd be in clover.'

'Maybe. Or perhaps I might have made a better fist of it.'

'Say that again!' Sam staggered to his feet, breathing heavily and with a face like thunder, but Arthur did not flinch. He saw no reason to apologise. 'You know, it ain't always been easy for me neither. There were times when I thought I might not walk, nor have any sort of life because of it. And it cost me my savings that I worked so hard for. Yes, the missus was good, but the mister had his moments, and plenty of them. I've had to fight for what I've come out with.'

'Of course, you're right. You're just better than me. Always were.'

Arthur could have served up a platitude but chose not to. Sam slumped back onto the bed. 'Go ahead, say what you like. There's no room to fight proper.'

'And nothing to be gained from it.'

The opening salvos were over, and a dead weight of silence descended on the tiny cell. Eventually, Sam began picking at a scab. 'You could have kept in contact…'

'So could you, if that's what you wanted.'

'You could have helped me out,' Sam accused almost pitifully.

'I didn't know you needed it.'

'We were pals once. We had each other's back.' Suddenly Sam was ten years old again.

'It was always me that had your back, never the other way

around.' It was the first time that Arthur had admitted he might have had a problem with this, and Sam was taken aback. 'Finding a safe place to sleep or somewhere to hide. Working out who to trust and who to avoid. Keeping in with the street gangs, not taking sides and taking all sides. Getting out of trouble with the right words. It was always down to me and, to be honest, I would have liked a break from it.'

'You never said.' Sam looked shocked.

'But then we come here, and I was as much out of my depth as you were. Might not have looked it, but I was. I couldn't think about no one else, I had my own life and that was quite enough. Every man for himself and make the best of your chances. I guess it was always that way, even as children.'

'You were never a child.'

Arthur smiled ruefully. 'I was never given the chance to be.'

After a brief pause in the duelling, Sam seemed keen to bring the meeting to a close. "You've not said why you're here.'

'I have a proposition for you to think on. You're out soon and you'll need somewhere to go and a way to put food in your belly, preferably something that doesn't land you back in here. I'll have work for you if you want it. I can't pay much, but you can live in and share what there is.'

'Don't want your handouts.' The voice in Sam's head made sure it got its answer in first, and once Sam had echoed it there was no going back.

'You know me, Sam, I don't do nothing unless I get something out of it. It's good for both of us. You'd be a man I could count on, unless you've changed beyond what I think you have. And it gives you a chance. You might not have too many of them.'

'So, you'll be bossing me around. Just like before.' The voice was in full flow and would not be interrupted. Sam was merely the messenger.

'Come on, it'll be like old times.' Arthur smiled in encouragement.

'Look, I'm not good at taking orders these days. I'm better on my own.'

'As you wish.'

And the self-destruction was complete.

They moved on. It could hardly be called a conversation, stilted as it was. They were close enough to feel each other's breath but otherwise so distant, tiptoeing around words that might have made a difference had they been said. Towards the end of their time, they shared some reminiscences in a way that was almost pleasurable, and for a few moments they forgot the awkwardness between them.

'You know, Sam, I miss it sometimes. Just the two of us. Living on our wits, celebrating our victories. Or licking our wounds – there was that too.'

'But there was always another day. That's what we said.'

'And then I remember how hard it was, and I'm glad it's over.'

Sam looked Arthur in the eye, but not in confrontation. 'It was my happiest time.'

As he was leaving, Arthur handed Sam a slip of paper. 'This is where I can be found if you change your mind.'

But as Sam stuffed the paper into his pocket, they both knew that he would never do so, and that if he did, no good would come of it.

Arthur strode out of the Big House without a backward glance. For some time, Sam stared at the space that his erstwhile friend had just vacated.

FIFTY-NINE

Michael Walsh's funeral was held at the church of St Joseph, and he was buried in the adjoining cemetery. The church was grander in scale than might be expected, given the local predominance of another persuasion; perhaps it had been built in the hope that one day the heretics would see the error of their ways and return to the true faith. Cold and oppressive, it demanded absolute obedience from those that entered, its walls radiating incense and hellfire to assault their senses and twist a supplicant's will into submission. There was no welcome to be found here, for the living or the dead.

Their heads bowed, the trinity of mourners approached the altar, the echo of their footsteps ringing out to every corner of the church. The coffin stood alone. It was a spartan affair, crafted in a rudimentary fashion from local pine and with an afterthought of plain iron handles, its simplicity at odds with the intensity of the mourners' gaze. There were no thoughts, no words, just feelings.

A solemn priest conducted the ritual, efficient and impersonal, reciting text he had rendered a thousand times to mark the end of different lives. It was largely an administrative matter between him and his God, a transfer of responsibility from earthly oversight to a celestial regime. It brought no comfort to those who witnessed it.

The cemetery was a place of peace and order. Stone tablets in obedient patterns dotted the immaculate greenery, each bearing a name, some dates and a handful of words that inadequately described those who lay beneath. In a distant corner a gathering of wooden crosses remembered those with insufficient means for something more permanent. A small number of excavations sat side by side, awaiting the day's business, and two gravediggers sheltered under a tree, partially camouflaged by tobacco smoke, spades at the ready for when the mourners had moved on.

Margaret stood before the open grave, oblivious to the rain that fell steadily from a sky that matched her mood. She let slip a small posy of flowers into the void, their luminous beauty a scold to the drabness of the earth and the bleakness of the occasion. She had barely spoken since Michael's death, nor had she spilled many tears, but now the shackles were broken and her howls of grief rent the silence.

'It is a cruel God that gives such wondrous hope and then snatches it away before it can be enjoyed,' she railed, beating her fists together in anger and frustration. 'Why has my beloved pa been punished so? And how am I deserving of such loss?' She glared at Daisy and John as if they were to blame.

'A clergyman would say that God moves in mysterious ways, but I never thought that was much of an answer,' Daisy ventured. 'Things just happen, good and bad, and there's rarely any rhyme or reason.'

Margaret barely heard the words. 'And that priest with all his talk of sin and repentance, and how if folks are lucky there might be some absolution at the end of it. I know Pa wasn't perfect, but it's not him that should be seeking forgiveness, not with the life he was given. It's them that hounded him on

Earth, and any God that allowed it to happen, they should be on their knees begging for pardon.'

And Margaret did not exempt herself. 'He would still be alive if he had stayed in England, I'm sure of it. His death is at my door for encouraging him to come here. I wanted him close by, and my selfishness has killed him.'

'Dearest, you are not to blame. Your father wanted to be here because otherwise he had nothing worth living for – he said so often enough.' John tried to hug Margaret, but she wriggled clear.

'It was only his desire to see you again that kept him going,' Daisy added.

'And when he was with us, he was truly happy. He would not blame you for your encouragement. He would thank you for it.'

'For two days. That's how long he was with us. He was truly happy for two days. In a whole lifetime.' Margaret stared daggers at new Ma and Pa. 'If he'd stayed put, I could have gone back to England when I was older. Looked after him, been with him. That would have given him something.'

John looked anxiously at Daisy. 'She doesn't mean it,' he mouthed. Margaret was in full flow, and they let her speak uninterrupted. There was nothing they could say to diminish her anger.

'From his first breath he was belittled and condemned – not for who he was, but for who folk thought he was. Where he came from and how he spoke and which God he favoured. The constant ridicule and bad-mouthing. The indignity of the workhouse and many worse places besides. He had to fight for every scrap, and he was never given a chance. Just like his father and his father before that.'

Margaret's tirade was briefly disturbed by a burst of laughter from the gravediggers as they shared a joke. She glared at them, and they fell silent again.

'He was an honest man, more decent and trustworthy than

many who saw fit to malign him. A good man living in bad times.'

The rain fell more heavily still, and the gravediggers pulled their coats over their heads for greater protection, but Margaret remained oblivious. 'But there was never an easy welcome, and it would have been no different here. Even in this town, I saw the looks of the faithful at our church. People like us are only ever judged for what we're not, not for what we are. And all this would have been my inheritance, but for his resolve that I should have a better life, even if it meant sacrificing his own happiness. And now I have a chance of that – thanks to you, of course, but also to him. He had a big heart, and his loss leaves a hole that can never be filled.'

Margaret looked into the grave, addressing her father directly. 'I am proud of you, and I will miss you so very much.'

Eventually she ran out of words and walked slowly away from the graveside, with John and Daisy trailing a discreet distance behind. The gravediggers extinguished their pipes and moved in to complete the job. The first load of dirt covered the flowers that Margaret had let slip.

'At the time when she needs us the most, she walks away alone,' Daisy whispered sadly, needing John's arm more than ever. 'What does that say about us?'

Margaret suddenly looked back. 'I want to be with my thoughts now,' she said in the emptiest of voices.

'May we at least sit with you?' appealed Daisy.

'I need to do this alone. In my own time. In my own way. I will have his memory for company.'

'Are we not enough for you?' John could not help himself.

Margaret smiled at the man who was now her father. 'One day you will be, I promise.'

'But not today?'

Margaret slowly turned to walk off. 'No, not today.'

SIXTY

In the summer of 1891, Sam Barney was released from the Big House, with just the clothes that hung off him and enough money for a one-way ticket to somewhere else. As he walked unsteadily through the prison, he hurled some final abuse at one-time adversaries and aimed a volley of curses at a jailer with whom he was particularly unfriendly. He shaded his eyes as he approached the unfamiliar sunlight. He was not in good shape, breathing hard and with stabbings of pain in places where it was usually considered dangerous to have them, a legacy of ailments he had collected and held on to for want of treatment. There was scarring around his face and arms, and one shoulder did not function entirely as it should. He had a hand that might have been broken, and which was struggling to heal, although he had continued to exercise it with regularity upon the skulls of others.

To his surprise, Alice Hamilton was waiting for him as he stepped out of the door.

'Didn't expect to see you, missus.'

Alice cringed at the epithet, but it was not worth challenging. 'Do you have any plans?' she asked innocently, being confident of the answer.

'An offer of work I don't want, otherwise nowhere to go and not much hope of a welcome in any town.'

'I have suggested this before, and perhaps this time you might be more amenable.'

'I'm listening.'

'There is a ship that sails from Quebec in three days. I will pay for your passage to England and will even see to it that you have a cabin.'

'Why would you do that, missus?'

'It is in your best interests. There is nothing for you here.' Alice also considered it money well spent to avoid future adverse publicity; Sam would always be seen as one of hers. She thought it best not to mention this.

'I will also furnish you with some clothes and other necessaries. And as you are now twenty-one, your wages are due, those you earned before your …' Alice struggled to find a word that would not antagonise him. 'Difficulties,' she settled on. 'After that, you are on your own.'

'That's how I like it.' His bravado was transparent; Sam was in no mood to bite this particular hand and asked no further questions. He was pleased to cut his losses.

And when he stood on the deck of the SS *Circassian* a few days later, gladly bidding farewell to Canada, Alice was finally able to wash her hands of him.

SIXTY-ONE

In the spring of 1892, Arthur Dilkes stood on a railway platform, bound for Winnipeg, his faithful trunk at his side. The possessions it contained had not greatly increased in number since its previous journey, but their adult size now made the box more difficult to close and keep secure. His copy of *The Pilgrim's Progress* had remained unopened in a drawer throughout his time with the Gaits, but it had been one of the first items he had packed; it was clearly a token of good luck.

The whole family had come to see him safely on his way. Robert Gait herded the two Gaitlets onto the cart then, delicately at first, but soon tiring of that, helped his wife aboard. The fact that she was expecting a third did not protect her from a good shove.

'Canada will soon be full, the way you two are going,' Arthur had joked when he heard the news. 'Save some room for us poor immigrants.'

And with Arthur and his trunk adding to the ballast, the horses earned their keep that day.

Soon it was time to say farewell. Gait appeared awkward, as he always did when displays of emotion were expected, shifting from one foot to another and making preparatory noises in his throat that implied fine words to come, but which always resulted in disappointment. He made as if to hug Arthur, then thought better of it and settled for a bone-jarring handshake.

Amelia was accustomed to rescuing the situation. 'What he means to say is we thank you from the bottom of our hearts for what you have done for us, and we will pray for you in your new life.' She laughed, making sure that her embrace was the equivalent of two. 'Perhaps one day you will bring your own children to see us.'

'And there's thanks due from me as well.' It was not clear if Arthur deliberately looked only at Amelia. He then turned to her husband. 'We've not always seen eye to eye, but overall I think we've been good for each other.'

'I would echo that,' Gait added after receiving a prod from Amelia.

Soon the train chugged out of the station, and Arthur left the past behind without a backward glance. It was time to look forward.

Amelia had laid on a spread for the journey: a large pie, a loaf of bread, some pickled eggs and a flagon of beer to wash it all down. Arthur smiled as he unwrapped it; this might be his last wholesome meal for some time. He had money in his pocket for his immediate needs, while other funds had been transferred to a local bank, but he was well aware of his financial fragility. Before he could break ground, he'd have to buy implements and tools, materials and transport, and all the other accoutrements he would need. He would have to patrol the boundary between necessity and luxury, but he had been there before.

The summer was a blur of activity. Arthur built a temporary structure to shelter him from the elements, and he made some progress in taming the wilderness, felling and hacking and digging until he had a patch that he could scrape a plough over in the spring. It was a start. Following Gait's advice, that first winter he would retire to the town and seek work there to eke out his savings, and he had already sounded out possible employers. By the next summer, he was confident that he could call himself a farmer.

It was soon apparent that while Arthur was good on his own, he would be even better in company, and a second pair of hands would push things along more quickly. He decided against employing a labourer, firstly in case Sam Barney changed his mind, however unlikely that seemed, then deciding that the money could be better spent. However, a more personal arrangement was a different proposition. One day he drove into Winnipeg and placed an advertisement with various newspapers, requesting a wife, although saying that he would consider a companion of either sex. To his surprise and delight, he received letters from several women who were languishing in various states of availability, not just from the western outposts but even in now-distant Ontario. Some enclosed likenesses, courtesy of the miracle of photography.

There was one applicant that stood out. A pretty face stared into the distance, framed by ringlets that had likely been created for the pose. Her smile would have melted the sternest of hearts, and it was made more appealing still by a trace of sadness that was just detectable beneath the façade of how she wanted to be seen. She wrote in a manner that hinted at being good company, and conveniently she was of farming stock, although currently in service to an important family in Kingston – the Hoggards. Apparently, it was a post she would very much like to vacate. She said her name was Charity Wright. She wrote about her family and her experience of working the land, describing the recent death of her mother with some ambivalence. She did not appear to be close to her father.

Arthur was particularly intrigued by one sentence.

We had a SAD boy once, she wrote. *But that's a story for another day.* And elsewhere she asked *Are you a man of music? I could sing for you if you would like it.*

Arthur smiled. 'I think I have found a wife,' he decided, and ticked another item off his list.

SIXTY-TWO

Sam Barney arrived back in London in a more positive frame of mind. No one would know him or be familiar with his misadventures, and he could start afresh in surroundings that were not foreign to him. Indeed, each familiar street revived memories of companionship and laughter and difficulties that were overcome. While it was a rose-tinted recollection, in his mind they were the best days he had known, although the competition for this accolade was not great.

Sam's hard-earned carpentry skills were a boon, and within days he found a position that was secure in tenure, and which paid better than many. Yet the voice in his head had not been silenced, and he was soon in dispute with his employer about wages and a perceived lack of respect. He walked out in protest and took to drinking, falling out with a second employer over his reliability, or lack of it. He stole from a third.

'He is a better craftsman than a human being' was how one man described him.

It was not long before Sam had worked his way through every potential employer in the vicinity, and his reputation now preceded him.

Some months later Alice Hamilton was reading the *Police Gazette*, as she was wont to do: it was a chronicle of crimes and misdemeanours, some solved and others in a state of mystery; a portrait of felons and accomplices, both apprehended and still at large. Aside from its entertainment value, there were instances when Alice, in the course of her work, happened upon information that would assist the police with their enquiries, and other times when it alerted her to certain children that might benefit from her attention. On this occasion, Sam Barney's name stood out from the crowd. He had been accused of a series of robberies and assaults, and his story took up the best part of a page. Alice's heart sank as she read on.

No longer employed, and with no desire ever to be so again, Sam had turned to crime to support what passed for a lifestyle. He mostly plied his trade in and around Leadenhall Street, in the heart of the City, where on a winter's evening he would find monied gentlemen brazenly walking about as darkness fell, perhaps en route to a railway station and thence homewards, or destined for an evening with like-minded others in a favourite club. Locally, there were a myriad of passages and alleyways in which a man might be detained if sufficient force were applied, or the threat of a knife were heeded, and Sam utilised these to the full, stalking his victim until he was sufficiently alone, and relieving him of his money, his pocket watch and whatever valuables might be about his person. It was daring to the point of reckless, but the rewards were sizeable, and he was past caring about the risk.

Sam's patch was a convenient walk – or a bracing run – from the maze of slums and tenements that he knew so well, and which had not changed one jot in his absence. There he could disappear without a trace until the next time, dossing down wherever he might find a bed, safe in the knowledge that no questions would be asked. And in the ale houses, he bartered his spoils for a fraction of their true value, and in return he enjoyed an evening of drink and a bite of food, and perhaps some female company.

Given the standing of his victims, it was unsurprising that the constabulary took an interest in Sam's activities, and they increased their vigilance. The *Police Gazette* described how a constable disturbed Sam in the act of pouncing, and a chase ensued. Sam outran his pursuer, but the constable's whistle aroused others in the area, and their answering calls confirmed that they were converging from all directions. Sam was now in Aldgate. He turned towards the river, hoping to find sanctuary in the labyrinthine streets that bordered St Katharine Docks and beyond. The brooding presence of the Tower of London loomed before him – he was nearly there, but three constables were at his heels, some with fewer miles in their legs, while more were arriving from the north and east. The only possible route was towards the new Tower Bridge, but still in the throes of construction, it did not yet offer passage to the other side of the river, and Sam's way was barred. He was trapped.

The constables were calling for Sam to stop and accept his fate, but the voice in his head was louder, refusing him the option of surrender. In desperation he began to climb one of the bridge's giant suspension cables, leaping onto it where it kissed the road and following its rise, his feet slithering on the polished steelwork, the rivets his only friend in keeping his balance. Several constables arrived at the foot of the cable and considered their next move.

'Hey, Sam Barney, best you come down. You can't get much further.'

Sam clung precariously to the cable with one hand and took his knife from a pocket, swaying in the wind as he waved it in the general direction of his pursuers. 'I ain't going to prison. Can't face that again.'

Perhaps there was one last fight in him, he thought, and the voice was egging him on, exaggerating his chances of success. But the constables were aware of the true odds.

'Should have thought of that before you went robbing innocent people. It's better to take that fall than the one you're facing up there.'

'Or you'll be coming down quicker than you went up.'

Sam heard the cruel laughter from below.

'It would be no great loss to the world, would it, lads?'

The constables laughed again, and Sam could not help but agree with them.

'I tell you, I ain't coming down. You'll have to fetch me.'

'No chance of that. But we can wait. All night if we must.'

And the constables made themselves comfortable at the foot of the cable, primed to apprehend their quarry should he descend. A light rain began to fall, and the constables donned their capes, but remained in place, cursing the English weather and occasionally reminding their prey that they were better equipped to withstand it. The hours passed. Sam stared disconsolately down at his would-be captors. Even the voice had abandoned him.

No one could say whether he jumped or slipped, but as midnight approached Sam fell into the unforgiving Thames and disappeared beneath the blackness of its waters. The constables strained their eyes to see if he might re-emerge, but there was no sight nor sound of him. Soon they returned to their beats, congratulating themselves on the success of their intervention. The next day, Sam's body was washed up nearby, and it was found by a group of young mudlarks who worked the shoreline, just as Sam and Arthur had once done.

He had come full circle.

*

'A number of outstanding cases have now been closed,' the article ended.

Alice Hamilton made some enquiries, which eventually led to an unmarked grave in the churchyard of St George-in-the-East. It was only identifiable due to having been recently dug. Alice commissioned a simple headstone so at least Sam's grave would have a name, should anyone choose to read it. She laid a posy on the bare earth and spent a moment in prayer.

Any boy that complains about good food that is freely given is bound to come to a sticky end, she thought, then returned to her business.

SIXTY-THREE

Mary Oliver sat by the window in her asylum cell and stared impassively into the distance – one of the few remaining activities available to those that were not physically restrained. The unchanging view barely registered upon her consciousness or triggered any thought or emotion. It was just there, as she was.

She rarely left the cell voluntarily. There were still the working parties, soulless hours in a cramped and draughty room, turning cotton into handkerchiefs and reeds into baskets, with not a friendly word exchanged. There was a compulsory period of exercise, a slow circular walk around the grounds in the company of other inmates, which was no company at all. Mary once had sung whenever the mood took her, but now she was silent; she left any melody to the birds. Her eating habits had become increasingly sporadic and her bathing most irregular. The cell was both a sanctuary and a prison, its walls seeming to contract each day, shrinking the room to a fraction of its original size. The door was always firmly closed. Yet it could be opened from the inside, if she so wished, such was her place in the hierarchy of lunatics. And this possibility, even if not exercised, helped her feel protected, not buried alive.

It had been a lonely winter, as all winters were, and now the spring thaws were in full swing. But this was a special year, and there was but one thought in Mary's mind.

'Percy will soon reach his majority, I'm sure of it. Then Miss Alice will arrive and let me out. I'll have a few days making myself look normal, and then I'll set off to find him. It's time I had a life.' So Mary sat by the window, awaiting her liberator's appearance, each day that passed a torment to her. But spring became summer, which matured into autumn, and suddenly it was winter again. Alice had not visited since their quarrel, far too proud to disobey the demand to stay away. Mary now regretted having been quite so angry and replayed their final conversation over and over in her head in the hope of a different ending. And she waited and waited until she could do so no more.

If she won't do it, I shall have to let myself out, she decided, although she had no idea of how that might be achieved. She imagined she would just have to ask.

The next morning Mary crept from her room and headed towards the central area, where the director would generally be found. She knew that the lunatics were not permitted to speak to him, unless he spoke to them first, and they certainly were not allowed to invade his inner sanctum, unless invited and suitably controlled, so she made her way there in secret, the importance of her mission banishing any nerves she might have felt. The director was sat behind his desk, devouring some biscuits in an effort to keep himself nourished until luncheon. He looked up when Mary entered the room, and in a panic, he instantly called out for help, shouting at the top of his voice and ringing a small bell. No help materialised. Mary wondered why a man many times her bulk might find her intimidating, but she did not wish to frighten him away entirely and maintained a respectful distance.

'Please, mister, I have a question for you.'

Through his fingers, the director looked suspiciously at the intruder. She did not appear to have a weapon about her person, nor was she threatening in appearance: she was scrawny, yes, unkempt, definitely, but not menacing. He would find out what she wanted.

'Spit it out, girl.'

'Easy one, really. How do I get out of this place?'

As they spoke, the director began to recognise his visitor. 'Get out? You don't get out. You are committed here indefinitely. Do you know what that means?'

'I think so, mister, I'm not stupid. So, how do I become uncommitted?'

'A medical man such as I would have to pronounce you sane.'

'So, can you do that, mister? You can see I'm all right in the head.'

'I see no such thing. I merely observe a young woman that has barged into my office, uninvited and unannounced, contrary to the strictest of our rules.'

This was not going according to plan. Mary edged closer to the director. He backed away from his desk.

'I need to be out, mister. My brother, he's eighteen years old now, and I need to find him.'

'I know nothing of your brother.'

'But Miss Alice Hamilton said that I would be placed into his care and he into mine when he reached an age, and now he has.'

The director knew of no such agreement, since it had been made with the previous director. However, he spotted an opportunity. 'There is, of course, a payment involved in becoming "uncommitted", as you put it,' he ventured.

'But I don't have no money, mister.'

'Then you cannot be sane.'

At this point, two burly men entered the office. Each took Mary by the arm and bundled her back to her room.

'Do that again and you'll be restrained,' one of them warned.

Mary lay on her bed and wept until her very soul was dry. Meanwhile the director celebrated his narrow escape with a pie that he kept for emergencies.

And so the waiting went on. Another year passed. The hopeful mornings became ever more desperate, the dismal evenings bleaker by the day, each sleepless night a personal Hell.

Surely, she wouldn't abandon me just because I spoke to her like that, Mary thought in her more rational moments. That would be too great a punishment.

But when her mind was fragile, as it often was, she could believe that it was exactly what Alice Hamilton might do, and she even came to think she might deserve it. Mary had no means of contacting her to find out; an inmate might say all sorts of things if allowed paper and pen.

Then on the first day of May 1892, a nurse appeared at the door of Mary's cell, not bothering to knock or ask for permission to enter.

'You have a visitor,' she growled. 'Didn't give his name and I didn't ask it. Said he will meet you by the big tree.'

Mary leapt from her bed. 'See, she hasn't abandoned me. Old Miss Alice said she might send someone else, and now she has. And a man, too.' Then she had a joyous thought. 'Perhaps he can get me uncommitted. Maybe that's why he's here.'

Her flustered mind was flooded by questions. The man had doubtless travelled out of duty and as a condition of his employment, but even so, what would he think of her? What would she make of him? How much did he know? How much should she tell him? It was overwhelming. And for the first time since Alice's final visit, Mary was conscious of her appearance. Her hair was dirty and bedraggled, not having seen water or a comb for several days. The uniform she wore was threadbare, so it barely covered her as it should. She was aware that others might not wish to stand too close to her.

'Oh, what to do? What to do?' She quickly ran a comb through her tangled locks, and that would have to be enough. Walking nervously across the grass, she could see a young man at the appointed place, tall and sturdy and, as far as she could tell, much younger than she had been expecting. When he heard her approach, he turned to face her.

Mary stopped in her tracks and for a few seconds they stared at each other, searching for the right words or, indeed, any words at all. Then she desperately rummaged in her pocket for the photograph of Percy that was always there and often looked at.

It was a match.

'I've never felt so twitchy as I was posing for that likeness. I've missed you, sis,' Percy said quietly.

Mary felt a cascade of confused and contrary emotions. An explosion of joy and shards of embarrassment that pierced her to the quick. She was ecstatic but mortified, euphoric and humiliated in equal measure.

'You cannot see me like this!' she shrieked, turning to flee across the grass to escape her shame, with Percy in pursuit, calling her name as he ran. He soon overtook her faltering steps and barred the way. 'You mustn't run, sis, not from me.'

'But look at me! How can you call me your sister? I never meant you to see this. You don't deserve to see it. Your sister, a lunatic.' She was shaking and sobbing so that each word was staccato, almost a sentence in its own right.

Percy smiled reassuringly, and her trembling abated a little. 'Sis, you of all people have nothing to be ashamed of. I know where you've been and what has befallen you. Every last bit of it. I thought I would find you in a state. And yet here I am.'

'But...'

'You have nothing to shock me with. Nothing that will make me think bad of you. And you are no madder than I am, although perhaps that is not a true measure.'

Mary laughed, a strange and unfamiliar sound. 'Are you real? People here swear they see things that are not there. Are you one of those?'

'I'm as real as that tree, sis, but sadly not as handsome.' Percy took Mary in his arms as proof of his existence, and the extent to which she had been reduced was all too obvious. Once she had been Big Sister, strong and determined, and as capable as any. He had followed and obeyed her without question. Now he towered over her. She had been made small and frail by her confinement and had no confidence even to stand straight or look Percy in the eye.

'Seeing you like this, in this loathsome place, so mistreated, fills me with such anger I can't think straight.' Tears filled his eyes. 'If I had known your true situation, I would have been here in an instant. You know that sis, I would have. But neither you nor old Miss Alice were honest with me. There's you weaving pretty stories and her always making excuses for why you couldn't even put pen to paper. How was I to know? But all I can think now is, how could I not see that something weren't right?'

'What could you have done? You were still a child.'

'Doesn't stop me feeling bad. Doesn't mean I didn't let you down, in my head if not in yours.'

Mary resumed the embrace, comforting her brother as she had in days gone by. 'I was too proud, and it has hurt you badly. And no doubt it has prolonged my own misery, and I have rightly suffered because of it. Can you forgive me?'

'There's nothing to forgive.'

A quietness settled upon them for a moment, each picking their way through a landscape of guilt and regret.

Finally, Percy broke the silence. 'So, shall we go, sis?' he suggested in a very matter-of-fact way.

'What do you mean? Go where?'

'Anywhere but here.'

Mary looked at Percy as a big sister might when explaining the obvious. 'But I cannot leave. They will not let me.'

'They will, sis. I have come to take you. Today, if you are willing to be taken.' Percy's smile returned and Mary thought she detected a wink. 'You are being discharged into my care. Miss Alice arranged it. She has given me some legal papers that I don't understand, and some money to pay off the scoundrel that runs this place.'

Disbelief and rapture flitted across his sister's face.

'You did so much for me when I was just a squirt. Put me first every time. Now it's my turn. They have broken you, but you will mend. I will see to it.'

'But where will we go? How shall we live? I detest this place, but I am almost scared to leave it.'

'We can be farmers, sis. True Canadians, proper SAD children. I'm applying for my own smallholding out west, and I'm told I should get something. It won't be much, but it will be enough for the two of us if we work it right. You'll have to do your share, mind. And it will be a hard slog too. I hope you've not got too fond of your lazy life here – all these servants scurrying around, waiting on you hand and foot, while you sit there, all regal like.'

Mary playfully punched Percy's arm, as she had often done when he was cheeky. 'But I know nothing about working the land. All I've done is live with a mad woman and her vile children, and I was so bad at that, I ended up here.'

'I've learned enough to get us by, maybe. And what we don't know we can learn as we go. Of course, you'll need to take orders from me, and do as you're told, and I'll wager you won't like that.'

Another playful punch.

'And if the farming doesn't pay, there will be something else. There's labouring or cutting down timber or digging the mines, and there's always work in the cities if you don't mind what you do.'

'Or we could head back to England.'

'Why not? The world is ours, and we can do as we please. Anyhow, wherever we are and whatever we do, before I know it, you'll meet some toff and turn into Missus La-di-Dah. And then you can employ me as your lackey, and I'll forever be having to doff my cap at you. I can see you having a liking for that.'

One final punch.

'So, will you come with me?'

Mary did not need to answer. She hugged Percy with all the force she could muster.

'Right, we'll sort that man out first, then we'll pack up your things. There is a train this afternoon, and it's quite a walk to the station. I brought some clothes so you can take off those festering rags.'

They marched over to the entrance hall to complete the formalities. After the briefest of knocks, they entered the director's office. He was in his usual place, attending to a plate of sandwiches.

'This won't take a minute,' Percy announced as the director tried to protest at the intrusion. Percy slapped the committal papers on the desk.

The director looked up at what he saw as two children. 'I do not recognise these documents,' he sniffed. 'Now kindly leave my office.'

'We're not going until you sign.'

The director raised himself from his seat – rather slowly, given the tonnage that was being lifted. As before, he shouted for assistance and rang his little bell. Within seconds, two large gentlemen appeared.

Mary screamed. 'Oh Percy, what are you doing? They'll put me in one of them jackets.'

'Don't worry, sis. I'm glad we've got some witnesses to hear what I have to say.' He smiled at the director. 'Miss Hamilton is a wily old bird, and she warned me you might try to pull a trick.' Percy's smile vanished and instantly he looked older than his years. 'I'm told there are plenty in Toronto that are very interested in how this place is run, particularly on the money side.' Alice had given him a script, which he had learned assiduously. 'And Miss Hamilton, bless her, is very thorough when it comes to recording what she has to pay. Every instalment is there somewhere, all added up nicely, and I doubt it tallies with what you have handed over to your masters.'

Suddenly the director looked concerned.

'All these important people paying more than they need to. They won't like that. I have a list of them and I'm sure they'll hear me out.'

'And you told me I could only be sane if I paid for it,' Mary chipped in. 'I don't see nothing about that in these papers.'

Of course, Mary had not read the documents, but the director was now too befuddled to consider that possibility. He signalled the men to leave, which they did, muttering to each other. They would be back later with their own proposition.

'There are costs involved in reversing a committal...'
'None that fall to you.'
'There is my signature and some additional paperwork...'
'Name your price.'

The director hemmed and hawed before quoting a figure.

'Done.' Percy slapped some notes on the desk. 'There you go, you can treat yourself to some savouries. You look like you need feeding up.'

When they left the director's office, Percy was grinning from ear to ear. 'He was so desperate to be rid of us, he only asked for half of what Miss Alice gave me.'

Mary laughed like the child she had never really been. 'She doesn't need to know, does she?'

'Gives us a bit of a head start, don't it?' Percy escorted Mary to her cell to collect what few belongings had not been lost or stolen over the years. Then he waited, relaxed at first but with growing impatience, while Mary commandeered the room where inmates were periodically sluiced down and deloused. But now she bathed and washed her hair in a far more civilised fashion, cleansing her mind and soul as much as her body. And for the first time in years she sang, the first notes in a faltering voice that soon became soaring and transcendent. Percy joined in, less confidently and often in a different key but joyous, nonetheless.

Inmates and staff emerged suspiciously, briefly listened then disappeared again, disquieted by the unfamiliar celebration of life. Finally, and taking care to transfer her precious photograph, Mary put on her new clothes, and the transformation was complete. They were not the greatest fit, hanging from her skeletal frame as if dangling from a branch, the result of Percy's understandably inaccurate guess as to what an appropriate size might be. But to Mary they were finery unsurpassed.

'You look a proper woman, sis.'

And so she was.

And soon Mary was walking down the approach road, glorying in the direction of her travel. The colonnade of trees formed a guard of honour, gently stirring in the Lake Ontario breeze, warmly waving her farewell. Then the forbidding gates creaked open in a final act of release.

The asylum receded into the distance, and Mary stood confident and straight, striding out and turning to check that Percy was keeping up with her, maintaining a constant stream of chatter and instructions.

She was Big Sister again.

SIXTY-FOUR

One spring morning Alice Hamilton was seated in her office in a state of nervous anticipation, a pot of tea for company. Papers covered her desk, but they were neatly arranged and clearly in some sort of order. The previous evening she had finally completed her epic project, and here it was in all its glory: the varied lives of her migrated children placed into one of several piles and judged a success or failure depending on where they came to rest. This was her legacy, the justification for all the battles she had fought, the miles travelled, the discomfort endured: vindication of the endless diplomacy, so unnatural to her, and the uneasy compromises that were even more so. It was payment for the personal sacrifices she had made; the void in her life where friends and family might otherwise have been; the absence of intimacy, which she now suspected she might have found tolerable, perhaps even gratifying, had she given it a chance. This was the means by which she would be remembered, and the light in which she would be seen.

Alice had set aside the day for a detailed study of all that she had found. Atop each pile was a list of names that fell within that category, and beneath it was the evidence for their inclusion. She had avoided keeping a running tally as her work progressed, in fear of either being unnecessarily discouraged or of claiming credit before it was due. Neither was the height of each pile an accurate indication of each case, as some outcomes generated more paper than others. She approached her task with some misgivings, her intuition telling her that it might be a difficult day. What if she did not like what she discovered? How would she live with that? Was it better that she did not know?

'Pull yourself together, woman, it will be whatever it will be,' she scolded herself and set to work.

She started on a positive note: the very young children who had been formally adopted, each sporting a new surname but with their previous existence also recorded. She moved her finger down the list, and it was almost as if each child waved to her as she passed, smiling and eager to tell their story, with cheery siblings by their side and proud parents standing behind them. They were secure and happy, loved and loving – proper families. Some might remember their past, but most would only have random memories, and that was just as well. Alice dwelt on the name of Margaret Walsh, now Bradley. It had been so sad about her father, she thought. Her birth father, that is. It showed the danger of not letting go, and that was a lesson to be learned. She had sent a note of commiseration when she heard the news, but she was unaware that Margaret had not yet felt able to read it.

Next, Alice moved on to those who had seen out their contracts as intended and had safely reached the shelter of their maturity. Certain names leapt out from the page, and Alice could immediately picture to whom they belonged. The children that always laughed and smiled, no matter what pain and sadness they had encountered. The boy who had graduated from a happy placement and brought her flowers in appreciation. The girl now wed and with children of her own, including one named Alice in her honour. The letters of thanks that were given pride of place in her filing system; she could always find those. At each of these reminders, Alice would smile and award herself a small pat on the back. These were as they should be. Arthur Dilkes was on this list.

There are some that you just know will do well, Alice thought as his name slid by.

And then there were those who had travelled in the opposite direction. The children too scarred by the past to hold down a placement for any meaningful time. Those who went awry for one reason or another, perhaps through no fault of their own. Those who grew up to know the inside of Canada's more challenging institutions – Sam Barney and too many others, finding brief notoriety in the pages of the *Toronto Herald*, allowing a certain type of person to say 'I told you so'. Mary Oliver was also in this pile, but at least she had her redemption, even if it was a long time in coming. And the ghost of Simeon Harding hovered over proceedings. However hard she tried, Alice could never quite shake off her guilt. She grieved for each child on this list, but in her calmer moments tried to reason that, whatever their fate, it might have been similar, or worse, had they remained in England. She could save children from all manner of perilous circumstances, but she could not save them from themselves. It was an argument that never quite convinced her.

And for those children who fell between these two extremes, those who had moved neither forward nor back, Alice's memory was often vague, and they occupied no more of her time than it took to read a name. Should they be counted a success or a failure? Perhaps neither. Perhaps both.

And then there were the invisible mites for whom there was no pile nor list, not even a scrap of paper as evidence of their destiny; they were a number, nothing more. For some there might be an echo of a life that once crossed her path, perhaps a vague recollection of a dark-haired boy or a pale-skinned girl, or a child with noteworthy freckles or perhaps a limp. Or a girl who was always hungry or a boy who cried excessively. Or some grievously inappropriate behaviour, the legend of which lived on, if not the name the child answered to. And for an unknowable number of children, there was nothing. No name, no defining features, no oddities, no memories. Just a number on a shipping list. Children who had come and gone, leaving no trace of their existence.

And the final pile was perhaps the most troubling: children known to have left their placement before maturity, often after just a short time, and who were never seen or heard of again. They were there, then suddenly they were not. Sometimes there were good reasons for their flight – perhaps a violent disagreement or a similar falling-out. Others absented themselves on a whim, or thought the grass was greener elsewhere, or fell under the influence of someone unsavoury. By now they might be solid citizens, or vagabonds, or felons – or dead. Or perhaps they had found a way back to England, to be reunited with those they had left behind, only again to languish in circumstances from which they had once been saved. Or any outcome that it was possible to imagine.

Lily Mudd had been the final name to be added to this pile. Until then, Alice had left her uncategorised, in the hope that she could be found, and she had made sporadic efforts to trace the girl, both in Canada and latterly in England. There had been a number of false alarms: a young woman in prison in Toronto; a girl in a morgue in Belleville; a harried maidservant in Kingston who had a different story to tell. But all leads had drawn a blank. Perhaps Lily might not want to be found. Or maybe there was nothing left to find. It was time to draw a line under the sorry tale. Alice shed a small tear and said a prayer, and then she added Lily Mudd's name to the 'Missing children' list.

And when she was done, Alice sat back in her chair and tried to make sense of it all. She counted the numbers that were on each list, but what did that tell her? How many successes equalled one failure? Or was it the other way around? And one child's success might be so much more so than another's that it surely could not have the same value placed upon it. And some were barely worthy of that description. Then again, a failure might only be relative and hardly worth a thought, or it might be Lily Mudd or Simeon Harding, or anywhere in between. And the unknowns hid a multitude of secrets that they would take to their grave – and perhaps some had already done so. It was not just a matter of addition. If it was, you would need a thousand categories, and even then, you might not do it justice. But one thing was clear, it was not the resounding success that Alice had prayed for, and largely believed, as she went about her business. That was troubling.

Over the following days and weeks, she tried to come to terms with what she had found. If this was her legacy, it was at best inconclusive and not what she had set out to achieve all those years ago. But neither did it represent a complete waste of her talents.

To improve just one life is a thing worth doing, she thought. And I have raised up so many. And yet…

Moments of buoyancy alternated with feelings of deep despair. At times she was the Alice that all were familiar with: energetic and domineering, pushy and pragmatic. But there were other occasions when she shut herself away and could barely lift herself from her bed. The reams of paper that she had so assiduously collected were consigned to a cupboard that she never had cause to visit – out of sight, if not out of mind. She did not publish the results of her efforts, as she had originally intended, and the exercise was not repeated.

Eventually Alice found a certain equilibrium, although

the matter never truly went away, resurfacing at each setback and when she had too much time to think. And whenever she was feted or praised or merely taken seriously, she could never fully enjoy the moment; beneath the surface, there was always a sense of disappointment and loss.

And the world was changing, at least the paths which Alice had trod for so long. As she complained one day in a letter to George Moore:

In my line of work, the days of the lone philanthropist are drawing to a close. The likes of myself and Clara Openshaw will soon be no more; well-meaning individuals with the children's interests at heart, making it up as we went along, challenging those that stood in our way, getting things done. It is now the age of the corpulent charities and the fattened offspring of the established churches, with their legally binding constitutions and their oversight boards and their endless reports on how each penny is spent, effort that should instead be expended on the children, who are almost an afterthought. And the national chains of orphanages that can never be seen to be standing still and who must continually make space for new recruits to boost their empires. So many ships now cross the Atlantic that I am surprised they do not collide. Too few patrons to go round. Too many rules. Too much risk of getting on the wrong side of the argument. Too many people with backs to protect – yes, I'm thinking of your former colleagues and their masters. There is no longer any room for the determined amateur. There is no place for a woman with a mission. There is no fun in it anymore.

SIXTY-FIVE

On a blustery July morning in the year of our Lord 1893, one hundred orphans and foundlings had been gathered outside the Alice Hamilton Home for the Salvation and Advancement of Destitute Children. The matron was in her usual state of befuddlement as she called a register. She might as well have tried to count the raindrops.

'Stanley Lubbock, I will have to tie your legs together if you don't keep still,' she screeched. 'Thomas Elliott, I shall swing for you if you're covered in dirt already. And where's your cap?'

Another shipment of SAD children was bound for Canada, and on their last day in England they were as skittish and contrary as any that had preceded them, shouting and singing, chasing and dancing, and tormenting any adult that crossed their path. It was a final celebration of childhood, and it was almost as if they knew it. Meanwhile, amid the rabble a boy stood unnoticed, rubbing his eyes and sobbing fitfully, while a girl sat quietly, perhaps hoping that someone might ask if she had changed her mind. A small crowd had convened to wish the children *bon voyage*. There was no family to be seen.

A carriage pulled up at the front of the bedlam and Alice Hamilton alighted, stumbling as she reached ground level and righting herself through the support of a convenient shoulder.

She smacked her umbrella on the frame of the carriage as her time-honoured way of attracting attention. A servant produced a box and helped her onto it.

'O happy travellers!' Alice bellowed, stretching her arms out as far as they would go. 'O happiest of days!'

And the well-worn script unveiled itself once more. To the casual observer, it was business as usual. But anyone familiar with Alice Hamilton might have noticed that there was less fluency in her delivery and that the words no longer rang as true as once they had. Nor did she command quite the same attention as before, and there was no sign that this unduly concerned her. And there seemed to be a tiredness in her eyes and a depletion in her vigour that could not be explained only by the passage of time.

And although she would have argued to the contrary, they might have concluded that her heart was no longer in it.

Acknowledgements

I am most grateful to the following people:

To Jonathan Myerson for your very helpful comments and for showing me that I didn't have a final draft after all. To Jane Hammett for your comprehensive and sensitive editing. And to both of you for your encouragement that I was not wasting my time with this project. Also, to George Green for your kind words and helpful comments before I even got to that point.

To Christine Hammacott for your atmospheric cover design; without you I would not have known where to start.

To all the staff at Troubador for turning a dream into reality.

To Ben Cameron and his team for helping to bring my novel to the attention of the world.

Most importantly, to my wife, Pauline, for her never-ending patience and support over so many years. I can never thank you enough. And also to Christopher and Rachel; all three of you have allowed me to have a happy ending.